THE LAST PARTY

ALSO BY CASSIDY LUCAS

Santa Monica

THE LAST PARTY

A NOVEL

CASSIDY LUCAS

HARPER

NEW YORK • LONDON • TORONTO • SYDNEY

HARPER

THE LAST PARTY. Copyright © 2022 by Cassidy Lucas. All rights reserved. Printed in the United States of America. No part of this book may be used or reproduced in any manner whatsoever without written permission except in the case of brief quotations embodied in critical articles and reviews. For information, address HarperCollins Publishers, 195 Broadway, New York, NY 10007.

HarperCollins books may be purchased for educational, business, or sales promotional use. For information, please email the Special Markets Department at SPsales@harpercollins.com.

FIRST EDITION

Designed by Jamie Lynn Kerner

Library of Congress Cataloging-in-Publication Data has been applied for.

ISBN 978-0-06-301848-8 (pbk.)

22 23 24 25 26 LSC 10 9 8 7 6 5 4 3 2 1

For Gary Louis Wolfson (1948–2021)
and Patricia Doherty Fierro (1942–2020)

And we would all go down together
We said we'd all go down together
Yes we would all go . . .

—BILLY JOEL, "GOODNIGHT SAIGON"

Raj (the Drifter)

THE NIGHT WAS FILLED WITH HOWLING.

Raj jolted awake in the cave that stank of his own unwashed body. Breath shallow, pulse throbbing behind the scraps of cotton T-shirt stuffed in his ears, he tore away the grimy sleeping bag and wheeled around to check the corners of the cave.

Perhaps a beast had crept in. A bobcat, a mountain lion, an animal with fangs ready to rip away flesh and tendon. Something even hungrier than Raj.

How-wooooo. How-wooooo. How-how-how-wooooooo.

The corner where Candace slept was empty but for the frayed blanket she refused to part with, wrapping it around her narrow shoulders each night when Raj was out foraging in the camouflage of dusk. He snatched it from the sandy ground. It smelled like the tangerine oil she dabbed on her delicate wrists.

He called her—"Candace!" He had sworn he would be silent when they came for him, but there was no life without Candace. He must find her, throw her over his shoulder, and run through the tangle of wild brush and thorny cacti if he must, whatever it took to get her far from the baying creatures.

How-ooooo.

Raj froze, listening. Since he and Candace had fled his Malibu mansion seven months ago, leaving everything behind, he had grown used to the sounds of the canyon. Coyotes screwing and fighting, owls screeching, mule deer scampering through the brush. But these sounds were different: maniacal laughter, yips strung into chattering cries.

They were human.

Raj's heart thudded in his chest.

What if he was too late? What if *they* had already found Candace?

He should never have let her leave the cave. But he'd had no choice. She had always viewed her independence as a sacred and necessary thing. One of her many qualities with which Raj had fallen head over heels in love.

Whenever she wished to go, he let her. Understanding the risks but not quite believing them.

And now, because of his weakness, they had found her. Hovered their drones in the sky above the ranch and spotted Candace's heart-shaped face. *Snap-snap-snapped* it with their long-range cameras, uploading the photos instantly to the net. An all-you-can-scroll buffet for their millions of sheepstream followers desperate to binge on the heartache of others.

His heartache.

Raj pressed his dirt-caked hands over his face. Candace. Her heart broken so she had not spoken a word since they had fled to the highest point of Topanga Canyon. A place so far above the scourge of Los Angeles that its owners had named it Celestial Ranch. On the night he and Candace arrived, Raj had stood panting in the moonlight and saw those words, carved into a wooden sign by the property's entry gate. Instantly, he had known this was the place. Here, close to the stars, he might keep Candace safe.

So, he had guided her by the hand through the slats of the gate and over the parched hills of the ranch until they had found the cave.

Now, Raj crawled across the sandstone floor to the cave's arched entrance and peered outside. Through the gnarled branches of a mighty oak, up by the old shed on Hydra Hill, he saw them: a circle of bodies lit an alien silver in the moonlight. Hands linked, they shuddered in and out of shadow, limbs windmilling, heads thrown back, necks stretched.

Raj inhaled sharply.

It was not the paparazzi parasites but the partyers. The group of trespassers (*guests*, the old man with the wolf dog who owned the property called them with a sneer) had congregated on the other side of Hydra Hill—*his hill*, Raj had come to think of it, though he had no right to be there, as he was a trespasser himself.

Still. They had no right.

The trespassers had seemed harmless yesterday when Raj watched them arrive through his military-grade binoculars, an old gift from Candace in the before times. Through their lenses, Raj saw city people buffed to a shine climbing out of luxury cars. Nameless, faceless, unimportant, like all the guests who visited the property on weekends, paying to stay in the small cabins that ringed the meadow.

But now, as Raj watched through his binoculars, it seemed a terrible force had transformed them from mere men and women into a ring of wild creatures howling at the sky.

Possessed like in the stories of the shape-shifting Rakshasa his Nani had told on his childhood trips back to India. The demons whose power was strongest with each new moon.

They were singing now. Or was it a chant, some dark prayer? A call for blood?

Surely, it was the work of the flame-haired Witch. She visited the ancient couple who owned the property every week, tricking them into believing she was a friend. But Raj knew better. She came to spread her black magic. To poison the sweet old woman with the long gray braid and her husband, the big, craggy old man Raj had first met shortly after he and Candace arrived at Celestial Ranch. Raj had opened his eyes one morning and the old man's weathered face hovered like a mirage above.

The old man had cupped the back of Raj's head, held a plastic jug of water to his split lips. *There, there, my man, take it slow.*

Raj knew instantly the man was special. He was Sheshnaag the Great, the thousand-headed serpent anointed by Brahma— his grandmother Nani's favorite bedtime story, especially on nights when heavy rain battered the clay-tiled roof of Nani's house in Chennai, storms that seemed apocalyptic compared to the sunny skies of Orange County back home.

Sheshnaag the Protector's sole eternal duty was to coil his tail around the earth and hold it steady. The old man became their protector, promising to shield Raj and Candace from dangers, as long as Raj completed certain assignments. And Raj had done everything the man had asked. Even the job with the bees! The proof was all over Raj's arms and neck and face, hot and swollen—he had not been able to remove all the stingers; and in the blood that stained his nailbeds pink even after he had scrubbed his hands in the bucket of fresh water the old man had left outside the cave.

The old man had given Raj a boning knife with a smooth wooden handle and curved, razor-sharp blade. Raj wore it belted to his waist and touched it often to remind himself he'd found an ally in the old man.

But why, *why*, was the old man absent now, when Raj needed him most? When a throng of trespassers crept closer, threatening to steal Candace from him?

Through his binoculars, Raj saw the trespassers still stood in a circle, but a new body had appeared in the center. His fingers trembled as he adjusted the focus knob.

The woman's features sharpened. Blue-black hair fanned her pale heart-shaped face. There was the cleft chin he had cupped and kissed. The petite and toned surfer's body that had been a perfect match for his own.

Candace.

They had imprisoned her.

A spasm of understanding edged Raj's terror.

He alone must save her. He had no choice. Even the old man had abandoned him now.

Raj heard a light breeze sift through the trees. The trespassers *aahed*.

"The goddess hears us!" a woman's voice squealed.

"Come to me, baby!"— a male voice.

How-wooooo. How-how-how-ooooooo.

A surge lifted Raj to his feet. He felt a strength he had not known since he and Candace had fled the poisoned world far below the canyon.

His hand closed around the handle of the boning knife. Raj now knew the knife's purpose. This was his astral weapon.

A knife made of stars. And when he was finished putting it to use, the next step would be revealed. The path that would carry him, and Candace, to redemption.

He crawled out of the cave. Overhead, the moon was a throbbing hole in the sky.

Raj walked up the hill, in the direction of the howling.

1

Dawn (the Birthday Girl)

ON THE EVE OF HER FIFTIETH BIRTHDAY, DAWN SANDERS SAT IN THE passenger seat of Mia Meadows's white Mercedes SUV, staring at the sun-sparked ocean and trying not to gasp as Mia drove through the clogged summer-beach traffic on the Pacific Coast Highway.

With each lurch of the big car, Dawn clenched her jaw and glanced to the back seat at her daughter, Quinn, who was surely edging toward a panic attack as a result of Mia's whiplash driving. Thankfully, Quinn seemed oblivious, her long legs drawn under her chin, pale face obscured by a thick paperback novel, tangled dark hair framing her open book. The cover bore the image of a chiseled, shirtless man atop a white horse and the title, *Unbridled Passion*, printed in swirly purple font. Dawn felt a twinge of satisfaction; she'd recently bought all eight installments in the Unbridled series for Quinn, each over five hundred pages. Quinn was obsessed with romance novels. They had a magically calming effect on her—the way thumb-sucking had when she was a toddler. Despite the books' awful covers, and abundance of poorly written sex scenes, Dawn was thankful for them. Quinn had been diagnosed with sensory processing disorder at four, Asperger's at six, obsessive-compulsive disorder at eight, and generalized anxiety disorder at eleven. Now almost twenty-two, Quinn still lived with Dawn. It had begun to feel like she always would. The books brought them both a rare peace.

Dawn glanced over at Mia, trying to gauge her current mood. Mia seemed content enough, though her grip on the steering wheel was tight, her long red nails digging in, and her oversized sunglasses made it hard to discern her expression. This was a tic of Dawn's—the insuppressible need to know that Mia was happy with her. Especially now, after so many years apart. After knowing the awful, vacant feeling of *not* having Mia in her life.

Never again.

Mia had cut off all communication with Dawn in 2011. A loss Dawn had never stopped mourning. Then, thirteen months ago, Mia had sailed back into Dawn's life at the height of the pandemic, when Los Angeles was in strict quarantine. A four-word text from an unfamiliar number had appeared:

Missing you Dawnie ♥ Meemers

The next day, they'd met for a walk along the beach. Dawn wore a mask. Mia didn't. *I trust my body*, she'd said with a smile, white teeth flashing. Dawn was so happy to see her old friend she hadn't even cared. They'd talked for three hours, walking all the way from Venice to Malibu and back.

Now here they were: Dawnie and Meemers, as they'd called each other during the first era of their friendship, two decades ago. Together again. Texting a dozen times a day, meeting for walks or coffee or Pilates. After a ten-year separation, the interminable and lonely months of the pandemic, the implosion of her career as an esthetician, *plus* a divorce and a daughter with special needs, Dawn was badly in need of a friend. She'd felt as if Mia had rescued her, reached into the abyss and pulled Dawn out.

And now, on top of rescuing Dawn from a despairing time, Mia was throwing her a party. An entire weekend in Topanga Canyon to celebrate Dawn's fiftieth (oh god, *fiftieth*) birthday.

The invitation had arrived in Dawn's mailbox back in April, done in custom letterpress on lavender cardstock—pure Mia.

A respite from reality.

In honor of Dawn Leigh Sanders'
50th Journey Around the Sun.

Please join us for a weekend of true
beauty & beautiful truth.

The top of Topanga Canyon
June 24–26, 2022.

Mia had insisted on handling every detail of the party weekend, a role she had always relished. Mia thrived on being Mia-in-charge. From the specific location—a private property high in the canyon named Celestial Ranch—to the cabin assignments, catering, music, and activities, Mia had planned it all.

And, by design, she'd shared almost none of it with Dawn. *I want you to truly experience your birthday,* Mia had explained, *not anticipate it. Your job is to simply show up. I'll take care of the rest.* She'd also insisted on paying for everything: *You only turn fifty once, babe. And I can afford it.*

It was true: Mia worked as a recurring character on various TV shows. Currently, she played the mom of psychic teen twins on the Disney hit *Double Vision*. She owned a huge house in the Palisades, another in Palm Springs, and a ski condo in Park City. Given that Dawn's finances were dwindling, her esthetician's license unrestored, her ex-husband, Craig, fighting her over alimony and custody, her life basically a disaster, Dawn had accepted Mia's generous offer.

It was embarrassing to accept such a gift at Dawn's age, but she felt she had no choice. She couldn't lose Mia again, and there was no saying no to Mia Meadows.

The guest list, Mia decreed, would be small, intimate: just four of her and Dawn's oldest mutual friends: Graham, Summer, Joanie, and Reece. The original group from the Nurtury Center for Child Development, where they'd all first met in 2007 in a parenting group led by Reece Mayall, a therapist who specialized in spectrum disorders. They'd been strangers to one another then, five young, bewildered parents of neuroatypical children (like Quinn, Mia's son, Nate, had Asperger's) in need of help. Under the gentle guidance of Reece, whose wisdom about children had seemed *right* to Dawn, the group had bonded and become like family. Essential to one another's survival. So united by their unique shared experience of parenting children with disabilities that Dawn sometimes felt they were a singular entity. That the six of them—Reece included—shared one brain. One soul.

One mission: to protect and defend their children.

And then it had all been ripped to shreds. The whole group—the friends Dawn had believed to be airtight, bound-for-life—burned to the ground like a California wildfire.

But that was long ago. Ancient history. Like new growth after a blaze, the friendships had reemerged. Dawn had reconnected with Graham five years ago, and Summer and Joanie shortly thereafter. All of them still lived in Los Angeles except for Reece, who had moved to Oakland. Dawn kept in touch with her with the occasional phone call and old-fashioned letters; Reece no longer "did the internet."

And now, with the return of Mia to Dawn's life, the old Nurtury group was complete. The dark days of the past forgiven, forgotten.

At least Dawn hoped so.

She'd pinned her birthday invitation to her refrigerator door and read it whenever she reached for milk or eggs or Quinn's probiotics, to remind herself the party was real. That her friends were actually doing such an extravagant thing for her. Each time, the phrase *true beauty & beautiful truth* lingered. Mia's choice of words struck Dawn as odd, but then, Mia was an actress, not a writer.

Now, Dawn gazed at Mia in the driver's seat, admiring her profile against the coastal backdrop: Mia's skin was taut and dewy, her pink lips lush and glossed, her mermaid hair colored in shades of wheat and honey, piled on her head in an artful topknot. As a career esthetician, Dawn well understood all the work that went into Mia's lustrous appearance: the injections and incisions, the serums and creams and acids, the lasers and microblades and exfoliators, all necessary in keeping Mia employed as an actress. Despite her profession, Dawn had given up the battle with middle age years ago, allowing gray hairs to thread her brown bob and laugh lines to spider her face.

"What's going on over there, Dawnie?" said Mia. "I can feel you staring."

Dawn quickly shifted her gaze. Outside, the June afternoon was cloudless and bright. On the wide sandy beach that stretched along the PCH, a team of ponytailed women in red bikinis jumped and dived for a volleyball. "I'm just—excited. I can't believe everyone's coming."

Traffic finally began to flow, and Mia accelerated with gusto.

"Believe it, birthday bitch," Mia sang, and Dawn smiled, despite the fact that Quinn loathed—practically feared—profanity. Mia considered *bitch* a term of endearment; coming from her, it made Dawn feel special.

"I believe it," Dawn said.

"Good. Because this weekend's going to be epic, Dawnie. I forgot to tell you, Graham's carpooling up with Joanie and Summer. Apparently, he's as wussy as ever about driving during rush hour. And Reece texted that she was heading up the Grapevine an hour ago, so she'll make it in time for dinner."

Dawn's chest fluttered at the mention of Reece. Seeing her in person for the first time in over a decade seemed momentous. That she was coming all the way to Topanga for Dawn was almost too much for Dawn to accept. For years after the Nurtury imploded, Reece couldn't drive at all. Or go out in public. Or be trusted with the possession of sharp objects; a social worker had routinely scoured her cupboards and drawers. Removed all knives and scissors, sewing needles and nail files. Even tweezers.

Reece had suffered more than everyone else after the Project failed.

Dawn, on the other hand, had been the least scathed.

But time had passed, and Reece had healed. She'd accepted the invitation and was driving down from Oakland. Mia had made it happen. Sometimes, Dawn thought, it seemed Mia could make *anything* happen. That the world bent to her will.

Mia-in-charge.

"I feel bad Reece is driving so far," Dawn said. "Probably eight full hours from—"

"Stop right there with the guilt." Mia jabbed a finger at Dawn. "Guilt is a *toxin*, you know. Are you already forgetting our rule? Do I need to remind you?"

"Oh god, sorry," said Dawn. "No, I haven't forgotten."

"Do you want to say it, then? Repetition is the best form of learning."

Dawn's palms felt damp, despite the car's chill A/C, and she cursed herself for the stupid mistake. In a group text to all the guests, Mia had declared that the weekend in Topanga would be one of epic joy only & NO TOXIC TOPICS. Not a single fucking mention. YKWIM

YKWIM: *You know what I mean.*

They did know. Dawn knew.

She took a deep breath. "No toxic topics."

Mia's smile was instantaneous. "Atta girl, Dawnie. I don't mean to be such a hard-ass. It's just because I love you, and I don't want you being unkind to yourself."

"Thank you, Meems. What I meant was"—she still had the urge to redeem herself—"I'm just so . . . truly grateful that Reecie's coming."

"That's what this weekend's all about," Mia said. "Gratitude, babe. Gratitude and *truth*. I just want you to relax and enjoy yourself, for once, even if . . ." She jerked her head toward the back seat, conveying the rest of the sentence: *even if you've got Quinn with you . . .*

"I will," Dawn promised, though the implication that Quinn was an imposition sent a pang to her chest. Mia had not been thrilled by the addition of Quinn to her carefully curated guest list—all the other guests had grown children also, and none of *them* were coming, but what else could Dawn do? Her ex-husband, Craig, an OB-GYN, referred to by his adoring celebrity patients as Doctor C., had bailed on his weekend parenting duties, claiming he needed to be at the hospital—and Quinn was incapable of staying in anyone else's care without melting down.

Dawn twisted toward Quinn in the back seat. She was still glued to her book, lost in some melodramatic world of implausible plot twists and clichéd characters that boggled Dawn's mind. Two nights of rustic accommodations in the woodsy, mountainous wilds of Topanga Canyon were sure to agitate every cell in Quinn's twitchy, anxious body. It was amazing that she had managed to stay this calm so far, given Mia's aggressive driving. Dawn was surprised Quinn wasn't picking at her cuticles or tapping her feet or chewing on the stretched-out collar of her T-shirt, her go-to ways of stimming when she was anxious, which was most of the time.

"Almost there!" Mia said, swinging the Mercedes onto Topanga Canyon Road, two narrow lanes that stretched flat for a quarter mile before ascending the flank of the mountain. The road ahead was wide open and patterned with shade; Dawn was glad to escape the clog of the coastal highway and the manic sparkle of the Pacific. The road steepened, and Dawn felt a fresh twinge of optimism in her chest. Her body relaxed.

"This is more like it," said Mia. "Happy birthday to you, Dawn Leigh Sanders. I hereby declare this moment the official start of an epically joyous weekend."

"Happy birthday to me," Dawn said, letting herself smile as the car climbed higher and higher, through the dappled summer light, up into the heart of the canyon.

2

Twyla (the Hostess)

TWYLA WAS RUSHING AROUND SIRIUS, THE LAST OF THE FOUR GUEST cabins she had to tidy and stock with extra towels and bath products and the complimentary bottle of wine, which a recent guest had called undrinkable in his four-star Airbnb review. The wealthier the guests, Twyla had learned in the eight months she'd been renting out the cabins at Celestial Ranch, the more impossible they were to please.

The sun slanted through the kitchen window of the lopsided cabin, catching flurries of dust in its golden light. Another guest had complained about the dust (three-point-five-star review). Twyla knew she should hire professionals to clean, but she couldn't afford to sink another dime into the ramshackle cabins, the yurt, the old barn, and the main house where she and her husband, Arnold, lived, all of which were worth nothing compared to the eighteen acres of prime canyon property they had owned for forty years, and which Twyla had converted to an Airbnb "experience," to Arnold's great irritation.

She imagined the guests making their way up the steep canyon roads, *oohing* and *aahing* at the sun-speckled oaks, the purple-tipped sagebrush, the craggy rocks. She knew they'd expect Celestial Ranch to be just as epic.

The guests often arrived together, a chain of silent luxury cars. Twyla had read somewhere that those fancy electric batteries were made from cobalt mined under horrendous circumstances by poor children in Cameroon. Just another instance of the mind-boggling hypocrisy common among her guests.

They were sleek city folk who yearned for a rustic getaway, then were often disappointed when they got what they wanted. Why was it, Twyla thought, as she hurried a rag over the cabin's scarred kitchen countertop, that her guests claimed to be most excited about the remote and rustic quality of the property, declaring in gushing messages that they were *dying to UNPLUG!* and *RECHARGE* and *RESET*, then proceeded to complain about the lack of amenities and cell service? What they actually wanted was to *tell* people they'd had a special, secluded weekend at the peak of Topanga Canyon.

Before the recent uptick in bookings, Twyla's trips to the Byte Me internet café down in the Valley had been the only time she allowed herself exposure to the harmful electromagnetic force fields radiated by computers. But she had ended up buying one for herself and added Wi-Fi when the trips into the Valley to check her email became too much.

Twyla slapped a Post-it note on the back of the cabin door (DO NOT FEED ANY ANIMALS ON PROPERTY). She couldn't trust her weekend visitors to do anything without explicit written instructions. Her guests tended to be such pampered urbanites, accustomed to automated *everything* (Twyla had heard even refrigerators were controlled with phones now), so removed from nature that their only familiarity with animals came from their genetically engineered dogs.

The details Twyla received on her guests (usually people linked to Hollywood) were often cryptic and filled with mumbo jumbo. Twyla requested the information under the guise of being friendly and curious, but really so she might personalize the little accoutrements, thus increasing her odds of a five-star review.

Twyla had been startled to see the name Mia Meadows pop up. The actress had long faded from the headlines. Ms. Meadows wanted to book *all* the guest residences for an entire weekend and was willing to pay a premium for *additional services*.

Twyla hadn't even needed to quote a custom price for the booking and Mia's accompanying list of somewhat odd requests; Mia had simply made an offer: six thousand dollars. Five times what the property usually earned on a weekend. They'd spoken on the phone for fifteen minutes, Ms. Meadows doing most of the talking, and shortly after they'd hung up, she'd transferred enough money into Twyla's account to cover months of utility bills, plus a bit extra to slice off a chunk of the property taxes Twyla owed. Giddy, Twyla had decided to spring for a bottle of wine to share with her husband, Arnold, and a bag of organic oats for their two goats, Nocturne and Diurn.

For a time, in the nineties and aughts, Twyla remembered hearing Meadows's name floated about, first for being a pretty face on a hit TV show, and then when she went from "autism activist" to jailbird for shenanigans related to her fierce opposition to vaccination requirements in public schools. Twyla hadn't been interested at the time; generally, she found the offscreen lives of actors boring and silly, especially those who fancied themselves "activists." Not that Twyla really understood what constituted "activism" these days, since much of it seemed to take place on phones and computers. Nothing like the antiwar protests she and Arnold had attended in the late sixties at the University of California at Santa Barbara, where they'd worn the soles off their shoes with miles of marching.

Still, even a disgraced celebrity could do wonders for Twyla's burgeoning Airbnb venture, and she resolved to make that weekend extra special for Ms. Meadows and her guests. However, Mia Meadows had proved to be, without a doubt, the most high-maintenance guest Twyla had ever hosted, and she had yet to arrive. Twyla had thrown in the yurt at a discount, hoping the woman would be grateful, only to receive an email asking if the yurt had air-conditioning.

She couldn't risk disappointing Mia Meadows. Who knew what a bad review from a TV celebrity would do to Twyla's budding business? Thank the goddess, Sibyl DeLoache, Twyla's friend and personal psychic, had agreed to help out. On their call, Ms. Meadows had asked Twyla if she knew a "talented and discreet" psychic available to guide the guests on "a spiritual journey." Sibyl, formerly *Sibyl, Seer to the Stars*, who had also suffered a doozy of a scandal, was likewise on her way into the canyon. Twyla had asked her to arrive early to go over Ms. Meadows's two pages of instructions.

Twyla needed Sibyl there in case anything went wrong. These days, Arnold was no help. And where had he disappeared to this time? Twyla wondered as she lifted the bed skirt to check for spiders, silverfish, and stray lizards.

She wished she could ignore these disappearances, but Arnold had changed so much the past year, growing confused, irritable, sluggish. Unrecognizable from the wiry, energetic man who, twenty years ago, had built the cabins that dotted their property. When he'd sold his cabinetry business in the late nineties, Twyla had hoped he'd invest his loads of free time in taking care of Celestial Ranch. Fat chance.

What if that Western medicine—obsessed Dr. Belk was right, and Arnold was showing early signs of dementia? It had been just a year and change since she and Arnold, double-masked in a windowless examination room down in the Valley, had listened to Dr. Belk utter that horrid word. *Alzheimer's.* Twyla preferred their longtime naturopath Zephyr's diagnosis that Arnold's decline had something to do with toxins in his spleen and required a dose of coral calcium twice a day, along with a hefty tablespoon of coconut oil.

The last straw for Twyla had been Arnold's shift in political leanings during the pandemic. A lifelong liberal, Arnold had started to agree with the Trumpers, even refusing to wear a mask on the rare trips they made to Topanga Natural Food Market. As Arnold's erratic behavior worsened, Twyla found herself, here and there, on Arnold's bad days, crushing one of the tiny *calming* pills Dr. Belk had prescribed for Arnold and stirring it into his oolong tea.

That Arnold had taken the dog with him, wherever he had vanished to, was a sizable comfort. Klondike was squarely Arnold's dog, the two of them bound by some ineffable energy, and Twyla trusted that Klondike would return to the house if something happened to Arnold.

As she swept the pile of grit and dust bunnies out the cabin door, she retraced the events of that morning: at nine she'd given Arnold his cup of fennel tea and toasted bread baked by Elaine, known as the Bread Witch, who sold her baked goods from a fluorescent VW bus. Twyla had made Arnold two soft-boiled eggs, slipping one into the pewter egg cup engraved with his name, one of the few items he had saved from boyhood. Usually, upon sight of the cup he smiled, even if just with a squint of his ice-blue eyes, but something had been off that morning.

Something had been off between her and Arnold for some time, Twyla thought as she scanned the cabin interior, searching for a stain, a dead bug, anything that might tarnish a potential five-star review. For years she and Arnold had languished in the gray muck of *maybe*, humoring each other: Twyla continued to nod when Arnold ticked off the endless reasons for leaving Celestial Ranch and the canyon, and he, in turn, accepted Twyla's vagueness when it came to committing to a decision date, her excuses for not being able to accompany him to visit yet another possible retirement community in the Valley. Awkward trips that always ended in tense arguments as the Vanogan chugged back up the steep winding road to the ranch. Arnold going on and on about how he *loved* the senior community's cafeteria, pointing out that there was a different dessert served *every night*! The thought of all that rubbery, processed food was enough to make Twyla nauseated.

Each of them was bluffing, a reality Twyla had been forced to accept after that last season of quarantine when it seemed as if Arnold lost more of his Arnold-ness every day. She had believed his resolve to abandon the ranch would weaken and eventually fade, or that he'd be sitting on the porch one morning, the red rocks and turtleback mountains rising around them, the hummingbirds darting in and out of the trees, the sun coloring the dry grass, and realize, *No, of course we cannot leave.* And he, in turn, believed she would simply give up. That she'd wake up one day and feel too old to do everything required to keep Celestial Ranch afloat. Not to mention all that needed to be reduced, such as her three decades' worth of unsold metal sculptures, rusted tools, cast-off furniture, and God knew what else, most of which were stashed in haphazard, dust-coated towers in their large basement.

Twyla stood in the middle of the small cabin and performed one last check of the room. No stains on the bedspread, no grime on the ancient cooktop or mini fridge. The foldout bistro table looked nice laid out with the bottle of wine, a box of shortbread cookies, and a small vase of periwinkle flowers she'd clipped from the bush behind the yurt. She had done a good job cleaning the cabins—*without Arnold's help.* She would find him and set him up in the living room of the house, give him his tea (one of Dr. Belk's calming pills crushed within), and make sure he didn't vanish again after the guests arrived. Who knew where and when he might pop up and disturb Ms. Meadows and her party?

She opened the cabinet under the narrow kitchen sink, reaching in to prop the dustpan and brush inside. A spasm rippled through her lower back. *Dear goddess, not now.*

The ancient pipes of the sink hissed. She groaned. She'd have to get the toolbox. She reached into the cabinet, her fingers just brushing the rusted pipes. There was a leak—her fingers touched something slick and cool but when she pulled her hand out, her fingertips were dry.

The hissing came again, along with a measured *tap tap tap* against the floor of the cabinet. A long snake slipped out. The brown and tan diamond-shaped ridged scales (they had always reminded her of a mosaic) were unmistakable. Twyla clambered backward on hands and feet. The snake seemed endless—its head slithering farther into the room, its tail still inside the cabinet.

Twyla grabbed the broom and attacked, at first using the bristles to bash the snake's head, then flipping it over to use the metal brush cap.

She didn't know how many times she brought the broom down, or how much time had passed. She stopped when her arms began to ache. She fell back into the wicker chair, the over-stuffed pillows she'd sewn herself let out a swoosh of air. The snake lay still in a small pool of blood. Its neck nearly severed.

She saw her mistake. With a sudden rage, she wanted to blame it on Arnold. He should've been there to help her, to stop her from killing the snake. It wasn't a rattlesnake after all but a harmless gopher snake.

She apologized to the snake—I'm so sorry, friend, so sorry—as she draped its glossy, limp body over the broom handle, whose bristles were red with blood. She had hurt one of her natural neighbors. Surely, the snake and his ancestors had lived on this land for ages—the land she knew was not hers to possess. Even if every tree and bush and agave spike; every hummingbird and rabbit; every hawk circling; every snake, even the venomous ones, were the only family she'd ever have. The family she'd chosen.

She should've known it wasn't a rattlesnake. Maybe, she thought, as she stood on the uneven top step outside the cabin, patting her damp forehead with a handkerchief, if she weren't so gosh-darned busy and stressed and worried about Arnold all the time, she'd have seen more clearly, and the freed snake would be on his way back to his home and his snake family.

She clutched the crystal dangling around her neck—a chunk of snowflake obsidian. A black stone speckled white that symbolized strength in overcoming difficulties. Sibyl had given it to her in their last session, instructing Twyla to rub the rough stone in moments of doubt. Twyla felt stronger immediately as her arthritis-stiffened fingers squeezed the stone. The healing energy like a heat passing through her fingertips and into her body.

She calmed herself with the mantra Sibyl had taught her.

"Be in the light! Be in the light!" Twyla repeated, until she realized she was practically shouting, her jaw clenched, face lifted to the bright blue sky. A family of mockingbirds rushed out from the drooping branches of a pepper tree, white-tipped wings spread, startling Twyla with a cry that sounded almost human.

"Sorry, guys!" Twyla called out to the birds. Look at how Arnold's bad behavior affected her! She was becoming a threat to the natural inhabitants of her precious land.

She scanned the landscape, looking for Arnold's lumbering, ursine shape, or the ghostly smear of Klondike's white-gray coat, her eyes catching nothing but earth, hills, and trees.

Damn Arnold.

She yanked her wide-brimmed straw hat over her head and set out to look for him.

She heard the bird call again. It was strange, bestial. The cry of an animal. Twyla froze. She *had* heard something—her hearing was, her naturopath Zephyr had told her, exceptional for a woman her age. There it was again, louder.

Except, Twyla was sure now, it was no bird.

Twy-la!

A gruff, baritone yowl.

It was Arnold, shouting from somewhere beyond the Andromeadow.

She didn't run toward his voice. Only chided herself for being stupid enough to worry about him, waste her time looking—again. *Of course*, he was messing with the damn beehive. He was newly obsessed with destroying it. Of all things, bees, an endangered species! She knew she'd find him staring at the hive that hung pendulous from one of the coastal live oaks in the woods beyond the Andromeadow. She'd named the ring of massive oaks the Family Circle many years ago, once she'd accepted that the trees and flowers, deer and coyotes, the poor snake she had murdered, were the only family she and Arnold would have.

"*Twy-la! Help!*"

She hated that word. *Help.* Since she was young, raised by a series of nannies, she had prided herself on her independence. Never asking for help. And now that she was old, she had promised herself she would continue refusing any offers of help.

Everything on Celestial Ranch, from the buildings to the art installations to the landscaping, Twyla—and once, Arnold— had created *without* help.

Help was poison. Help was what had slowed down Arnold, so he'd given up on life. On moving and doing, living and fighting. Wasn't *action* the definition of life at its core? she thought, as she strode down the lavender-and-rosemary-hedged walkway and the clearing opened in front of her, the five gnarled trunks of the massive oaks a nearly perfect circle, as if nature truly did have a divine plan.

3

Raj (the Drifter)

THE BEES WERE ANGRY. RAJ WAS AFRAID OF THEM.

He hid in the ferns near the ring of live oaks, binoculars around his neck, hand sweating around the corroded rubber grip of an ancient golf club. The old man had given Raj the rusted nine iron when he'd issued Raj's latest assignment.

A weapon.

Raj adjusted his grip on the club and, with his free hand, lifted his binoculars through the fern fronds to focus on the massive hive lodged between the largest tree's trunk and its lowest branch. A giant, lumpen pod affixed to the crook in the bark. The hive trembled with the bees' rage. Its surface a pulsing, shifting mass of tiny gold-brown bodies.

At the base of the tree was an open ladder tipped on its side. Which meant, Raj knew, that the old man had been right here, not long ago, visiting the hive.

For a moment, Raj doubted he had the courage to complete the mission.

Then he thought of Candace, curled beneath her frayed blanket in the cave, her once-strong swimmer's shoulders thin and trembling, and his will returned.

If he did not do as the old man, Sheshnaag the Great Protector, asked, then bad things would happen to Raj—worse, to Candace.

He lowered the binoculars and closed his eyes.

He reminded himself these were special bees. Like many things he had encountered at Celestial Ranch—the cave, the trees, the hummingbirds, even the wolf dog and the old man himself—the bees were sacred. Touched by the gods. In his Nani's fat book of the Vedas scriptures, the richly colored drawings showed Lord Vishnu and Krishna, and Indra, the king of heaven himself, as golden bees. The nectar-born ones. Raj was but eight or nine when his grandmother showed him the image of Vishnu as a blue bee lit upon a lotus flower, explaining to little Raj that bees were no enemy but the symbol of life. Of resurrection.

Perhaps the bees would not hurt him, but save him?

He lifted his binoculars again just as the old woman, Sheshnaag's wife, with her long gray braid, marched into the ring of trees and stopped a dozen feet short of the hive.

Raj held his breath and watched. The old woman was part of the assignment. Raj tightened his grip on the golf club.

"Arnie!" the woman shouted. A startled sparrow darted up through the branches.

Raj was grateful Candace was in the cave. The old woman's anguish would surely sadden Candace, whose heart was too big, and what if she wanted to help, to pull the old woman into a hug and rub her back? He warned Candace again and again to be careful. To remain invisible. He reminded her, every chance he found, of the paparazzi parasites who had infested their happy life, fed on their misery, forced them to flee their home with Candace in Raj's arms begging him to *Stop! Please, Raj, no!*

"Arnie, please!" the woman called. "Sweetie, where are you?"

Raj watched her stand still, listening, until a low sound, a creaking groan, came from overhead.

From the trees.

The woman tipped her face to the sky and swiveled her neck, tracking the source of the noise. Raj wanted to look too, to push away the fern frond covering his head and stand up, but he dared not move a muscle.

Then he heard her gasp: "Oh my god!"

She darted over to the oak and stood on the side opposite the hive, looking up, hands cupped over her mouth.

Raj could no longer restrain himself. He dropped onto his stomach and rolled onto his back, scooting toward the edge of the ferns, so if he angled his head just so, he could see to the top of the oak.

The old man was in the tree. High up, a good half-dozen feet above the hive. He stared down at his wife, a look of fear-tinged shame on his weathered, white-stubbled face.

"Twy," the old man croaked. "Help me."

Raj maneuvered the binoculars to his eyes and, as best he could from his awkward position, brought the old man's face into focus.

Sheshnaag the Great, Raj and Candace's only defender, appeared frightened. Nothing like the courageous protector who had brought them food and water and supplies. Now he hugged the branch like a frightened cat. Where was the man Raj had depended on those past seven months? An inferior spirit had possessed the old man's body. The distant look, the dead eyes, were the very opposite of the fever-bright focus Raj had seen during the old man's visits to the cave.

The thought of their protector weakening, going soft in the head to the point that he could not see the great danger in getting stuck at the top of a tall tree, was too much for Raj. Without the old man, Raj and Candace would be forced to return to the corrupted world far below the canyon.

He twisted back onto his stomach, moved by a powerful urge to spring from the cover of the ferns and help the old man down from the tree.

Even if it meant being spotted by the old woman.

Even if it meant outing himself to others lurking on the property: the trespassers who came on the weekends to Instagram themselves, or the media roaches on the hunt for another viral photo to sell to TMZ with a trending hashtag:

#MurdererRajPatel

The old man knew nothing of Raj's past. Raj had only identified himself as Rāha, an approximate translation of *traveler* in Hindi, and the man had simply nodded his big, furred head and repeated *Rāha,* in his deep, scratched voice. He was incurious and accepting. He asked no questions. He simply helped Raj and Candace survive.

Sheshnaag: their miraculous ally.

In turn, Raj did whatever he could to help the old man.

He was about to jump from the ferns when the woman spoke.

"Good god, Arnie, you brought the ladder all the way out here? How on earth did you manage to carry it?"

Raj saw her ropy arms reach for the ladder and maneuver it upright, propping it against the base of the tree, moaning with the effort.

She loved the old man, Raj understood. He knew this because she was taking care of him the way Candace had taken care of Raj. Supporting him, even when he'd done something stupid. Hurtful, even.

Memories flashed: Candace, adding cream to the crabmeat and asparagus soup she'd made for him, after he had complained that it was too salty. (How ungrateful he had been, in his old life!) Candace, begging *Don't hurt yourself, baby, please,* when he had forced her out of the Malibu house in the middle of the night, lifting her over his shoulder so she could not stay behind. Giving her no choice but to follow him up into the wilds of the canyon.

Now he watched the old woman coax the old man from the high tree branch with the same loving tone Candace had used, even when Raj deserved it the least.

He listened, his eyes brimming with tears.

"Okay, Arnie. You're going to keep both hands on the branch and scoot yourself toward the trunk. Very slowly, love."

The old man inched forward along the branch until his big stomach pressed against the trunk.

"Now you'll wrap both arms around the trunk, like you're giving the tree a big hug, and swing your leg . . ."

Raj watched as the old man followed his wife's every instruction, until finally, his big, booted feet reached the top rung of the ladder.

At the bottom, his wife reached out her arms until she could hold his ankles and help him to the ground.

Then Sheshnaag was in the old woman's arms shaking like a terrified child, nothing like the Great Protector deigned to hold the world steady, and the two of them crumpled to the ground, holding each other.

Raj's face heated with shame. He was spying on a moment of devotion.

And yet, he could not lower his binoculars.

"What were you thinking, Arnold?" the woman said.

"I was," the man stammered, "I was . . . just trying to . . . help."

"Help *how*, Arnie?"

"I wanted to surprise you, Twy. Make the bees go away. Fix the problem."

Raj was confused. Had he waited too long to carry out the old man's assignment? It was impossible now. Mission *not* accomplished. Perhaps, in his stupid, childish fear of the bees, he'd shaken the old man's confidence in him.

He groped at his side for the golf club he'd dropped, locating the coarse rubber grip. He closed his hand around it.

If only he could have another chance, he would not fail Sheshnaag again.

"Fix the problem?" said the woman, with scorn, as she detangled from her husband's embrace and stood, brushing off her overalls. The tenderness in her voice had vanished, Raj heard, replaced by fresh irritation. "Actually, you create all kinds of *new* problems, Arnie."

"That cockamamie exterminator," the old man said, "he wanted a fortune to get rid of the hive. What a crook! I wanted to help."

I'll help! Raj wanted to shout. *I will, really!*

But he did not utter a word, remembering how the old man had instructed him to "stay invisible." How, in return for hiding, Sheshnaag had guaranteed Candace's safety.

So, Raj would stay hidden and silent.

As absent from the world as a dead man.

The world wanted him dead, anyway.

#GoodRiddanceRajPatel the media leeches would say. Never mind that he had been a luminary of the tech world. Number three on the 2020 Forbes 30 Under 30 list. His bank account so bloated he could not have spent the money in many lifetimes.

None of that mattered now. Nothing mattered but pleasing Sheshnaag, so that Candace could survive.

Beside the tree, the woman reached for her husband's hand and helped him to his feet, wobbling against his heft. The bees hummed behind them.

"If you really, truly want to help, Arnold, you can stop getting yourself in situations like this." She flung a hand toward the hive.

"I'm sorry, Twy." The old man hung his head and curled his fists like a child bracing for punishment.

Raj felt again that he might cry.

Twyla swatted her neck. "Ow! Now look what I've done! Killed a bee—an endangered species."

"I've been trying to save them," the old man muttered. "That's why I let the hive go so long in the first place."

Raj heard dejection in his voice. He was no longer the righteously angry man who had, on so many nights in the cave, sounded off about the political correctness devouring the country like a second plague, his deep voice a roar. He had given Raj the language to make sense of why he and Candace had lost everything. *The cancel culture woke mob! The self-righteous snowflake know-it-alls!*

"You know what, Arnold?" Twyla placed her hands on her narrow hips. "Sometimes, *I* need to be saved too."

"I'm sorry, Twy."

"I forgive you. Again. But only if you promise me you'll stay close to the house this weekend. Stay out of the guests' way. This group is paying a premium."

"I promise."

"And no more fooling around with that hive. We'll deal with it when we have the—resources—to do it properly."

Raj heard the old man grunt in agreement.

"Now let's go. I'm late to meet Sibyl at the house, and you know she hates when I'm late."

Sibyl.

The name the old woman used for the Witch.

Raj's pulse quickened.

The Witch had returned.

He waited until he was certain the old couple was gone. Then he stood from the ferns, golf club swinging from his hand, and stomped his legs to wake them. He would complete his assignment soon—very soon—but first, he must visit the Witch. He had witnessed the power she cast over Twyla, how the old woman emerged from their meetings transformed. Renewed. Her eyes sparkling with new clarity.

As if, Raj thought, she had drunk a magic elixir.

He must convince the Witch to do the same for him. To show him the clear path forward, to infuse him with her power. The old man alone was not enough. Until today, Raj had believed him all-powerful, but the sight he'd just beheld—Sheshnaag hanging in the tree branches, quaking like a terrified animal—had revealed weakness.

Raj needed more help. He could not risk the media roaches finding Candace. Or risk Candace delivering on her threats to leave the cave, leave the canyon, and return to the wicked world down below.

Perhaps the flame-haired Witch could guide him.

He tossed the golf club into the ferns, memorizing the spot where it landed, and ran in the direction of the old farmhouse.

4

Sibyl (the Visionnaire)

SIBYL SAT ON THE SAGGING FRONT STEPS OF THE TWO-STORY FARM-house, which was badly in need of a paint job, the original white exterior overtaken by the brown-gray wood underneath. The afternoon was sweltering, and Sibyl fanned her face with the skirt of her peasant dress. She searched the parched meadow for signs of the rusted golf cart Twyla drove.

Where the hell was Twyla?

Sibyl knew what her more difficult clients might say. *Thought you were Sibyl the Seer. Can't you just see where someone is?* Usually, Sibyl's contrarian clients were male and over forty, the sessions arranged by their fed-up wives. Men were often challenged by Sibyl's ability. Worried she had X-ray vision and could see through their jockey shorts.

As Twyla might say, *goddess forbid*. Sibyl had sworn off men (and women) around her forty-fifth birthday. Why deal with the drama and heart hurt and the loss of all that time and money spent in couples therapy when subscriptions to Bellesa

Porn by Women were ten dollars a month, and vibrators fifteen on Amazon.com with next-day shipping?

Relationships always ended badly for Sibyl, who chose domineering alpha types. She knew only a couple of psychics (she preferred *seer, reader, visionnaire*) who were married. Few people can tolerate life with a super empath capable of reading the hidden meaning of every gesture, intonation, and quip. How could any relationship work when Sibyl could *see* from the first moment that it was doomed?

She didn't need visionary powers or a therapist to know her shitty partner picks meant she was chasing her father, the Supreme Reverend Crabb of Harmony Church back in Beaver County, Pennsylvania. She'd left home at seventeen, changed her name, and rewrote her past in Los Angeles, all to get out from under her father's allegedly divine thumb. To be rid of the gold polyester robe, the Lamb of God embroidered across the back by her meek mother, that Sibyl had worn up at the altar of Harmony Church since before she'd lost all her baby teeth, reading the hopes and fears of the believers desperate for holy intervention. Admission had been ten dollars but no matter how many heads showed up each Sunday, her father had never been satisfied.

Twenty-six hundred miles and three decades away, she found herself wondering if she'd managed to escape after all. Her father, her mother, and the six siblings she'd left behind had been on her mind too much these days. It was all those damn texts at crazy hours.

She'd begun double-checking the locks on the windows of her Silver Lake bungalow.

A spooked psychic, what a joke.

On cue, her phone vibrated.

"Don't look," she whispered. "Just ignore it."

Another vibration came, then another. She yanked the phone out of her pocket and powered it off without looking at the screen.

Not now, when she needed to be Sibyl, calm and composed visionnaire. Unflappable seer of secrets.

She began to pace, smacking her hand against one of Twyla's recycled sculptures—a star-shaped mishmash of soldered steel and iron. The rusted metal left a brown stripe across her palm and she let out a "Fuck!," her irritation flaring.

Maybe she should just go home. Inch through the sure-to-be-miserable slog of Friday afternoon traffic. The arrival of new texts had escalated her mood from irritation to nearly unbearable panic.

Twyla had begged her to come for the weekend to work a "big-time" birthday party, even though, as the brief message on her website, voicemail (set up after she'd changed her phone number—*twice*), and every one of her social media handles stated:

Sibyl, Visionnaire to the Stars,™ *is on hiatus from her work and is taking time to recenter and reacquaint herself with the many mysteries of our shared universal interrelatedness. Her work will continue in 2022 when all Sibyl has manifested in this year of "heart work" will be shared.*

What the message should state, Sibyl thought, was far beyond *hiatus.*

Sibyl is finished. Kaput. Over. Canceled. Sibyl the Seer has gone dark.

Now she was here in the canyon, doing what she swore to her manager, her agent, the PR consultant who'd bled Sibyl's savings ("reputation management") she would *not* do after the scandal. But Twyla had pleaded with Sibyl to do readings for the guests that weekend, her voice cracking with desperation over the phone. Sibyl was genuinely worried about her friend, and especially Arnold, who seemed to age a year between Sibyl's visits to do readings for Twyla. Twyla was Sibyl's last remaining client and paid with the little cash she had on hand and, sometimes, jars of canned preserves.

Sibyl knew that in order to keep Celestial Ranch at a bareminimum level of habitability, as well as stave off Arnold's demands they sell (a fear that dominated Twyla's sessions with Sibyl), Twyla needed every penny she could earn.

Sibyl visored her eyes against the sun to scan for Twyla's golf cart but saw only those detestable rodents darting back and forth across the rutted dirt lane. *Beechies*, Twyla lovingly called them. Sibyl's brothers back in Harmony Township would get their rocks off bursting those tiny skulls with pellet guns. Her stomach roiled at the thought.

She worked the tips of her old red boots into the dry ground, willing Twyla to hurry the hell up. Likely, Sibyl thought, the couple was off at some far-flung part of the property, tending to some grueling work they'd created for themselves: the halfdozen chickens that lived in the coop or the pair of obstinate goats Twyla had adopted on a whim. Recently, Twyla had been complaining about a *godforsaken beehive*.

Sibyl hadn't done a live "seeing" in three years—Twyla's didn't count—and now she was facing an entire weekend of sessions, booked by none other than Mia Meadows. Sibyl had not worked with the Hollywood set since 2019, pre-pandemic, on that bright, clear February day when *The View* talk show host Merry Williams had flashed a double thumbs-up from the open hatch of a plane and hurtled down. Since then, Sibyl had funneled a vast chunk of her net worth into legal fees—her lawyers trying to prove that Sibyl was legally blameless. The skydiving company had taken the hit, closing all seven of its locations, declaring bankruptcy, and awarding the Williams family fifty million dollars in restitution.

The tragedy, technically, was *not* Sibyl's fault: Merry Williams had been more than willing to face her fear of heights on national television. But Sibyl's reputation was another matter. There was no escaping the media speculation that Merry Williams would have never scheduled her ten-thousand-foot jump from a plane had Sibyl not encouraged her to face her greatest fear.

It had all been scripted, of course, Sibyl and Merry's teams collaborating over a series of conference calls, ultimately functioning as a massive promo to both the talk show and Sibyl's business, but after the jump went horribly wrong, the network turned on Sibyl, framing her as a goading, risk-pushing fraud who'd bullied Merry into the jump.

The truth no longer mattered. Sibyl was a pariah, a hoax, a circus performer who'd stop at nothing to thrill an audience. Every client had severed ties; the highest-profile ones did so publicly. My heart is LITERALLY BREAKING, tweeted Gisele Bündchen, for #MerryWilliams and her family. Tom and I are devastated by her loss and deeply regret our former connection to @TheVisionnaire. RIP Merry and we love you ALWAYS.

Even Gwyneth Paltrow, who'd once told Sibyl she considered her a *cosmic sister*, had taken to Instagram with a picture of Merry and the caption:

In the spirit of solidarity with and compassion for #MerryWilliams, the @goop team and I renounce any affiliation with @TheVisionnaire. Merry was a true #SpiritWarrior and this world is a lesser place without her.

Plus, the tabloid and gossip-site headlines:

SIBYL DELOACHE: PSYCHO-TO-THE-STARS?
FRIENDS SAY MERRY JUMPED WITH "PUSH" FROM
SO-CALLED VISIONNAIRE

By the time Sibyl emerged from her fog of shock and dismay, it was too late for her to explain that Merry had co-engineered the skydiving stunt, certain it would be a boon to ratings and secure her spot on the show for several more seasons, which she'd heard through inside sources was at risk, with Lindsay Lohan waiting in the wings. Sibyl, Visionnaire to the Stars™ (also the title of the Lifetime reality series that had been slated to begin production in spring 2020), was kaput. Merry Williams's freefall had gone viral and, per *People* magazine, was memorialized as one of the "Most Moving Moments of 2019."

At forty-eight, Sibyl found the rug pulled from beneath her twenty-plus-year career. The only job she'd ever known, built on nothing more than hustle and internet research. Her savings would not last much longer. She had no marketable skills, no family to fall back on. She'd never graduated from high school and had few friends left in LA.

You'll make a comeback, her (now-ex) PR consultant had told her. *Just give it time. America is a great amnesiac.*

Then she'd sent Sibyl a bill for four thousand dollars.

The truth was, she might have refused to work this weekend had it not been for the guest bios Twyla had forwarded. When Sibyl saw Mia Meadows on the list, she was in.

Mia Meadows had described herself in the bio as "a career lead in some TV shows you've probably seen!" Sibyl, and anyone who had a pulse in the early nineties, knew the story was bigger—Mia had made a comeback after four months in prison for forgery of medical records, just over a decade ago. The headlines had been every bit as scathing as Sibyl's. But here was Mia now, appearing routinely on a number of popular shows, her followers on social media in the hundreds of thousands. Toting a hot young actor-boyfriend with James Dean eyes, to boot.

Jax Dupree was her boyfriend's name. A fake name if Sibyl had ever heard one.

His Instagram bio had made Sibyl snort with laughter. *Humble inhabiter of my character @VLADVANDERMEER on the CW show #WICCANS!!!!* Another actor airhead teeming with self-satisfaction, utterly serious about the forgettable, derivative nonsense (*Wiccans? Really?*) that he referred to as *his work*.

And yet, Sibyl found herself lingering on his abundant social media photos. The guy was gorgeous, that was for sure, but so were a million other people who worked in Hollywood. She'd switched back to Google and searched for interview footage of Jax Dupree. There was plenty, lightweight fare on TMZ, E!, People. He spoke the usual canned lines with the usual carefully rehearsed blend of charm and self-deprecation that all actors use to make themselves *relatable*.

There was nothing special about him, Sibyl decided. Just another pretty face fueling the Hollywood content factory.

And yet. There *was* something. Something about Jax Dupree's sculpted cheekbones and scalloped lips, something in the faux-soulful gaze of his long-lashed eyes, that Sibyl could not dislodge from her mind.

She looked at his Instagram daily.

Lately, Mia Meadows was all over it, draped over Jax's muscled shoulder, curled on his lap.

Mia might be fifty, well past the age of extinction for mid-tier TV actresses, but she seemed to be doing just fine. Sibyl knew Mia had enough disposable income to pay her a thousand dollars a day to hang out and do a few readings whenever it struck the fancy of her guests at Celestial Ranch. It made Sibyl a little nauseated, to be relegated to an on-demand party favor, but she was in no position to be choosy. Plus, compared to her old work schedule, which sometimes involved as many as eight sessions a day, Mia's requirements were easy: no more than six sessions total.

Sibyl didn't need to be Seer to the Stars again, didn't need their ridiculous gifts of diamond-encrusted dream catchers (Gisele/Christmas 2018) or a ten-thousand-dollar eBike (Taylor Swift/Sibyl's forty-fifth birthday). She only needed to scrape together the down payment for that two-bedroom house out in Joshua Tree with a big tin hot tub so she could watch the star-studded sky like a real cowgirl. It had been *the* dream that had carried her through the aftermath of the Merry Williams mess. The future she wished she could see clearly like an honest-to-goodness psychic prediction. She would be safe out in the desert with the old hippies and roadrunners and miles and miles of nothing but armies of twisted cacti. She yearned for the silence, the stillness, the spotty cell reception that would block those cryptic texts.

Perhaps a weekend reading for the likes of Mia Meadows and her friends was just the thing Sibyl needed to breathe new life into her asphyxiated career. She'd scanned the other bios optimistically: among the guests was a "literary novelist and screenwriter, a "visual effects designer," a "Big Data engineer for a major streaming platform." Film and TV people had once been her bread and butter; they'd come to her in droves, referred their glamorous friends, tagged her on social media, and supplied a steady stream of testimonials. As much as Sibyl loathed the narcissism of actors, she knew her own profession was not far removed. She, too, had devoted her life to pretending to be someone else.

Now, someone from one of those past lives had found her.

She'd gotten the first cryptic text back in March: UR LIFE IS A LIE, and they'd continued to arrive a few times a week, usually in the middle of the night. Each message was a repetition of the last, but with an additional line.

UR LIFE IS A LIE / LIES DON'T LAST / U THINK U CAN RUN / AWAY FROM UR PAST

Stupid, clumsy messages riddled with shorthand Sibyl associated with young people, but still. They rattled her. She deleted each message promptly, and blocked the number, but the messages always returned, longer each time, and from a new unidentified number.

What bothered her most: the area code of the sender. The source number always changed, but never the area code. Always 724. Harmony Township in Beaver County, Pennsylvania.

She ignored and deleted, ignored and deleted.

The mystery texter grew bolder. He (she knew it was a *he*) found her on social media, filled her DMs so she'd had to deactivate her accounts on Twitter, Instagram, and Facebook. LIAR LIAR. PANTIES ON FIRE.

Copied and pasted thousands of times.

Stupid. Childish. Terrifying.

Sibyl squinted down the hill at the faded barn beside Twyla's weed-choked vegetable garden. The sun sparked off the single solar panel Twyla had installed on the barn roof before realizing she couldn't afford to convert Celestial Ranch to solar power. Sibyl hadn't been thrilled to learn that one of Mia Meadows's many stipulations was that Sibyl conduct her sessions in Twyla's decrepit barn.

Her feet sweated inside her red cowboy boots. Her entire outfit—the boots, flowy bohemian dress, and wide-brimmed felt hat—suddenly seemed pathetic. It had been her signature style, and a major part of the branding campaign that had transformed mousy Pennsyltucky church girl Deborah Crabb. She'd been an idiot to wear the boots in the middle of a hot summer day. Of course, she'd hoped to summon the Sibyl *Vogue* had anointed as "The Psychic Who Guides the Stars."

She eased back down on the creaking front steps and yanked off her boots. She knew she had no choice but to do what Mia Meadows wanted. The money she made this weekend might give her the courage to do something about the cryptic texts.

UR PROBLEMS DIDN'T DIE W/ MERRY
How does it feel to live in the dark?
How does it feel to be SEEN, Debbie?
#NEVERFORGIVE #NEVERFORGET

She placed the dead phone facedown on the steps. She repeated the mantra she used to calm her most anxious clients. It was surprising how many people panicked in those first moments of blindness, so much so that Sibyl had begun blindfolding herself as well, albeit after they chatted a bit. Sibyl was a collector—of people's gestures and facial tics, of the secrets people hid behind toe tapping, leg jiggling, hair twirling, lip biting; their *oh my god*s and *hmm*s and *uh-huh*s. "*Repeat after me*," she'd say as she held the blindfolded client's hands, making sure one finger rested close to the client's wrist. "*Be. Here.*

Now." They repeated those words together until Sibyl felt the client's pulse slow. Only then did the vision session begin.

She closed her eyes and took a deep breath, holding it until her chest began to ache, then exhaled. *Be. Here. Now.* She slipped into the quiet place at once, the gentle clicking of the hummingbirds coming from a distance. The journey from outside to inside had always come easily for her. After all those hours she'd spent as a child lying in bed, curtains closed tight, waiting for the headaches to subside, visualizing the pain like waves breaking against the shore. When, at six years old, she climbed the stained carpeted steps to the altar/podium/stage at Harmony Church, slipping in and out of the trance, called the Spirit by her minister father and devout mother, had been a piece of cake.

A rustling rose from the overgrown bushes between the house and the tangled path of lavender and sage that led to the meadow. A warning that pulled her to her feet.

"Twyla?" she called.

Someone was there. He—she knew it was a *he*—smelled of sweat and wood smoke and peppermint.

"Twyla, I swear to God—if you're messing with me."

The sound of wood cracking. Something scampering over dead leaves.

"Whoever you are . . . there's a gun in the house. And I know how to shoot it!" Both lies.

She grabbed her phone, nearly dropping it, fumbling with the buttons.

"Come on!" she shouted as the glowing white apple appeared on the screen and began to load.

Then he was gone. A whiff of peppermint left behind.

She sat, dropping her phone onto the wood step.

Sweat dripped from her chin into the cleavage she hid with a tasseled tie-dyed scarf. She would need to redo her makeup in the cloudy mirror in Twyla's guest bathroom.

Her phone pinged on.

As it rattled across the scarred wood, text after text arriving until it seemed they would never end, she heard the rumble of the golf cart from across the meadow.

Twyla, at last.

5

Raj (the Drifter)

RAJ CONCEALED HIMSELF AGAIN, THIS TIME IN THE THICKET OF SPINY aloe stems on the side of the old couple's house, and watched the Witch sitting on the front steps leading to the sagging porch. She tapped her cowboy boots on the splintered wood and twisted her long, gauzy skirt around her hands. Impatiently waiting, Raj knew, for her friends to return home. So that, together, the three of them could face the trespassers, the so-called *guests*, soon to arrive in their gleaming cars for the weekend.

The old woman had been preparing all week for the guests' arrival with an intensity bordering on the frantic, crisscrossing the property carrying bins of supplies to the cabins, her ropy arms straining under the weight. The Witch, Raj knew, had come to help the old woman keep the guests happy.

And in turn, Raj would help Sheshnaag.

The weak moment he'd witnessed in the old man at the beehive had not shaken Raj's loyalty. Weakness in the presence of a woman—in the old man's case, his wife—was different from other weaknesses.

Raj knew this firsthand. It was his own weakness around Candace, his vanity, his insecurity, his childish need to impress her with lavish gifts and parties, that had caused so much wreckage. Had invited the media roaches right into their lives, cameras *snap snap snapping,* drones swerving overhead.

#CancelRajPatel

#RIPRaj

If only he'd had a chance to speak, before the hateful internet mob had driven him out, he could have told them that all he'd ever wanted, all he'd ever intended, was to keep Candace's love.

A love so pure and transcendent, he did not deserve it.

Perhaps, he thought now, as he lifted his binoculars to bring the Witch's face into view, the old man felt the same about his wife. That his fear of losing her was so great, it made him do crazy things, just to retain the privilege of her attention.

Yes. Raj understood.

Zoomed into his lenses, the Witch's dragon-red hair glinted in the afternoon sun beneath her wide-brimmed hat. He could even see the sweat clinging to her sharp, straight nose. Raj's hands trembled. He'd never had the opportunity to watch the Witch like this, at such close range, sitting still. Her oval face appeared older than he'd expected. Her pale skin creased around her mouth. Faint wrinkles trailed from beneath her sunglasses.

Despite her hat and sunglasses, Raj could see that the Witch was weary.

And then, for the first time, he realized he recognized her. Not only from these past months at Celestial Ranch, but from the long-ago days before the pandemic.

His breath quickened as he adjusted the focus knob.

Yes. It was definitely *her*.

He bit his bottom lip until he tasted blood, his memory clicking into place.

Like Raj, the Witch had once been a person in the regular world.

Like Raj, she'd been a victim of the cancel culture woke mob.

Years before the virus, he remembered now, he'd seen her on TV talk shows and, later, her fiery hair splashed across the covers of supermarket checkout rags, never guessing that his face (and sweet Candace's) would adorn those same trashy magazine covers. The tabloids had many names for the Witch—*shamed seer, disgraced psychic, charlatan*. Just as they had many names for Raj—*superspreader, billionaire brat, death party host*. Raj and the Witch were compatriots in the battle of truth versus the politically correct liberal elite know-it-alls!

His breath quickened with indignation. For the Witch, and for himself. He wanted to run to her, to tell her he understood. To beg her to come with him to the cave and cast her magical spells over Candace and him, to clear their minds and light their eyes, the way he'd seen her do with the old woman.

But then, he heard the whirr of a motor and the old couple lurched up to the house in their golf cart. The old woman leaped to the ground and ran to the Witch, weaving through the twisted metal sculptures dotting the front yard with the agility of a child. The mere sight of the Witch seemed to fill the old woman with vitality.

He watched the Witch rise to meet her. The two women embraced with the ferocity of long-lost lovers.

Raj felt a sudden, vast emptiness in his own body.

He needed to hold Candace in his arms.

Desperately.

It was almost time to return to the cave. To gently lift her sleeping body from its darkest corner and pull her close, their hearts thrumming in sync.

Soon, he would feel her heart.

But first, he would need to see the newly arrived guests. To take inventory, to gauge the fresh infusion of danger.

Silent as a deer, he backed out of the tangle of aloe, the spikes of a long stem snagging at his threadbare shirt. Near the house, the women chattered, oblivious in the sunshine, as Raj disappeared into the woods.

THE SUN WAS beginning to slide down the sky above Hydra Hill when Raj heard the crunch of car wheels on the dirt road below. Finally, the trespassers.

From the cover of scrub oak leaves, he watched the cars ascend the steep gravel road. Clouds of coppery dust billowed behind. A Mercedes SUV followed by a Tesla sedan stopped in front of the locked front gate.

And on cue, from the other direction, the old woman approached the entrance to Celestial Ranch in her rusted golf cart.

The Mercedes's driver's-side door opened and the first guest, a blond woman in too small denim cutoffs and cowboy boots, stepped out. She strode to the rickety gate secured to its post with frayed rope and began to dislodge it, acting as if, Raj thought, she owned this hallowed land. He despised the way the thoughtless guests treated the land of his redemption.

The old woman braked the golf cart a dozen feet from the gate and hopped to the ground; Raj knew it was the Witch's work, the way a woman of her age could move so nimbly. But just before the old woman reached the gate, the wolf dog blazed in front of her, knocking the old woman to the ground and springing toward the blond demon at the gate.

"KLONDIKE, NO!" the old woman screamed from the ground. "HEEL!"

Raj's binoculars tracked the wolf dog bounding toward the blond demon, flying over the ground, strong flank muscles rippling under blue-silver fur.

Hallelujah! The fierce animal spirit of the wolf dog would save them from this woman who might be beautiful on the outside but, Raj just knew, hideous inside.

The blond woman released the gate with a terrified scream and darted back toward the Mercedes. The old woman scrambled up from the ground, but it was too late: the wolf dog had gotten to the woman and begun barking. The barks were just hellos of excitement, Raj could tell from the way the dog wagged his tail, but the blonde continued to scream "Help!" She reached the driver's door of the Mercedes, then wheeled around, holding a red canister.

Raj heard a sound like a goose honking.

The dog yelped in pain, then cowered on the ground, grinding his head into the dirt.

Pepper spray.

The dog tore off into the brush.

The old woman shouted to her husband: "Arnold, do something!"

Raj's heart swelled for the wolf dog, for his unjust pain. How dare the blond woman hurt this gentle creature whose thick gray coat had warmed Raj many a night in the cave.

Keeping under cover of the scrub oak, Raj made his way down the slope where the dog had gone, through the trees, and down farther.

He saw the dog writhing on the ground in the clearing at the bottom of the hill, whimpering and mashing his snout into the patchy grass.

Slowly, Raj approached, humming softly so as not to startle the dog, holding out his hand in peace.

"It's okay, buddy," he said to the dog. "Let me take a look."

"It was the bitch with the fake tits," came a deep voice from the trees.

Raj looked up to see the old man standing less than a dozen feet away. He wore a battered fedora like an ancient Indiana Jones, his face stubbled with white beard. A leash dangled from his hand.

"Blond bitch got him. Pooch ran out to say hi, and she went and pepper-sprayed him."

"I saw," said Raj. He reached for the canteen on his belt and uncapped it. Then sluiced the water over the dog's face. He kept pouring, directing the cold stream over one eye and then the other, until the whimpering stopped.

"Appreciate it," said the old man. "The people my wife brings up here, they're a bunch of goddamn idiots." He limped down the slope to the dog and snapped the leash to his collar. He stood to face Raj and jabbed a finger in the direction of the road. "Can't even tell when an animal's being friendly. They have to go and burn his eyes."

The old man turned and heaved up the slope, the wolf dog at his side.

"Maybe put a little yogurt in his eyes," Raj called, surprised at his disappointment that the old man was leaving so soon. "Neutralizes the pepper faster."

The man stopped and glanced back at Raj.

"You don't worry about the dog anymore. Worry about the things you're supposed to do."

"I—" Raj began. *Don't leave yet,* he wanted to say. *Come with me to the cave. Sit with Candace and me, just for a short while.* "I will."

"Good. And you best look out for that blond bitch who sprayed Klonnie. She's the one to watch. She's the ringleader."

Then he charged up the hill with his dog, leaving Raj alone in the waning afternoon.

6

Dawn (the Birthday Girl)

"I JUST CAN'T APOLOGIZE ENOUGH," TWYLA REPEATED, HALF YELLING into the warm breeze stirred up by the rusted golf cart she drove with surprising aggression over the bumpy, toast-colored ground. "Klondike is usually a pooh bear! I don't know *what* got into him."

In the back, Dawn clutched the vinyl edge of the seat to keep from flying out. Beside her, Quinn kept an iron grip on Dawn's upper arm. The late afternoon sun was beginning to dip down toward the steep mountainside beyond the trees. Despite the long drought, the parched landscape was just as beautiful as the Airbnb listing had promised. Dawn glanced at Twyla, who leaned forward over the steering wheel.

"Please don't worry about the dog!" Dawn yelled into the wind. "Mia's very understanding!" This, of course, was a lie—Mia was a champion grudge-holder. All Dawn wanted was to get out of this golf cart, into her cabin, and settle Quinn down for the evening, so she could shower and ready herself for dinner. Mia and Jax were hosting a catered dinner at their yurt—*in the authentic Mongolian style!*

"Animals are just erratic sometimes," said Twyla. "I'm so very sorry. I just hope Ms. Meadows can forgive me. She seemed very upset." The older woman's long gray braid flared behind her.

"Oh, I'm sure she already has," lied Dawn, cringing. *How many times was Twyla going to apologize?* Then again, Dawn could relate. How many times had Mia demanded that Dawn not apologize so much, claiming it *diminished her power?* "You have nothing to worry about!"

"Thank the goddess," said Twyla, gunning the cart up a rocky slope. Quinn's grip tightened around Dawn's arm.

"Who's the goddess?" Quinn whispered.

Dawn heard her daughter's rapid breathing. She was glad she'd remembered to tuck some Ativan into her purse, never mind that both Quinn's psychiatrist and Craig disapproved. *They* weren't the ones spending the weekend with Quinn in the middle of nowhere at the apex of the canyon. In every direction Dawn looked, there were steep drops into seemingly bottomless ravines.

"It's okay, baby," Dawn said, rubbing Quinn's knuckles. "We're almost there."

"Almost *where?*"

"Our cabin, Quinny. It's called, um—"

"Betelgeuse!" Twyla chimed in. "Everything at Celestial Ranch is named after the stars."

"Betelgeuse?" Quinn sounded alarmed. "Like the dead guy in the striped suit in that movie?"

"No, honey, not like that," said Dawn. "It's just a cabin. A cute little house."

The golf cart hit a bump and bounced hard; Quinn moaned and clutched Dawn's arm tighter.

"Sorry!" yelled Twyla.

"No problem," said Dawn, loosening Quinn's grip. It seemed like ages since they'd dropped Mia at the yurt, where she'd bounded into the arms of Jax, her thirty-year-old actor-boyfriend with muscles on muscles and a chiseled jawline. Dawn had felt a pang of envy—when was the last time she'd been embraced like that? Not since way before the pandemic, before the divorce.

The late afternoon sun gilded the meadow with honeyed light as the golf cart flew downslope toward the woods. Dawn had a sudden memory of being out of control on skis as a kid, how the impending crash felt sickeningly inevitable. She reminded herself that Twyla was practically a mountain woman, an ultra-capable, latter-day pioneer. How many pioneers would die of something as silly as a golf cart crash?

Dawn squinted across the meadow for a glimpse of their cabin, but no buildings were visible, only an expanse of down-trodden earth, flanked by trees. *"All the guest quarters are spaced out intentionally!"* Twyla had explained. *"So each guest feels a sense of total privacy."*

Dawn wouldn't mind a little less privacy. She hoped she'd be able to find Mia's yurt with the hand-drawn map Twyla had given all the guests, with NOTE: PHONE MAPS SUCH AS GOOGLE WILL NOT WORK HERE printed across the top.

"We're here!" Twyla stopped at a sagging wooden bungalow with a slanted front porch.

"It's . . . charming," said Dawn, though the bungalow seemed to slouch to the left, and growth around the foundation—weeds and wildflowers—gave it a long-abandoned look.

"Let's go inside, Quinny-bee," Dawn said, prying Quinn's fingers from her arm and stepping out of the golf cart. "Thank you so much for the ride, Twyla!"

"My absolute pleasure." Twyla hopped from the driver's seat and shot to the back of the cart, where she retrieved Dawn's large duffel without the slightest strain.

"It looks haunted," said Quinn, not budging from her seat. "I don't want to go in."

"Quinn!" said Dawn. Poor Twyla had already gotten enough grief today.

Slowly, Quinn climbed out of the golf cart.

"I'm sorry," Dawn said to Twyla. Now *she* was the one apologizing.

"It's all right," said Twyla, smiling. "Nothing at Celestial Ranch is haunted, my young friend. Only magical." Then she handed Dawn her bag, hopped into the golf cart, and sped into the darkening woods.

BETELGEUSE WAS WORN but tidy inside, its walls and ceilings made of wide pine slats. The living room was furnished with a faded brown couch and a corduroy-upholstered loveseat situated around a blue rug. On the battered wood coffee table, Dawn spotted a bottle of wine, Costco-label cabernet, beside folded cardstock reading WELCOME TO BETELGEUSE! MAHALO FOR REMOVING YOUR SHOES in Twyla's elegant cursive.

God, the poor woman really *was* trying.

Quinn sank onto the couch and pulled out her phone. Dawn carried two Trader Joe's grocery bags to the kitchen, its beige linoleum floor peeling up at the edges, and set them on the chipped Formica countertop, then turned the dial on the mustard-yellow oven to four hundred to heat Quinn's dinner: the same frozen tater tots and chicken tenders (not *nuggets* or Quinn would not touch them) she ate over and over and over. That plus baby carrots (steamed, to silence their dreaded crunch) had comprised the majority of Quinn's diet for the past decade.

"Mom." Quinn looked up from her phone. "There's no cell service. Only Wi-Fi."

Dawn nodded. "Yes, honey, Twyla told us that. No signal way up here."

"What's the password?" Quinn sat up straight, stricken by the notion of no internet.

"Tell her you don't have a password," came Mia's voice in Dawn's mind. *"Think of what a great learning experience for her to be without the internet for a few days."*

Dawn crossed the room to her purse and pulled out the handwritten "property guide" Twyla had given her. She unfolded the brown butcher paper and read the Wi-Fi password to Quinn: "CELESTIAL90290."

"Works," said Quinn, sinking back into the couch. "It smells bad in here."

"Let's try not to complain, okay, sweetie?" Dawn pulled open a cupboard that was missing a hinge and shoved three bags of Corn Nuts—Quinn's favorite snack—inside. "This is a really beautiful place, and we're lucky to be here."

"It smells like poo."

"It does not," said Dawn. Actually, she *did* smell something vaguely intestinal. "I'm going to take a shower, honey. Then I'm going to walk over to Aunt Mia's place for dinner. It's just on the other side of the meadow."

"I can come with you," said Quinn.

"We talked about this, remember? Not tonight. It's just an—an old-person thing. You'll have all your regular dinner foods, and you've got a bunch of your favorite stuff downloaded, and we packed enough books for a lifetime. I'll just be out for, like, two hours."

Quinn trained her eyes on Dawn, unblinking, then dropped her head down toward her phone. Dawn sighed and pushed through the beaded curtains toward the dated bathroom with salmon-colored tile covering the wall beneath a cloudy mirror. It looked reasonably clean. The stack of white towels on the sink appeared fresh. Dawn exhaled with relief—she was dying to clear her head with a blast of hot water. Hopefully the shower had decent pressure. She pulled off her clothes, pushed back the green vinyl shower curtain, and stepped inside the stall.

Then she saw it. Two inches from her foot: an oblong brown lump of—*Jesus, what was it?* Dawn stared at it for a few disbelieving seconds. *Oh god*—it was some sort of shit.

Dawn leaped from the shower stall and snatched a towel off the sink, then bolted out of the bathroom and back down the hall to the living room.

"Mom! What's happening?" Quinn jumped from the couch, her phone clattering to the floor. Quinn covered her eyes. "Mom, please! What's happening? Why are you naked?"

Quinn was terrified of nudity.

"I'm sorry, Quinny, so sorry!" Dawn hurried to her suitcase by the front door, unlatched it, and located the oversized T-shirt she slept in. She pulled it on with a shaky breath as Quinn curled into a fetal position on the couch.

"I'm really sorry, baby. I overreacted! I just saw . . . something in the bathroom that startled me. I know there's animals here. I guess something got into the shower."

"There's an animal in the shower?" Quinn bolted off the couch and over to the front door.

"No, sweetie! No animals in the cabin. I went to step into the shower, and there's this giant brown . . . *log thing* in the corner of the stall."

"Log thing?"

"It's some kind of . . . animal poop, I guess. I'll just text
Twyla, and she'll clean it right up."

"I don't want to see it!"

"And you won't. Twyla will take care of it." Dawn entered
the Wi-Fi password into her phone and fired off a text: Bathroom issue—need some assistance ASAP! So sorry!

Soon Dawn's phone pinged with a reply: All bathrooms were
deep-cleaned this morning! I'll be there in 5 minutes!

"She's on her way," Dawn said to Quinn. "Everything's under control."

"Are you wearing underwear, Mom?"

Dawn draped her arm around Quinn and squeezed. "Nope.
You got me. I guess I'd better go put some on. And maybe some
actual clothes."

She lugged her duffel into the bedroom, slamming the
bathroom door shut on her way, and looked out the window
facing the meadow, hoping to see Twyla bouncing back to the
cabin in her golf cart. She saw nothing but a sea of grass and
wildflowers beneath the dimming sky, the bleached earth
abutted by deep-green trees and craggy flanks of mountain.

Dawn opened the window. The air was warm and still, the
afternoon silent but for the occasional trill of birds. She felt
an excitement she hadn't in years. It was hard to imagine her
friends here to celebrate her. She imagined Summer and Joanie,
squabbling over dresser drawers; Mia, already changed into
some Topanga-chic outfit, firing orders at the caterers; Graham
forcing his pretty young wife, Cecily, to listen as he quoted a
passage from Wallace Stegner he felt spoke to the landscape. Or
had marriage and a baby on the way changed him? Graham was
a literary novelist, prone to flares of pretentiousness, and back
when he and Dawn were a secret couple, he had brandished a
bumper sticker reading MAKE ART, NOT CHILDREN.

And Reece—what was she doing right now? Communicating with Reece was different than with other people: no short, choppy texts, no emojis, no links to stupid memes, no links of any kind, because Reece was not online. When they talked, they really *talked*. Or rather, Dawn talked and Reece listened. That was Reece's gift: her ability to listen, to really hear you, and then, only after she'd thought deeply about your situation, did she offer insights.

That was what Reece had given Dawn and her friends back at the Nurtury. She'd listened and listened, week after week, and only after the group had met for years—from teething to toddler tantrums to elementary school—had Reece led them to the Project. In retrospect, Dawn had come to realize that *they*—she and Mia, Joanie and Summer, Graham—had been shaping the idea all along. Reece had simply brought the plan into the world.

But that was ancient history. And, according to Mia, *not* to be discussed this weekend.

No toxic topics.

Fine. As it happened, Dawn had plenty of her own *toxic topics*, none of which she planned to discuss with her old friends this weekend either.

For example: only Reece knew about Dawn's stupid mistake during the pandemic. She'd written it in a letter, having been too ashamed to tell anyone else, and confessing on paper felt safer than saying it aloud or sharing in a text to Mia or Graham. She'd written it all down after she'd spent the morning in virtual court.

"And Ms. Sanders, is it correct to say that you administered several medical-grade cosmetic procedures from your own home, when a state mandate had placed a temporary ban on such services?"

Dawn knew to say nothing more than *yes*. Her lawyer had coached her well.

Verdict: a ten-thousand-dollar fine and one-year suspension of her esthetician's license.

Plus, an avalanche of humiliation. On top of her divorce, which had not yet gone through.

Dawn knew only one other person who had been ruined professionally. Pushed to the brink. Reece Mayall.

Dawn wrote the letter. Four single-spaced pages. *I don't think I was capable of comprehending what you went through with the Project. But now that I'm older (though probably not wiser), I think I understand what you went through. And I want to say: I'm so, so sorry.*

She'd dropped the letter in the mail, heart pounding as the blue metal hatch of the mailbox clanged shut with finality.

Two weeks later, she'd received a letter back.

No one else knew what Dawn had done. Not even Craig. Once the first surge in Covid deaths hit, LA County Public Health had shut down all "personal-care establishments."

In the course of a year, she'd managed to lose her husband, her career, and her dignity. She didn't have the money for therapy—Craig micromanaged their shared bank account, was a joint partner in the LLC for her esthetician work, and line-checked their credit card statements.

Her friends were mortified that she could be so trusting, so *enmeshed* when it came to her and Craig's money. But the truth was, all Dawn had room for—in addition to the facials and injections she administered to Brentwood stay-at-home moms— was Quinn. She'd never been interested in money or bothered to learn anything about it. Of this fact, she was ashamed, but how was she supposed to change when she was nearly fifty and earned a fraction of her husband's income?

The divorce was supposed to have transformed her. In running a "personal-care establishment" operation out of her home while Covid was raging, she'd been preparing for her own independence, believing she was doing something brave.

Her clients, rabid to have their new wrinkles erased, their blackheads extracted, were happy to pay a premium for the government-banned services. Dawn tripled her rates. She wore two masks—an N95 under a surgical one. She bought a thousand-dollar UV-light-sterilizer cabinet. Since she was working out of her home, she didn't have to give the commission to the med salon where she usually worked. She even opened her own bank account, unbeknownst to Craig.

Her clients made promises: *I'll not breathe a word. You're an angel.*

Her Prohibition-style salon, which she ran out of Craig's former home office, since it was accessible from the backyard, was an instant success. She'd intended to share it with only her oldest, most trusted clients, but the money was too enticing. She expanded her list, using a new cell phone she'd bought for the business to reach out to nearly anyone who'd been a client. She ran out of Botox. She ran out of Juvéderm. She ordered more from Tijuana. And then Alison Auslander, a woman Dawn had been injecting with god knows how many units for eight years, had a *reaction.*

Bell's palsy on the left side of her face. Significant swelling, especially her nose. One eye sealed shut. She texted the photos to Dawn's new phone, irate. I'M ELEPHANT WOMAN WHAT THE FUCK ARE U GONNA DO ABT IT

Of course, Alison Auslander didn't die. She wasn't permanently disfigured. Her face unfroze, her features returned to normal, her eye reopened. In three days, no one would have ever guessed what had happened.

Her anger at Dawn, however, was permanent.

A week later, two policemen knocked on Dawn's front door.

It wasn't the first time the authorities had come for her but, god, she hoped it would be the last.

DAWN STEPPED AWAY from the window overlooking Andro-meadow, smiling at the thought of Twyla's little-girl pride in the names she'd given various areas of the ranch. She unzipped her bulging duffel. With dismay, she examined the clothes she'd packed minutes before Mia had picked her up, too frazzled from the last-minute addition of Quinn to think about fashion. She held up a gauzy dress in sage green, then a flowy black jumpsuit she'd purchased from Instagram, falling for the caption "*Who says you can't be #SEXYTILDEATH.*"

The purchase seemed pathetic now; she dropped the jumpsuit back onto the pile and hung the green dress in the bedroom's small closet. She felt grubby and overheated, in desperate need of a shower. Where the hell was Twyla? And how had the poop gotten into the shower?

"Mom!" shouted Quinn. "The golf cart lady is back."

"Be right there!" called Dawn, tugging on underwear and leggings.

Dawn pushed through the beaded curtain to see her daughter standing at stiff attention beside the front door.

She hoped the night could only get better.

Sibyl (the Visionnaire)

"PEACH BREAD?" TWYLA ASKED SIBYL, BALANCING A THICK SLICE OF yellow loaf cake on a serving knife.

"Like I'd say no," said Sibyl, pushing her plate across the strawberry-print oil cloth–covered kitchen table.

"I made it this morning," Twyla said. "Peaches I got at the farmers' market on Wednesday—they were already going soft."

There was no fruit Twyla could not adapt into a moist, delicious cake, which, Sibyl thought, partially accounted for the expanding reach of Arnold's gut over his waistband. Twyla, on the other hand, remained spare and lithe as she'd ever been, her spine as straight as a ballerina's, the picture of a woman who proffered delicious treats constantly without partaking herself.

Sibyl noticed a subtle trembling in Twyla's hand as the older woman lifted the delicate bone china teacup to her dry lips. Chamomile—made with flowers gathered from the parched kitchen garden Twyla worked so hard to keep alive.

The same dogged determination, Sibyl thought, the older woman put into sustaining every acre of the ranch, every corner of the crumbling house and ramshackle cabins. As if, by pure effort and desire alone, she could force Celestial Ranch to thrive. The house, though still holding its rustic charm, had reached a new stage of disrepair, Sibyl noticed with dismay. The kitchen ceiling was growing a ring of mold and she wasn't sure if she should point it out. Maybe the older couple couldn't see it; maybe they chose not to.

She adored Twyla, who'd been a client, and then a friend, for over a decade, after she'd read about the Visionnaire in a profile Topanga's weekly paper had done on Sibyl, but when would the aging woman accept that enough was enough? That, as strong and fit and independent as Twyla was at seventy-two, it was not reasonable for her to keep up nearly twenty acres of mountaintop property practically by herself alongside caring for her husband, Arnold, who was probably, Sibyl feared, in the early stages of dementia.

It was too much for any person, of any age, to shoulder alone. As a result, Celestial Ranch was crumbling around Twyla, and even the simplest chores, like feeding the goats and turning them out each morning, were neglected.

"You okay, hon?" Sibyl asked and a look passed over Twyla's face, as quick as a cloud moving past the sun on a windy day. As if she'd been caught. Seen.

Twyla's toothy smile broke the suddenly somber mood.

"Who, me?" Twyla asked. "If I wasn't okay, I bet you'd already know." She winked at Sibyl, who had to laugh. Twyla looked into her cup, studying the liquid, as if, Sibyl thought, reading the tea leaves. "Problems—little ones, big ones, and everything in between—they seem to come out of nowhere day after day."

Sibyl knew there was more to the topic but respected when

people wanted to share and when they chose not to. The whole story, or at least the parts that mattered, she'd learned, came out when they were ready. No use in forcing it.

After an early dinner of lentil stew and home-baked bread, Twyla had flown out of the house after receiving a text from one of the guests. It was incredible, Sibyl thought, how needy the Airbnb people could be. Of course, they knew how desperate Twyla was to please them—Sibyl was sure they sensed that immediately and took advantage of it, complaining about everything from the thinness of the bath towels to the raucous noise of the coyotes fucking and fighting in the early morning hours. As if poor Twyla could press a button and mute the canyon wildlife. She'd returned from her errand at the guest cabin flushed and clearly upset, but had waved her hand when Sibyl asked for details, and busied herself serving dessert. Sibyl took a bite of cake; it was delicious. Twyla served Arnold a far smaller slice, placing it in front of his drowsing form with a "Here you go!" as if he were wide awake. Sibyl understood—her friend wasn't ready to see her husband's decline. If there was anything Sibyl had learned in the decades she'd spent reading people inside out so that, in her eyes, they wore their secrets on their skin, it was this—acceptance was the bitch of all bitches.

"This is crazy-good, as always," said Sibyl, washing down a bite of cake with the lemonade Twyla had poured into a mason jar, mason jars being the receptacle of choice at Celestial Ranch; Twyla must own a thousand. "So, tell me what I need to know about this fiftieth birthday gang that trekked all the way up into the canyon—"

"Away from their *smart* homes!" Twyla interrupted with a snort.

Sibyl laughed, "Good one, Twy," knowing Twyla had no idea what a *smart* anything really was. Twyla, whom Sibyl had only just convinced to put in Wi-Fi, and who'd bought her first cell phone in 2020 at the start of the pandemic, was convinced the device gave off toxic rays that would poison her and Arnold.

Twyla rose to locate a worn composition notebook on the kitchen island. Tucked inside it were two sheets of printer paper. Settling back at the table, she handed the loose sheets to Sibyl and opened the notebook to a page covered in her spidery handwriting. "*JUNE 24–26 GUEST INFO*," Sibyl read in large letters across the top.

"The printed stuff is Ms. Meadows's special instructions for you," Twyla said. "You're their main attraction!" She lifted her eyebrows, "For a bunch of Hollywood glamoramas. How fun. I'm a tad jealous."

"Don't be," Sibyl said, glancing through the text-cluttered pages. A *lot* of instructions for so few sessions. Some of them were expected—be prepared to do sessions with clients on demand, whenever the urge strikes them—others were more cryptic: Sibyl was not to leave the barn between sessions if she had an hour or less between clients. Sibyl was not to eat or drink during the sessions.

What. The. Fuck.

Then she heard her mother's voice: *Beggars can't be choosers.*

This was true; after the Merry Williams disaster, Sibyl could not afford to turn down work. Or to displease another celebrity. Even if Mia Meadows was a minor celebrity decades removed from the brightest spotlight.

"Mia said there will be some additional stipulations that she'll discuss with you privately," Twyla said, adding, "but that they're not a big deal, nothing outside your expertise."

"*Additional* stipulations?" Sibyl said. Alarm bells.

"Oh, you know," said Twyla. "Probably just confidentiality

stuff. We know how these Hollywood types stick to their own kind. And fancy themselves oh-so-important. She probably just wants you to promise you won't leak the names of her famous friends, or take pictures of them, or what have you."

Arnold cleared his throat, suddenly roused. "Bunch of assholes, probably."

Sibyl laughed. Arnold's on-the-nose criticism, which some dismissed as typical old-man crankiness, was what she loved about him. A counterbalance to Twyla's rose-tinted optimism.

"Arnold!" Twyla planted an admonishing hand on his arm. She turned to Sibyl. "Someone's in a *mood* today."

"I'm right here," said Arnold.

Twyla put on her glasses and began reading the guest information from her notebook aloud.

"Let's see. We've got the birthday girl, Dawn, and her daughter, Quinn—what sort of name is that?—in Betelgeuse. Then Mr. Graham Caldwell, who's a published author, in Sirius. Gosh, I hope the bed in there is comfy enough for him. Evidently he's quite famous."

"I've never heard of him," Sibyl couldn't help inserting.

Arnold snorted. Twyla ignored him.

"We've got the two ladies," she went on, "Summer and Joan, who goes by Joanie, in Vega." Twyla slid a hand across the table and gripped Sibyl's forearm. "I think the super-bright Vega energy is the perfect fit for lesbians, yes?"

Sibyl nodded, knowing there was no point in arguing with Twyla's often romantic notions, and added, "It *is* the star of forbidden love according to Chinese legend."

"Oh perfect!" Twyla clapped her hands. "And of course, Ms. Meadows and Mr., er—"

"Jax?" said Sibyl.

"Guess I left off his last name," said Twyla. "But yes. Ms. Meadows and Mr. Jax are in Orion. Mia specifically requested the yurt."

"Naturally," said Sibyl.

"And finally"—Twyla lifted the notebook closer to her face—"we've got Reece Mayall—all the way from Oakland, goodness!—in Ursa Minor."

"I shall not disappoint," said Sibyl, standing from the table and transferring her plate and glass to the sink. She knew better than to try to wash Twyla's dishes. She retrieved her purse from its hook by the kitchen door. On cue, her phone buzzed with a text alert from inside the bag.

Please, no.

She turned back to Twyla and Arnold, her heart beating too fast, and gave a jaunty salute. "Okay, my loves. I'm off to my room to prepare for the *glamoramas.*"

"Give 'em hell," Arnold called as Sibyl made her way up the creaky staircase.

Panting on her way up to the landing, she pulled out her phone, chest tightening with dread as she read the text:

KARMA'S A BITCH / A BITCH IS NO FUN / ESP WHEN
SHE'S UNDER YR BED / WITH A GUN

She gripped the curved end of the banister, fighting to catch her breath, willing herself to calm down.

The text was as stupid as all the rest, on par with bad bumper stickers, and still, each one shook her more deeply than the last. Left her paralyzed with anxiety as she tapped *Block Contact* yet again.

She thought about hurrying back downstairs and telling Twyla, then imagined the fuss her friend would make. *No sirree.*

Could Sibyl call the police based on threatening texts alone? Would they do anything more than tell her to change her number, block the caller, let them know if anything real happened? Then they'd hang up and have a good laugh: *Guess who* just filed a report about—wait for it—text harassment . . .

She was already a laughingstock. No need to fuel the fire. No need to bring her name to the attention of the authorities again. She'd already pushed her luck too far.

8

Dawn (the Birthday Girl)

WELCOME TO ANDROMEADOW, PLEASE STEP LIGHTLY!

Dawn squinted to read the words carved into the wooden sign staked at the periphery of the meadow. Then she began to walk across the open field of scrub grass and rocks, punctuated by frizzy bushes and patches of wildflowers, hoping she'd read Twyla's map correctly.

"Don't be late for dinner!" Mia had reminded Dawn earlier. *"I know you're going to want to make everything perfect for Quinny, but it's the opening night of your birthday, bitch."*

The *opening night* phrase had made Dawn nervous. A reminder that tonight was just the first in a long list of activities Mia had planned for the coming days.

And now, of course, Dawn *was* late. Before she left the cabin, she *had* made everything perfect for Quinn, right down to ensuring *Dune* was downloaded on Quinn's iPad, the Unbridled novels stacked on the coffee table, Quinn's favorite snack (ranch-flavored Corn Nuts) laid out on the kitchen counter, and her favorite pajamas (blue plaid, their ancient cotton threadbare) folded atop her bed.

Mia wouldn't approve, would call it "coddling" or "enabling" or whatever, Dawn thought as she hurried across the darkening meadow, praying she wouldn't step through the poison oak Twyla had pointed out earlier, or—*oh god*—the rattlesnakes Twyla had called *"shy and mellow, as long as you don't surprise them!"*

Since they'd reconnected, Dawn had discovered that Mia's parenting philosophy, which had once been so aligned with her own—and with that of the whole group at the Nurtury Center—had changed, now that their children were grown. Once-doting Mia was now hands-off with Nate, who was twenty-three and lived in his own studio apartment and worked as a software developer in Culver City. He bought his own groceries and even went on dates with women he met on Tinder and Hinge.

These developments, which Mia had revealed to Dawn on their beach walks during the pandemic, had stung. Quinn had made no such progress.

Of course, Mia attributed Nate's independence to her refusal to coddle him and encouraged Dawn to do the same with Quinn, to *"step back"* more often, to *"let go."* This was nothing new. Dawn had been getting similar feedback from Quinn's therapists and doctors, from her own friends, and, of course, from Craig, for years. *Stop helicoptering. Stop lawn-mowing. Stop anticipating her every need. Let her discover how capable she actually is.*

The advice stung Dawn, every time, but especially coming from Mia, who at one time, along with the rest of their friends who would be at dinner tonight, was part of the group unified by the unique demands of their *atypical* children. Unified by their shared understanding of just how hard it was for their kids to get through the basic mechanics of a day—shoe tying, tooth brushing—let alone connect meaningfully with others. Were all the people encouraging Dawn to let Quinn *do it on her own* blind to how hard that was when the most benign daily encounters filled Quinn with fear, when she didn't have a single close friend in the world—other than her mother?

God, what Dawn would do to be able to turn her daughter out to pasture and watch her gallop away, frolic with others, *thrive* without constant oversight. But it wasn't that easy.

Which was why, just before leaving Quinn alone in the cabin, she'd pressed half an Ativan into her daughter's palm. Of all Dawn's parenting choices today, Mia would disapprove of this the most.

For the past thirteen months, they'd managed to avoid the topic of medical intervention.

"Nate and I had Covid," Mia had casually mentioned on one of their first calls after the initial forgiveness text. *"Back at the very beginning. It was no picnic, but that's Mother Nature for you."*

Dawn had murmured something about being so glad they were okay and left it at that. She'd made no mention of the three-plus hours she'd waited at Dodger Stadium to receive her Covid vaccine—and she planned to keep it that way.

She'd gotten Quinn vaccinated too. *That* she'd never share with Mia.

Or Reece. Or anyone this weekend. Surely, no one would bring up the topic of vaccines. Never mind that the topic of *"to vax or not to vax"* had taken center stage in the national psyche, since vaccines had played such a critical role in subduing Covid.

Dawn thought of Mia's decree to the guests: *Not a single fucking mention.*

What had Reece thought of Mia's mandate? What had the

others thought? Would they really get through the weekend without mentioning any of it?

Dawn walked quickly in the direction of the yurt, her breath coming faster, weeds biting at her ankles and the last dregs of sunset draining from the sky.

And then, there it was, at the base of a long gentle slope: a large, rounded structure rising from the grass, like a carousel wrapped in a giant Band-Aid, with glowing oval windows and pretty string lights lining the edge of the roof.

The yurt. She'd found it.

It was time to be the birthday girl.

"DAWN LEIGH SANDERS!"

A silhouette stepped from the yurt's tied-back canvas door and began charging up the hill toward Dawn, a curtain of braids dancing behind her.

It was Reece.

"Reecie!" Dawn broke into a jog, and then they were in each other's arms, hugging with the ferocity of lovers long separated by war. Dawn's joy at the sight of her old friend was so pure that forgoing the usual pre-hug courtesy—*"Is this okay? I'm vaccinated, of course"*—did not faze her. Never mind that Dawn had prefaced every single hug she'd given a friend in the past year and a half with these approval requests, which were basically the societal norm now.

"Let me *look* at you," said Reece, stepping back from their embrace but keeping her palms on Dawn's shoulders. "You know, I don't really *do* the internet, so I need a minute here."

"You look amazing," said Dawn, meaning it. "Exactly the same." Except for some gray hair threading her signature

braids, Reece was just as Dawn remembered her from years
ago: tall and lithe, her unlined, broad-cheeked face open and
curious, her dark skin smooth as river stone, offset by her
pretty yellow dress.

She did not, Dawn thought, with relief, look like a woman
who'd suffered a great deal of damage. Dawn had expected something different: a bitter edge, a haunted look in Reece's eyes.

But no. She looked like Reece: calm, wise. Open and accepting. No judgment.

"You've only gotten more beautiful, Dawnie," Reece said.
"Happy birthday."

"Thank—thank you," said Dawn, swallowing the lump in
her throat. "I just can't believe you're here. That you'd drive all
the way down from Oakland—for me."

"I wouldn't miss it for the world. We have so much to catch—"

"Yoo-hooo!" a familiar throaty voice interrupted, and Dawn
turned to see Summer Hemsworth beckoning at the bottom of
the hill. "Are you guys finished making out yet? Because we're
all *starving* in here."

Behind her, Joanie Ahn, Summer's wife, glossy black hair
loose at her shoulders, dressed in an impeccable taupe sheath,
waved at Dawn. "Hey, b-day girl," Joanie said in that effortlessly
cool way she had, as if they'd seen each other just yesterday.

"Here we come," Reece returned, grabbing Dawn's hand
and pulling her down the hill toward the yurt. They reached the
bottom and fell into a four-way hug with Summer and Joanie.

"Thanks for schlepping all the way up here," said Dawn.
Her face felt hot from all the attention, and she hoped her
makeup wasn't a smeared mess.

"Are you kidding?" said Summer. "It took us a half hour.
I've been counting the days. Nothing like Reecie's heroic effort coming so far. Plus, I adore Topanga. Joanie, on the other

hand"—she elbowed her wife affectionately—"is acting like she got dropped on the set of *Naked and Afraid*."

"I am *not*," said Joanie. "I just happen to possess certain basic standards of hygiene."

Dawn caught a whiff of Joanie's perfume, something delicate but earthy. Even in the dry wilds of Topanga, Joanie was as civilized as ever in her simple linen dress, her face as fresh and unlined as it'd been eighteen years ago. Although she'd grown up in Los Angeles and was as American as anyone Dawn knew, Joanie's parents had immigrated from Korea, and her mother had instilled in her the traditional Korean reverence for skin care.

"You look beautiful, Jo," Dawn said.

"My face feels like a desert," said Joanie.

"No complaining, Goose," sang Summer.

"Who's complaining?" asked Joanie. "I'm positively thrilled to discover I won't have to shit in a hole in the ground."

"Isn't plumbing the best?" said Reece.

"I spy with my little eye . . . the birthday girl!" a voice sailed from the yurt, and Dawn saw Mia standing at the entrance in a powder-blue apron over an all-white ensemble, quite similar, from what Dawn could tell, to the flowy black #SEXYTILDEATH jumpsuit she'd almost worn. Thank god she hadn't—with Mia's blond hair tumbling loose around her shoulders, her arms tanned and sculpted, the cinched apron showcasing her still-tiny waist, Mia evoked the authoritative hotness of a *Melrose Place*—era Heather Locklear.

"Get in here, lovelies!" Mia beckoned, fluttering her long nails. "Don't just stand there waiting for rattlesnakes to bite your ankles!"

"Still got her talons," Summer said under her breath.

"Let's do it," said Reece, taking Dawn's hand again—

wrapping Dawn in a much-needed cocoon of safety—and they made their way to the entrance of the yurt.

"You're late, Dawnie," said Mia, kissing Dawn's cheek as she ushered them into a cavernous space with a high-domed ceiling lined with more strings of lights. "But I forgive you."

The interior was significantly nicer than Betelgeuse's, its softly lit living area furnished with a newish-looking midcentury couch and two matching chairs, plus a round tiled table covered with crackers, spreads, and nuts. Thelonious Monk dipped and bobbed over the room. Dawn wondered why Mia hadn't given *her* the nicer place for the weekend—could it be punishment for bringing Quinn along?—then quickly pushed the thought from her mind, chastising herself for being anything but grateful.

"Sit, sit, relax. Dinner'll be up soon. We're sitting outside. Jax is mixing drinks, Graham's on the deck FaceTiming with Cecily, and—"

"FaceTiming?" Dawn couldn't help interrupting. "Did Cecily stay back at her cabin?"

"More like back at her house in Bel-Air," Summer said.

Mia nodded. "Cess decided that an adventure weekend in the woods was *not* what the doctor ordered for her third trimester."

"Understandable," said Reece. "Nearly all mammalian species experience intense nesting instincts before giving birth."

"Of course, makes total sense," said Dawn. "I was just looking forward to getting to know her better."

"I'm sure you were," said Mia, without sarcasm, though Dawn knew her friend was onto her. She'd confessed her feelings about Cecily to Mia on one of their beach walks. Confided that while Dawn no longer felt possessive of Graham, she felt he just wasn't himself around his wife. It was as if, Dawn had confided in Mia, Cecily's sunniness had banished the wry, ironical, dark-tinged sensibility that made Graham *Graham*.

"Ma'am?" a stressed-looking man in a black uniform called to Mia from the small open kitchen along the far wall. "Could I speak with you for a moment?"

Mia rolled her eyes. "Caterer's being a little high-maintenance. Be right back. Make yourself comfortable, darlings, the night is young!"

Dawn settled on the couch beside Reece, marveling at how Reece *still* had the ability to make her feel at ease in any setting.

"Evening, ladies!" Jax appeared in a ribbed tank top and olive jeans, balancing a tray of pale-green drinks with mint sprigs jutting from the glasses. "May I interest you in a cocktail? It's a special drink I made up for the birthday girl." He extended the tray toward Dawn. "Sort of a mojito with a kick. I call it—" He paused and swept his free hand toward the tray. "The Dawn Treader."

"Oh?" Dawn brightened. "Like the C. S. Lewis book? My daughter adored the Narnia series when she was younger." She reached for a drink.

"What?" Jax looked confused.

"The name of my drink. It's a reference to a novel of the same name, right?"

"Hmmm, no." Jax shook his head. "Must be a coincidence. It's a reference to the new J. J. Abrams film I was just cast in. It's actually called *The Voyage of the Dawn Treader*."

Clearly, Dawn thought, Jax had no idea his own movie was based on a book.

"Adore your braids," Jax said as he extended a green drink to Reece.

Reece held up a hand. "Oh, no thanks. I'll just take some club soda."

Jax nodded. "I'm sober-curious myself. Just haven't quite gotten there yet."

Dawn cringed, feeling the urge to smack him. How could Mia be dating such an airhead?

"You'll get there if you need to," Reece said. "It's been ten years, nine months, two weeks, and six days."

Dawn did a quick calculation. That would put the start of Reece's sobriety right around the time Mia got out of jail and Reece was released from the hospital for the second time.

Right around the time they both stopped speaking to Dawn.

"A decade, wow," Jax said. "Props to *you*." Then he offered the tray toward Summer, who grabbed two drinks and handed one to Joanie.

"Thanks!" Summer said with an overbrightness that implied *Now go the fuck away.*

Jax complied, wishing Dawn a "Happy big five-oh" before gliding off to the bar.

Dawn took a long sip of her drink. It was tart and delicious, with a ping of heat at the finish.

"No words," said Summer, leaning back in her chair and crossing her thick, muscular legs. Joanie, Dawn thought, was childlike next to her wife. "Meadows has outdone herself with this one."

"Please be nice," said Joanie. "Mia and Jax are *hosting* us."

"Relax, Goose." Summer drained her drink.

Joanie gave Summer a withering look and set her full glass down on the table.

Dawn scanned the room for Graham; still no sign of him.

Reece turned to Dawn, drawing a leg underneath her flowing yellow skirt. "So, Mia tells me you brought Quinny-bee along?"

Hearing Reece speak Quinn's old nickname from toddlerhood made Dawn feel teary again. Her mind flashed to a memory of the Nurtury: Reece bouncing a red-faced Quinn on her knee, humming in her ear, magically coaxing her into calming down from a tantrum.

"Yes. It sort of just—happened. My ex-husband—" Dawn stopped, hearing Mia's voice in her head.

No toxic topics.

Craig was a toxin.

"You know," Dawn went on, "never mind. Yes, Quinny's here. Back at our cabin."

"I can't wait to see her," said Reece, reaching to touch Dawn's arm. "I bet she's the most amazing person now."

Now Dawn worried she was really going to cry. It was so nice, so *rare*, for someone to have such an uncalculated, positive reaction to Quinn.

She swiped at the corner of her eye, hoping a tear wouldn't escape.

"She'll be happy to see you too."

"Hey, where's Grahammy-boy?" Summer cut in, already sounding tipsy.

"Talking to his *wife*," said Joanie.

"No way in hell is he *still* talking to her," said Summer. "Men have an eight-minute limit when it comes to FaceTiming. He's been out there for half an hour. You can bet your ass he's sipping his whiskey and sneaking a smoke. But really, this *is* our weekend to cut loose, isn't it? We're old, our kids are grown and gone—" She caught herself and looked at Dawn. "*Mostly* grown and gone. What I mean is, why shouldn't Graham indulge a little? You know, when in Topanga, without your pregnant wife . . ."

"One should start a forest fire?" Joanie finished.

Reece threw back her head and laughed. "I've missed you guys."

Dawn laughed too, awash in happiness. The drink was getting to her, for sure, but mostly, it was Reece. It felt so good to be back together again—far better than she'd dared to imagine.

But where the hell *was* Graham?

"I think I'll pop outside and find Graham," Dawn said, standing with her drink. "You know, shame him for smoking. How could he have missed that giant Smokey the Bear statue at the bottom of the canyon? Be right back!" She set off toward the deck, touching the top of Reece's head as she went, thanking her.

Santa Monica

AMONG THE FIVE CORE DEVOTEES OF REECE MAYALL'S parenting support group at the Nurtury, envy was a serious problem. Not of one another but of parents of "neurotypical" children. Parents of kids on the "trad track at school," as Reece called it—the traditional, general-ed path.

Dawn would always remember the enormity of her relief when, sometime in her second year of attending meetings every Thursday morning, Mia had stood up during WOW (*Wide-Open Words*—Reece's name for the "judgment-free invitation to share anything on your mind") and declared, her voice forceful but shaky at the edges, *"I'm so fucking sick of being jealous of other parents. This morning, my neighbor, who's got three kids, including a son who's eight, just like Nate, casually tells me that they're taking a trip to fucking Europe this summer. The five of them are going Eurorail. Which is something I've always wanted to do!*

But now I'm thirty-five and divorced, and I can't even take Nate shopping at Trader-fucking-Joe's without—" She covered her face and burst into tears.

Reece knelt beside her, looping her arms around Mia's narrow, quaking shoulders.

Soon the rest of the group was crying too.

One by one, the other parents spoke, confessing their own locked-away anger over the limits their children had placed on their lives. How jealous they were of the freedoms that families with neurotypical children took for granted.

When it was Dawn's turn to speak, she said the things she'd never dared utter to anyone. Not even to Craig.

She told the group that some days—okay, at certain times nearly *every day*—she resented Quinn. How some days, as much as she loved the girl, and god, she did love her, mothering her simply felt too hard.

How sometimes, she felt she could not go on.

How she felt like a permanent failure of a mother.

Of a human.

When she finished, Dawn wept with a relief deeper than any she'd known. She let Reece hold her, and she was not ashamed, thinking, as she so often did lately, that the Nurtury was saving her life. That without her new friends—especially Reece—she might die.

9

FRIDAY, JUNE 24, 2022

Twyla (the Hostess)

IT WAS TIME TO FIX ARNOLD HIS BEDTIME CUP OF TEA.

There were three pills left. Twyla dreaded the inevitable trip down into the Valley on Monday to see Dr. Belk to ask for more. She might be refused a refill without Arnold present, but she couldn't bring him along. A calm, compliant Arnold was necessary for her business to be a success. There had already been too many incidents that threatened her host ratings.

She tightened her bathrobe against the night chill seeping in through the windows and made her way down the hallway, past the closed door of the guest room where Sibyl was staying, down the stairs, careful to avoid all the creaky patches. This was how well she knew her old house: every sagging step, every splintered floorboard.

She crouched over Klondike, curled in slumber on his ancient dog bed by the kitchen door. She rubbed the crown of silver between his ears and whispered, "I'm sorry, buddy."

Poor loyal Klondike. She'd wanted to slap that Mia Meadows

across her perfect face, make the woman feel the pain poor Klonnie with his red and runny eyes had felt. What kind of monster pepper-sprays a playful dog? Arnold had wanted to call the ASPCA, file charges against the woman. Twyla had felt like a traitor apologizing to Ms. Meadows. They all had to sacrifice to make life on the ranch feasible, even the dog.

She made her way through the dining room, passing the table strewn with detritus pertaining to Arnold's unfinished art projects: a mosaic from old garden tiles, a watercolor of a seascape, which she'd had to nag him to start. Where had Arnold *the doer* vanished to? The man who'd spent so many nights in his workshop sanding wood, carving dowels by hand, all of it resulting in beautiful Shaker-style chairs and stained art frames.

Arnold was asleep in the recliner in the dimly lit family room. She had always resented him calling it that, *the family room*, when it was and always would be just the two of them. He'd been asleep since after dinner when she'd left to feed the goats and make sure the holes the beechies had made in the rotting barn wall were stuffed tight with shredded steel wool. That's all she needed—a bunch of rodents interrupting the serenity of Sibyl's sessions with guests tomorrow.

She'd have to wake Arnold and risk his anger. What if she couldn't coax him into drinking the tea? A whole pill would go to waste.

In the kitchen—it still smelled sweetly of the peach bread she'd warmed in the oven—Twyla set the kettle to boil, reminding herself to pull it from the flame before it whistled. It was important to stay extra quiet, as Sibyl was a light sleeper and prone to stormy moods if she woke before her "natural emergence into consciousness."

From its place beside the fridge, Twyla pulled out a step stool and stood on the platform, gripping the edge of the countertop for balance. It was depressing how cautious she'd become with her body after all the years of unabashed use: entire mornings spent crouched and digging in the garden, afternoons loosening hay from the bale with a pitchfork to feed the goats, climbing ladders to repair roofs, riding uncooperative horses on uncleared mountain trails; what used to be everyday living had become a lineup of risks, any of which could knock her out of commission.

If Arnold had his druthers, she thought as she lifted onto her toes to reach for the herbs—chamomile salvaged from her dried-up garden, plus lion's mane—some previously mundane chore would knock her down so hard they'd have to leave Celestial Ranch altogether. Not that Arnold consciously wanted her to break a hip or blow out a knee. But her husband was, clearly, looking for a reason for them to leave Topanga. He was ready for someone else to do the work. Preferably a staff member at some godforsaken *senior living community* in the Valley. He'd actually started sharing "literature" with her—pamphlets, websites, reviews on that Yelp site!

She didn't hesitate to remind him of the 200,000 Covid deaths that had occurred in nursing homes. They were death traps, spiritual and otherwise.

She didn't deny the obvious—Celestial Ranch had issues. Still: it wasn't simply the place she'd lived for forty years. It was the only home her *soul* had ever known. It was an extension of Twyla herself, the Twyla she'd become after fleeing Connecticut and the suffocating cage of her conservative, status-quo-loving parents, for UC Santa Barbara back in 1968, where she'd met Arnold at the peak of radical love and antiwar protests, all-night euphoric celebrations spent dancing to rock 'n' roll. She could still feel the ache in her muscles after those long ocean-soft nights moving in sync with the music of Arnold's band, No

Shrinking Violets. Not caring how her flesh jiggled, freed from
the full-form bra and girdle her mother had insisted she wear.

Celestial Ranch was the culmination of that freedom. She
deserved to spend the last years of her life in dignity.

She wasn't quite sure she, the liberated Twyla, would survive anywhere else. So, she'd done whatever it took to keep the
ranch intact, even if it had involved driving down to that awful
computer café in the Valley, studying the godforsaken Airbnb
website, and figuring out how to take "flattering" photos of the
crumbling cabins. Even if it had involved cashing in an old favor with Griz and that sketchy friend of his, Tom Something-
or-other, to build a yurt, the only modern structure on the
property, and the one Twyla showcased on her Airbnb profile. Once potential guests got an eyeful of the yurt, with its
stainless-steel kitchen and freshly stained redwood deck—
plus the photos of the ranch's prettiest spots: the ridge, the
meadow, the grand oaks, and the massive agave in full bloom,
its ten-foot-tall stalk reaching from the center of the plant up
into the sky—they skimmed right over the heavily edited photos of the other structures.

If she continued to have money for the upkeep of the
ranch, Arnold's argument for leaving would grow consider-
ably weaker. She wasn't there yet, but she was moving forward.
The party this weekend, regardless of that twit Mia Meadows,
was her biggest earner yet. Which is why the appearance of
foul-smelling animal crap in the bathroom of Betelgeuse had
nearly sent Twyla into a fit.

The log of shit was a mystery. How could an animal that
large—it must have been a black bear or a bobcat—get into the
cabin and manage to shit on the bathroom floor, then leave
without destroying furniture or scratching walls? She had
heard from Dr. McAllister, the homeopathic vet she insisted

treat Klondike and the goats, that the pandemic had caused big changes to the wilderness areas around Los Angeles—the months of decreased human presence had made animals much bolder. Coyotes in downtown LA, falcons circling the subdued skies of the airport, and even large families of deer grazing in empty lots in South Central.

Perhaps a rare mountain lion had slid into Betelgeuse sometime yesterday and taken its formidable dump as some sort of marking technique? Animals, after all, possessed extraordinarily high degrees of intelligence and canniness. Humans, on the other hand, Twyla thought, not so much. She'd known the city women wouldn't question whether Klondike had been responsible for the shit. And she'd been right, though Twyla felt a little bad about pinning the mess in the bathroom on her innocent dog. Then again, she desperately needed this weekend not to result in any refund requests.

Steam shot from the kettle, and Twyla moved it from the flame. Arnold snorted from the family room, and the springs of his old recliner squeaked. She poured the scalding water into the mug and paused to inhale the fragrant steam.

She dropped a small pill into the ceramic mortar bowl and hummed as she ground it with the pestle, hoping her low drone covered the sound. A movement at the kitchen window made her lean forward, scan the rolling hills of the meadow, lit blue in the moonlight like a shimmering sea. A dark shape ran across the meadow.

It must have been one of the guests, she decided as she carried the mug into the family room. The thought of the guests running through the moonlit property pleased her. Like a scene straight out of *A Midsummer Night's Dream*. How romantic.

Twyla was careful when opening and closing the swinging door to the family room to avoid its creaks. When, *when*, would

Arnold WD-40 it, as she'd asked so many times? Whether he was incapable of making the smallest efforts to keep up the property or simply unwilling, Twyla was unsure, though how he'd sprinted after Klondike yesterday afternoon hadn't escaped her. And how did *that* Arnold jive with the Arnold who seemed too weary to locate the canister of WD-40 in the garage and hold down its button? Who had suggested they sell, even donate, the goats they had loved like children for years? The first Arnold, the dog-chasing sprinter, thought Twyla, as she unfolded the tray table and set it next to Arnold's recliner, did not make so compelling a case for deserting the home they'd tended for forty years for a "gated community" with a bleach-filled swimming pool, starchy dinners served at five p.m., and giant-screen TVs on every wall.

She brushed her lips over the coarse, dry cheek of sleeping Arnold, and placed the steaming cup of tea on the tray.

"Wake up, Arnie," she whispered. "You need to take Zephyr's bedtime tea if you're going to get a good night's sleep."

Arnold startled awake, flailing his arms. His hand smacked the mug off the tray. Twyla lunged for it, her knees landing hard on the cold wood floor. The tips of her fingers brushed the mug, one she'd hand-thrown herself at the wheel in the barn, before it shattered across the floor.

10

FRIDAY, JUNE 24, 2022

Dawn (the Birthday Girl)

STEPPING OUT OF THE YURT, DAWN SPOTTED GRAHAM LEANING against the deck railing, staring out to the tree-lined ridge. Smoke drifted over the shoulder of his short-sleeved button-down shirt, patterned with various types of fruit; well into middle age, Graham stood by his signature style of wacky hipster shirts paired with professorial blazers.

There it was now. Dawn saw a tan jacket draped over the railing next to a tumbler of scotch. She smiled, finding comfort in the familiarity of his form: six-three, narrow shoulders, that boyish lankiness. And was it just Dawn's angle, or did he look a little heavier from behind?

Perhaps, now that he was with Cecily, he felt he could let himself go a bit. Graham's first marriage, at fifty-two, was to a woman thirteen years younger with green eyes and dark curls. Dawn was surprised at how much the news had stung. She and Graham had been purely platonic for over a decade, and even back in the days of the Nurtury, had slept together only in furtive stretches when lonely. There had been periods when Craig was absent from the house—Dawn not sure if he was simply working or avoiding her, or Quinn, or the state of flustered panic that had settled over their home, thickening as they realized they could not soothe their baby girl. Graham had been there for Dawn when Craig had not. She and Graham had lost touch for only a short time after the disaster with the Project, then Dawn found herself coaching Graham through a grueling breakup, which involved negotiating ways to see Ethan, Wendy's son, whom he adored but had no legal parental rights to.

That was *then,* Dawn reminded herself.

A lifetime ago.

Now Graham was married to Cecily Goshen, heiress to a Napa wine fortune, not yet forty and seven months pregnant. He'd be chasing a toddler around in his fifties. Dawn couldn't believe it.

Graham dropped his cigarette into his empty scotch glass.

"Busted," she said.

Graham wheeled around, startled. "Jesus, Dawnie! You scared me. I was communing with nature. *And* trying not to start a wildfire."

"I guess whiskey and tobacco are technically natural. Sorry to interrupt."

Dawn wasn't snarky by nature, but Graham brought it out in her. Teasing was their mode of communication.

"Very funny," he said, grinning. Crow's-feet fanned around his eyes, and his hair was almost entirely gray, but the changes suited him. "I realize it's uncouth, stubbing a cigarette into a glass, but I do have backup." He lifted his blazer from the railing and worked a silver flask out of one of the pockets.

"How old are you, twenty? Is this a frat party?"

"Frat boys could never afford this stuff," he said, uncapping the flask and taking a sip. "Plus, it's the only way I can handle Mia Meadows for an entire weekend." He beckoned and opened his long arms. "Come hither, birthday girl."

She stepped into his embrace. He held her tight, and she let her eyes close, breathing in his scent of cedar and cigarettes.

"I'm sorry Cecily couldn't make it," she said.

He released her and took a step back.

He shrugged and leaned on the railing. "I was too, but now that I'm here, I think it's a good thing. She's not really one for the rustic mountain vibe. It'll give her a chance to actually relax. You know Cess, she always has to be *doing* something."

"Do you think that's a rich-person thing? The need to prove internal worth?" She and Graham had always been able to dive right into it—no need for small talk.

Graham waved a hand. His gold wedding band caught the glow from the string lights. "Rich-person thing, no-day-job thing, heiress thing, woman thing, it's hard to say."

"Graham!" She shoved his shoulder. This was a foundation of their friendship: the freedom to say things they'd say to no one else. Testing the boundary of that had been a kind of foreplay when they were younger—and several times, after a Nurtury meeting, they'd failed the test. Ended up in Graham's apartment in Westwood, the sex always rushed, bordering on frantic, as Graham calculated how long it would be until he needed to get Ethan from physical therapy, and Dawn the number of minutes required to speed back to Santa Monica in time for Quinn's school pickup.

"What do you mean by *woman* thing?"

"Oh, come on, Dawnie. Don't you think women are more demonstratively industrious than men? It's not an editorial. Just an observation."

"Not *demonstratively* industrious, you pig." It felt good to

test him. Made her realize how bored she'd been. Stuck at home
with Quinn during the pandemic. "Just plain old industrious.
I'm sure Cecily's at home painting the nursery or something."

"Nah. Paint fumes—not good for the baby."

"You're missing my point."

"You're hearing me wrong."

Was he challenging her? She had an urge to push her face
closer to his, make a joke. She remembered Quinn, once her
baby, and now this other baby—a gift to Graham and Cecily.
Sure to be *typical* in every way that Quinn and Ethan were not.
She hated these thoughts, hated herself for having them.

"Are you excited? For the baby? Is Ethan . . ."

"It's okay. You can just spit it out. Am I excited, as a fifty-
two-year-old, to have a newborn?"

"Yes."

Graham had always been averse to having children; he believed it would impede his ability to create books. But then he'd
fallen in love with Wendy, ten years his senior and the divorced
mother of Ethan, a shy, wide-eyed boy with a host of develop-
mental issues that Wendy's travel-intensive job prevented her
from properly addressing. Graham had stepped in to help, and
he'd surprised everyone by becoming even more smitten with
Ethan than he was with Wendy.

"I'm stupidly, pathetically excited for the baby," Graham
said, taking a swig from the flask and offering it to Dawn. She
tipped it to her lips and drank. The whiskey was rich and mellow. She felt happy all over again. A blush of something youthful and illicit.

"I'm glad," she said. "I never thought you'd do it, honestly.
Have one of your own."

"I just needed to meet the right person. You told me it
would happen."

"Even you, a contrarian dick and a romantic at heart." Dawn felt a tinge of sadness.

"I fell madly in love with Cess, and having a baby no longer seemed anathema to my happiness. It's so cringingly cliché, isn't it? But we're all just embodied clichés when you get down to it."

"I guess." She'd heard more about Cecily Goshen than she needed. She looked up at the darkening sky and saw the first pinpricks of stars emerging. "Hey, how's your cabin?"

"Promise not to tell Mia?"

Dawn smiled. "Promise."

"It's kind of a shithole."

"Mine too."

"Well, it's our secret then. Mia would flip. She's obsessed over every detail of this weekend. You don't even know the *half* of it, since she left you off most of the planning emails."

"Mia-in-charge," Dawn said, then froze. That had been Mia's name during the Project.

Not a single fucking mention.

She was relieved to see that Graham appeared not to notice her slip. "I think if she knew my cabin was an utter fucking dump, she'd skewer that sweet old lady with the wolf who owns the place."

"Twyla. She *is* sweet. And already terrified of crossing Mia."

"Can you blame her?"

"Nope," she said. "You know, there was actually some sort of disgusting brown sludge in my shower when I got here. Poor Twyla had to clean it up."

"What? That's *disgusting*. I went to put my own sheets on the bed and found—get this, dude—" Graham paused for dramatic effect. She knew he was drunk when he started calling her *dude.*

"Wait, hold on, you brought your own sheets? Marriage *has* made you soft," she teased. Allowing her face to inch closer to his. "Okay . . . *what* was on your bed?"

"*Pine cones!* The mattress was covered in pine cones!"

"What?"

"Pine cones, dude. Like a giant *nest* of them. All over my bed. Some were crushed into pieces, so it took me like a half hour to get rid of them."

"Bizarre," said Dawn. "Sounds like a summer-camp prank. I think that would've freaked Quinn out even more than the brown—"

"What? Quinn's here?"

"Yep. Courtesy of Craig's self-centeredness."

"And, uh, she's staying—overnight?"

"Yes." Dawn felt a spike of irritation. Couldn't he simply be glad that Quinn was here? Hadn't their children brought them together in the first place? "Where else would she stay? You know how she is. Refuses to be with anyone but me and Craig."

"Right. I just thought—" He was fumbling for words, which was out of character. "This was supposed to be *your* weekend of, you know, total freedom. Mia said it was the Nurtury group only, and a few plus-ones. No kids."

"Well, Quinn is here," said Dawn, feeling hurt. It was unlike Graham to question the presence of her daughter. "Mia's well aware." Dawn pictured her daughter alone in the drab cabin right now, hunched over her book, sucking her Corn Nuts and spitting them into a cup, a habit Dawn barely tolerated, and the happy feeling Graham had sparked in her was dead. "Quinn can fend for herself," she fibbed. "It's *me* who might not be able to find my way back to the cabin, thanks to all this whiskey you're making me drink."

"Don't worry, I can help you find your way back after dinner. It's your birthday. Let a *man* handle the logistics."

Dawn groaned and shoved him. Though . . . was that an invitation?

Mia's voice sailed from the yurt. "Dinnertime, bitches! Come sit down, pronto."

Graham sighed. "Am I really being summoned to dinner as a *bitch* by Mia Meadows?"

"I'm afraid you are. I probably shouldn't have abandoned Reece in there."

Graham's posture seemed to stiffen. "Reece seems . . . *good*, though, doesn't she? Solid? I've only spoken to her a handful of times since . . ."

Since everyone's lives were shot to hell after the Project.

Well, Dawn thought, except her own.

"Grahammy and Dawnie!" Mia's voice came again. "*Now.*"

"Lead the way, birthday girl." Graham reached for his whiskey glass on the railing and missed, knocking it onto the ground below.

"Shit," he said. "Let me go grab that. Mia brought a fucking Waterford set up here."

"Of course," said Dawn. "And we'll get it *after* dinner." She would not be late for Mia twice in the same night. Dawn grabbed his hand. "Let's go, *bitch*," she said, and Graham laughed as she led him toward the yurt and twilight gave way to darkness.

11

FRIDAY, JUNE 24, 2022

Sibyl (the Visionnaire)

SIBYL ROSE FROM THE SAGGING BED IN THE SECOND-FLOOR GUEST room of Twyla's house, too jittery to sleep. She was nervous. About the texts, no shit. More surprising, she was nervous about the upcoming sessions. How silly was that? At the peak of her career—before Merry Williams went splat—Sibyl was giving readings ten hours a day. She'd read for kings and queens, pop idols and rock legends. She'd read for Oprah! And here she was, butterflies in her stomach about a few readings in a barn.

She stood at the open window with a west-facing exposure, muslin curtains tied back. The house's position at the top of the long slope offered a sweeping view of the property, across the meadow to the dark army of trees and a glimpse of the ridge beyond.

The guests' dinner party had ended. The sound of their self-satisfied laughter thankfully replaced by the canyon's awesome silence. It reminded her of home. Not that she'd thought of Harmony Township as *home* in god knows how many years. Maybe the only good thing about living in the middle of no-wheresville was the quiet nights. When her father, the Supreme Reverend Crabb of Harmony Church, was drinking, she had lugged her stained mattress out across the patchy backyard and into the old shed, whose roof had caved during one nor'easter. A freedom worth the price—countless no-see-um bites and as many bugs as stars winking at her through the hole in the roof.

Her father got drunk on grape-flavored Malt Duck and on the bad nights ended up on his knees in front of the altar in the living room as dozens of the little seven-ounce glass pony bottles rolled around him. If he drank enough, he'd plead with her mother to pray with him, staring up at her with watery eyes and purple stained teeth. If she refused, he'd yank on her mother's arm, the hem of her dress, even twist her delicate ankles until she had no choice but to drop to her knees.

On those nights that seemed to go on and on like the agonizing eternity of Hell her father preached about on Sundays, little Debbie Crabb had to escape to the shed in time, or else her father's drooping eyes would fall on her, and she'd have to pray too, her knobby knees aching as they pressed into the hardwood. She thought of sweets to get through the pain and boredom—hot apple pie squares from McDonald's, custard-filled donuts from Dunkin' Donuts.

A breeze carried the scent of flowers thirsty for rain into the guest bedroom. Something else—the dry, mineral essence she had detected outside Twyla and Arnold's house that afternoon. An unwashed body. Crushed peppermint. The tang of fear.

There *had* been someone watching her from the thick brush.

She felt a migraine coming on. The aura was growing

stronger—the halo of light above the bedside table lamp pulsed with the pain—so she knew she had no choice but to pop a few ibuprofens. Even if her gastro, Dr. Sassi, after her last endoscopy had told her *absolutely no pain meds.*

After decades of swallowing up to three pills a day, often *before* she felt a headache coming on, her stomach was bleeding enough that she'd had to have an iron infusion last year. Weekly treatments hooked up to an IV bag filled with rust-colored liquid in the UCLA hematology and oncology unit. She had tried to shut off her senses, her mind, tried not to see and hear during those hours surrounded by chemo patients. She'd listened to her favorite true-crime podcasts and read a chapter of the newly released sequel in the trashy romance series she binged, Unbridled. She even downloaded one of those stupid Candy Crush games. The pain had seeped in regardless. A discordant symphony had washed over her and she'd had to ask the nurse to remove the IV so she could rush to the bathroom and throw up. Hearing, seeing, *feeling* the pain of all those dying people had drained her in a way she hadn't believed was still possible.

The migraines had increased after *The View* incident—two or three a week—so Sibyl had spent hours and hours in bed, blackout curtains drawn, eye mask on, foam plugs stuffed in so deep her ears ached. She had welcomed the pain that blotted out the ability to think, worry, wonder what everyone was saying about the disgraced psychic.

Now she popped two Advil and swallowed the pills dry. She couldn't afford to be distracted by pain tomorrow, not when so much—for her and Twyla—was at stake.

At the window, Sibyl watched as the nimbus of light beyond the trees, from the yurt where the actress and her boy toy were staying, shuddered. The auras that announced the arrival of the migraines played tricks on her—fireworks of light in the corner of her sight, a flashing technicolor rainbow zigzagging the air. Sparkles like raindrops, dots strobing so she felt motion sick. The special effects the auras created were quite pretty, if only they weren't the harbinger of impending agony. Her father had declared them *signs*, refusing her mother's pleas for little Debbie Crabb to see a doctor. It was only after she'd made it to Los Angeles, gotten health insurance, and finally seen a neurologist that Sibyl knew the medical terms to describe what her father had advertised in the Pennysaver Coupon Book as her "*Spiritual Visions*," attracting visitors to Harmony Church from across Pennsylvania and beyond to see her.

She'd thought about calling her father more than once, breaking the news that *hell no*, she hadn't been communing with the angels on high after all! God Almighty had never spoken to little Debbie Crabb. Her *visions* had been little more than the activation of nerve cells within her brain stem. The dilation of blood vessels that triggered a thunderstorm of activity traveling across her brain. Her mother had taken care of her after the auras passed, sitting by little Debbie's bed, patting at her flushed face with a cool washcloth, catching the little girl's vomit in a wastebasket.

Still, Sibyl thought as she pulled the thin guest room curtains closed, suddenly aware of how visible she might be, her mother could have stopped her father, could've brought her to a doctor. Instead of feeding her pain pills.

She climbed back into bed, knowing she wouldn't sleep.

Someone had been watching her that afternoon, and, surely, they were there, right now, at Celestial Ranch.

SIBYL'S GIVEN NAME was Deborah Crabb. She had grown up in Harmony Township, Pennsylvania, the second of seven brothers and sisters—eight if you counted the baby girl who died from complications during labor that nearly killed Sibyl's mother, Amity. Her parents had named the baby Charity and buried her in the woods behind the family's double-wide.

Then there was Mathias, Sibyl's older brother, who rarely spoke. *"Mathias is just as God wanted him to be,"* Sibyl's mother would say, when Mathias sat through dinner staring off into the middle distance, holding his fork over his plate but not touching a bite, as if mesmerized by some invisible force. But when Sibyl was older, and began to teach herself about computers, and found a machine at the Harmony Public Library that allowed her one hour of access to the World Wide Web for a dollar-fifty, she learned that Mathias's silence and slow-limbed way of moving were probably less a matter of God's will and more of reduced oxygen to his brain during his home birth; perhaps he'd gotten stuck for too long or the umbilical cord had been wrapped around his neck.

Sitting in front of the hulking Compaq desktop on a beige Formica table at the library, she knew why her brother was the way he was. Because her parents were too selfish and stupid and stubborn to have bothered going to the hospital.

The information made seventeen-year-old Sibyl sick with rage. What was *wrong* with her parents? It was the 1990s for God's sake, not the eighteenth century. Surely her mother could have managed to give birth in the presence of someone with basic medical knowledge. She also could have managed to pay a little attention to her children. It wasn't as if she had an actual job, beyond singing off-key at top volume inside the rat-gnawed walls of Harmony Church, then flopping on the floor and jerking around like the bodies of the copperheads Sibyl's father decapitated in the summertime.

She'd always felt sorry for her mother, a servant to her father's random whims (what Sibyl would later, after years of therapy, diagnose as bipolar disorder), but that day at the library, everything changed. Scream-singing, bucking on the floor, speaking in tongues, and being at her husband's constant service, were Sibyl's mother's top concerns. Whereas feeding and bathing her children, or sending them to school or the dentist, were electives, like unpleasant chores.

And then Sibyl had learned, shortly after the afternoon she'd spent on WebMD, that her mother was pregnant *again,* with baby number nine, just as Ephraim, the youngest, had made it to age six. Six was a relief to Sibyl, because it meant he could ride the little yellow school bus that pulled up to the end of the lane at seven a.m. on weekdays and shuttled them to a small public school that, while probably one of the worst in Pennsylvania, would keep him safe and fed.

It was not right, teenage Sibyl had decided, to bring another child into the world. Not when you couldn't be bothered to put your existing children to bed at night, remind them to brush their teeth and change their bedsheets so they weren't stained yellow. Make sure they wore clean underwear, or any underwear at all.

One afternoon at the library, she discovered IRC—Internet Relay Chat—and came up with a plan.

The plan had worked. Or at least, for the past twenty-plus years, she'd believed it had. Because her past had stayed in the past, silent and lifeless.

But then, just three months ago, decades after she'd handed her infant brother—her mom had named him Abel, but Sibyl would not call him that; she'd wanted his slate to be truly clean of his past—to the couple she'd met on IRC, in exchange for enough money for Sibyl to escape Beaver County, get to California, buy a computer, change her identity, and start molding herself into the woman who would become the Visionnaire™, psychic to the stars, the texts had begun to arrive.

What's worse than a fraud? A fraud who's also a kidnapper.

Somebody knew.

12

Dawn (the Birthday Girl)

"CHIN CHIN, EVERYONE!" MIA CLINKED A FORK TO HER GLASS AND rose from her chair as the servers cleared the dessert plates. "Listen up!" Mia looked svelte and willowy in her white jumpsuit, yet imposing too. Her eyes were huge with mascara and liner, her face haloed by bouncy, golden hair.

"CEO Barbie," Graham whispered into Dawn's ear. "Midlife edition."

Dawn giggled. She was definitely *more* than tipsy.

"Good evening, my *bébés*. My old friends and fellow nurturers. We've come together this weekend to honor one very special woman, mother, esthetician extraordinaire, friend, and human being—"

Dawn winced. Shifted in her seat.

Mia held up a finger and frowned. Dawn thought she detected a flicker of anger cross Mia's smooth face. "No self-devaluing, Dawnie. Not this weekend, okay?"

"What she said," said Summer.

"Oh—okay," managed Dawn, her cheeks flaming. Beside her, she felt Reece's hand on her arm. A soft, reassuring squeeze.

"Look, you'd better just get used to the compliments," said Mia. "Because we're going to make you love yourself *all* fucking weekend, babe. If it kills us."

The table burst into laughter. Dawn tried to join in. The sounds seemed to ricochet off the domed ceiling and return twice as loud.

"I'm so . . . so touched and happy that you all made such an effort to be here," Dawn said. She looked at Reece, hoping she knew Dawn was most grateful to have *her* there.

"Our pleasure, love," said Mia. "Now, before we adjourn I wanted to help us set our intentions for the weekend."

"You mean set them *for* us," said Graham.

Dawn suppressed a chuckle. She was surprised by how relieved she was to have Graham there, his charming snark a balance to Mia's intensity.

Mia ignored Graham. "This weekend is a sacred space for relaxation and pleasure. Sleep late. Lay around. Gaze upon the flocks of hummingbirds. Soak up the beauty. There are hammocks all over the property. Food will be available all day here in the yurt."

Mia's ceremonious monologue sounded almost scripted.

Graham whispered, "They're actually called a *charm*—a grouping of hummingbirds."

"Thank you, Professor," Dawn whispered.

Mia said, "The only timing detail I want you to pay attention to is 10:34 p.m. tomorrow night."

"Could you be a little more precise?" asked Graham.

Summer barked a laugh.

"Go on, Mia," said Dawn.

"Ten thirty-four, my loves," Mia said. "It's the *precise* time

Dawn Leigh Sanders was born. The actual moment, one-half century ago—"

"Now, that's just *cruel*," said Summer.

"Age is nothing to be ashamed of—it's the accumulation of life in all its joy and pain that creates wisdom," said Reece, nodding.

"Yeah, shut up, Summer," said Joanie.

"No, it's okay, I like it," said Dawn, "Reece is absolutely right."

"As usual," said Joanie.

"We'll be gathering at the shed on Hydra Hill. Use those handy maps our friend Twyla gave out, because you won't find it on your phones."

"So old school!" piped Jax. Dawn did *not* want to know what year he had been born—probably around the time she'd graduated from college.

"And, prior to the main event tomorrow night, we've got a few special group activities planned for the birthday girl, selected by"—Mia swept her hand around the table—"none other than *our younger selves*."

"What?" Dawn blinked up at Mia. "What does that even mean?"

"List please, Jax," said Mia, and Jax handed her a folded piece of paper.

"What the hell is *that*?" said Graham.

Mia giggled and held up the paper. It was a list, in several different handwriting styles.

"It's our very own F-List," said Mia. "Straight from the archives of 2011."

"No *fucking* way!" said Summer. "You found the Freedom List?"

Dawn started. *What?* The yurt felt stuffy and warm.

"Where on earth did you find that?" Joanie said.

"Was this *your* doing, Reece-Piece?" Graham smiled. "I'm impressed."

"Pleading the fifth," Reece said.

Dawn felt suddenly alone. Of course, Reece had helped organize the weekend—why wouldn't she?—but Dawn had always disliked surprises. Reece's involvement made her feel a bit betrayed.

"It's our commandments to ourselves!" sang Mia, eyes glittering with delight. "The things we swore we'd do once we were free. And this weekend, my *bébés*"—she raised her champagne glass—"we are *free*."

Dawn searched her memory—what was on that list? She wished she hadn't drunk so much.

"Dawn," said Mia, extending the creased paper across the table. "Could you do the honor of reading the list to us?"

Dawn stood and reached for the paper, swaying a little as she angled toward Mia. The aged paper felt soft and mealy between her fingers.

She squinted at the list and winced in recognition of her own prim, slanted handwriting. She cleared her throat and began to read.

THE FREEDOM LIST—OCTOBER 14, 2011

o   Travel! Far and wide
o   Epic backcountry camping (where no children can
    get in touch w/ me!)
o   Run marathon(s) / Be in great shape
o   Trip! (psychedelically) in a beautiful remote location
o   Hang out on a nude beach w/ no shame
o   Skydive

o   Trek in Nepal
o   See a psychic REGULARLY
o   Lotsa sex in woods, or on beach, or at all HAHAHA.

Dawn stumbled over the last line, laughter floating over
the room, as she felt herself blush—who had written *that one*?
She handed the list back to Mia and sat down, slightly woozy.

"Thank you, Dawnie. And thank *you*, Reece, for assign-
ing the list in the first place. The Freedom List is our *theme* for
the weekend. I've planned a number of activities for us, all of
which are adaptions from this original list."

"Adaptations, right," said Joanie.

"Straight talk, please, Meadows," said Graham. Dawn
thought she heard a ripple of worry in his usually droll tone.

"I can't give *too* much away," said Mia, pressing a finger to
her lips. "But first off, tomorrow morning, we're going to meet
up in that big open meadow and run around in the sunshine.
In honor of the *marathon* entry on the F-List, of course."

"Sounds kind of pleasant," said Joanie.

Mia arched a brow. "Oh, yes. It will be. *Quite* pleasant."

Dawn had seen that look on Mia's face.

"You're scaring me, boss," said Summer.

"Nothing to be afraid of, Summer. All you need to do is
show up in Andromeadow—as named by our kooky hostess—at
ten tomorrow morning. And there's more."

"Lord, help us," said Reece, smiling.

"I'm really excited about this," said Mia. "Our second point
of inspiration for the weekend will be sessions with one of the
foremost psychics in the country. Right here, in residence all
weekend on Celestial Ranch!"

The group was quiet.

"Not thrilled about the psychic," said Graham—then, catching Mia's glare, he raised his hands in surrender. "Just being honest, Meemers. Don't worry, I'll play along."

"Good boy," Mia said, irked. The group was giving Mia a surprising amount of pushback—Dawn felt sorry for her.

"Let's hear Mia out," Reece said, and, Dawn saw, just as back in the Nurtury days, Reece's steady voice calmed them. "She wouldn't bring us all the way up here to simply torture us."

Or would she? Dawn thought.

"Thank you, Mother Superior Reece," said Mia before she blew her a kiss. "As I was saying—before I was so rudely interrupted—finally, inspiration number three. A combination, I'd say of traveling, skydiving, and, well"—she gave a dramatic pause—"tripping!"

Okay, now Dawn was in line with the rest of her old friends. Drugs? This was too much. She thought of Quinn back at the cabin.

"No fucking way," Summer said. "I'm *not* shrooming. I quit going to Burning Man in my twenties for a reason."

"No, Summer," said Mia. "You will *not* be shrooming."

"Spit it out, Mia," said Graham. "What, then?"

"DMT," said Mia, with a note of triumph in her voice.

Dawn began thinking of excuses she might use to get out of *whatever* crazy drug adventure Mia had planned: like, Quinn wasn't feeling well and Dawn had to stay and care for her, or Dawn had picked up an out-of-control poison-oak rash.

"DMT?" Summer said. "Isn't that some hard-core drug? No thank you. I can't even handle pot gummies. We're far too old for that. We've got kids. Graham's about to have a fucking *baby.*"

"Good thing he's not the one giving birth," Reece said.

Reece's laid-back reaction to Mia's crazy plans stunned

Dawn. Back in the Nurtury days, it would've have been Reece's job to talk Mia off the ledge, thus protecting the rest of the group from the consequences of whatever risky adventure Mia had dreamed up. Except, Dawn remembered, the Project. Every one of them had been *all in*, even Reece.

"Take it easy, Summer," said Mia. "It's not a hard drug. It's a psychedelic distilled from the ayahuasca plant, which has been used in spiritual ceremonies for thousands of years. It's very common in South America."

Graham nodded. "I read that piece in *The New Yorker* about ayahuasca."

"Me too," said Joanie. "I read up until the part about the vomit troughs, then put it down."

"Vomit what?" asked Dawn, suddenly wishing she were back in her cabin with Quinn.

"I just remember the stuff about how the drug makes you"—Graham air-quoted—"'plumb the swamp of your soul.'"

Was *her* soul a swamp? Dawn wondered.

"You guys should just do a normal, fun drug, like molly," Jax offered.

"That's enough, darlings," said Mia. "You think I wouldn't have done *exhaustive* research on this? Have I ever led you wrong on our countless journeys? I've got everything under control. The beauty of DMT is that it only lasts *fifteen minutes*. It's not like shrooms, which last all night, or all the freaky effects of ayahuasca. Trust me, I'm not interested in vomiting or swamp diving. This simply gives you access to your own deep consciousness for a few minutes."

Dawn wasn't sure she wanted access, not when there had been so much to forget. The hours she'd spent fucking Graham while still married to Craig. The divorce. The myriad ways she felt she'd failed Quinn. The last thing she wanted to *plumb*

Page 110

was the disastrous aftermath of the Project. Mia's hard stare as she was led from the court in handcuffs. Reece being lifted into the ambulance. She felt the walls of the yurt close in. The candlelight shuddered among so many open mouths, so many voices competing.

"What about—" Joanie started.

"Yes, Jo Jo?" said Mia, impatient.

"Well, I know Reece can speak for herself, but it seems inconsiderate to—"

"Thank you, Joanie," Reece said. "That's very thoughtful. You guys know I'm sober. I haven't ingested an altering substance since September sixth, two thousand eleven, marking the end, shall we say, of a certain chapter in my life, and the beginning of another."

Dawn felt dizzy. She leaned on Graham for support. She squeezed her eyes shut to banish the memory that had flashed in her mind, brutally clear: Reece on a stretcher, blood soaked through the white sheet covering her body, braids swinging over the edge as the EMTs lifted her into an ambulance. The image still returned to her regularly in dreams; more than once, she'd woken screaming, *"I'm sorry, I'm sorry."*

Her stomach churned. She forced herself to look at Reece, healthy and radiant, very much *alive.*

It's okay, Dawn told herself. *Everything turned out okay.*

No one spoke. The yurt felt stiflingly hot.

Dawn knew she had to say something. "We love you, Reece." Her voice cracked. "So much."

For a moment, Dawn could almost believe they really were *okay.* Even after all that had happened. Here they were, at the top of the world, golden candlelight catching tear-filled eyes. Reece was the truest mother Dawn had ever known, and she knew the other Nurtury parents felt the same. They had survived so much, and now, they'd survived a year spent hiding from a raging virus, one so different from the viruses they had researched and questioned and debunked back in their anti-vax days.

Mia said, "And for the record, Reece and I already spoke at length about how this is going to go down. It's perfect, actually, because we can't *all* take DMT at the same time. We need some-one to stay in the grounded world as our guide. And Reece has been our guide in the past, has she not?"

Dawn picked up her water goblet and took a long drink. She felt Mia's eyes on her.

"Has she *not*, Dawnie?"

"I'm sorry?"

"I said, has Reece *not* been our guide in the past?"

"Y-yes," Dawn agreed. "She has."

Why would Mia call her out like that? No one had been more dedicated to Reece than Dawn. She doubted any of the others had been in contact with Reece in years.

"Thanks, Dawnie," said Reece, lifting her braids from her shoulders.

"Dax Shepard does this for Kristen Bell!" said Jax, sound-ing triumphant.

"*Huh?*" muttered Summer. "Is your boy Jax already trip-ping?"

Mia said, "Look, you guys, I know it may sound radical. A bunch of us old-timers expanding our consciousnesses in the woods. Just trust me. Or rather, trust *us*. We're only doing what we promised ourselves we'd do. And having a total blast in the meantime. Lighten up, this is just a *theme party*. The theme be-ing our younger selves!"

"They say youth is wasted on the young, yadda yadda," muttered Joanie.

Dawn's wooziness intensified, the alcohol swirling in her veins.

"I think I'd better go to bed," she said. "Sounds like I'll need my rest."

She did not add, *and Quinn is probably freaking out.*

"We shall release you," said Mia, raising her empty champagne glass, "but first, one final toast. To Dawn!"

"To Dawn!" chorused the group, clinking their glasses.

"I'll walk you home," said Graham, as he took her elbow. "Like I promised."

"OH MY," SAID Dawn, "Is this tobacco, or crack?" They stood a dozen yards off the deck behind the yurt, sharing a cigarette, Dawn's first in who knew how long. They'd descended from the back deck to look for the tumbler Graham had dropped.

"You've always been a lightweight," said Graham, taking the cigarette back. "But drugs are for tomorrow night, apparently."

"I can't even tell if Mia's serious," she said, trying to gauge Graham's level of concern.

He took a drag, and the cigarette tip glowed orange against the black night. She tipped her head back. "God, look at the stars."

"Dammit. Where'd that thing go? Who brings crystal to a rustic getaway?" Graham aimed his phone's flashlight at the ground. "There it is." He picked up the glass and examined it. "Perfectly intact." He brushed it off and set it back on the railing. "I'm pretty tired. Not used to swilling a half-dozen drinks before ten. My cabin's sounding pretty cozy about now. Or I suppose I should say *Sirius.* That Twyla chick—"

"*Chick?*" Dawn planted her elbow in his side. "She's almost eighty!"

"Ow," said Graham. "For the record, by *chick* I meant youthful, energetic, full of life. It's a compliment."

Dawn laughed. "You always *were* such a feminist."

He slipped an arm around her. "Would you prefer *septuagenarian matriarch?*"

"How about just *Twyla?*"

"Fine. Either way, she's got moxie. Like part astrologer, part real-estate hustler."

"Mia was a real bitch to her," Dawn said, then looked over her shoulder toward the yurt, which glowed like a paper lantern. "Over the dog thing. I think the poor woman's traumatized."

"Classic Mia. Gotta assert her dominance anywhere she can."

"*Chicks*, you mean," said Dawn, smiling into the darkness.

"There's my Dawn," said Graham.

There was a hum in her voice that she recognized from long ago. A hunger.

He tightened his arm around her shoulders and held her against his side. "She's being cool with you, though, right? Mia?"

"She is. I mean, she's always a little scary. But I love her. I think we've finally moved past—"

She hesitated.

"The whole *Shawshank Redemption* thing?"

"Jesus, Graham, that's not funny. She was in *jail* for four months, separated from her kid."

"I remember." He sounded annoyed. "Ethan was only twelve. But that doesn't mean we can't find a little humor in it, does it?"

"You're the worst." She sighed and leaned her cheek against his blazer.

"*We* are the worst," he said. "That's why I love you, Dawnie."

"Even after—" She stopped herself. *Not a single fucking mention.*

She sighed, enjoying the feel of Graham's body against her. Dawn suddenly realized how touch-starved she'd been for so long and pressed closer to him, closing her eyes.

"Hey," she said, impulsively. "Are you vaxxed?"

"Are you asking me a question about a *toxic topic*?" His tone was joking, but she felt his body go rigid.

"Sorry." She'd broken the rule again.

Graham was silent. Some night animal scurried through the darkness.

"Yes," he said. "I got the shot."

He sounded sad. She wanted to tell him it was okay. He'd done nothing wrong.

"Me too," she whispered. And then, moved by some force outside herself, she tipped onto her toes and kissed him.

He jumped back, as if she'd shocked him. "Dawn. *No.*"

The woods around her began to wheel. She wobbled, disoriented. Unable to process the rejection. She blinked hard. The trees stood still again. "What does it matter? You're committed. Cecily's rich and gorgeous. I'm just your dubious ex-girlfriend with a ton of wrinkles and a twenty-two-year-old daughter who—"

"You're drunk."

"So are you. All I'm saying is, I'm no threat. Cecily wins. She got you to have a *baby*, Graham. Truly achieved the impossible. So, what's a little of *this*." She kissed him, quickly. "Between old friends? It changes *nothing*."

"You're a pain in the ass, Dawners," he said. "Always have been."

"I'm also wet," she said.

He let out a small gasp, and she knew it was inevitable they'd fuck. Had been since Mia sent her the birthday invitation.

He lowered his face and kissed her. She tasted cigarettes and a faint hint of hazelnut from dessert. Their tongues worked together. His body was an old friend who reminded her of who she'd been before—before she'd made so many mistakes, before she'd lost faith that her daughter would ever lead a so-called "normal" life, before she'd given up on her marriage, herself.

She felt his hardness through her summer dress.

"Your shirt is so dumb."

She giggled and fumbled with the button of his jeans, got it open, and lowered herself to the ground, using his body for balance. When she'd steadied herself against the hard earth, she pulled him down beside her.

"I'm married," he said, as she kissed his neck. "I'm with Cecily forever. If this is going to happen, I need you to tell me right now that you understand."

"I understand," she said, breathless, climbing on top of him, pulling up her dress, yanking her underwear to the side. In a fluid motion, she worked him inside her, closing her body over his, settling into motion.

"Quick," he moaned. "It's got to be quick. Jesus, oh Jesus."

She rocked into him, shutting out the rocks digging into her knees, the faraway chorus of coyotes, the moon that had, just now, found a way to pierce the black night. There was only flesh against flesh, their ragged breaths synced, and the rise and swell of twitching heat in her center.

They gasped and moaned, Graham peppering the final seconds with *fuckfuckfuck*, just as he had fifteen years ago in Wendy's big bed overlooking the Wilshire corridor.

It wasn't until Dawn had rolled off him, her knees smarting, her skirt twisted and covered with dirt, Graham scrambling into his clothes, that she felt the presence of someone else.

Someone there, watching. In the throes of pleasure, she'd heard it—for *sure*—a crunch of branches underfoot, a clearing of a throat.

Hadn't she?

Graham leaped to his feet and extended his hand to Dawn. "Let's go."

"Wait. Listen. I think I heard something."

"Cut it out." He was annoyed. How could that be after what they'd done? "Let's go." He bent and grabbed her hand, pulling her to her feet. She knew there would be no tenderness now.

The night was silent but for insect chirps and the faintest sound of voices from the yurt.

"It's just the others at the yurt," said Graham. He let go of her hand and walked ahead. Dawn felt the thing they'd just done dissolve. A hollowness took hold.

She *had* heard someone. Not from the yurt. Right here, in the clearing.

"Dawn, I'm fucking serious, come on," said Graham, over his shoulder.

Dawn took a small step. "Reece?" she called out. "Mia?"

"Dawn! Don't do this."

"Do *what*?"

"You know *exactly* what I mean." His voice was dark. Accusatory. She knew that whatever he was saying, it was far bigger than what they'd just done.

A light jumped from the ground. Her phone. She picked it up and looked at the screen.

Quinn: when are you coming back its late.

Dawn typed as she walked: RIGHT NOW

She broke into a jog to catch up with Graham, fearing she'd ruined everything, yet again.

13

Raj (the Drifter)

AGAINST THE NIGHT SKY, THE DOMED YURT GLOWED.

It reminded Raj of the paper lanterns he and Candace had lifted into the tropical air at that *other* party two winters ago on Sanibel Island. When Raj had been no different from the trespassers swilling champagne in the yurt right now, uncorking one bottle after another, *pop sploosh, pop sploosh.* Back on Sanibel Island, in early 2020, he'd done the same, a giddy fool drunk on the certainty that he and Candace would be together always.

Now, Raj sat in the tangle of overgrown rosemary near the yurt. Close enough to smell the partiers' food, the scent of it nearly knocking him on his back. He could see it: bubbling cheese, roasted tomato, basil, onion, and—*salmon?* The sweet tang of balsamic and nutty olive oil. Toasted bread lathered with garlic paste. The meat (a grill sizzled and spit) made his stomach twist. How he missed meat that was not the gristly threads of the beechies he occasionally hunted. He had survived on canned food—beans, tuna, peas, and pineapple chunks in syrup—whatever the old man left at the mouth of the cave.

Candace had loved to cook for him, despite how picky he was, another part of his rigidity only she had ever accepted—unlike his ex-girlfriends, his mother, and especially Nani. His grandmother once smacked him with a wooden spoon dripping sauce for refusing to eat her chapati.

But for Candace, he had eaten all. Abandoned his protein shakes, protein bars, and peanut-butter-and-jelly sandwiches. He had deemed most foods unclean as a kid—refused to eat anything oily, fried, pungent, and absolutely no fish.

Candace was a pescatarian. He ate every dish she cooked for him. Red curry soup. Egg-and-shrimp dumplings. Seafood and scallion pancake, despite his suspicion that fishcake had nothing resembling organic fish in its makeup.

He would have done anything for her.

He *should* have, he thought now as the scent of slow-cooked pork (and freshly chopped cilantro?) joined the heavenly cloud wafting from the yurt.

He should have been on guard. He should have protected her. He should have made every decision solely for her well-being. Instead, he had been as cocksure as the trespassers whose party grew louder and more abrasive against the night. It mocked him—this playful banter of people satisfied with their lives, with themselves, their careless laughter ebbing and flowing.

Bang sploosh, bang sploosh.

WHEN HE'D FIRST brought Candace to Topanga, seven months ago, they'd almost died of exposure. Then Raj opened his eyes one morning—or maybe it was afternoon, time did not exist in

the dimly lit cave—to see the old man's craggy face. His heart
a chittering wind-up toy, beating so fast he knew he was near
death. The old man said Raj had been seizing. Gave him water
while cradling Raj's head in one of his hairy-knuckled hands.
Raj drank and drank. The old man gave him a pair of worn hiking boots two sizes too small and wool socks. Plus, a light blue
fleece blanket that Raj gave to Candace. She cradled the blanket in her arms like a baby night and day in her corner. There
were gifts of food—canned vegetables and boxes of chicken
broth and jugs of water. Bags of dried beans Raj soaked overnight in a rusted pan just as he'd seen his Nani do. The old man
visited the cave each week with food and water. A heel of bread,
bruised pears, and split tomatoes. The dog, Klondike, curled
up next to Raj and let him run his fingers through the thick and
wiry silver-white fur. The sandpaper tickle of the dog's tongue
on Raj's cheek was pure ecstasy. Candace laughed as the dog
nuzzled Raj's new beard. What joy the sound had brought Raj!

RAJ HAD CHARTERED two private planes to Sanibel for every em-
ployee of Plasteeq, after the company's Q2 of 2020 had been its
most profitable ever. The price of Plasteeq shares had tripled
in the pandemic—all that faux-plastic needed for food deliver-
ies to those quarantining at home. Raj had benefited from the
virus, Candace made sure to remind him. To which he always
responded, "Well, I have the best marketing director—her
name is Candace Lu."

A perfect balmy night on an island where he'd rented
a villa to thank his employees. He'd had another motive as
well—he hoped to impress the woman he loved. At first, he
(with Candace's prodding) had insisted all employees stay
outside on the beach, or on the deck of the palatial villa, masks

on, but as the champagne bottles were uncorked, the mai tais replenished, the bonfires stoked, and the amps turned up (Raj had hired Post Malone for the night), masks came off. A surprise rain shower sent all seventy-two partiers scurrying to a rounded structure similar to the yurt. Windowless.

After a steamy half hour of bodies pressed tightly together (Raj had been grateful for the warmth), they returned to the beach. As Raj had carefully planned, the Plasteeq employees sent a hundred paper lanterns aloft, the candles within lit so each floating globe held an ethereal amber light. Raj dropped to one knee in the sand, velvet jewelry box open to reveal the two-carat Sri Lankan Padparadscha sapphire ring, the pinkish orange stone the color of lotus blossoms. The same color of the chain of paper lanterns ascending behind Candace as she looked down at Raj, her cheeks wet.

She said *yes*.

14

Dawn (the Birthday Girl)

DAWN TWITCHED AWAKE INTO FULL-BLOWN MORNING SUNLIGHT.
She'd fallen asleep without removing her contacts, and
her eyes felt tacky and dry. Her head was throbbing, her throat
parched. She blinked into the brightness and checked the twin
bed across the room for Quinn, who was sound asleep. Quinn
never slept under the covers—all bedding, to her overactive
senses, was too scratchy, too heavy, too crispy, etcetera. The sight
of Quinn sleeping peacefully gave Dawn a momentary sense of
calm, tinged with pride—her daughter had made it through the
night in an unfamiliar cabin without incident.

Then, *bam*—Dawn's memory of her own night came crash-
ing down on her, and she bolted upright. Pain shot to her tem-
ples, and she groaned, kicking off her blanket to find she was
still wearing her gauzy summer dress, now rumpled and caked
with dirt.

And her knees were practically on fire, both scraped and
raw. Her left calf was covered in scratches.

Pieces of the night drifted back: the sound of her friends' raucous sing-along wafting from the yurt. Her cheek against Graham's fruit-patterned shirt. A button popping off as she yanked it open. The coarse hair of his chest, the booze-sweet smell of his skin and smoky taste of his mouth.

No. They hadn't—had they?

She remembered the slashes of moonlight through the branches, crossing his face as she climbed on top—

Oh god. They *had.*

The walk home flashed back: her drunken, stumbling gait, leaning into Graham to keep from falling on her face. He'd held her steady, but she could sense his touch was only necessity; all his flirtation and teasing affection had vanished the second he'd come, replaced by admonitions, practically reprimands:

"Cecily can never-fucking-ever know. I need to trust you with this. We're way too old for this bullshit. We're agreeing it never happened. And if Mia fucking Meadows finds out . . ."

Would he be able to act normal today? As if nothing had happened? Would *she?*

"Idiot," she hissed to herself under her breath. "Grow up."

Then Dawn remembered: she *was* fully grown. Today—well, technically tonight at 10:34 p.m., as Mia had reminded her last night, Dawn would turn fifty.

She eased her feet to the wood floor. Everything hurt. An ache of shame throbbed in her gut. How could she have gone off the rails so easily?

She ran her fingers over her scalp, trying to massage away her headache.

Her phone pinged with a text—thank god she'd managed to hang on to it—and she located it under the bed.

Quinn stirred and resettled.

The text was from Mia to the group:

Morning bebes! TODAY'S THE DAY. HBD to our birthday
bitch DAWNIE! Also: killer coffee and breakfast yumyums
in the yurt. See you by the firepit in ANDROMEADOW
(lol!) at 10am sharp. BRING YOUR PHONES.👄

Shit. It was already 9:06 a.m. Dawn needed to clean herself
up, leave some breakfast and a note for Quinn, and go meet her
friends at the meadow.

She heaved out of bed and limped into the salmon-colored
bathroom. She peered into the shower. Blessedly, there was
nothing more offensive than a few streaks of mildew. She turned
on the water and stepped out of last night's clothes. It wasn't
until the hot water streamed over her body, stinging her fresh
scrapes, that she remembered something else from last night:
her sense that someone had been watching them. The feeling
had been strangely palpable, as unmistakable as Graham's lips
on her (*ugh*) nipples.

Had it been a trick of her addled mind, soaked with whiskey
and champagne? Or had one of her friends followed her and
Graham? Could it possibly have been—*oh god*—Reece? It was
the sort of thing she would have done, back in the Nurtury days.
Followed Dawn to make sure she was okay. Reece had been such
a caretaker, a giver. A *nurturer.*

Dawn lathered shampoo into her hair, hoping to Twyla's
goddess that this wasn't true.

If she and Graham had gotten away with such a stupid mistake, well, then she could handle pretty much anything this
weekend. Skydiving, a marathon, psychic readings—whatever
the hell was on that list Mia had ticked off last night.

And if they hadn't gotten away with it, well, she'd survive.
Maybe.

Santa Monica

"NO, QUINN. POINT TO THE RED DOG, NOT THE BLUE DOG. Try again!"

"No, Quinn. Hands are for helping, not hurting. We don't use our hands when we're mad, we use our words. Try again!"

"No, Quinn. The blocks go on top of each other, not next to each other. Try again!"

How many times had Dawn stood alone outside the playroom when Craig was off at work (attending to the needs of other women) and sobbed as she listened to yet another therapist fail to connect with Quinn? Why—*why* was it so hard for her four-year-old daughter to simply follow the rules of the world, to engage with other people as they wished? Quinn's brain functioned so beautifully in some situations— building Legos, identifying the make and model of practically any car, sorting confetti by color, and reading every word of *Frog and Toad* aloud when

most of her peers only looked at the pictures. Why
was answering basic questions, following simple
directions—never mind putting on shoes, eating a
decent lunch, or *using her words*—so impossible?

It was after the third day care had "kicked out"
Quinn—suggesting that Quinn *take a break until she
learned to use her words instead of her hands, and, on
occasion, her teeth*—that Dawn began attending a
weekly parenting support group at a place called the
Nurtury Center for Child Development. She'd seen
it advertised in a stack of business cards on the reception desk at Quinn's pediatrician's office. "Facil-
itated by Reece Mayall, MS, Integrative Health."

At Dawn's first meeting, Reece, a strikingly
beautiful Black woman in her late twenties, had
taken Dawn's hand and led her to a chair in the circle
of four parents. Dawn had spent most of the meeting fighting back tears as she listened to each parent
share stories of the challenges they'd had with their
own children—situations nearly identical to those
Dawn had suffered with Quinn.

"*My girlfriend couldn't be here,*" said the tall guy
in the hipster newsboy hat, who'd introduced himself as a novelist and "quasi-adoptive dad" to an
"amazing, brilliant, and atypical" five-year-old boy
named Ethan. "*But I wanted to come on her behalf,
because, honestly, this group is what holds my relationship together, and I don't even believe in support groups.*"
They had all laughed.

One woman, a free-spirited redhead named
Summer with a loud voice and a tendency to use
it, sat clasping hands with her wife, Joanie, a styl-

ish seemingly unflappable Korean woman with a
bone-dry wit that, Dawn would learn, belied her
extra-sensitive soul. The couple told stories of the
heartbreak they had felt in discovering that one of
their twins, Maisie, was neuroatypical, while the
other, Audrey, was "as mainstream/traditional as
neurology gets."

And Mia had been so vulnerable then. Unrecognizable from the bubbly blonde Dawn had
seen on TV. Her skin sallow, dark moons beneath
her eyes, freshly separated from an "emotionally
handicapped" husband and unable to mitigate her
four-year-old son Nate's epic tantrums that occurred several times a day. *"I just can't soothe him,"*
Mia wailed, her cornflower eyes glassed with tears.
"If his mother can't soothe him, who can?"

Reece had guided them. *"My heart aligns with
your stories. I, too, am so-called neurologically atypical. But I'm also trained in both Eastern and Western
healing methodologies, and I want each of you to understand that you're not alone and that much of what
your pediatricians, teachers, and therapists may have
told you, though well meaning, is not in service to you
or your children . . ."*

Her gaze latched on to Dawn's. Something
passed between them.

What a relief it was, for Dawn, to imagine Quinn's
issues weren't her fault alone. Before the Nurtury,
before Reece, Dawn had never questioned the di-
agnoses and often conflicting advice of the army
of psychologists and pathologists; occupational,
speech, and physical therapists; neuropsychiatrists

and nutritionists who had evaluated Quinn—poked at her, prodded her to stack alphabet blocks, pick out the horse from a page of barn animals, slip a plastic star in the right hole. *"No, Quinn, not that one. Try again. No, Quinn. Wrong one. Come on, you can do it."* Until Quinn's frustration overflowed, and she threw the tests disguised as toys across the room. Until Dawn's beautiful freckle-faced, ponytailed little girl bit the evaluator's hand.

Each week, at least one parent in the group—all of whom soon became Dawn's close friends, maybe the closest she'd had, so complete was the comfort of their shared experience—would inevitably ask Reece, usually during a crying jag, *"Why is my baby like this?"* They all knew the science, of course, dispensed to them ad nauseam by pediatricians, therapists, magazine articles, the AMA, the AAP, the CDC.

Translation: Nobody really *knew* what caused autism, or Asperger's, or any of the so-called spectrum disorders.

Reece had been the first person, the *only* person, to offer Dawn and her new friends a clear possible answer. The five parents had been meeting with Reece for more than a year, their fussy babies now tantrum-throwing preschoolers, when Reece's single question set the Nurtury parents on a path that would change their lives. Her brown eyes were wide and inquisitive as they panned around the Nurtury, making eye contact with each parent as she spoke, her voice gentle and free of judgment.

Had any of them, Reece asked, happened to notice any changes in their children after they'd gotten their MMR vaccine shots?

Mia raised her hand. "Actually, yes! I also read an article. And then a book. I carry it with me everywhere now." She leaned over to rummage in her giant Gucci tote, pulled out a book, and held it up.

Defeating Autism Naturally, by J. McCartney and Gerry Kartzel, MD.

"That's an interesting book, Mia," Reece said.

"But it's written by a freaking D-list actress," Graham added, but Dawn saw he'd straightened in his chair, come to attention. "You know she paid that doctor to use his name."

"No judgment in the Nurtury, please," Reece reminded him. *"Now, my friends, has anyone heard of Dr. Andrew Wakefield?"*

Dawn's heart began to thud. She leaned forward in her seat.

Perhaps a *shot* was the answer to *why*? Perhaps a *shot* had made Quinn—and Maisie and Nate and Ethan—the way they were?

15

Twyla (the Hostess)

THE SKY WAS A DULL GRAY, THE RANCH WRAPPED IN A BAND OF LOW clouds and fog.

Even though the planet was burning up, winter with its replenishing rainstorms a thing of the past, Antarctica on rapid thaw, Twyla was relieved that the phenomenon known as "June Gloom" in Southern California, the weeks of early summer when the mornings started gray and misty, did not appear to be going anywhere.

On Saturday morning, Twyla sat on the porch in the teak rocking chair Arnold had made long ago. She blew on her tea (a peppermint-licorice-fennel-calendula blend Zephyr had recommended as a digestive aid), careful not to spill as she rocked the chair while gazing at the meadow. It was the same down-sloped expanse of brush and grass punctuated by grand old oak trees she had looked upon every morning, thousands of times, her mind traveling down the dark tunnel into wondering exactly how many mornings she had left.

Morning mist threaded through the sparse trees. The colors were even starker and browner than they'd been last summer, the grass the color of hay, the aromatic shrubs—lavender and purple sage and rosemary—crisped black at their tips. The dense thickets of evergreen chaparral carpeting the canyon's hills and cliffs, and every crevice in between, seemed doomed. It wasn't yet high summer and even the leaves of the hardy black walnut trees were wilting.

Would rain ever be more than a fleeting anomaly that happened a few times a year, for a scant hour here and there? Twyla thought of the guest family who'd visited back in April, an attractive couple in their thirties who lived in Calabasas with cherubic three-year-old twin girls who'd squealed and clapped over the goats. Twyla had been in the barn with the mother and the little girls, who fed the goats handfuls of alfalfa, when the sky had suddenly darkened and unleashed a torrent of rain that made gorgeous pattering sounds on the aluminum roof of the barn, then intensified into a loud thrum.

Suddenly, the twin girls, who had been giggling and stroking Diurn's soft black-and-white coat, began to scream. They scurried to their mother and burrowed against her.

It had taken Twyla a while to realize what was happening. Then she heard the pretty blond mother murmuring to her hysterical daughters: *"Oh, baby girls, it's just rain. That's all. It's just Mother Nature watering the earth."*

The scene had depressed Twyla for days. What future was there for an earth inhabited by little girls who yowled in fear over a summer rain shower, one Twyla's beloved and parched canyon so desperately needed?

Of course, after decades in Topanga, she had witnessed the miraculous resilience of nature. Just when she was ready to tear out a withered hummingbird trumpet vine, its blackened stems produced a bevy of crimson tubular blossoms. The plant had only been sleeping, patiently restoring itself for a stunning return. She had watched branches sprout from the basal buds of trees whose bark had turned chalk white.

Every one of the canyon's human inhabitants feared wildfire, Twyla included. Yet the flora of Topanga had evolved so its cycle depended on it. Like the fast-germinating leafy ephemerals tipped with bright pink and purple wildflowers that carpeted the charred ground after a fire. While the trees' burned limbs mourned above, the backup seeds stored in the forest floor began to germinate. Nature wasn't wasteful like humans—the goddess's pantry was always full. Twyla's favorites were the jack pine and lodgepole pine seeds whose shells were so hard they needed the high temperatures of wildfire to crack open. She hoped to live like those seeds, to thrive even in the harshest environs. And here was Arnold demanding she live in a one-room apartment in a senior home where the residents weren't trusted to cook their own food.

During her sessions with Sibyl, she had often envisioned herself as a tree—not one she'd seen in the canyon but a tree from back home, the graceful weeping willow in the yard of her childhood estate. She'd felt the wind sifting through her drooping branches, the ants and millipedes and worms tickling her roots deep in the cool, loamy Connecticut soil. She'd wept after those sessions, even begged Sibyl to bring her back into the vision, let her return to the tree and the peace she felt there. This was a vision about death, Sibyl had explained in a quiet voice, careful not to scare Twyla.

"*The trees*," Sibyl had said, "*will outlast us all.*"

What Twyla said next had surprised the psychic: "*Good. The trees deserve to have the planet to themselves.*"

The perilous state of the planet had been a mighty justi-
fication for her and Arnold deciding, decades ago, not to have
children. Or, at least, Twyla had told herself this at the time.
Why would she bring new life into a world inevitably bound
for suffering? Just to appease her selfish fears of dying alone,
her yearning for a tiny body, as warm as a loaf from the oven,
to cuddle on cold nights. She'd been no different from other
women, she'd felt those pangs, a longing to make a face similar
to hers, one she could look into each time that pesky wave of
existential dread swelled over her.

The decision they had made was so far in the past, she
couldn't remember the details. She would not go so far as to say
Arnold denied her a child. But he'd done a good job of convinc-
ing her that it was a good and noble choice. Now, four decades
later, she recognized a similarity in his argument for selling
Celestial Ranch. Keeping the property was not economical, it
required far too many resources. A waste of time and money
and effort.

But what if the most meaningful parts of life weren't nec-
essarily the most useful?

Dawn (the Birthday Girl)

DAWN RUSHED ACROSS THE MEADOW TOWARD HER FRIENDS, CLUS-tered beside a crumbling, overgrown fire pit near the center of the field.

"Oh yeah!" sang Mia, looking rested and cheerful in tiny red seventies-style track shorts and a white tank top, making Dawn wish she'd worn something less age-appropriate than her loose palazzo pants and linen tunic. "There she is!"

"Birthday girl in da meadow!" hooted Summer, flashing double peace signs. Dawn was relieved to see both Summer and Joanie dressed in their usual style—Summer in a snug track suit that had an Olympics circa 1976 vibe and Joanie in a tank top and skin-tight workout pants with an iridescent sheen.

"You missed my bloodys!" said Jax, flashing a snow-white grin from beneath his green trucker hat. He was wearing a loose tank top that showed off his tattoo sleeves—a mishmash of tribal rings that seemed to pulse atop his tight muscles and,

surprising Dawn, religious icons. Crucifixes, a heart crowned
with thorns, Latin phrases inked in Gothic script.

"Sorry, guys," Dawn said, embarrassed by her lateness.
How long had they been waiting? Here it was, only ten-thirty,
and she was already screwing up.

Graham waved, his face obscured by sunglasses and a baseball cap that read SCHITT'S CREEK. Dawn sucked in a breath and
waved back. *Normal. Like it never happened.* She spotted Reece
in colorful, wide-striped pants and a sleeveless white shirt that
tied in front, braids piled on top of her head. She swooped in
and smothered Dawn in a fierce embrace.

"Baby girl," she sang. "There you are. You look beautiful.
You *are* beautiful. Inside and out. Happy birthday."

A warmth spread through Dawn's chest. If Reece was disgusted with her, or disappointed, well, she was doing a good job
of hiding it.

Mia jostled between them. "Let me in here," she said, hugging them both. "Happy birthday, bitch!"

"Goodness!" said Reece. "These hugs feel transformative
after a year with no lovin'."

"Sorry I'm late," said Dawn. "I overslept. God, I'm not used
to drinking that much."

"No apologies, chiquita," said Mia. "Not today. I don't want
to hear a single *sorry.*"

"Okay," said Dawn, as Summer and Joanie moved in for a
joint hug and effusive *Happy Birthday*s, followed by Jax, who
double-kissed her cheeks, European style.

Graham stepped over and hugged Dawn too.

"Here we are," he said, releasing her a beat too soon, "together again. Happy birthday, Dawnie."

"Thanks," she said, her heart speeding. "You"—she looked
up at him but could only see her reflection in his lenses—"okay?"

"Never better," he said.

"Great," she said when she was thinking, *Fuck*. She had ruined yet another friendship. She stepped back and cleared her throat. "This is so nice, you guys," she said to the group. "You're almost making me forget I'm officially old."

"Don't worry, we'll keep reminding you," said Summer, and everyone laughed.

Dawn began to relax. Everyone seemed—normal. Nothing but a touch of standoffishness from Graham. For the first time all morning, she noticed how nice the sun felt on her face. Warm and gentle. The air smelling faintly of honey.

"Okay, people!" called Mia. "Gather 'round, please." She bent over the brick edge of the fire pit and lifted what looked like a large metal lunchbox. She opened the clasp and held it out toward the group. "First things first. Everyone brought their phones, right?"

"Phone, what phone?" said Summer innocently.

"You're making me nervous, Meadows," said Joanie.

"Hell yeah, I've got mine," said Jax. "I'm already blowing up Insta today with this scenery."

"Well, time to take a break from all that," said Mia. "This is a handy-dandy lockbox. And I'm asking each of you to drop your phone in it for the next twenty-four hours."

"Gladly." Reece stepped forward and extended an ancient flip phone to Mia.

"Retro," said Jax, sounding impressed.

"Thank you, Reece," said Mia, placing the flip phone in the box. "Now, everybody, see how easy that was? Who's next?"

From the group, groans of protest. Dawn's heart rate accelerated again. She couldn't relinquish her phone, not when Quinn was in Topanga with her, excluded from the activities.

"Are we grounded or something?" said Graham.

"Yes, actually," said Mia. "You've been a very bad boy, Graham."

Was Mia *implying* something? Dawn slid her eyes to the pebbled ground.

"*Kidding!* No one's being punished. This is a birthday party, not *Survivor*. In fact, I'm not forcing anyone to give up their sacred devices. I'm just strongly encouraging it. It's a measly twenty-four hours. I just think freedom from our phones will make us all so much more present and *attuned* to each other and this gorgeous setting. This time is precious. Our togetherness is precious." She paused and looked at Dawn with the kind of brimming emotion Dawn had seen Mia use in her most dramatic TV episodes. "*Dawn* is precious. So, I hope each of you will follow Reece's lead and place your phone in the box."

"And what's happening with the box?" asked Joanie.

"Our gracious hostess, Twyla, has agreed to stash it in her house until tomorrow morning. Your little darlings will be safe and sound until then. Consider this a birthday present to Dawn."

Dawn looked up and flashed what she hoped was an appreciative smile. "Aw, thank you, Mia! I'm blushing. But seriously, I don't mind a little distraction."

"Oh, come on!" Mia said. "We made it through practically half our lives without little computers in our pockets. Would we even have bonded back at the Nurtury if we'd had phones? If we'd had access to a barrage of other options, twenty-four-seven?"

At her utterance of the *Nurtury*—the first time Dawn had heard it spoken aloud all weekend—the air around them seemed to go still. As if a cloud rolled over the meadow. Dawn's heart began to canter.

Hadn't Mia said it: *No fucking mention?*

Then again, Mia was *in charge.* If she wanted to break her own rules, she would.

Summer held her phone in the air. "All righty then, I'll feed my phone to the box. What's the big deal? Joanie's the only person who texts me anyway, and she's here." She stepped forward and placed her phone in the box.

Joanie followed suit, but Dawn could see she wasn't thrilled about it.

"I love it," Jax said, dropping his phone into the box.

Without a word, Graham did too.

Dawn was shocked—he had a pregnant wife at home. "Are you sure, Graham? I mean, with Cecily—"

"I'm sure," said Graham, too quickly. As if he didn't even want Dawn to say his wife's name.

Dawn felt for her phone. She thought of Quinn, waking up in the overheated cabin, pouring her sugary kid cereal and opening one of her fat romance novels. The thought triggered a wave of sadness. Quinn was *fine.* Dawn reminded herself she was hungover, which always made her emotions unwieldy.

Phone in hand, she eyed the metal box, now at Mia's feet.

She just couldn't. She knew it was ridiculous. That Quinn was twenty-two. But still.

"Guys," Dawn said. "I don't mean to be odd woman out here. But since Quinn ended up having to come along at the last minute, and she's really skittish about new environments—"

"I get it, honey," Reece said. "You know I do, but Quinn is—"

Mia interrupted. "Quinn's twenty-two. She's perfectly capable of not texting you for twenty-four hours."

"I hear you," Dawn said. "It's just that it wasn't planned for me to bring—" She faltered—oh god, was she going to *cry?*—and looked to Reece for comfort, but Reece averted her gaze and stared off toward the high ridge in the distance.

As if, Dawn thought, Reece wished she were anywhere but here.

Get it together, Dawn commanded herself.

Mia spoke with impatience. "Look, of course you can keep your phone, Dawn. But let me ask you this: is being able to send a text in a place like this *truly* necessary? This is an Airbnb property in Los Angeles County, not the actual wilderness. We all know where Quinn will be, and we'll all be looking out for her."

"Do what *you* want to do, Dawn," said Reece.

"Thanks, Reecie," said Dawn.

She stepped forward, took a breath, and dropped her phone into the box.

"Okay, lovelies!" said Mia. "Gather 'round." She beckoned with both of her gemstone-adorned hands. Mia received copious gifts from LA jewelry designers in return for posting selfies of her glittering fingers on Instagram.

Dawn and the five others shuffled into a loose ring around her.

"The time has come for our first activity, inspired by the F-List. As promised, I've combined and adapted some of the items for us to partake in together, in honor of our collective friendship. Of *moving forward* into the second act of our lives. In honor of learning to live for ourselves, which, of course, is the path to true generosity."

Mia looked at Dawn and beamed. Dawn felt a knot of anticipation forming in her chest. What was Mia talking about? Why did she suddenly sound like an amateur life coach?

"I think it's the third act, technically," Joanie said. "Not the second."

"That's my Goose," said Summer. "Nothing gets by her."

Joanie glared at her wife.

Dawn was reminded how much she did *not* want to fall on Joanie's shit list. Never again. After the Project had fallen apart, Dawn had opened her front door one day to a paper bag. On fire. She'd stomped on the bag—Quinn screaming in the hallway—until the doormat was a mess of ashes and pieces of paper and dog shit. Each time Dawn wondered if it was Joanie who'd left it there, then heard Reece's voice in her head: *"That's your own guilt putting this craziness in your mind."*

Mia ignored them. "This weekend, we'll embrace the F-List in honor of learning to live for ourselves. The six of us were once a group so tightly knit, we felt like one person."

Dawn snuck a look at Graham, but his eyes were still hidden behind those awful *Top Gun* sunglasses. Joanie, Summer, even Reece, seemed unfazed by what seemed like Mia's inevitable excavation of the past. Of the Project.

Mia's voice rose. "Our bond was our children, and in turn, each other!"

She sounded like a new age priestess at one of those glam born-again Hollywood churches Dawn knew were all the hype with recovering LA quasi-celebrities.

"Intense!" said Jax.

"Exactly," said Mia, blowing him a kiss. "A fucking magical intensity. Wouldn't you all agree?"

Reece spoke, her voice strong and clear. "Yes, I would."

The others murmured in agreement. Dawn's cut-up knees began to sting again, her headache returning.

"Of course," Mia went on, "that sort of magic can't last. We've all moved on, forged our own separate paths. Our children have grown and g—" Mia caught herself, but Dawn knew what she'd been about to say: *grown and gone.* "—gotten strong. As have each of us. But I believe we can still reclaim the magic!

And to be clear, it doesn't matter who added what to the list. By turning our old list of collective dreams into real rituals, by manifesting—"

"Could you get to the point, Meadows?" said Graham. "It's hot as hell out here. And the suspense is killing me."

"Well, we need you alive, Grahammy," said Mia. Dawn saw the irritation simmering below Mia's eyes, right under her iridescent highlighter. "So, I'll cut to the chase. If you'll remember, two of the goals added to our list of yesteryear involved, *one*"— she held up an index finger, lacquered red nail gleaming in the sun—"nudity without shame."

Dawn's throat went dry.

"Oh, come on," Summer said, "that's the dumbest one on the list. I know because it's mine. Maisie was refusing to nurse, and my boobs were like rocks, but my stomach was like bread dough, and I read this article about a nude beach in Thailand especially for new m—"

"That's enough." Mia raised a palm. "Perhaps you didn't hear me say *it doesn't matter* who wrote what."

"She never listens," mumbled Joanie.

"My bad," Summer said, staring at her feet. Dawn had never seen Summer silenced like that. Mia-in-charge apparently had some kind of super strength up here in the canyon.

"Moving on to number two," Mia said, flashing two fingers, "the wish to run a marathon."

Dawn's face heated. She'd written that one in the throes of jealousy over the moms at school—mothers to so-called neurotypical kids—who were training for the LA marathon. Moms who could leave their children in the care of nannies, grandparents, friends, and not worry that both their kid and the caretaker would be in tears when they returned.

"So, here's the deal. We don't have time to get to Thailand, or run twenty-six miles. We'll work with what we've got! And what we've got is this beautiful meadow"—she flung out her hands—"and our beautiful bodies."

Dawn heard Joanie suck in her breath.

"We're going to *run*, people. Right here, across this glorious field."

"I run," moaned Graham, "and I puke."

"Go ahead," said Mia. "You won't get any puke on your clothes . . . because we're running *in the nude, and free of shame!*"

Dawn laughed, certain Mia was just messing with them, but when she saw Reece smiling, looking at Mia with what seemed like total agreement, a wave of panic crashed over her.

"Come on, everyone, clothes off!" Mia shouted as she pulled off her tank top and bra in a single motion. Then she pushed down her shorts and underwear and tossed them over her shoulder. Dawn could only stare in disbelief. Mia was *naked*, in broad daylight, her body taut and supple as a teenager's. "We're going to prove that we love and appreciate our bodies, even at freaking fifty! Now, strip!"

Dawn turned away, her face aflame. The heavy food and alcohol from last night threatening to rise. Had Mia lost her mind? And how could her body look this way, at nearly fifty—her small breasts standing at pert attention, her stomach drum-tight. Bracing herself, Dawn turned to Reece, who looked placid, nearly beatific, gazing at Mia with a smile.

Then Reece pulled her yellow sundress over her head and let it fall to the ground.

"That's the way, Reecie!" Mia shouted. "See that, everyone? Now it's your turn. Let loose and *let go,* people. Free yourselves of the shackles! In honor of the F-List, bitches! For Dawn!"

"Jesus!" said Summer. "And Jo says *I'm* an exhibitionist!"

"You are!" said Joanie, sounding uncharacteristically merry

as she—*oh god*—began unbuttoning her sleeveless blouse. In seconds, she was naked too.

"Right *on*, Jo!" yelled Mia. "See, that wasn't so hard! And *damn*, the sun feels good." Mia, to Dawn's shock, wiggled her bare ass. "Now the rest of you are going to strip down to your— *ahem*—birthday suits, and we'll race to the other side of the meadow and back." She pointed across the field. "See that big-ass oak tree? That's the midpoint. You run to it, kiss the bark, and I mean *lips to bark*, don't dare turn around before you've done it. Then run back. Got it, birthday girl?"

"Um," Dawn said, "I guess I'm worried about—my feet." *And my boobs and ass and—*

"You can leave your shoes on," Mia said. "I'm not a monster."

"Hol-eee!" said Summer. "So, we're doing this?"

What if Twyla saw them?

Summer had already stripped down to her bra and underwear and, Dawn was relieved to see, looked more like a naked woman nearing fifty. A lifelong swimmer, her tan and freckled arms were muscled, but the loose skin of her belly was crisscrossed with pink-white stretch marks. A reminder of the babies she'd carried, Dawn thought, suddenly missing Quinn and fearing she might see them. The sight of her mother and aunties and uncle streaking would only increase her aversion to nudity, maybe even prevent her from having an intimate relationship.

"You know, I did something similar to this at Burning Man," said Jax. "It was rad. Got first place. So"—unbuttoning his shorts—"what the hell, right?"

Off they came. Joanie erupted in an uncharacteristic spurt of giggles having gotten a look at Jax's hefty endowment.

"Of course you got first place, ya young buck," said Graham, tossing his baseball cap to the ground. His gray hair was half-plastered to his head. Dawn remembered the night before and shuddered. "Anyone bring sunscreen?" added Graham, grinning, his face shiny with sweat.

What was happening?

"I—can't," said Dawn, gluing her eyes to a rock on the ground.

"Look up, Dawnie," said Mia. "Don't be afraid."

Dawn looked up. She was the only one wearing a stitch of clothing.

"Here," said Reece, "I'll help you." She walked over, her long, leonine body gleaming in the sunshine, and helped Dawn undo the buttons running down the back of her tunic.

Slowly, Dawn stepped out of her palazzo pants. Then her bra and underwear. The breeze, softened by the marine mist, felt nice on her skin.

"She did it!" yelled Mia. "A round of applause, please, for the birthday girl in her *splendid* birthday suit!"

The group whooped and cheered. Mia blew Dawn a kiss.

"Dawnie, as a birthday gift, we're giving you a three-second head start."

"What?" said Dawn, stricken by the suggestion of everyone watching her from behind. "I don't need to, um, cheat."

"Too bad, it's decided!" said Mia.

"It's not cheating, hon," said Reece. "It's a gift."

"I said *no*." Had she ever spoken to Reece so sternly? "I'll go when everyone else goes."

"Sorry, Dawnie," said Mia, "but *sometimes you don't get to pick.*"

Dawn froze; it was, word for word, advice Reece had taught them at the Nurtury, to use when their kids challenged their parental authority: *Sometimes you don't get to pick.* She looked to Reece for a reaction, but Reece was looking at Mia and smiling.

Mia addressed the group again. "When I yell *go*, Dawn goes. Then I'll count to three, and the rest of us will try to catch her. Ready?"

"Ready!" yelled Jax.

"Can't hear you!" said Mia.

Catch her. Dawn hoped she had misheard. Goose bumps sprung across the backs of her arms at the thought of their hands on her naked body.

"*Ready,*" yelled the group.

"Wait! No!" Dawn shouted.

But they had taken away any choice she had.

"On your mark." Mia shaped her thumb and index finger like a gun. "Go!"

"Ahhhh!" Dawn heard herself cry, and she ran.

"Get her, guys!" Mia yelled, and Dawn ran faster, seized by an animal instinct, her sandals flying over the rock-strewn meadow, weeds biting at her toes, foxtails burrowing in her ankles, lungs burning.

Go! Get her! The sounds at Dawn's back seemed to amplify, to rise and surround her, a roaring noise bigger and louder than the five people behind her could possibly make.

She pushed faster, the sun pounding on her shoulders, her knees throbbing. The buzzing was everywhere.

Could she be having a *stroke*?

She thought of Quinn, alone in the cabin, and a wail escaped her lips.

She'd made it halfway across the long meadow; the oak was drawing closer, its big branches like thick, splayed arms ready to catch her. The roar was getting closer too. Dawn stretched out her hands, willing herself forward, closer to the tree, to the midpoint of the race, though she was desperate to turn around now, to run back to her clothes, back to Betelgeuse, to Quinn.

But Mia's words pressed down on her mind: *Lips to bark, don't dare turn around before . . .*

Ludicrous commands, but Dawn knew Mia was serious.

You didn't cross Mia when she was serious.

Dawn tried to run faster. The flesh of her stomach shuddered. Her breasts bobbed. She didn't care. She just needed to reach the tree.

But then, the noise behind her shifted. Suddenly, the whirring sounds were *in front* of her.

Above her.

Dawn slowed her stride and looked up.

And then she saw it: a dense flock of tiny birds overhead, flying erratically. The cloud-shaped mass dipped and rose, constricted and expanded, dipped again. Its buzzing sound loud and crazed and—

Dawn stopped running. Her mouth fell open.

It wasn't a flock of birds sailing over the party guests running nude through the meadow, but a massive swarm of bees.

17

Twyla (the Hostess)

TWYLA TOOK A LONG SIP OF TEA, THEN ROCKED A LITTLE HARDER IN her chair. It was all too much, the last two years, with the virus and the rage in the streets and the toxic politics and the economy in the toilet, and the inability of the sky to rain. It was incomprehensible to her that Arnold would vie to leave Topanga now, of all times, when the world out there, at the bottom of the long winding road out of the canyon and into the parched Valley, was scarier and more volatile than ever.

Well, she thought, planting her foot against the uneven wood floor of the porch, then pushing off hard, *she* was not going anywhere. And how could Arnold possibly go anywhere alone? It had been more than fifty years since he'd known a life without her. She was quite sure he did not want to. Wasn't she?

She drained her tea, wincing at the bitter leaves at the bottom, and set the mug down on the floor beside the chair. She'd give herself a few more minutes before getting to her morning chores: sweeping, feeding the goats, fixing the rope on the gate

Ms. Meadows had so inconsiderately taken apart. Then she'd make eggs and buckwheat toast for Arnold, who could sleep until noon if she let him, and see about Sibyl.

She should also, she remembered, check on the guests. From afar, of course. According to Ms. Meadows's detailed itinerary (not that Twyla needed to know exactly what the guests were doing at all hours), there was some kind of sports game planned for that morning, and apparently the guests would be wearing nothing but their birthday suits. Well, that was if "Nude Footrace" was to be interpreted verbatim. Twyla was chuffed by the image of the middle-aged guests, feeling free and secure enough to throw off their worldly vestments, racing through the Andromeadow. It was exactly the kind of alternative to the constraining outside-Topanga city life she'd hoped to provide for her guests.

She sat back in the rocker, let her eyes drop closed for a few seconds, and breathed in deeply through her nostrils, letting the still-cool midmorning air flood her lungs. In an hour, they'd be roasting (*thank you, fossil fuels*). Even if the world *was* in a continuous state of falling apart, the canyon at this hour felt like heaven, like an untouched place, all her own. Eyes closed, Twyla smiled to herself. Just as she felt herself drifting into a light doze, she sensed a shift in the meadow that made her eyes snap open. She bolted upright in the rocker, moved by instinct.

Then she saw a form descending the curve of Bone Tree Hill up near the caves Arnold had only just closed off that spring, claiming he'd found evidence of animals (coyotes, maybe even mountain lions) making a burrow. It had been the last time Arnold had been helpful on the ranch without her having to nag him.

The figure hurried down the slope—no, he ran. She could

tell it was a man by the broad shoulders and bearded face. Long dark hair pulled into a ponytail. Too tan and ruggedly dressed to be part of the group of guests.

She was fortunate to have good sight at her age and could see the figure was the same thin young man Arnold had been talking to the day before, after poor Klonnie had been sprayed.

What on the goddess's green earth was the hiker—wasn't that how Arnold had described him?—doing on the ranch, sprinting down Bone Tree Hill as if something were chasing him?

It was then she heard the screams coming from the direction of the meadow.

18

Sibyl (the Visionnaire)

SIBYL SET DOWN HER SUPPLY BAG, LIFTED THE WOODEN LEVER ACROSS the barn's entrance, and pushed open one of the sliding double doors. It opened with a loud groan of disuse, mixed with a strange, nasally keening sound: Twyla's goats, Nocturne and Diurn, braying for their lunch. Instantly, the smell of musty, stale air and something more fetid hit Sibyl's nostrils.

"Hi, little friends," Sibyl called out uncertainly. Twyla had told her, apologetically, that while she'd "cleaned and tidied" the barn to prepare for Sibyl's sessions, she had nowhere else to put the two goats, who slept together in one of the stalls. Could Sibyl be a doll and just let them into the outside pen and feed them real quick, before her first client, then she could have the barn completely to herself? And if they wouldn't go outside, well then, Sibyl could simply loop the leather straps hanging on the wall outside the stall—*shanks,* she called them—around the goats' necks (*"Gently, please!"* Twyla had said) and lead them out into the sunshine.

Of course, Sibyl had said yes, though her shoulders had tensed with annoyance. She heard her mother's voice: *Beggars can't be choosers, Debbie girl*.

Sibyl tapped on the flashlight on her phone and located a bank of light switches on the wall, which she flipped on. The barn leaped into light, and the goats' braying grew louder.

"Settle down," Sibyl muttered.

She shoved open the other half of the sliding doors and surveyed the barn's interior with dismay: the concrete floor was cracked and filthy, the windows and skylights hazed with grime, cobwebs everywhere.

How on earth could she do a session here just forty-five minutes from now? Jesus, the *smell*. She'd brought lavender spray but doubted it would make much of a difference.

Well, she had no choice. She'd already signed up for this.

She found the bin of goat food, filled a coffee can with the foul-smelling brown-gray pellets, and walked around the back of the barn to the outside pen, where she dumped it into the feeder beside a trough of water. Then bracing herself, she unlatched the outside door of the goats' stall, as Twyla had instructed, freeing them from the barn. As Twyla had predicted, the two animals, larger than Sibyl had expected—the size of Doberman pinschers (Sibyl was a dog person, not a goat person)—bolted into the pen and beelined for their feed, burying their faces in the dusty meal as if they hadn't eaten in weeks.

Sibyl double-checked the latch to the pen to verify it was secure, so that the goats could not escape out onto the property. ("*They don't exactly get along with Klondike*," Twyla had explained.) She had just enough time to sweep before her first client. Hopefully the guests would not be too disgusted by the setting. Sibyl didn't want anyone, especially not Mia Meadows, demanding refunds.

Her first session, scheduled to start soon with a novelist named Graham Caldwell, would need to go well. From the small amount of internet research Sibyl had done, she knew he was going to be tough to please. For a time, she had scorned preemptive research on her clients, but the truth was, it had been a while since she'd read for anyone other than Twyla (open book that she was), and Sibyl was more than a little nervous to read for the likes of Mia Meadows and her friends. So, she'd also glanced at Graham's Amazon.com page and author website, studying the black-and-white photo of the intensely serious, half-scowling middle-aged man in a tam-o'-shanter (to hide his thinning hair, she guessed) and thick-framed Warby Parker glasses. Talk about *open* book—the scrivener was trying way too hard. Insecurity galore. Sibyl had memorized the titles of a few of his novels—*The Last Sommelier, Elysian Park*—wondering who the hell wanted to read such books.

But the biggest clue about Graham Caldwell she'd gleaned from Twyla's Airbnb guest log, in which Twyla had jotted down the names of her visitors in spidery blue script.

On this weekend's page, Sibyl had read:

"Graham Caldwell & ~~Cecily Goshen~~."

Graham was supposed to have had a companion at Celestial Ranch this weekend.

Sibyl had played the name over in her mind, *Cecily Goshen*— it evoked a sort of WASPy, tennis-skirted wealth—on an instinct honed from years of absorbing strangers' personal minutiae. Cecily's crossed-out name was *the detail,* Sibyl decided, that she'd utilize in the session with Graham. Clearly, Cecily had canceled last minute; surely, Sibyl thought, Graham was not thrilled. Even if her reason was benign—a summer cold, a pollen allergy—Sibyl would use it to open a door to Graham's psyche. In general, romantic partners were the easy route to entry—lovers or mothers, really—and once Sibyl was *in the door*, well, her subjects did most of the work for her, inadvertently guiding *her* through the session. This was Sibyl's only true trick: creating the illusion that she was in control of the conversation, when nine out of ten times, her subjects led the way, guiding her to relevant conclusions without realizing they'd handed her all the clues.

The little she'd learned about Graham Caldwell in advance was enough to boost her confidence, to turn her apprehension into excitement for the session. Even though it was taking place in a crumbling barn reeking of goat shit, she felt an expansion of her consciousness as she awaited Graham's arrival. The feeling of being truly present buzzed at the base of her neck, her throat, starting its slow journey down her shoulders, her arms . . .

She covered the hay bales that doubled as seating for her sessions with blankets and turned on a few electric candles, the kind that appeared to flicker. It killed Sibyl not to light real ones for a session—cedarwood were her favorite—but it was fire season in Topanga, as Twyla had reminded her many times, and Topanga usually stayed in the high-risk zone all summer.

A delicate *tap-tap* came at the door of the barn, and then Graham Caldwell appeared, glancing warily around the barn, as if he expected bats to swoop down from the rafters. "Hi there. I'm here for my, ah, appointment."

"Welcome." Sibyl summoned her most generous smile and indicated the hay bale across the table. "Please, have a seat."

Graham stepped gingerly toward her. Sibyl saw he looked a bit ragged, perhaps hungover, and that he bore a strong resemblance to the aging, ex-hipster dads Sibyl often saw at the farmers' market on Sundays. He wore a wrinkled beige linen blazer over a white T-shirt, jeans, skateboarder sneakers, and the sort of newsboy cap Sibyl associated with the Great Depression. His graying hair matched the scruff shadowing his lined face, but he was still handsome in the worn, affable manner of an English professor or a latter-day Hugh Grant.

On his ring finger, Sibyl noted, he wore a gold wedding band.

"It's best if we forgo introductions, to maintain the integrity of our session, but I'm Sibyl, and it's a pleasure to have you."

"With all due respect," said Graham, frowning at the hay bale and skimming his palm across the blanket before sitting down, "I'm here because the host of the birthday party I'm attending already paid, and it seemed rude to decline. Also, I'm hungover and have PTSD from nearly getting stung to death by a swarm of bees this morning, so we can make this quick?"

"Oh, yes," Sibyl said. "I heard about the unfortunate incident with the bees."

He leaned in and she smelled the faint odor of booze leaking from his pores. "Couldn't you have given us a heads-up?"

"I'm sorry. I don't know what you mean." She lied, knowing exactly what he was about to say.

"The bees. You're a psychic, no?" He crossed his legs with effort. She could see he was not yet accustomed to the extra weight around his thighs. Was it the "Quarantine 15," as the talk show hosts called it? The alcohol? Newlywed bliss? Perhaps his last novel had sold poorly.

"If you're not in an open frame of mind, Graham, we won't be able to do our best work, anyway."

Graham laughed dryly; Sibyl heard the note of condescension. *Silly psychic!*

"Look," he said. "I know who you are. From—you know, the news. So we don't need to play any games here."

Sibyl's happy buzz vanished.

She'd been expecting some of the guests to know about her disgrace. Of course they would: Her name and face and a clip of the live *The View* footage had gone viral for weeks, maybe even months, after the accident, seemingly front and center on every news app, social media, live TV.

Sibyl, Seer to the Stars, scandal!

And the infinite, forever-on-the-internet memes of Merry Williams . . . Merry in her jump gear ascending the plane steps, Merry giving two thumbs-up from the open door ready to jump, even Merry plummeting to earth—they were legion.

Of course Mia Meadows's friends would know.

She just hadn't been prepared to be called out in the first ten seconds of her very first session.

Graham's words stung worse than she'd imagined they would. *I know who you are.*

Sibyl wished she could tell him to fuck off.

Instead, she forced a light, knowing chuckle. "Well, Graham, it is good to know you haven't been living in a cave. But we've all got a past, do we not?"

"Well—" Graham fumbled. "Yes, that would be true."

"Good. Listen, I'm glad you told me you know who I am. Transparency is necessary to a successful session, no? So, I'd like to state up front that I also know *you*. In fact, I'm a great fan of your work. I've only read *The Last Sommelier*, but I thought it was truly brilliant."

Instantly, she felt the air soften between them. Graham leaned ever so slightly forward, training his tired blue eyes on her.

"Could we just be gloves off here?" he said. "No disrespect, but I've never embraced this sort of thing."

He had that quality she'd observed in writers over the years:

desperately insecure, while somehow simultaneously radiating superiority.

"And what sort of *thing* is that?" Sibyl was used to this kind of opening; her lines came back to her like muscle memory.

"As in, uh, mystical—or, I guess, spiritual activities? Mia told us she gifted everyone a session and made us promise we'd use them. And you just don't say no to Mia—it's more trouble than it's worth."

Sibyl filed that detail about Mia Meadows away even if it wasn't any surprise after the woman's attack on Klondike the day before—still, it could be helpful in the session Mia had scheduled for herself later that afternoon. The most important session of the day, as Ms. Meadows was supplying Sibyl with that month's mortgage payment.

"So here I am," Graham said and sighed. "I'm a curmudgeonly skeptic by nature, so I'm wondering if we can do away with the pageantry and maybe just have a conversation? You're getting paid either way."

So, he was one of those, Sibyl thought, the guy who pays for a prostitute so they can *just talk*, and then ends up asking for a blow job. A man who needs to believe he's different, better than those other men. She'd dated too many guys like that. Her ex, Steven, two exes before Darryl, her last ex, had been addicted to massage parlors, a fact she'd discovered after he'd charged three thousand dollars' worth of "massages" to her Amex.

"Why don't we do this?" said Sibyl. "What if we do five minutes of a real session? Just give it a small chance, and if it's not interesting to you, we'll switch over to a regular conversation. Does that sound reasonable?"

Graham shrugged. "I suppose so."

"Wonderful." She reached into her bag at her feet and

pulled out two blindfolds, blue and green. She handed Graham the green one. "I'll ask you to tie this over your eyes. I'll do the same. It's best if you can't see anything, but if that makes you too uncomfortable, or you have issues with darkness, you can tie it any way you like."

She found this was a surefire way to motivate her subjects to block their eyes entirely; no one wanted to risk being perceived as a coward. Even, she thought, by Sibyl the disgraced psychic.

"A blindfold?" Graham laughed. "You're not going to make me walk a plank, are you?"

There he goes, she thought, putting in a little more effort. Even turning on the charm. They were getting warmer. This was her favorite part of the work—the subtle shift in the dynamic between two people, an electric sizzle in the few feet of air between Sibyl and her subject. The change burned extra hot with challenging subjects—atheists, lovers scorched too many times, the devoutly religious—as it did right now.

He tied the blindfold tight around his head. *Good boy,* she thought, and then she did the same, leaving the smallest opening that would allow her to see his hands if she cast her eyes downward. Usually, the hands of her subjects were all she needed to see to know she was on the right path. Hands and jawlines were where people held their feelings. Given Sibyl's gauze trick, she'd become especially adept at reading hands. And the stories they told.

"No planks, I promise," she said, tying on her own blindfold. Sibyl always used an imperceptibly sheer navy blue covering for her own face. Clients hardly ever noticed the slight transparency of the fabric, and if they did, Sibyl said something about her insurance requiring a modicum of visibility, for safety reasons, which was not true. If they asked to look through it, she let them. They almost never did. "To start, we'll just breathe together. Ready? One, two, three . . ."

Graham's breath was shallow and quick.

"Let's slow down," said Sibyl. "There's no rush here. I want you to make your exhales twice as long."

"I'm not a yoga person," mumbled Graham. The wobble in his voice, the sudden vulnerability, almost (*almost*) had her forgiving him for that shitty *I know who you are* comment at the start of the session.

"That's okay," said Sibyl softly, soothingly, "neither am I."

She waited a few more counts, until Graham's breathing had slowed down.

"A woman is presenting herself to me," Sibyl began. *Thank you, Cecily Goshen.* "Lithe and athletic, attractive, medium height, blue eyes."

Blue eyes or *brown eyes* were always safe, as the vast majority of the population had one or the other, so Sibyl always used whatever color her actual subject had—that way, if she was wrong about what she "saw," she could easily explain herself out of the mistake. *This person wants to see things your way, through your eyes,* etcetera.

"Um, okay," said Graham. "That's not entirely off track. Go ahead."

Sibyl had forgotten how easy this could be, how pleasing the gradual acceptance of her subject as he or she felt the details of their life accumulate in the prettily wrapped gift (their unique *truth*) Sibyl would have ready to present very soon.

"You're having relational tensions," she continued (who wasn't, at any given time, especially during the claustrophobic confinement of the pandemic?). "It's thrown off your equilibrium. This person is physically absent, but also very present."

In her narrow window of vision, Sibyl saw Graham's hands

link together on the table. A sign that he was engaged with the session, at last.

"Go on," he said.

"There's another force at work here," she said. "An oppositional one"—as if, she thought, this wasn't the most basic law of nature—"that is taking shape . . . as another woman, though it could also be a nonhuman entity with feminine energy—"

"What the hell is *that* supposed to mean?"

His defensive tone told Sibyl she was on precisely the right track.

"I'm not sure yet," she said. "I only know I'm seeing two women." She thought of the gold band on his finger, considered her original deduction that he was probably on his second wife, or possibly his third, and her gut told her to proceed with the hunch. "Or—possibly three. Are there three women who have been very important to you, at various times in your life, or even concurrently?"

Graham seemed, she thought, like the type of artiste who left his longtime devoted wife for a younger, bohemian woman, then wrote essays (praised by literary critics) about how the choice tortured him.

His breathing quickened again. "Kind of."

Bingo. Typical self-involved artist/cheater, Sibyl thought, whose commitment to monogamy lasts only as long as his partner's pert ass and belief in Graham's brilliance.

"One is younger, one is older, and the third—" Sibyl paused, pretending to be scrutinizing the images in her own head, when, on cue, Graham jumped in: "Jesus. Don't say it! She's African-American, right?"

Sibyl exhaled, as if he'd validated her precisely. "Yes . . . exactly. That's correct. The third is a woman of color. The three of them are standing together, in my mind's eye, asking no more of you than to— Wait a moment, while I listen to them—" She paused and counted silently to five. "Okay. They're asking you for courage and decency to take responsibility for your past, and to make strong, true commitments going forward. Only one— the younger, I believe—requires your ongoing love and devotion, but the others are just asking for, well, respect. Honesty."

She was, Sibyl thought to herself, simply speaking on behalf of all women everywhere who'd suffered the romantic vagaries of self-important men like Graham.

On the table, she could see Graham wringing his hands.

"This is fucking bizarre," he muttered.

"Shall I go on?" said Sibyl.

"I'm not sure," said Graham. "Yeah. I guess. I mean— whatever you want." In his voice, she heard defensiveness mixed with intrigue. Her subjects always desired more, even as they feared the truth.

"What? Have I touched a nerve?"

"Maybe. But you're also being pretty vague. Like I said, I'm familiar with how this stuff works—I'm a novelist, for *chrissakes*—so if we're going to stick with the session, I'd like you to tell me something really specific."

Oh, but she was ready for this. As soon as Twyla had told her there was a novelist (a male, to boot) in the group, Sibyl had known, with a tingle of anticipation at the possible challenge, she'd have to counter his doubt. It was the creatives who were tougher to guide. Novelists, screenwriters—poets were no problem, they existed in the ethereal zone—those who believed their imaginations so vast there were few mysteries they had yet to crack.

They were also so egocentric; they were happy to apply virtually *anything* Sibyl said to their own lives. She'd found, over the years, that with writers especially, she could be daringly

specific, simply plucking from a memorized list she'd composed years ago of common human scenarios, based on no one
in particular (perhaps she, too, was a writer!). All she needed
to do in her sessions was choose a scenario from the list and
apply some highly specific details: hair color, street names,
song titles, foods, and *boom*—her subjects would fold them,
somehow, into their own lives.

In an instant, she decided on one of her go-to favorites
from the list, one that seemed just right for Graham.

"I'm getting a very pointed message about you, Graham. It's
distilling now—hold on, let me see—" She took one long, slow
breath, pretending to concentrate very hard. "Are you ready?"

"Hit me."

She spoke haltingly, as if struggling to read small print in
low light. "I'm seeing that you've lost a lover but kept a friend.
A child is involved. So is . . . dignity. *Family* dignity, it appears.
You are struggling to see a path. You're grappling with grit versus glamour, past versus present, and transcendent love versus sexual desire. I see a Spanish-style house on a tree-lined
street. Bougainvillea and jacaranda trees. A woman sits in the
window, weeping quietly. Her hair is long and shiny, or once
was, and her eyes are light. She is not the woman for you."

Through her blindfold, she could see his hands had begun
to tremble. She smiled to herself. As expected, he was hearing
prescient observations about his own life. Via a basic Shakespearean plotline, adorned with ubiquitous LA flora and hair-
styles.

"*Goddammit.*" Graham dropped a balled fist on the card
table; it shuddered, toppling his water bottle. He stood and
pulled off his blindfold. "Fucking Dawn," he said—almost spat.
"Couldn't even keep her mouth shut for twenty-four hours. I

can't believe she'd bring Cecily *and Ethan* into this." He jumped to his feet, knocking back the hay bale. "We're done here."

"I'm sorry?" said Sibyl. She removed her blindfold. Sunlight angled through the slats of the barn roof. Faintly, she heard from somewhere in the stalls the rustle of those little rodents that were plentiful as roaches. Twyla called them beechies.

"Dawn must have put you up to this. Or was it Mia? Of course, I should've known better than to let those two rope me into a goddamn psychic session." He looked down at Sibyl, his eyes blazing. "I'm sorry. This has nothing to do with you. I actually feel we had a bit of a connection. But it's fucked now."

She watched him whirl around and stomp over to the double doors of the barn, where he heaved them open—with considerable effort, Sibyl noted. There were few sights more satisfying, she thought, than a haughty intellectual in the wilderness.

"By the way," he yelled over his shoulder as he left the barn, "it stinks like hell in there!"

The heavy barn door shut. The barn shook—Sibyl was sure the roof was about to collapse in on her. Instead, her phone announced a new text.

19

SATURDAY, JUNE 25, 2022

Raj (the Drifter)

ONE, RAJ CREPT CLOSER TO THE SEETHING BEEHIVE LODGED IN THE crook of the live oak. He swiveled his binoculars around so they hung at the center of his back.

Two, he lifted the driving iron the old man had given him behind one shoulder, gripping it with both hands like a batter stepping up to the plate.

He stood a few feet from the trunk of the tree, so that the pocked orb of the hive was a foot overhead, at an angle.

He flicked his eyes up to the blue sky blipping between the broad leaves of the tree, and asked Nani to help him.

Then he looked at the hive, told the bees he was sorry, and—

THREE—swung the golf club at the hive with all his might.

It cracked into thirds and hurtled to the ground, kicking up clouds of dust.

Raj dropped the club and groped for his binoculars so they would not slam his back. Then he whirled and ran as fast as his legs would carry him, blinded by panic as the bees' buzzing

filled his ears, and he felt the fiery stings on his arms, the back
of his neck. A few on his calves.

He ran faster, in the direction of the meadow and his cave
beyond, his need to see Candace so urgent he could hardly
contain it. His flesh itched and burned as he sprinted, and he
fought the urge to scream at the top of his lungs.

To plead for help, like the coward he was.

Instead, he pushed faster as the wide expanse of the
meadow came into view, and on the other side, the rocky hills
where his cave was lodged.

Where Candace was waiting, he hoped, *prayed*, her ratty
blue blanket twisted around her.

Unless she'd gone off wandering again. Unless the media
roaches had found her while Raj was gone to complete his mission with the bees.

As he reached the edge of the woods, the meadow sweeping
before him, just a hundred yards or so separating him from
Candace in the cave, Raj saw them.

The trespassers.

In the center of the meadow.

Running in a zigzag pattern, arms flailing, their wild
laughter sailing through the air.

They were, Raj saw with horror, completely *naked*.

He stopped short at the edge of the trees, unable to look
away from the bare bodies in the sunlight, his face heating
with shame.

What were they *doing*?

Was it some perverse ritual concocted by the Witch?

Raj did not want to find out. He would have to take the long
way back to the cave, through the woods again, past the dry
creek bed beside the giant oak tree with the decayed tire swing
hanging from its thickest branch.

He walked fast, wishing Candace could be with him right
now. She loved to hike. But he could not risk exposing her beneath the open sky of the ranch where the drones might see her.
Instead, he left her in the cave when he went out each day, and
brought her presents he'd found while roving on the faint trails
of the property. A fiddlehead fern. A heart-shaped rock. A
beechie skull picked clean by ants. She loved them all, clapping
her soft hands over her mouth with delight when he revealed
each little gift.

He kept his eyes down as he walked, searching for Candace's newest surprise, scanning the rocky earth for any glim-
mers of delight.

And then—he saw it! A smooth white stone. Was it heart-
shaped? He crouched and swept it into a pocket.

When he stood, the giant oak with the tire swing was just
ahead.

Someone was using the swing.

Raj stopped in his tracks, his heart surging to his throat.

Was she *real*?

The person—a woman—swung from one side of the tree to
the other, head tipped back, long dark hair flaring behind, as
she stretched her legs to the sky, feet bare, body lithe and muscular, sinews jumping from her calves and thighs. A low *woooo*
rose from her throat. A happy sound.

Candace.

20

Sibyl (the Visionnaire)

"OKAY, LITTLE FRIENDS," SAID SIBYL, OPENING THE STALL DOOR TO, once again, release Twyla's goats into the large, fenced pen at the side of the barn. The creatures had somehow found their way back into the barn. "Diurn, Nocturne, whoever you are. Out you go." She shielded her eyes from the glaring midday sun with one hand—and waved the animals forward with the other.

"Get *out*," she said, kicking toward one of the goats' haunches, and it bucked and shot into the pen. The other followed, looking back at Sibyl disdainfully as it trotted after its friend. The goats stopped in the shade of the small tree at the center of the pen and stared at Sibyl, threads of straw stuck in their little tapered beards. They *were* kind of cute, Sibyl thought, in their wizened, furry, triangular way. She felt like she might cry.

Get it together, she commanded herself, sighing and stepping back into the barn. She did not want to get emotional over goddamned goats. Not when she still had more than half the guests' sessions ahead of her. But the failure of Graham's reading had deflated her. His disdain. The lack of connection. Usually, even a few sparks of understanding between Sibyl and her subject buoyed her.

Graham had given her nothing.

Then a new text had landed on the rectangular screen of her phone:

All work & no crime makes Deb a dull girl.

Hardly clever. Hardly *scary.* Yet Sibyl's hands were trembling when she resettled on her hay bale to wait for the next party guests to arrive, fake candles flickering on the table before her, straw slicing into the backs of her legs.

"Yo, *hello?*" A throaty, assertive voice came from the barn's entrance. "Any bees in here we should know about?"

Sibyl stood to greet the two women making their way down the center aisle of the barn: the compact, muscular redhead followed by the serious, reproving Asian woman. The redhead walked with purposeful, nearly aggressive strides, while her partner shuffled behind her, eyes downcast.

"No bees!" Sibyl called out brightly. "I heard about the incident, and I can assure you we're bee-free in here."

She delivered her most generous smile to the women as they arrived at her table, the redhead with a forceful smile, the other averting her gaze into the middle distance.

Relational tensions, thought Sibyl. *Obviously.*

Instantly, there it was: the tang of possibility in the air. Lifting Sibyl.

"Summer and Joan," said Sibyl. "I have been provided with your names, but nothing more. Sessions work best when I've been given as little context as possible."

"She goes by Joanie." Summer nodded toward her wife.

"I can speak, thanks," said Joanie, stone-faced.

"Summer and *Joanie*, then," said Sibyl.

The two women sat on opposite sides of the bale across from Sibyl. She handed them fresh blindfolds, explained the basics of her method, and tied the fabric over her own eyes. She felt herself relax as she led them through the breathing exercises, her old pre–Merry Williams confidence returning. Sibyl rarely did couples sessions—she'd found that individual subjects *wanted* to believe her, whereas two people introduced a sort of self-consciousness, an inability to let down their own guard for fear of appearing more gullible than their partner.

But Summer and Joan—*Joanie*—were obviously in a funk at the moment, each in no mood to appease the other. In this case, Sibyl decided, stealing a glimpse of each woman through the tiny gap in her blindfold as she counted their breaths, it made sense to use the Random Imagery Approach. Her subjects were in an obviously heightened emotional state, making them more likely to see meaning in nearly everything. Of course, it was a gamble; sometimes RIA backfired, and the subject closed off, but Sibyl had a hunch that would not be the case with Summer and Joanie—and she was ready to dig herself out if it was.

"Now, let's count our breaths aloud," she said now, to Summer and Joanie. "One . . ."

The women drew in breaths. Through the imperceptibly sheer fabric of her blindfold, Sibyl watched them as she counted. At around thirty, Summer placed her hand over Joanie's. Joanie did not move a muscle.

At fifty, Sibyl glanced down and saw one of the yellow-and-brown barn spiders Twyla called her "artful eight-legged friends" scurrying across the table.

When they finished counting, Sibyl told the women she'd received the clear vision of a spider. Asked them if the image *resonated*.

Joanie and Summer fell silent.

"Our twins," said Summer, finally. "They've had pet tarantulas."

"That was ages ago," Joanie said.

Sibyl was not really surprised; this happened more often than not with RIA: whatever image she offered could be applied meaningfully to a subject's life. She was simply tapping into the abundance of interconnection *everywhere*. Her body tingled with harmonious feeling.

"I see that," said Sibyl. "Twins, yes. They are girls, yes?" Like blue eyes or brown, Sibyl routinely chose daughters or sons for her subjects with children; if she was wrong, she simply explained that biological sex was sometimes different from *energy*, which all beings embodied in both masculine and feminine forms.

"They are," said Summer. "Our daughters."

Sibyl heard sadness in Summer's voice.

"The spiders are a source of both controversy and joy," said Sibyl. "Your daughters tell me this is a theme in your household—much friction but also much happiness. Does this resonate?"

Was there any normal family, Sibyl thought, that wasn't steeped in both? The observation was wildly vague, and yet to her subjects, would seem startlingly personal.

"Yes," said the women, nearly in unison, sounding amazed.

Sibyl heard a rustling sound in the far corner of the barn near the goat pen. As if something were running in place in the hay, or digging a hole; a frantic, scratching sound.

"Go on," said Summer. The eagerness in her subject's voice was food for Sibyl's malnourished mind. She hadn't realized how much she'd missed the intimacy of the sessions. How they restored whatever faith was left inside her.

The rustling sound grew louder. Through her blindfold, Sibyl strained for some glimpse of the source, which was somewhere off to her right, but all she could see was rusted metal slats crisscrossing one of the stall doors.

They reminded Sibyl of a jail cell.

"A prison," Sibyl free-associated. "I've received the image of a prison."

"What the hell," began Summer, then faltered.

The air around the two women had stilled. Had she gone too far too quickly? Let the thrill of the hunt—for information, for clues, for communion; god, what a terribly lonely time the past year had been—make her too eager?

"Did you—" Joanie faltered.

"Go on," said Sibyl, as placidly as she could, though her face was burning. She was stumbling, groping more than usual, clearly riffing, but the rustling sounds were distracting her—was it the goats, digging or scratching? Had they somehow gotten back into their stall?

"Did you say—prison?" finished Joanie.

"Well—yes," said Sibyl. "But do not assume the image is literal. Sometimes what I'm shown is metaphoric—"

"Jo, relax," said Summer, squeezing her wife's slender hand. "You know this is some sort of guesswork."

Through her blindfold, Sibyl saw Joanie's lips were pressed together in a tense line.

"Joanie?" said Sibyl. "Is something I've said resonating with you?"

"Not *resonating*," said Joanie. "Creeping me out. Spiders, jails—it's all so obviously relevant." She turned to her wife. "Did you prep her for this, Summer?"

"What?" said Summer. "No! Of course not!"

"Please don't be alarmed," said Sibyl. "The sessions can be disarming, But the purpose is always deeper understanding, and often, to open a path to healing."

"I've heard enough," said Joanie, standing up. "I never wanted to be here this weekend, anyway. Summer knows it. I've told her for *years* I never want to see Dawn Sanders ag—"

"That's *enough*, Joanie." Summer stood up too.

Sibyl forced herself to remain seated.

The scratching sounds were louder and closer—no, it was definitely *not* the goats.

"What the hell is that noise?" said Summer.

"We're in the middle of the wilderness. We share this place with many creatures." Sibyl recited the words Twyla had told her countless times. Words Sibyl had scoffed at.

The scampering seemed to be closing in from multiple directions. Could it be rats?

Then Joanie screamed, a sharp peal of terror, and Sibyl ripped off her blindfold.

21

SATURDAY, JUNE 25, 2022

Twyla (the Hostess)

TWYLA WAS PASSING THE BARN, IN SEARCH OF ARNOLD, WHO'D MAN-
aged to wander out of the house in the two minutes she'd left
him to fold the clean towels, when she heard the scream.

The guests' caterwauling from the Andromeadow had surely
been heard all over Topanga. Twyla knew she should be grateful—
the goddess had *truly* been watching over her this morning,
when the bees had swarmed but not actually *stung* a single guest
during their bizarre naked footrace. She had found the wrecked
hive cracked open at the edge of the meadow, still buzzing with
a handful of bees. Surely the work of a black bear, lured by the
prospect of honey. Twyla hoped the queen bee had survived and
that not too many workers had drowned in the pool of honey.

The big black doors of the barn were closed, as Sibyl was doing a session with two of the guests, the beautiful Asian woman
and her sporty redheaded wife. Nocturne and Diurn were in the
pen outside their stall, splashing each other with water from
their trough.

"Arnold?" Twyla called out. Could he have stumbled into the barn?

Twyla hurried over. When she was a few paces from the barn door, it swung open and the Asian woman—Jodie? Janie? Twyla hated how her brain was no longer good with names—stumbled out, blinking in the weak sunlight, the blindfold Sibyl required in her sessions dangling from the woman's slender hand. Summer (that one Twyla could remember) ran out, nearly pushing her petite wife to the ground.

"There's some *things* in—in there!" Summer shouted, pointing into the dimly lit barn.

Sibyl appeared behind her, looking flustered, her blindfold pushed up on her forehead, her mass of bright red curly hair half escaped from the bun.

"Twyla!" Sibyl called. "Hi there! Joanie, Summer, and I were just taking a brief interlude to relocate—"

The woman Joanie (apparently) said, "There's some sort of *critter* in the barn. Like, vermin. A *lot* of them. An entire nest or something."

"Loads," Summer said. "I'm not sure, but I think one of them ran across my sandals. The top of my foot stings. Like, what if it bit me?" She looked to her wife—the way a child might look to its mother for reassurance. "What do you think, babe? Should we go to the ER? Just to be safe."

"No one needs to go to the hospital, Summer," Sibyl said. "It's probably just a few beechies—they're like chipmunks' cousins."

It couldn't be, Twyla thought. She'd been so careful to chase them out. She'd swung the broom at them, which went against her pacifist nature, calling *shoo, shoo!* Then she'd stuffed the holes through which they'd entered the barn with wads of steel wool before nailing squares of plywood over the openings.

So how had they gotten back in?

She must have missed a hole.

She cursed herself for being careless. Arnold was to blame—giving her so many *extra* worries.

Topanga was overrun with the weird little rodents that hopped like kangaroos. They were technically ground squirrels but looked like a cross between a chipmunk and a capybara. Harmless, but certainly a nuisance, and constantly underfoot during the summer. Twyla had allowed a little family of beechies to bed down in a corner of a stall in the barn. She'd shooed them out at first, but then realized they were hungry. The drought had curbed the abundance of the nuts and berries and insects they preferred, so she'd taken to leaving almonds and dried cranberries in a corner of the stall that had holes. It was another task Arnold had abandoned—sealing the many cracked boards of the old barn. It was Arnold, she thought now, who had basically *created*, out of sheer laziness, egress for the beechies. But yes, she was at fault too—she'd basically *trained* the rodents to live in the barn.

She enjoyed watching the beechies crawl into the barn, tentatively, vigilantly, then lose themselves in a feeding frenzy upon finding Twyla's offerings. Like a weak mother, letting her toddler crawl into bed with her night after night, well aware of the bad habit she was creating.

She had put the money she'd counted on making from her cut of Sibyl's earnings in jeopardy, and she'd failed Sibyl as well.

"Joanie, Summer, I'm *so* sorry!" Twyla said, flinging her palms for emphasis. "That's just a little crew of beechies. They're actually very cute, sort of like dandier squirrels. They find the barn really cozy, and I don't have the heart to exterminate." As if she would *ever* do such a thing, but she reasoned that she might appeal to the women's softer sides.

"Hold on," said Summer. "These little rats are your *pets*?"

"If you give me just a minute, I'll have them vacated in no time."

"That's quite all right," said Joanie. "I think I've had enough of my session."

"But we weren't even at the halfway mark," Sibyl protested. She flashed a look at Twyla. Translation: *Get those fucking animals out of the barn so I can get back to work.*

"I don't think I can do it," said Summer. "I have a thing with—rodents. I spent a summer in New York City."

"You deserve your whole session," Twyla said. "Give me just two seconds and I'll have those little guys out of the barn." She stepped to the broom leaning against the side of the barn.

Joanie hesitated, considering. "I just feel kind of rattled now."

"Sometimes, an incursion during a session can actually be useful," Sibyl said. "It can stir the pot, so to speak, so we unlock other elements of our unconscious mind."

"Maybe," said Joanie uncertainly, taking a step away from the barn. "But I'm also happy to go back and join my friends."

"Right," said Summer, and Twyla saw a look exchanged between the two women. "We still have to, um, get the cake ready. And other stuff."

"Twyla can make sure all that gets done in time for the big b-day celebration," said Sibyl.

"Certainly!" said Twyla, wondering what this meant—was she supposed to offer herself as a servant to Ms. Meadows? Arnold would be needing his lunch, for goodness' sake.

"Uh," said Joanie. "Okay then. Let's just do it."

Twyla hurried into the barn, flooded with relief and impressed with how Sibyl had managed to salvage the session. Perhaps they'd each get their payment, after all. Every bit was critical to keeping Twyla in the canyon where she belonged, and away from the gates of a godforsaken *senior living community.*

She whacked the broom against the barn wall, her standard warning to the beechies.

"Hey ho, it's time to go!" she called out, and whacked again. On cue, the rodents rustled.

She whacked again.

Hey ho, hey ho!

She heard the scamper and scrape of little claws and smiled. They *were* nearly her pets, the way they responded to her. How silly that Joanie, and especially Summer, who'd seemed so hardy, had actually been *screaming* over them. Then again, city dwellers were so full of fear, so prone to skittish, extreme reactions to benign components of the natural world.

"Hey ho, it's time to go!"

There was a hole in the back of the stall where they entered and exited; she would chase them out and patch it the second Sibyl and Joanie and Summer finished their session.

Then, from outside, came a startled gasp.

Then Sibyl's voice: "It's okay, Joanie! Twyla will be right back. She'll, um, make them stop." Then, "Twy, we need you! Like *now!*"

Good god, these city people! Twyla was irritated now. What *didn't* scare them? She'd managed to chase three of the beechies into the hole, but still needed to find the other two.

Clutching the broom, Twyla rushed out of the barn.

Sibyl had one hand on each of the women's backs trying to coax them into the barn.

"Back to it, ladies," said Sibyl. "I'm sure it's beechies-free now. Right, Twyla?"

Joanie and Summer didn't answer, their eyes fixed on the goat pen. Twyla heard a low bleating, and her heart sank.

Invigorating herself, she shifted her eyes to Nocturne and Diurn, knowing what she'd see: Diurn on his hind legs over Nocturne, mounted and thrusting.

"Are they," said Joanie, sounding repulsed, "*mating*?"

"Oh! No. Certainly not! Don't mind them. They're fixed. Plus, they're both boys. It's just a game they play. Many animals do it. It's harmless."

"Okay, then!" Sibyl cut in. "Intermission's over. Let's continue, Joanie and Summer!" Sibyl was nearly pulling the women toward the barn. "Follow me," she said, beginning to sound desperate. "We don't want to pause our work for too long—it could disrupt the flow."

Twyla's cheeks flushed with heat, and she cursed herself for saying too much.

Sibyl gave Twyla another sharp look. "Twyla, you'll stop by the yurt, yes? To see if the rest of the guests need help with tonight's birthday arrangements?"

"Of course!" said Twyla. She would have to *pray* the remaining beechies in the barn stayed quiet. At this rate, Joanie would be demanding all sorts of refunds, and who knows what Ms. Meadows would do. God forbid she said something bad about the ranch on that Twitter website.

"Oh—okay," said Summer, taking a step toward the barn.

"Hold on, babe," Joanie said, pulling her arm out of Sibyl's grasp.

Summer froze.

"You know, I think we're good," said Joanie. "And ready to get back to our friends. Sibyl, thanks for the half-session. Maybe we can talk about the, ah, logistical details later."

And with that, Joanie grabbed Summer's hand and hurried away, leaving Twyla and Sibyl to watch her snow-white shirt disappear into the trees.

Dawn (the Birthday Girl)

DAWN JOGGED AWAY FROM THE MEADOW AND ONTO THE TRAIL LEADING through the woods back to Betelgeuse. The midday sun was gentle on her face, and a fresh breeze feathered the air. Her birthday weather could not have been lovelier, but she was unable to focus on anything except getting back to Quinn. The bees hadn't stung anyone, miraculously, but the seething, buzzing swarm had scared the shit out of Dawn and made her frantic to check on her daughter.

The group had been rattled by the sudden swarm over the meadow. The dark, humming cloud that had zoomed furiously toward them, then veered away in the direction of Hydra Hill. Still, the bees had killed the mood.

Dawn slowed to a speed-walk on the trail, her chest still burning from the terrifying nude sprint. Had she really just *done* that? Gotten buck naked in front of her friends and sprinted, boobs and ass flapping—and, oh god, what about that weird skin pouch right above her twenty-two-year-old C-section scar?

When the bees had disappeared, they'd all hurried back into their clothes. Even Mia had rushed to cover herself.

Dawn caught her breath and resumed her jog. She had a few hours to herself until dinner and *whatever* Mia had in store for them afterward. A few hours to spend with Quinn and put her into the calmest possible frame of mind—Dawn pictured the white tablet of Ativan, then felt ashamed—before Dawn took off again with her friends. As if *she* were the young adult.

It was irrational, Dawn knew, to have such anxiety over leaving Quinn alone in a rented cabin for a couple of hours. But the combination of running around naked and Mia's decree that everyone turn over their phones had made Dawn feel unnaturally removed from her daughter. Quinn's need for her had been the steadiest factor in Dawn's life. Even though Quinn rarely texted anything more than *Where are you?* and often when Dawn was right upstairs at home, and the occasional flurry of cute memes (pandas hugging, bunnies holding heart-shaped balloons), the baseline of Quinn's need was as much a comfort to Dawn as an irritation. Her need for Dawn was always there, insatiable, waiting to be filled.

Dawn slowed to a walk again; she'd run enough for one day. To think she'd been a runner once, covering miles and miles of the path along the beach, from Santa Monica all the way to Temescal Canyon. And now, because she'd been so consumed with mothering Quinn, a short sprint across a meadow and a trot over a trail left her panting. Maybe now, at fifty, she would finally get back in shape, although she remembered saying the same thing around her fortieth. As she walked, working the clean canyon air back into her lungs, she had the sense of another presence—someone behind her on the trail. She wheeled around. The trail was empty but for a few scampering chipmunks, although they didn't look like any she'd seen before.

She reached the end of the trail, and there was the shabby cabin.

"Hey, Quinny, I'm here!" she called out.

The door of the cabin was wide open. Odd. Open doors made Quinn uneasy. Dawn hopped up the stairs to the small porch, feeling the ancient wood shudder under her weight, and rushed into the cabin.

She nearly crashed into Quinn, who was wearing her backpack. Quinn's face was flushed, as if she'd been running too, and her hairline was damp with sweat. She looked startled.

"Honey! Hi! I'm sorry I was gone for so long."

Quinn took a small step back. "That wasn't long."

"Oh?" Dawn was confused. "I thought I said I'd be back at noon, and it's almost—"

"You're never back when you say you'll be. Last night you were three hours late."

Dawn's face went hot. "I know, sweetie, like I told you, last night was a—an unusual situation. I hadn't seen my friends in ages. We lost track of time. It won't happen again. I'm going to be off doing things a lot this weekend, but that doesn't mean I'll—"

"I'm going on a hike," Quinn said.

"A—hike?"

Quinn never voluntarily hiked. She didn't even walk around their Santa Monica neighborhood unless Dawn insisted. Usually, she had to bribe Quinn with the promise of a strawberry milkshake from the Brentwood Country Mart to get her to agree to a short hike up in Mandeville Canyon.

"You told me to walk around and explore," said Quinn. "I'm going to do that."

"You are? I mean—great! Where are you going to walk, exactly? Do you want me to come with you?"

She heard Mia's voice: "*Give the kid a fucking break, Dawnie. Don't smother her!*"

Then Reece: "*Congratulate your child when she or he shows independence.*"

"I'm proud of you, sweetie," Dawn said.

"You're standing in front of the door, Mom."

For a moment, Dawn considered closing the door behind her, offering to buy Quinn some romance eBooks for her Kindle, another bribe but this time, to stay inside.

Dawn took a step to the side, freeing Quinn's path to the door.

"Oh! Sorry. I'm just . . . surprised. What's in your backpack?"

Quinn stared at Dawn as if she were very dim. "A water bottle. Corn Nuts. The map."

"Oh—okay. Yeah, that was a dumb question." Dawn laughed.

What did she think Quinn had in there—a bottle of vodka and a pack of cigarettes?

"When will you be back?"

"Later on."

The open-endedness of Quinn's responses knocked the wind out of Dawn. It felt as if something had drastically changed. Her Quinny-bee. Her baby. What if Quinn had seen her and everyone else running nude across the meadow?

"Well, how about—let's say—by two?"

Quinn shrugged. "Okay." She took a few steps forward, out the front door and onto the porch. "Happy birthday, Mom." She walked down the steps and into the scrub grass, toward the trail that led deeper into the canyon, as if she knew exactly where she was going.

"Be careful!" Dawn called out, as she watched Quinn's long, angular frame disappear.

Dawn sat down on the step and rested her elbows on her knees, fighting the urge to follow Quinn. Trying not to think of bobcats and mountain lions. Might a pack of coyotes attack a grown woman? Graham had implied they were vicious in a group. And who knew what kind of people might be squatting in the tangled wilds of Topanga Canyon. Why had Graham felt the need to mention the Manson family last night?

She knew she should be happy to see her daughter displaying such rare independence. She closed her eyes and tipped her face to the sky, willing herself to relax, to appreciate that, somehow, this place was inspiring a sudden wanderlust in her fearful, indoorsy daughter. Twyla, as flaky as she may be, was right. Celestial Ranch *was* magical.

Dawn opened her eyes. Mia stood in front of her.

"Jesus, Meemers! You scared me!"

"Sorry, baby doll! I was trying to catch up with you on the trail, but you were jogging so fast. I'm impressed you had so much pep after our sprint across the meadow."

So, it hadn't just been the beechies back on the trail with her. The presence Dawn had sensed had been real after all.

"Why didn't you just yell for me to wait up?"

"Oh, I don't know." Mia tipped her head. "I thought you might be having, you know, a *moment* after that experience and being freshly divorced from your phone. I didn't want to interrupt."

"I wish you had. Maybe you could've helped me talk to Quinn." As soon as the words came out, Dawn regretted them.

"Talk to Quinn? About what?"

"Get this," Dawn said, trying to embody a more carefree attitude. "I got back from the meadow and caught her leaving to go on a *hike*! She doesn't even like walking around the block at home. I have to bribe her to take a walk on the beach."

"A hike?" Mia beamed. "That's amazing! Why are you making it sound like it's a bad thing?"

There she was—Mia the critic. Dawn couldn't mention any sort of worry or Mia would try to convince Dawn her fears were silly (or plain wrong) or force Dawn into a long therapy session in which Mia did most of the talking and offered up a solution. Often, Mia did both!

"I—I'm not making it into a *bad thing*. It's just really unusual behavior for her. She doesn't like *nature*."

"Does she really not, though? Has she ever had a chance to experience it like this?"

Stop being such a fucking contrarian, Dawn wanted to say. "Well—no. This is her first trip to Topanga. In case you forgot—she wasn't even supposed to be here. I know my daughter. Trees make her nervous. She hates walking through that community garden on Main Street—she says the plants look like the monsters in some video game—"

"Listen to yourself, honey. It sounds like you're—unintentionally, of course—validating these anxieties. Subtle cues like that can be really influential to kids like ours. Remember how I used to think Nate hated water? And then I signed him up for that ocean-swimming class, just to see what would happen."

"Of course I remember." Dawn felt the back of her neck tighten. *Here we go*, she thought, Mia's habit of using her son's experience as a one-size-fits-all for every other kid. Dawn knew she wasn't alone—every member of the Nurtury had, in confidence, confessed to being irked by the way Mia used Nate as a comparison. "Well?" Dawn said. She felt like she had no choice but to play along. "And what happened with Nate at the swim lessons? He hated it."

"Wrong," Mia said. "He hated it *at first*. And then what?"

"And then he got used to it."

"Not just *got used to it*. He fell head over heels for it. Now he does open-water races down in Marina del Rey once a month."

Great. Not only was Nate neurotypical, in other words, *normal* (the word was taboo in the special-needs world), unlike the rest of the Nurtury kids, but he was also some kind of extreme-sport athlete.

"It took me years to realize it, but *I* was feeding his fear of water. Constantly reinforcing it by letting him avoid water and telling other people that he was practically aquaphobic. A fiction of my own making!"

There it was. A waste-of-time lesson masquerading as a chat between friends was really about one thing: blame.

"So, you think I'm actually making Quinn afraid of the outdoors?"

"God, no, sweetie! That's not at all what I meant. I'm sure Quinn does have some innate aversion to wild settings. But the best thing you can do for her is support any sign that she might be the tiniest bit open to overcoming that fear. The human brain is astonishingly flexible. Extraordinarily *forgiving*, if you will. "

"I—I guess you're right."

"Of course I'm right. I'm so happy Quinny-bee went hiking. Consider it her birthday present to you."

"I'll try."

"That's my Dawnie."

"It would be such a great help," Dawn said, taking advantage of the moment, "and allow me to chill and enjoy my day, if I could get my phone—just so I have a way to stay in—" .

"Absolutely not," Mia said, wagging a finger. "Jax insisted on clipping the lockbox key to his undies to prevent desperate screen addicts from trying. He's so naughty. And here's another upside!" Mia pointed at Betelgeuse. "We've got a quiet, empty cabin to hang out in and have some girl time. We need to rest up before your big night. Let's go inside and kick back on Twyla's nasty old couch. I have to meet that psychic in an hour for a sesh."

Dawn summoned a weak chuckle, though the prospect of the "big night" ahead made her dizzy with anticipation. What had she gotten herself into?

2010

Santa Monica

THEIR CHILDREN WERE TEN NOW, AND MIDDLE SCHOOL was looming. And with it, a slew of new vaccine requirements, mandated to parents in a list of disease names and acronyms Dawn could never keep straight.

> *Meningococcal disease (MenACWY)*
> *Tetanus*
> *DTaP*
> *Diphtheria*
> *Whooping cough (pertussis)*
> *Influenza*

NO SHOT, NO SCHOOL! read the marquees of middle schools—public, private, and charter—across Los Angeles County in the summer of 2010.

Dawn was scared to let Quinn get the shots. So were Graham and Mia, Summer and Joanie. They'd all read that British doctor's article linking vaccinations to autism, especially the dreaded MMR. What if this next series of shots made Quinn even more withdrawn, her moods even more erratic? What if it made all the Nurtury kids worse? Not that any of the Nurtury parents would dare phrase it this way—like Dawn, they had, years ago, accepted their child as extraordinary. Given up on finding a cure (again, a word never spoken lest it imply their child was sick, broken, incomplete). Not that it stopped Dawn from trying out every diet and supplement and therapy under the sun claiming to help alleviate the symptoms associated with autism. Despite money Dawn spent on bottles of fish-oil capsules, weighted vests and blankets, and every organic-plastic fidget toy known to man, despite the elimination of sugar, wheat, dairy, and nearly every category of food at one point or another, Dawn knew her daughter was *perfect* just as she was, even if it was hard to remember that on the bad days.

She knew of parents, even those with neuro*typical* children, who interviewed pediatricians (sometimes *before* giving birth), searching for doctors who bent the rules, allowed parents to delay their child's vaccination schedule, sometimes by six or twelve months. Just in case. It was this *just in case* that kept Dawn up at night the summer before Quinn entered middle school. Quinn's appointment to receive the MMR vaccine, required for kids entering sixth grade, was already in the calendar. Dawn and the other Nurtury parents confessed their fears to

Reece at the Nurtury, where they still met every Thursday, while their children were in camp.

Reece said: "Sadly, admission to our public education system, one of the tenets of American society, supposedly the right of every citizen, requires one critical piece of paper verifying that you've had a chemical injected into your child's body, by mandate of the government." She gave a low, bitter chuckle. "That's freedom, right?"

"You guys, I have an idea," Mia said. "Well, it's more like a project. That we can all do together."

Everyone in the room—Summer, Joanie, and Graham—looked around, found one another's eyes, and seemed to collectively understand what they were all thinking. Maybe there *was* a way to avoid the vaccines—the poison—and still send their children to middle school and give them the *normal* lives they deserved.

Mia turned to Reece and spoke with the organic force born from the instinct to stand up for one's baby—they all felt it, each time they met. It was the energy that bound them together: "Let me ask you this. Is it the actual shot they're concerned with? Or is it the paper?"

Reece: "I'm not getting what you mean."

Instead of answering Reece's question, Mia turned to Dawn. "You're a whiz with computer-design stuff, right?"

"I—I used to be pretty good. Back in college."

Before she'd dropped out to get her esthetician's license, Dawn had been pursuing graphic design.

Sometimes, late at night, when she couldn't sleep, she played around with Photoshop, for fun.

Mia: "Can you make creative adjustments to documents?"

Well, yes, Dawn could.

In her chest, she felt something rising. A force bigger than herself. A call to action.

Dawn, who'd never done anything "activist" beyond signing a petition for more meat-free options in the Otis College dining hall, soon felt herself transformed by *the movement*.

A part of something bigger than herself.

23

Sibyl (the Visionnaire)

PING-PING-PING.

Sibyl's phone unleashed chime after chime, which reminded her of the sound of shooting dainty bullets, when she arrived back at the barn for her session with Mia Meadows herself. She had turned the stupid device back on in a lapse of self-control. She'd kept it off most of the day, including during her late lunch break at Twyla's house, where she'd been hungry enough to scarf down the rather awful tempeh and barley stir-fry Twyla had served. The older woman had been distracted, worried that Arnold was ten minutes late returning from his usual midday walk. *"I knew I should have gone with him— especially after the bees escaped. He just gets so resentful when I try to interfere with the dog, or the . . ."*

Sibyl had tried to listen, to pretend she was enjoying the bowl of hard, chewy grains and crumbly soy, but her mind was elsewhere: She was nervous about the upcoming session with Mia Meadows, for starters—it had been a long time since she'd worked with an actress, and Mia exuded a brassy confidence that required a certain finesse on Sibyl's part. Could she summon the old Sibyl of unwavering faith to pull it off?

Her phone was destroying any concentration she had left after such a colossal fuckup of a day in which, not one but *three* subjects had stormed off mid-session. When her phone was on, she jumped at the sound of every text, and when it was off, she imagined the texts waiting to assault her when she resumed her signal. Lately, she'd had the impulse to hurl the thing into the ocean, out her car window on the freeway, into a dumpster in some neighborhood far from her own, or, in the past twenty-four hours, over the precipice of the canyon.

The thought of destroying the noisy, glowing little box brought her instant relief—how *easy* it was to kill a machine—but then, she imagined how afraid she'd be without it: What if the person, or people, or *whoever* it was, behind the menacing messages came to find her, and Sibyl didn't even have a phone to call for help?

She was miserably tied to the goddamn thing, stuck in a never-ending toggle of turning it on and off, on and off, looking away and back again.

Now, she cursed herself for lacking the willpower to wait until *after* her session with Mia Meadows to power her phone back on. Because here they were, a fresh spate of messages, greeting Sibyl in the barn when she was about to start her most important session of the day.

Ping-ping-ping.

Do not look, she told herself, sitting down for the third time that day on her godforsaken hay bale—her ass would probably have permanent straw imprints—and smoothing the muslin tablecloth over the card table, but then, as she always did—

She looked.

Roses r red, pussies are pink, I know the REAL YOU &
just how U THINK
Babes in the woods! Babes in the woods! Snatch one for
yourself—really U SHOULD!!!
It should be called a Sibyl Alert not an Amber Alert

Jesus. Sibyl's hands went slick and cold around her phone, despite the stale, overheated air of the barn.

The texts were becoming longer, more singsong, as if written by some demented Dr. Seuss.

"Darling! Finally, it's *my* turn!"

Sibyl turned to see Mia Meadows clopping toward her in cowgirl boots and cutoffs, her pink T-shirt cropped just enough to reveal a ribbon of her flat, tan belly, giant sunglasses propped atop her loose spirals of butter-and-gold hair. Sibyl fought the urge to cringe; she'd been removed from her usual client base of Hollywood women for so long that she'd nearly forgotten how they disregarded their chronological age. Why did they refuse to acknowledge that ineffable, unmistakable quality of middle age that no amount of snipping and injecting and exercise could erase? It hurt to look at them sometimes, the fifty-year-old women parading as teenagers.

It hurt to look at Mia a little, but Sibyl made eye contact and summoned a big, welcoming smile.

"Mia! I've so been looking forward to it," said Sibyl. "Take a hay bale. I'm afraid it's all we've got in the way of seating."

"The others have reported being quite"—Mia sat down and adjusted several times on the hay bale, wriggling with a grimace—"affected by their sessions with you."

"It can take a bit of time, for the insights to set in," said Sibyl. *Affected* was not exactly positive. But it wasn't especially negative either, was it? "Especially when it's a single meeting.

Usually, I encourage my clients to commit to a minimum of three sessions, in order to derive the full benefits."

"Smart lady." Mia nodded. "Going right for the triple billing."

"Oh—that's not what I meant." Sibyl felt her face flush.

"No need to backpedal. I admire good business decisions. We do what we need to do, right?"

Sibyl couldn't tell if Mia was commiserating, one fallen star to another, or if she was insinuating something much darker.

"I'm just grateful to be a part of such a meaningful weekend," said Sibyl as brightly as she could muster. "I hope everyone's having an amazing time. Now, shall we begin? I'm sorry to forgo niceties, but—"

"Oh, don't apologize for *that,* of all things," said Mia, cutting into Sibyl's usual introduction. "Women need to get better at forgoing niceties, don't you think?" She tipped her head to one side and arched her scythe-shaped brows at Sibyl.

"I—I suppose." She handed Mia a lavender scarf to cover her eyes. "You're probably familiar with my sight-blocking method? In obstructing your field of vision, we allow your inner eyes to truly *see* the hidden—"

"Got it," said Mia, grabbing the scarf from Sibyl. "I did my homework on you already. You don't think I'd just drop a few grand on *any* old psychic, do you?" She chuckled and tied the scarf around her head. "Let's do this, oh Visionnaire."

"Your energy is very intense," Sibyl started. It was an observation she often made of actresses, who always took it as a compliment. "I'm getting radiant light, a golden glow, some sort of . . . crown."

"Oh wow," said Mia. "Sounds pretty . . . religious."

"Oh no, no," said Sibyl. "I'm seeing it more as your inner light, radiating."

"Come on, Sibyl," Mia cut in, her voice tinged with amusement. "It's okay if it's, like, a Jesus thing. I want to know the truth."

"Jesus, Buddha, Muhammad . . . all the leaders of great world religions inform my work, but on a very general level."

"So, you've never been religious? It's funny, I did a bit of research on you, as much as I could find that wasn't related to that horrendous Merry Williams accident—sorry to even mention it. I found zip about your background. There're a million interviews with celebs saying how much they adore your work, but—"

Sibyl needed to nip this in the bud. While she badly needed the money Mia would pay her that weekend, *she* was the one in charge. Sibyl was the guide, Mia merely the subject.

"I'm sorry, Mia, I hate to interrupt, but I'm just worried that we're getting a little sidetrack—"

"You're right, you're right. I'm *so* sorry. Please go on. Your way."

"I run my sessions according to a strict code of conduct."

"Ah." Mia laughed—a cackle. She leaned over the card table, so close Sibyl smelled the chemical berry fragrance of her tinted lip balm.

"Don't worry," she whispered. "I'll keep your secret safe."

"I don't know what you are talking about."

"Look, I get it. From one actor to another." Mia laughed. "We're scrappy. We do what we need to do."

"I—"

"Please, do *not* worry. We all manifest our talent in different ways. That you've managed to pull off all that you have and still be here right now, free as a bird, well—" Mia lifted her ropy, muscular arms into a goalpost shape—*praise hands,* Sibyl realized. "Respect."

A wave of nausea rolled through Sibyl. At the same time, she was flooded with something like relief. *Mia. Mia fucking Meadows was sending her the texts.*

Sibyl pulled off her blindfold. Then she reached over and pulled off Mia's too. Moving so fast made her head spin. "You can cut the cryptic shit now, Mia," she said. "I know what you're up to. And it's technically verbal harassment, what you've been doing. Punishable by law, you know."

This was a fib, of course, but Sibyl didn't care. She just wanted to put an end to the texts, once and for all.

For the first time since she'd stepped into the barn, Mia looked truly puzzled.

"Don't play dumb," said Sibyl. "I know what you've been up to. I have to compliment you on your texting skills—you're unblockable."

Now Mia threw back her head and laughed. "I have no idea what you're talking about, you cute little scam artist. All I meant was, congrats on being a master scammer. It's pretty remarkable to bounce back from manslaughter the way you have."

Sibyl's fist slammed onto the flimsy table. An electric candle toppled over. She needed to stand, walk to the barn doors, and leave. Leave her stuff behind, stumble her way to Twyla's, and spend hours in the cool dark bathroom—close to the toilet because she'd certainly puke. Screw the money. Screw Mia Meadows and her friends.

"Oh-kay then," said Mia, rising from her hay bale. "Seems I've touched a nerve." She took a step back. "I know I've already prepaid for this session, but honestly, I'm not in the mood to get punched by an angry psychic today. Escaping a swarm of bees was—"

"That's enough!" Sibyl leaped up and gave the table a hard

shove toward Mia. It flipped over and landed legs up in front of her. "What did I ever do to *you*, Mia? I was hired to be here. I am *the help*. Why in God's name are you torturing me with fucking text messages? Are we fourteen years old? You don't see *me* sending you semi-illiterate threats about how you went to jail for being a crazy anti-vaxx—"

"Bring it on, psycho!" Mia cut in, sounding almost gleeful as she flung a sharp-nailed hand through the air. "Just keep on ranting, oh Visionnaire. Keep trying to take me down. It's truly pathetic. You think you can scare me with my own personal history?" She laughed, a delighted cackle. "No, baby girl. That's *you*. You're the one terrified of your own past. Not me. I have nothing but pride for the things I've done." She locked her ice-blue eyes on Sibyl's. "*Everything.*"

Sibyl fought to control her breath. She counted to five, forcing herself to calm down. Her head was throbbing. The dim light of the barn unbearable—how would she walk through the late afternoon light to Twyla's?

"Then why, Mia?" she said, finally. "If everything is hunky-dory with you, then why bother harassing me with stupid text messages? Why do you care? Don't you have better things to do, like, oh, *I don't know,* screw your barely-legal boy toy?"

Mia tipped her head and squinted at Sibyl, looking truly perplexed.

"You're even more batshit than I thought, Seer Sibyl. I might think you're a total fucking fraud, but trust me, I have never sent you a single text. I wouldn't want to waste my *thumb* energy."

On cue, Sibyl's phone chimed. Mia broke into a white-toothed grin. "Wanna look at that? I think I just texted you with my mind." She threw back her head and laughed.

Hands shaking, Sibyl picked up her phone.

The text read Fool 'em once / shame on you / Fool 'em twice / SHAME ON YOU. U BETTER RUN CUZ I AM COMING 4 U.

"I think we're done here," said Mia, ice-cold. She turned and walked away from Sibyl and the upended table. She'd gone a few paces, the clops of her boots echoing through the barn, when Sibyl heard a familiar deep voice boom from the doors.

"HALLLLO! Anybody in here?"

No, Sibyl thought. *Not him. Not now.* She needed to lie down and close her eyes. Even if it was on the goat and beechie crap–covered barn floor.

Sibyl hurried after Mia's tiny, fast-retreating form. She caught up with her a few paces before the open doors, where a hulking, bearish form blocked the entrance.

It was Arnold, backlit by the golden afternoon sun, and naked from the waist down.

24

Raj (the Drifter)

OF COURSE, RAJ SAW NOW, THROUGH HIS BINOCULARS, THE WOMAN IN the tire swing was *not* Candace. Candace would never be so careless as to expose herself on an open trail in broad daylight.

The woman on the swing, he saw now, was one of the tres-passers. The youngest one. The green-eyed girl who had emerged from the back seat of the car driven by the blond demon.

She was one of *them*.

Go, Raj commanded himself, but his legs would not budge, and then, it was too late: the girl's gaze wheeled straight over to him.

Idiot Raj! He had stood in the open like a dumb steer, when the most important of his missions was to remain invisible.

He raised a hand in greeting. What else could he do?

Odd—the girl continued to swing, reaching her legs out and tilting her torso back as the tire lifted to the sky. Was she telling him he was free to move on, that she was content to pretend she had not seen him?

But she *had* seen him. Not knowing what she might do next troubled Raj. If he simply walked on, she might report him. Tell the other trespassers of the grimy bearded brown man in the woods who'd appeared on the trail and watched her with *binoculars* . . .

Surely, then, they would find him. Take him away. And then what would happen to Candace?

He swallowed and summoned his voice. "Hi."

She did not answer, but swung higher. He walked toward the swing.

The girl dragged her feet against the ground to stop the swing, and in a quick, fluid leap, dislodged herself from the tire.

"You can—keep swinging," Raj said. His voice sounded thick and slow. "I am lost. In the woods."

She faced him, one hand on the swing, the other jammed in the pocket of her denim shorts. Her green eyes studied him but still, she did not speak.

"I'm Raj." A fleck of spit shot from his mouth. "I'm sorry if I scared you."

Finally, she spoke. "You want a turn? This isn't my swing."

"It's not my swing either," he managed. His heart was galloping. When had talking become so difficult? He had to pause and think about what words came next. "Swinging makes me—seasick."

"Seasick?"

He tried again. "I'm—just out for a hike. I like hiking . . . in Topanga." His words felt thick and dumb. "And, uh, watching birds." He pointed to his binoculars, bracing himself for her inevitable next question: *Were you watching me?*

"I want to see animals here," she said, instead. "But there's nothing but those red squirrels everywhere."

"Beechies." Raj nodded, relieved. "They're harmless."

"And the old people have a wolf."

He's half malamute, half wolf, Raj wanted to tell her. *His owner is Sheshnaag, the Great Protector.*

But of course, he could not let on any familiarity with Celestial Ranch. He was just a day hiker passing through.

"What's your name?" asked the woman.

"Raj."

"Mine is Quinn. It's short for McQuinn or MacQuinn," she said quickly, as if she had shared this information often. "Most notably Niall Ó Cuinn, who was slain at the Battle of Clontarf in 1014."

Raj laughed; real laughter from deep in his chest. The reflex felt warm and sweet. He realized he was no longer hungry, that the gnawing sensation in his gut had subsided.

"A warrior name. That's—romantic," he said.

She stared at him. Her eyes placid. Free of judgment. She was special, Raj understood. Like the old man and his dog.

"I like romantic stories," she said finally, pushing the tire lightly with her palm, then stopping it.

"Who doesn't?" Raj said, struck by the casual chitchat tone his voice had adopted, as if it had a mind of its own. He sounded like a character on TV.

"My mother doesn't."

"Doesn't what?" asked Raj.

"She doesn't like romance stories." She revealed herself with a total absence of discomfort. A purity the opposite of the guests he had listened to in the yurt last night. Before Raj could respond, she asked, with no inquisitive upturn, "What time is it?"

"I'm not sure." He looked to the sky, then panned his eyes around the woods, gauging the light, but it was flat and muted by the dense overgrowth, so he could not gauge the angle of the sun. "Eleven, maybe?"

"I need to go back," said Quinn, but she did not move.

"Back where?"

"Betelgeuse. The place my mom and I are staying."

"Sounds fancy," said Raj, though he knew the little cabin was shoddy, practically falling down. He did not want her to leave, not yet. He liked her placid green eyes, her tumble of dark hair. How she'd simply stopped swinging to talk to him, without apprehension or suspicion.

As if they were two old acquaintances who'd run into each other at the park.

He should not be here, standing idle, talking to a stranger. Candace had already been alone in the cave too long.

Strangers, after all, had nearly killed them before. If they could do it on the internet, how much worse would it be now, when they surrounded him in the flesh?

"Fancy?" She sounded confused. "No way. The cabin is gross. When we got there yesterday, there was a bunch of poop in the shower. My mom was sad. It's her birthday."

Raj's cheeks flamed. *I'm so sorry,* he wanted to say.

Instead he asked, "How old is she? Your mom?"

"Old. Fifty."

Raj laughed. "That's not so old. How old are you?"

"I will be twenty-two years old on the twenty-seventh day of August. Former President Lyndon B. Johnson was born on August twenty-seventh. So was the actor Paul Reubens, otherwise known as Pee-wee Herman."

"I was born on April third, nineteen ninety-one," Raj offered.

"You've been alive for thirty-one years."

"That was fast. Are you a mathematician?"

"No. Are you?"

The question was deadpan, completely earnest.

The desire to be honest welled in his chest, pushed into his throat. To tell her exactly who he was, and why he had to live here, in the canyon. But of course he couldn't. She might tell the other trespassers and then, who knew what they would do to Candace? He thought of the hard blond woman in the skimpy shorts—the *ringleader*—and felt his stomach turn.

"I'm not a mathematician," he said finally. "I don't have a job."

"Me neither," said Quinn, shrugging. Her lack of curiosity— no, her total lack of judgment—made Raj want to keep standing in the filtered sunshine beside her.

"I have to go," she repeated.

"Can I walk with you? We might see animals." He lifted his binoculars from his chest.

"Okay."

"Lead the way, Quinn—of the warrior tribe O'Quinn." He folded forward in a bow, one arm tucked behind his back.

She giggled and, for the first time, Raj thought, sounded like any young woman from the world below.

He had made a joke. He had made her laugh. He had talked with someone. To a pretty girl with clear green eyes.

She stepped down the trail, and he followed.

THEY WALKED IN silence toward the meadow, in the opposite direction of Raj's cave. Away from Candace, but Raj told himself he was doing the right thing by escorting Quinn back to her cabin. He would not walk her all the way, of course, that was too dangerous, but close enough to ensure she'd get back to Betelgeuse safely. Candace would not have wanted him to abandon a young woman lost in the woods. Candace herself struggled to say no to anyone in need. She'd lured Raj out of his brain and a little closer to his heart, talking him into donating money to help migrant children imprisoned by ICE at the border. She'd plastered the windows facing the long driveway with posters pleading: MAKE AMERICA KIND AGAIN. She had convinced him to attend BLM protests and canvas in Orange County before the 2020 election. Candace had made him a better person.

For a moment, as he walked beside Quinn, their strides matching, he felt guilty. Would it hurt Candace, make her jealous, if she knew of the flash of enchantment this green-eyed woman Quinn had triggered in Raj's chest?

Sunlight sliced through gaps in the trees. They'd rounded the second-to-last bend before the meadow when they came face-to-face with a mule deer, standing smack in the middle of the trail. A buck the size of a horse, easily the largest Raj had ever seen.

"My god," said Raj.

Reflexively, he reached for Quinn's arm, so that she would stand still. Mule deer often charged when they felt threatened. Could turn aggressive on a dime, trample you flat, bite through your skin all the way down to the bone.

Quinn pulled away from his hand and continued to walk toward the animal.

"Quinn, be careful." He dropped his voice to a whisper.

She kept walking.

He clapped his hands together and called out to the deer: "Move along, friend!"

The animal did not move. Did not even *blink*. It stood as still as the old woman's steel-forged statues, appraising them with its big oval eyes.

Raj clapped again, harder.

"Don't do that," said Quinn, without turning back.

"I have to. It's the only safe way to pass him."

"He'll move himself." She was just a dozen feet from the mule deer now, then eight. Then six.

The animal did not move.

Quinn stretched out her hand.

She was going to *pet* it, Raj realized, with horror. A wild animal that weighed well over a ton.

He spotted a pine cone on the ground and snatched it up.

"Quinn," he called out sharply. The pine cone was heavy with sap. "Stop. That's a wild animal. You don't know what—"

She didn't stop.

He hurled the pine cone.

It struck Quinn squarely in the back.

"Owww!" Quinn yelped, jerking forward.

The mule deer broke from its trance, lurching backward. It whirled around and bolted off into the trees.

"I'm so sorry!" Raj called to Quinn. "I didn't mean to hit you!"

Quinn kept her back to him, bent into a squat. He ran to her and lowered himself down beside her. "You okay?"

Her face was buried in her arm, and she kept it there. Had he *hurt* her? *Stupid Raj, stupid stupid!*

"He was trying to tell me something," she said, her voice low and hard. "He was just about to tell me, and you ruined it."

He had hurt her. Made her angry.

Stupid Raj.

"I know I did," said Raj, touching her shoulder with his palm, very lightly. "I'm sorry."

"Go away."

"I know where the mule deer live." The lie flew from his lips. He would make it up to her. Fix his mistake. "There's like a whole . . . herd of them. I can show you."

Quinn did not answer at first, but he felt the interest in her pause.

"I can show you. Tonight. Can I see you tonight?"

The question was absurd. Dangerous. How could a casual day hiker, up for a few hours from the city, return for a secret mule deer show at night?

But the words had tumbled from inside him. He could not take them back now.

Quinn pushed herself up from the ground in a single fluid motion. She latched her green eyes on to him, her flare of anger extinguished, replaced by her usual stolid, neutral expression.

"Okay, tonight," she said, and set off down the trail to the meadow without looking back, leaving Raj too shocked to speak.

25

Twyla (the Hostess)

ONCE AGAIN, TWYLA WAS OUT LOOKING FOR ARNOLD. SHE WAS ON THE edge of the meadow, nearing the barn, praying to the goddess that Arnold was elsewhere. Ms. Meadows was scheduled to have her session with Sibyl right about now.

She couldn't handle another disaster. Not after the bees. It was almost as if the ranch had fallen under some wicked curse.

Twyla was bone-tired. Searching the sprawling property for Arnold, nearly every day, drained her. Aged her. She let her mind wander—what if this disappearing act was intentional, a ploy to break her so she'd cave to his demands?

Arnold had always been a vindictive sort. Like that time, nearly fifty years ago, back at UC Santa Barbara, when a guy at a beach party came on to Twyla, grabbed her ass so hard she'd had bruises. Arnold had found the guy's car and slashed his tires. At the time, Twyla had been flattered, even impressed, but—

A shriek came from the barn.

Twyla ran as fast as she could. A woman was laughing—a cackling trill that seemed to go on and on.

The charcoal-colored barn looked black against the western sky afire with the sinking sun. She ran past a pile of cloth on the path. She stopped and scooped up the tangle of muddy—what was it? The yellow plaid looked familiar.

"Oh no."

Her chest was heaving when she stopped in front of the barn.

In the entryway, Arnold stood, backlit by the fading sun.

He turned to her and called out, with more cheer than she'd heard from him in years, "Good morning, Twy!"

"Arnold!"

Her husband was naked from the waist down, his penis swinging from ample gray pubic hair.

Behind him, in the barn, Ms. Meadows's cackling continued. Sibyl stood a few feet from Arnold, hands in the air as if Arnold were armed.

"This is unacceptable, Arnie," said Twyla as she knelt to put his feet into the muddy pajama pants, pull them up, and tie them around his waist. She felt Sibyl's discomfort permeate the air, nearly as palpable as the gamy scent of Nocturne and Diurn in the nearby pen.

"I'm so sorry, Sibyl," Twyla whispered.

"All that matters," Sibyl said, "is getting Arnold back to the house so he can get warm."

Ms. Meadows laughed and laughed. Arnold joined her—the *Bwahahaha!* of a madman—and Twyla wanted to scream, *Stop! Both of you!*

Arnold didn't resist as Twyla secured the pajama pants with a knot, her bare arms rising with gooseflesh in the cool air.

Damn you, Arnie.

They walked back to the house, arm in arm, Arnold going

on about what a beautiful *morning* it was, Twyla clobbering him with questions. *"What's gotten into you? Do I need to be worried? Should we call Dr. Belk?"*

At home, she settled him in his recliner with a cup of tea—this time helping him take a few sips to avoid wasting a pill. There was only one left in the bottle.

He finished the tea and fell asleep. She knew she should've made him change out of the mud-stained pajamas he'd been wearing since the night before, but she was exhausted from the godawful beechie scene, the bees, the animal crap in the Betelgeuse shower, and now this.

Later, at the downstairs kitchen table, Twyla heard the creak of Arnold's footsteps across the bedroom floor above. Why had the pills stopped working?

She pushed away the almond-butter toast she'd just sat down to eat and hurried up the stairs. Eating, sleeping, emptying her bladder—it felt as if she'd never have a break.

"Arnie, I'm here," she called out, nearly tripping on the wobbly stair halfway up.

She reached the landing just as he was stepping out of the bedroom, clad in a robe and slippers.

"Hi," he said, smiling. "What is it?"

"What is what?"

There was no denying it any longer—Arnold wasn't well.

She clung to the banister, frustrated by how out of breath a single climb had left her. Arnold looked disheveled in a post-nap way she'd once found endearing: his tufted white hair standing off his head to one side, pancaked on the other. Faint imprints on his cheek from the chenille pillow sham. Between blinks to adjust his vision, his eyes were at half-mast. How fast this state of his, emerging from deep slumber, had shifted from indicating an old man waking into a possible diagnosis of dementia. From a moment that had charmed her into one that terrified her.

"Why are you looking at me that way?" he asked.

"What way?"

"As if you're catching a teenager climbing out his bedroom window." He smiled roguishly, like he had the first time he'd asked her out back in 1970. They'd been at a party making signs for the May 4 nationwide student strike after the United States expanded the Vietnam War into Cambodia. His sign had read: FUCK NIXON: END THE WAR NOW. Hers: UNITY IN OUR LOVE OF MAN.

"What? No! I just heard you wake up and thought I'd come see if you, ah, wanted dinner."

"Geez." Arnold placed a hand on the banister. "It's already dinner? Why'd you let me sleep so long?"

Twyla cleared her throat. What good would it do to remind him that the clock in his brain was off by ten hours? "I thought you needed it. After what happened at the barn."

"Don't let those city folks get you down, Twy. Bunch of slicksters, this crew."

Was it possible he could remember?

"What do you mean?" she pressed. "Who are the slicksters this weekend, exactly?"

She figured testing him might be a good place to start.

"Pretty boy with the muscle shirt," he said. "Tan lady with the blond hair. And the Oriental."

"Arnold!" she cried, horrified he'd use such a word to describe Joan Ahn, yet relieved that he'd accurately recalled the appearance of several of their guests. "That word is no longer used. It's terribly offensive. Asian-American."

He shrugged. "Asian-American, then. Still a city slicker. Can't be trusted."

"Why don't I make you dinner? How does a BLT sound?"

"It's Saturday, yes?"

"Yes."

"We have the appointment at eight a.m. tomorrow. The tour. Down the hill. I called a few days ago, and those vacancies have opened up."

"What?" She feigned confusion, concealing her incredulousness that he'd remembered. It was back at the end of April, nearly two months ago, that Arnold had insisted they drive down to the Valley and drop into the residential purchases office at the Your Life, Your Style Senior Community in Reseda; they'd been told they were *anticipating vacancies* soon, a menacing euphemism for the impending death of residents. Twyla had assumed Arnold would forget.

"You—you made an appointment?"

"I did."

"Arnold, we've got guests this weekend!"

"We don't need to babysit them."

"No, but I need to be here in case anything goes wrong. Look at all the problems we've had since yesterday!"

Arnold squinched an eye. "Problems?"

Twyla reminded herself to stay calm, despite her rising disbelief, tinged with indignation. "Do you not remember, honey? Yesterday, Klondike charged one of our guests? And then the . . . *mess* in Betelgeuse?"

"Of course I remember. But that was yesterday."

"Well," Twyla said, "*today* was even more eventful. Do you not remember?"

He looked pensive, blinking and shaking his head.

"Maybe something with the beechies, those little fuckers."

"And . . ." Twyla said.

"Nada."

She knew she must call Dr. Belk. This was a problem for an

M.D. What if it was *her* fault he was like this? The pills. She'd read the side effects on the complicated instructions the pharmacist had given her. She never thought he'd actually suffer from any of them.

"It's a big group, Arnie," she said. "Lots of little things can go wrong. We can't afford the negative reviews. I need to be here, in case."

"Screw the reviews! If we don't go tomorrow, someone else will take our spot. Do you know how rare it is for this place to have vacancies?"

"Listen to yourself," she said, trying to control her frustration. "A couple of people die in an old folks' home, and your idea of an urgent errand on a Sunday morning is to go sniff around the rooms they were just carted out of?"

"It's a senior community, Twy. Not an *old folks' home.* It's a nice condominium where we could relax and enjoy ourselves without having to worry about *all this.*"

His disdain for Celestial Ranch stung. "I'm sorry that this heavenly mountaintop acreage with hundreds of species of animals and trees, not to mention some of the rarest flowers in California, plus a network of creeks and—"

"Twy, those creeks have been dry since before my hair turned gray."

"That's not true." She was reassured by his gross miscalculation; in 2018, the winter and spring had been so rainy there'd been mudslides in Santa Barbara County. They'd marveled at the transformation of Celestial Ranch that year, how the palette had changed from beige to verdant, life-giving green, and the cicadas and crickets and clicking chirp of the towhees that usually dominated the acoustics of the property were drowned out by the soothing sound of running water in the creeks.

Surely if Arnold had forgotten that magical season, he

wasn't lucid. Therefore, his determination to fulfill their appointment at the Reseda senior community wasn't a sound decision.

"How about this?" she said, noticing Arnold's gaze shifting toward the window, "I'll talk to Sibyl about being on-duty while we go down the hill. If she's game, we'll go. If not, I'll call them and reschedule."

"You promise?"

The directness of his gaze, how he could toggle so quickly from absorption in some faraway thought, then snap back, was troubling. When, exactly, did her husband's mind become so . . . transitory? The only topic really anchoring him these days, it seemed, was the fixation on moving away. While his web-browser history reflected the website of every senior living community in Los Angeles, her own research patterns were unsearchable since Twyla loathed the web and searched instead at the Topanga Living Café, where there was a bulletin board, ink configured into letters, stitched into sentences by an actual human hand, written on index cards affixed to the board with thumbtacks and organized into columnar categories, one of which Twyla checked every Wednesday during Arnold's nap: *caregivers*.

Yes, it was dishonest the way she allowed him to believe she was considering some horrendous move *down the hill*. But while Arnold believed it was a new beginning, Twyla saw it as the beginning of the end. The entryway to a monotonous, anonymous death, indistinguishable from the hordes of other septuagenarians living out their dull "third act" in the godforsaken San Fernando Valley.

Hell if Twyla would die at one of those places.

She reached for Arnold's hand; it felt large and gnarled and dry.

"Let's go downstairs and eat, dear. Sibyl's joining us for dinner, so we'll talk to her about holding down the fort."

"Okay," Arnold said and fell into step behind Twyla. Just as they reached the first floor, a knock came on the door, and Sibyl called out, "Hi guys, it's me."

Her voice sounded a bit strangled.

"Come in!" Twyla said, reaching for Arnold's elbow. "Go on and sit down for dinner, honey. I'll be right there." He padded in the direction of the kitchen.

Sibyl was bent over on the porch, her long hair in her face.

"Sibyl, what on earth?"

"Sorry. I tried to wait until I got to the bathroom."

Twyla saw the puddle of vomit on the porch steps.

"Oh, sweetness!"

"My head—" Sibyl looked up, one hand shading her eyes. "Can you—sorry—turn off that light?"

Twyla hurried to help. "Of course!" she said, switching off both the porch and hallway lights, helping a blind Sibyl through the door—she had both hands cupped over her eyes now. "Is it one of your migraines? Oh, my dear Sib, the stress of this weekend . . . If I'd known it would harm you—"

"*Stress* is one word for it." Twyla heard the sharpness in her friend's voice. "It's a little early in the weekend to make them mad, don't you think? The beechies, the goats, Arnold—"

On cue, Arnold swung open the kitchen door and announced, "Dinnertime!"

"I just need," Sibyl said, with a soft groan, "to lie down for a bit. My pain meds are upstairs."

As Twyla steered Sibyl toward the stairs, she tried to deflect her relief that Sibyl was in no shape to manage the guests in the morning. Twyla and Arnold certainly would *not* be traveling down the hill tomorrow.

Dawn (the Birthday Girl)

"PICK UP THE PACE, BEAUTIFUL PEOPLE," SAID MIA, SWINGING HER lantern as the group began to ascend Hydra Hill, a low mound of earth that rose along the ridge of the canyon like a sleeping turtle. "The hour of Dawn's birth is nigh!"

"Didn't know you spoke Middle English, Meadows," said Graham, stumbling over a pile of rocks.

"There's *lots* you don't know about me, Grahammy," said Mia, linking her free arm through Dawn's and tugging her up the slope.

Dawn didn't feel like a late-night hike, but involvement was mandatory. She kept pace with Mia and tried to focus on the beauty of the summer night, the bright stars sprayed across the velvet sky and a yolk of full moon hanging heavy above the trees.

Mia drew Dawn closer to her. On Dawn's other side, Reece took her hand, giving Dawn the not-unpleasant feeling of being hemmed in. Just over a year ago, she had neither of these women in her life. Had believed their absence permanent. Now, here they were, all together, on her birthday.

The night had already been perfect. It could have ended an hour ago and Dawn would have gone to bed happy. For her birthday dinner at the yurt, there had been sushi (Dawn blanched at the thought of just how much Mia had paid for Sugarfish to deliver all the way up to Topanga). Then, for dessert, a green-tea ice cream cake—Dawn's favorite flavor—blazing with candles arranged in the shape of an *L*—the roman numeral for fifty. As the group sang "Happy Birthday," Dawn fought back tears and a fresh wave of awe. Her friends had come so far and done so much for *her.*

After all this time. After everything that had happened.

As she closed her eyes to make a wish, she made a promise instead. She would be there for each of them the next time they needed her. Especially Mia.

"Happeeee birthday, deeeear Dawnieeeee."

Mia's voice had soared above the rest, bell-bright and clear. Full of love.

As the caterers were clearing the cake, Jax stood and, to Dawn's pleasant surprise, bid the group farewell with a jaunty wave, saying he'd booked his session with the "psychic or whatevs." Then he blew Dawn a kiss, gave Mia an actual one on the lips, and sailed out of the yurt.

Mia beckoned. "The time has come, my darlings. Gather your lanterns, and follow me."

Now, as they ascended the hill, Dawn glanced at Reece. She'd been worrying about her friend's enjoyment of the weekend, her comfort with being around people she hadn't seen in so long who still drank alcohol to excess and made poor choices. Reece shouldn't have to tolerate such behavior. She'd always been the best of them: kinder, more generous, and compassionate. She existed on a higher plane, really, Dawn thought, glancing at her old friend. Profiled in the moonlight, her braids piled atop her head, Reece looked serene, almost beatific, Dawn was relieved to see.

Dawn leaned toward her. "Thank you for being here," she whispered.

"Now, now, no secrets, birthday girl!" Mia said. "Tonight, we shall be totally *unified.*"

"Sorry, Meemers," Dawn said.

Reece squeezed her hand. Dawn squeezed back.

The good feeling dissipated as they hiked farther up, replaced by a more familiar anxiety. The distance to the top was short, but Dawn was unnerved by the sheer drop below. Beneath the bright stars and big moon, the vertical slab of mountainside seemed suspended over a dark abyss. Dawn remembered a detail from Twyla's map, a wobbly arrow and a caption about the drop: "Approx 300 feet USE CAUTION!!!!" Dawn thought of Quinn, cloistered in the cabin, nose deep in the microscopic font of an Unbridled novel.

Dawn was nervous—something was up with Quinn. She knew she should be happy. Quinn had never been so calm, so unneedy, and had seemed uncharacteristically nonchalant at the prospect of another night alone, barely even looking up from her tater tots when Reece arrived to pick up Dawn. Quinn had actually gone out on a *hike* that afternoon, and returned with high color in her cheeks, a slight softness permeating her usually cautious shell.

"Don't question positive developments, honey," Reece had advised, when Dawn expressed her puzzlement over Quinn's altered behavior. "Celebrate them. Who knows, maybe Topanga is Quinny-bee's happy place. Maybe she's finding her inner calm."

Still, she'd instructed Quinn to take half an Ativan at eleven. That way, she'd be relaxed and drowsy—if not sound asleep—by the time Dawn got home. She did her best not to think about how much Craig would disapprove. And Mia. And Reece.

As Mia guided the group to the top of the hill, the grade became steeper, the grassy ground giving way to a rockier surface. Dawn tried to keep her gaze straight ahead as they ascended, avoiding any glimpse of the empty space just beyond the ridge. Tried to push away thoughts of taking a bad step, losing her footing, tumbling down the hill and over the edge. She focused on the touch of her friends anchoring her, the tight tuck of Mia's elbow with hers, Reece's warm hand.

Her friends wouldn't let her fall.

Still, Dawn's heart cantered. She wished for the false courage of a booze buzz, still annoyed, and puzzled, by Mia's merry decree at dinner that each guest would be limited to "*a maximum of one drink, if you absolutely must.*"

"There it is—the shed!" Mia said, charging toward the boxlike structure ahead.

Mia arrived and then wheeled back toward the group, arms spread, face lifted to the starry sky. The structure had three walls of thick timber planks, with one side so rotted that the entire building slouched to one side, and a tin roof draped by an overgrown curtain of pepper tree branches. It reminded Dawn of the set for a low-budget horror movie, the place two teenagers would stumble upon and, inevitably, go inside while the audience cringed, thinking, *No, don't go!*

"We've arrived at our destination!" said Mia, as if she'd just led them to a beautiful, secret beach.

"Wow," said Summer. "Real rustic charm we got here."

"It used to be Twyla's toolshed full of hedge trimmers, shovels, machetes—"

"Reminds me of *Saw*," said Graham. "The Chris Rock one was actually pretty dec—"

"Those films are sadistic and vile," Reece said.

"In we go, lovelies," sang Mia, stepping around the edge of the wall. "Though, it's really only *half* inside. A roof over our heads, if you will."

"Not to mention rats' nests," muttered Summer.

"*Why* do you feel the need to say that?" snapped Joanie.

"No bickering!" came Mia's voice from the shed. "Kind vibes only, kiddos."

Reece let go of Dawn's hand. "I guess we're doing this."

Reluctantly, Dawn followed her into the shed.

Inside, Dawn was relieved to find the space was cozy with yoga mats and pillows strewn around the periphery. Where the fourth wall would have been was an opening to the hillside leading to the drop-off, lending a view of the trees and sky. The light from the electric lanterns they had carried from the yurt threw oblong shadows on the ceiling. In the center of the room was a small round table bearing an assortment of mismatched mugs on a silver tray.

"Atmospheric," said Summer.

"Meadows can set a scene," said Graham.

"Spread out," Mia said. "Lie back, give yourselves room." She wriggled out of the large backpack she'd been wearing, set it carefully on the floor. Then she removed a blue camping kettle, a small foldable camping stove, a water bottle, and a small plastic bag. "No more talking, *bébés*. I'm going to step outside and prepare our tea ceremony."

Dawn waited for Summer to make a crack about Mia's no-talking rule, but she only reached for Joanie's hand and guided her to a spot on the far side of the shed. Dawn took a spot on a purple mat and beckoned for Reece to sit beside her. Reece lowered herself next to her, and Dawn leaned into Reece's body, trying to calm herself.

Why was she so edgy, anyway?

Reece said, "It's just a birthday party," as if she'd read Dawn's thoughts.

On the other side of Dawn, Graham sat with his back against a large pillow, legs stretched out. She reached out and touched his shoulder—it was the first contact they'd had since last night—and he clasped his hand over hers.

27

Sibyl (the Visionnaire)

SHE SENSED THE WARNING SIGNS THE MOMENT JAX RAPPED ON THE barn door. The last of Sibyl's scheduled sessions, mercifully, but sure to be the most difficult. She could feel it. You didn't need to be psychic, real or otherwise, to sense the menace in a person's presence.

The pretentious author, the lesbian couple, they were harmless enough—the vibe she got from them was self-involved, insecure, weak-willed. Qualities that should have dissipated in middle age, but that, here in Los Angeles, Sibyl had learned, morphed from the egocentrism of youth to something that *appeared* to be more evolved. They were some of the least introspective people she'd ever known, even though they used phrases like *looking inward* and *doing the work* with abandon. They were looking inward, Sibyl thought, but not seeing themselves. They were doing . . . *work*, but by middle age shouldn't you have already done it?

Jax exuded something else entirely. She sensed it right

away, his slippery quality, as soon as he'd knocked on the open door of the barn—*"Yoo-hoo, anyone home?"*

Sibyl had nearly nodded off. She was typically a night owl, but this evening all she wanted to do was burrow into the sagging poster bed in Twyla's guest room, slip her blackout eye mask on, and sleep until the sun rose. The pain meds had tamed the migraine, now more of a tension headache, the pain consolidated at the back of her neck. She stretched and cracked and massaged the muscles of her neck, and still they felt like they'd been filled with cement. Stuck in the gauzy in-between fog that followed a migraine, she felt dulled and out of focus. Not the best state in which to perform a reading.

She reminded herself of that bitch Mia's contract: *"Services must be performed in an on-call capacity through sunrise on Sunday, June . . ."*

Mia had instructed her to wait in the barn until she was signaled to leave, explaining she'd promised her friends they could drop in for a session anytime that night. Like Sibyl was a fucking all-night diner. They'd be in a "headspace," Mia had said, that might compel them to seek Sibyl's visioning at odd hours. Translation: The group would be out of their minds on drugs and might want to tack a psychic reading onto their trip. Sibyl feared tonight could be a long one. Mia had been adamant—*this* night was what she'd hired Sibyl for.

This was another thing about middle-aged Los Angelenos Sibyl had learned: It was never too late for drugs. The drugs they took just became more obscure and harder to source, taken in the name of spiritual enlightenment instead of merely to get fucked up.

"Good evening, good evening," Jax said, pushing the barn doors open with both arms. The old wood groaned. "Here she is, the twenty-four-hour psychic!"

"Hello," said Sibyl. "It's good to see you. I'd grown a bit tired of talking to the goats." She summoned a chuckle.

Jax, his voice tinged with a theatrical lilt, said, "I'd love to be your goat, Ms. Sibyl, Seer to the Stars." He made a bleating noise that was disturbingly goat accurate.

Sibyl had learned, from years of working with the Hollywood set, that actors never took a break from acting. The handsome man's true self, Sibyl saw, was locked away. The Jax he showed her floated like an oil slick over the surface. His compliments were a bit too effusive, his jokes too on point. As if he had rehearsed.

She hesitated for a beat, then swept her hand toward the hay bale across the table, an inviting gesture. "Please, then, sit. And just Sibyl is fine."

"Okay doke, *just* Sibyl." He stood over her, his hands tucked in the pockets of his black skinny jeans. His big green eyes were blank. They allowed her no entry. Kept her in the shallows. His high cheekbones were tinged with color, the fringe of his lashes so thick she wondered if he was wearing mascara. He really *was* beautiful, in the way of a statue, or a creepy family portrait from the Renaissance—apple-cheeked children and hunting dogs, chiaroscuro lighting, fruit on the table, and a dead rabbit.

Somewhere in Sibyl's mind, there was a man—a father—off shooting a musket.

Jax, the most beautiful of a large brood raised in a drafty old stone house, one who survived the diseases and the winters. Inscrutable and self-possessed, trained by his environs, his distant, miserable mother and cruel father, to suppress himself.

Yes: the connection was valid. Sibyl could feel the certainty rising in her chest.

"Sit down," she said. Kindly, but firmly.

He lowered himself onto the hale bale across from her; a smile slid across his face, his cheeks rising, accentuating his tapered chin.

"It's just you and me now, sister," he said.

"Yes," said Sibyl, unnerved by his sudden familiarity with her. Then again, she reminded herself of millennials and their faux familiarity, how they professed adoration, obsession, *love* with no real underpinnings, just a flare of affection, an aesthetic appreciation.

Sibyl reached under the table and located her blindfolds. She handed one to Jax.

"I use a blindfold method. By diminishing external sight, we deepen our capacity for looking inward. It's a basic principle of sensory deprivation, of course. Suppress one, heighten the other."

"Makes sense." Jax kept his eyes on Sibyl, unblinking. Sibyl thought of *A Clockwork Orange*.

"But I know sitting in darkness with a relative stranger—me—can be unnerving."

"You're no stranger," said Jax.

"So, I use these semi-opaque bands. They simply blot and dim your vision, without eliminating it altogether." She nodded to the plastic dispenser on the table. "If you could sanitize your hands, please. And then put on the blindfold."

Jax squirted the alcohol onto his hands, rubbed them together and pulled the gauze band around his eyes; even with a third of his face obscured, his beauty was still evident.

Sibyl did the same. Eyes covered, she reached for Jax's hands. They were cool, a bit clammy even, usually the qualities of women's hands. Men's hands tended to be warm and dry.

"Sibyl, we appreciate you keeping these unorthodox hours for us."

"It's my pleasure," said Sibyl, wishing she could add that her *unorthodox hours* had nothing to do with her pleasure and everything to do with her bank account.

"First, we will breathe together for a count of one hundred. It will feel long, but the duration is necessary to get us in sync and release the fullest possible vision. Are we ready?"

"More than ready," said Jax.

"We'll start on the exhale," said Sibyl. "And one."

She heard air move from Jax's lips.

"Two," said Sibyl, pushing all the air from her lungs.

The barn was eerily quiet, except for their breathing. The beechies were gone; Twyla had stayed true to her word and gotten them out. The absence of their rustling should have been a relief, but Sibyl found herself wishing for their company; she felt acutely alone with the young actor and his big, vacant eyes.

"Fourteen," said Sibyl.

Something was off. In her mind she tried to locate the disturbance. Beneath the hipster millennial exterior, something angry and dark hid inside the man, as if his taut, tan skin were strained by *the thing* inside him. Whatever it was, Sibyl knew it was barely contained, pushing against his burnished surface.

She squinted through her gauze at Jax; he looked relaxed, almost serene.

No matter how long Sibyl lived in LA, she never forgot where she'd come from. Pennsyltucky ran through her veins. She could smell other outsiders, sometimes like perfume, others, like the tang of a chemical. Jax was sulfur. She'd detected it when he leaned over and took the blindfold.

"Twenty-five, twenty-six," Sibyl counted softly as Jax sat still across from her. She could see little but the shape of him, the tendrils of his hair springing from the top of the gauze, his supple form backdropped by the dingy wall of the barn. She sensed that his stillness was evidence not of his calmness but of his discipline. He was waiting her out. Squirrelly and restive beneath his placid surface.

Sibyl might not be truly psychic, if you defined it as the gift of prediction, of seeing the future. Truth be told, she did not believe in visions. But she believed in intuition. Twenty years of focusing so intently on another person in an attempt to *read* what they needed to hear from her had honed her ability. Then there were all the years she'd spent onstage (Daddy had made her call it *the altar*) at Harmony Church in Beaver County, Pennsylvania. There, in the white robes that were too long and made her trip on the steps to *the altar*, she'd given the worshippers something a little different. Instead of listening for what they wanted to hear, she'd given them what they'd wanted to *feel*. Whether it was a woman in a broken-down charity wheelchair who begged little Debbie Crabb, gripping her tiny fingers tight so it hurt, to *take away the pain*. Or an old woman waving a faded Xerox paper with a young girl's face—*find my baby*. Mostly what they needed to feel was comfort, even if it only lasted for the forty-five minutes of her father the Reverend's service. In that way, the work she'd done as a child was the same as the work she'd done (*was doing*, she thought) as Sibyl.

She squinted through her gauze at Jax's hands. What story would this man's hands tell?

Sure enough, his well-shaped, square-nailed, pristine hands were curled into fists. Loose fists, but still. He was withholding.

"Forty-one, forty-two," counted Sibyl.

The barn was so quiet she heard Jax breathing.

"Fifty," said Sibyl.

She stopped counting, realizing what was wrong.

The goats were missing.

Diurn and Nocturne had been nestled in their stall, circling and snorting before they'd curled against each other, hoof to head, and fallen asleep.

But they should have woken when Jax arrived. He'd made a racket, rapping on the barn doors, projecting his actor's voice as if they were in a shitty Shakespearean play.

"I thought we were going to a hundred," said Jax.

"Sixty," said Sibyl. "But please excuse me for just one moment while I check on something. It will not interfere with our session; I've already received a number of interesting signals, um, points of entry." She cringed at her own incoherence. "I'm just going to glance into the stall down at the other end of the barn. I'd like you to sit here and continue to breathe. We'll continue counting in just a moment."

"Points of entry," said Jax. "Rad!"

"It should be," said Sibyl, standing up. "I appreciate your patience, Jax. Please focus on your breathing with your eyes closed until I return to the table."

Sibyl removed her gauze and set it down; the dim barn around her came into focus: the soaring ceilings that ended in darkness between the rafters, surely home to a family of bats, spiders spinning glorious webs. The grimy floor of the aisle, old dirt packed over concrete. The slice of darkness where the door to the tack room stood open.

Sibyl's boots tapped over the floor as she made her way to the goats' stall, her stride quickening as she covered the length of the barn. Her heart rate had already spiked when she reached the last stall and saw what was inside:

Sawdust. A pile of hay in one corner, pellets of shit everywhere.

The goats were gone.

28

Dawn (the Birthday Girl)

DAWN STARTLED WHEN MIA STEPPED BACK INSIDE THE SHED HOLDING the kettle.

"Oh, this is silly," she whispered to Reece, "but I'm a little scared."

"You got this," Reece whispered back.

Mia strode to the table in the center and poured a small amount of steaming brown liquid into each mug. Then she lifted the tray and offered a mug to everyone except Reece. Dawn selected a chipped white mug and sniffed the steam. It smelled loamy and vaguely rancid, like something rotting under soil. She burrowed closer to Reece, suddenly jealous of her friend's sobriety.

"Listen up, peeps," Mia said. "I just have a few short opening remarks. Some of which I *may* have gotten from the YouTube channel of a Peruvian ayahuasca priestess."

"Remind me to subscribe," said Graham.

Dawn didn't want to drink the tea. She set the mug on her

yoga mat and cleared her throat, summoning the courage to tell Mia.

But then Reece turned to her, eyes wide with concern. She held Dawn's gaze, then whispered, "It's okay. You can do it."

"Thank you," Dawn whispered back. "I don't feel right drinking something like—"

"I mean, you *can*," Reece interrupted.

"What?"

"I meant, *it's okay, you can drink the tea.* You'll be fine. I'll be watching."

"But—"

"Shhhhh." Reece raised a finger to her lips. "Trust me, Dawnie. *Drink the tea.* It's for the greater good." Her voice was soft but unyielding. A memory snapped to Dawn's mind: the group, twenty years younger, sitting in a circle at the Nurtury. Reece had spoken nearly identical words, used the same gentle yet commanding tone: *Trust me. It's for the greater good.*

"Ladies?" Mia returned the empty tray to the table in the center of the shed. "Anything you'd like to share with the rest of us? No secrets, remember?" Mia lifted her mug. "As I was saying, via my favorite Peruvian priestess, tonight, my dear old friends, we'll be taking a high-speed train to some faraway, hidden places deep below the surface of our psyches. Chronologically speaking, the journey will be brief; just fifteen minutes on our external clocks, but eternal and infinite on the stopwatch of our souls."

Dawn heard Graham whistle under his breath at the flowery sentences.

"In other words, we're about to *trip balls*, yo," said Summer.

"Babe," said Joanie. "Don't sully the poetry."

Mia ignored them. "My advice to you is to attempt total passivity. To simply *receive* this experience. We spend our entire lives in motion. It's now time to trust the vastness of your inner world, your inner knowledge. Most of all, your inner *truth*."

She looked at Dawn, her blue eyes piercing.

Reece squeezed Dawn's hand.

"And now, my lovelies," said Mia, lowering to sit on a purple mat between two shaggy white pillows, "we *drink*."

Dawn drank.

Sibyl (the Visionnaire)

SIBYL STOOD STARING IN DISBELIEF. THE DOOR AT THE BACK OF THE stall was unlatched and stood open. *"Please triple-check that their stall is latched,"* Twyla had reminded Sibyl. *The coyotes.*

Twyla and her goats. Sibyl found the animals quite repulsive but was aware of her friend's outsized attachment to them, so she'd checked and tested the latches.

Twice.

They could only be opened from the outside. Designed to allow exit from the barn to the adjoining outdoor pen.

Sibyl lifted the latch of the stall, stepped into the filthy square, and crossed to the opposite door. She checked the pen, confirming what she feared: the gate leading outside was open.

Someone had let the goats out. Set them free on Celestial Ranch, where the coyotes would *"sniff them out in a heartbeat,"* according to Twyla.

"Shit," said Sibyl, under her breath.

But first, *Jax.* The man—it was hard not to think of him

as a child, in the way extreme vanity evoked the young and unevolved—was waiting for her, gauze pulled over his eyes, at the table back at the barn's front entrance.

Sibyl pulled the outer stall door shut and crossed back to the main aisle of the barn. She'd simply end the session with Jax, she decided, and go search for the goats. They likely hadn't gone far—they were ravenous and distractible, cloven-hooved gluttons. Surely, she hoped, they would've stopped at the first edible plants, the first pungent scent.

She thought of her contract with Mia. It bound her to remain on call for the duration of the night, until sunrise, which would happen at who knows what time. She'd have to ask Twyla. Or check the weather app on her phone. Payment was contingent upon fulfillment of the terms.

Well, her friendship with Twyla mattered more than the payments. Even if the money would allow Sibyl to make her one dream left a reality—her little house among the twisted cacti out in Joshua Tree.

She thought of Twyla's grief at discovering something had happened to the goats. How little, it seemed, the woman had left to live for.

It was settled: Sibyl would end Jax's session right now.

She broke into a half-jog down the aisle of the barn. She'd been so occupied with weighing her options that she didn't notice Jax's empty hay bale until she was just a few paces from the table where she'd left him sitting.

He was gone.

"Jax?" she called out. "Sorry for the disruption. I'm back now."

She waited a beat, listening for his voice. Nothing.

The sandalwood candle in the center of the crate she was using as a table glinted softly in the low light of the barn. The table looked oddly bare. The gauze band she'd left there before going to check on the goats was gone.

Was it? She checked her pockets. Nothing.

"Hey, Jax?" she tried again.

From behind, hands closed around her neck. They were large and warm.

She smelled him. *Sulfur Creek.* It was what her daddy had called the dead stream that ran through the woods by Harmony Church. The water was a deep orange from the town mine's drainage. Not even the long-whiskered catfish survived.

In her ear, a low, commanding voice. "Do not make a sound. Do not turn around. Keep looking straight ahead."

Reflexively, her breath snagged in an inhaled shriek.

The hands at her throat contracted. She felt pressure on her windpipe, gasped for air.

"I said, *zip it.* Not a sound."

The hands released for a moment, and then fabric was yanked down over her eyes. The blindfold she'd left on the table.

The hands shifted to her wrists, encircling them tightly.

She was going to die.

Then, warm breath in her ear. Jax's voice was familiar but changed. The theatrical affect had vanished, replaced with a lower, graver sound.

His *real* voice.

"Not a sound," said Jax, as gooseflesh sprang down her arms. "Just do as I say, got that?"

"Yes," she whispered.

"I'm going to hold your hand, and you're going to walk with me. You're going to keep walking with your blindfold on until we've reached our destination. All clear?"

"Yes."

"That's what I like to hear, Debbie."

Sibyl's voice froze in her throat.

"Wh-what?" she whispered.

"You come with me now, Debbie," said Jax. "I'm in charge. We're doing things according to *my* vision now. Okay?"

"Okay."

"Now, that's a good big sister."

30

Dawn (the Birthday Girl)

THE TASTE OF THE TEA REMINDED DAWN OF DIRT AND FEET. BUT SHE'D been steeling herself for something truly vile, and the warm, gritty liquid was not as bad as she'd feared. She downed it, set the mug on the floor, and lay back on her yoga mat, trying to be *open and receiving*. The others lay back too, except for Reece, who sat cross-legged beside Dawn, palms on her knees, gaze forward like an elegant Buddha.

Dawn breathed slowly, waiting to feel *something*, but she felt normal. In fact, she felt hyper-normal: sober, relaxed, aware of the ordinary sounds around her—the shush of the branches stirred by a light breeze over the roof, a faint creak of the decaying walls, an orchestra of insects outside. The room had darkened, the lanterns dimmed to a faint glow. Reece sat sentry nearby. Watching over Dawn. Protecting her. Just as Reece had watched over all of them at the Nurtury, long ago, when they were young and bewildered by the challenges of raising their extraordinary children, pushed to their limits—

past their limits—by the tantrums, repetitive behaviors, chronic bedwetting, food refusals, and wild fears of benign, everyday experiences. Graham's son was terrified of stepping off sidewalks. Joanie and Summer agonized over little Maisie's fear of their gourmet oven.

Dawn had been the biggest mess of all. She'd been the last to join the group, stumbling into the Nurtury playroom with swollen, bloodshot eyes, too shy to make eye contact. Quasi-hysterical over what four-year-old Quinn had just done, but also over having just left Quinn with Craig, whom she'd had to page at the hospital and beg to come home.

"Go take care of yourself," Craig had said, too evenly, when he'd arrived home to find Dawn curled on the couch sobbing, the wreckage of porcelain chunks and shards still all over the kitchen floor, the remains of their good dinner plates, a wedding gift. Quinn had grabbed a plate and thrown it, then another, after some stupid fight with Dawn—Dawn couldn't even remember what started it. Only that she'd been screaming, and that Quinn was covering her ears, and that Dawn could not *stop* screaming, though she knew she should.

And then, the sounds of pounding and shattering.

Dawn screaming. Quinn screaming.

"Her hand is bleeding," Craig had informed Dawn after he'd found Quinn in her bedroom, burrowed under her weighted blanket with her Simon game. *"Don't fuck this up any further. I'll handle it. You go take care of yourself. Somewhere other than here."*

Dawn had gone to the Nurtury. She could think of nowhere else. She'd been crying so hard she could barely see when she stepped through the door and collapsed into Reece's arms.

"What do I do?" she'd sobbed.

"Right now, you do nothing," Reece had said. *"You're here. That's as much as you need to ask of yourself."*

Reece's words returned to Dawn now, as she lay on her back in the shed, her mouth dry from the chalky residue of the tea.

Do nothing, Dawn told herself.

She shifted onto her side, hands tucked in prayer beneath her cheek, knees drawn to her stomach. Beyond the opening of the shed, Dawn saw a slice of the night sky, stars spilled like salt across it. The shed was a warm hand, and Dawn was cupped in its palm, held safe against the night. Her body relaxed. Every muscle, every *molecule.*

Then the room shifted.

Dawn had the sensation of the ground canting and jerking, like during a small earthquake.

Around her, the shed disappeared.

Dawn disappeared too. She felt her body melt, pooling like a snowman in the sunshine. Freed of the clumsy weight of her flesh and bones, the *rest* of Dawn was transported into another room. Far, far away from Topanga Canyon and the shed on Hydra Hill, this place was sun-blasted and plant-filled, back-dropped by the sounds of traffic and the smell of baking bread. She knew her friends were there with her—Graham and Mia, Joanie and Summer—though she couldn't see them. Only Reece was missing.

Reece, Dawn tried to say, but stripped of her mouth and throat, she couldn't make a sound.

A knock came at the door of the sunny room. Dawn tried to say *Come in,* but the words came as a scratchy, warbled sound, somewhere between that of a cat and a bird. The knock came again, and Dawn moved to the door. The cat-bird noise came from her throat again. The knocking was insistent now, pounding, the door reverberating, and Dawn felt desperate to open it.

But she was handless.

The door began to open.

31

Raj (the Drifter)

DRY LEAVES CRUNCHED UNDER RAJ'S BOOTS LIKE TINY BONES AS HE neared the shed on Hydra Hill, following the terrible noises that had assailed him in the cave.

How-woo. How-woooooo.

Strung around his neck, the binoculars knocked against his chest. He found a spot in a burst of elderberry with a direct view to the open side of the shed, and tucked himself into the leaves.

Through the lenses, he could see the trespassers congregated outside the shed, on the open-air side of the structure itself. On the packed dirt floor inside, Raj identified a table, pillows strewn on the floor, and—

He squinted into the lenses as his heart rate surged.

Jutting into his view were a pair of human legs. Drawn up in a V.

He could not see the rest of the body. It was either obscured by the wall of the shed, or lost in shadows, or—

Raj shuddered convulsively.

—or the legs were *not* attached to a body.

He moved the binoculars back to the group of trespassers outside the shed, his disgust for them displaced by a sickening fear. Had they killed one of their own?

The ringleader's voice sailed through the night, gleeful.

"About five minutes, party peeps! I've got a timer set. Let's get back into character and *celebrate!*"

Raj watched as the group began to sway and gestate, breaking their circle. Their argument over, they returned to their careless, greedy revelry. The ringleader suddenly threw back her head and cackled, punching her fist into the air.

"*Dance*, bitches! *That* is totally unbelievable. Dance like you mean it, please. Like you're tripping balls!"

Quinn, Raj thought, as he listened to the blond bitch's unhinged laugh, thinking of the legs folded in the shed behind her.

He lifted his binoculars again: the legs were still there. He looked hard; they were *not* Quinn's legs. They were shorter and softer.

"Come on, Reece," the blond bitch said. "You can try a little harder than that, sweetie."

Raj began to wriggle in reverse down the hill, elderberry branches snagging at his long hair. He needed to get to Quinn *now,* to make sure she was safe.

The universe was counting on him.

Where was the Witch? he wondered suddenly. Could the folded legs in the shed be hers?

If they'd gotten to the Witch, surely they'd get to Quinn too.

From the dancing group came more noise, their laughter turning primal and raw. They were, he realized, mimicking the coyotes.

How-wooooo. How-how-how-wooooooo.

Raj sprang to his feet and sprinted down Hydra Hill. As he ran, he turned his boning knife around on his belt, snug against his hip.

He needed to get to Quinn, so that she could be kept safe.

He'd failed with Candace. He would not fail again.

32

Dawn (the Birthday Girl)

IN THE PLACE WHERE DAWN HAD GONE, FAR BEYOND THE SHED, BEYOND the canyon, a door opened. Standing on the other side was Reece. Unlike Dawn, she had a body: long and lithe, skin supple and smooth, nearly aglow against the bright pattern of her floral dress, the marigold-colored cloth wrapped around her head. Her eyes shone. She smiled, showing Dawn pearled teeth.

In the place where her heart once was, Dawn felt a lifting sensation. It was only Reece, knocking at the door! Beautiful, wonderful Reece. Their *guide*.

Mama! came a voice from behind Dawn. *Mama, I'm here!*

Quinn. Her baby was here too. Dawn moved in the direction of her voice but couldn't find her little girl.

Mama, mam-aaahhh. Aahhh-ooooohh.

How-wooooo.

Quinn's voice devolved into a howl. A mournful, two-note wail that gathered and multiplied, as if she'd been joined by many more Quinns.

How-wooo. HOW-WOOO.

Dawn was seized with panic—no, she *was* the panic. She wanted to go to her daughter, but she didn't know how to find her. Perhaps Reece could help. Dawn and her panic, dawnthepanic, turned back to Reece, standing in the doorway, to plead for help.

Reece *always* helped.

But Reece was gone. Instead, Dawn found her lying on the floor, the yellow scarf on her head now a plastic bag lowered over her face, stretched tightly over her nose and mouth. A crimson circle spread beneath her body, growing wider as Dawn looked on.

Dawn screamed. A deep and anguished bird-wail that was the accumulation of all the pain of life—animal, human, plant—over sixty-five million years of agony.

A cool, wet blast hit Dawn's face. She was blind.

When she opened her eyes, she was back in the shed on Hydra Hill. Everything looked bleary, as if the room had been submerged in water, and as she blinked, voices sharpened.

"Dawn! Stop it!"

The room snapped into focus, illuminated by lantern light.

Reece was standing over her, holding a water bottle, her braids falling around her face.

"Dawn! Jesus! Are you okay?"

Dawn looked up at Reece. Her eyes were saucers, filled with alarm.

"I—" Dawn's voice had returned.

"Sorry I threw water in your face," said Reece, breathless. "You were just really freaking us out."

"You sure fucking were," came Mia's voice. "You were having a real coo-coo-for-Cocoa-Puffs moment, babe."

Dawn lifted her hand and placed it on her cheek, relieved

to find her regular face was there. She patted her stomach, her legs, her hair.

Everything was there and, as far as she could tell, intact. Her hair was wet from the water Reece had thrown on her, but otherwise, she seemed fine.

"Thank god," she blurted, feeling she might cry with relief.

"Honey?" Mia said. "Seriously, are you okay? Because you were making the most disturbing noises. They cut right into my trip. Which wasn't much of one. Honestly, I think I might be immune to DMT. It's rare, but some people are."

"Disturbing sounds?" said Dawn. "I'm so sorry."

"I've never heard anything like it," said Mia.

"Don't be sorry, Dawnie," said Reece. "You were definitely having a *moment*, but you're back with us now."

"Where—" Dawn began, still shaky, not quite trusting her own voice. "Where's everyone else?"

"Summer and Joanie are right there," said Mia, pointing to a blanketed form in the far corner, "all cozied up. Screw couples therapy. Evidently all they needed was a little DMT."

"Ha," said Dawn weakly, shivering despite the warm night air.

Reece grabbed a blanket and draped it over Dawn's shoulders.

"Thank you," Dawn murmured, finally starting to relax. *Only a dream.*

"Well, that was fucking bizarro." Graham unfurled from his mat and stood, rather unsteadily, using the crude wall of the shed for balance. "I don't know *where* I just went, except that it was very, um, *kaleidoscopic*, and when I got back, you were making Chewbacca noises."

"Sorry," mumbled Dawn.

"Be *nice*," said Mia. "I was actually a little worried about our girl."

"I had her back," Reece said.

"Of course you did!" Mia said. "I wasn't worried-worried, but, Dawnie, you were out a good five minutes longer than me. And clearly experiencing some intense shit. But, hey, everyone's brain chemistry is different. I mean, those two over there are *just* coming down." She nodded at the lump of Joanie-and-Summer in the corner. They began to stir and shift.

"Makes sense," said Dawn, though she felt the experience had been anything *but* sensical.

"Oh and, hey!" said Mia. "Happy birthday, babe. Like, *officially*. You're five-oh. How does it feel?" She slung an arm over Dawn's shoulder. Instinctively, Dawn pulled away. Usually, Mia's affection gave her a little thrill, but now it felt harsh, like a touch to a sunburn. "A little skittish? I get it. I felt a little strange when I woke up too. Did you have a nice, um, time? Despite whatever was making you yowl?"

"I guess I need some time to . . . process," said Dawn.

"Of course," said Reece. "It takes time to figure out what the trip means. Or you might not ever really know."

"I'd prefer to start processing in the company of a stiff drink," said Graham. He turned to Mia. "What do you say, Captain? Can we head back down to the yurt and do normal, age-appropriate party activities?"

"For sure," said Mia. "Jax must be getting lonely."

Dawn grimaced; all she wanted to do was go back to her cabin and see Quinn.

"I need to see my daughter," she said to no one in particular.

"I know you do," said Reece.

"I need to see my Quinn," Dawn mumbled, rising to all fours, then slowly climbing to her feet.

"Whoa, birthday girl," Mia said, holding up her palm. Dawn noticed she'd broken one of her long nails. "We have fun things to do! The night is young."

The lump of Summer-and-Joanie was rising into a seated position. The blankets fell away. Dawn heard the unmistakable, rare sound of Joanie's earnest giggle.

Dawn was soothed by the sound; soon, she told herself, at least she could leave this godforsaken shed and return to the relative comfort of the yurt. Drink some champagne, nibble on the leftover ice cream cake.

Tonight was the last party she would ever allow to be held in her honor.

Dawn squinted into the darkness. She blinked and waited for her eyes to adjust. When they did, she saw only Joanie had emerged from the blankets and was sitting cross-legged on her yoga mat, rolling her neck, mouth hanging open.

"She lives!" sang Mia. "Welcome back, Jo! You were making some really cute noises."

"I—I was?"

Dawn cut in. "Where's Summer?"

Joanie stared at her, head tilted. "What?"

"Where's Summer? We thought she was next to you."

"She was," Reece said. "She was beside Joanie the whole time. I watched them pull the blankets over their heads."

"Well, where'd she go then, Reece?" Graham said. "Since you were watching the whole time, you must have seen her leave."

Dawn didn't like the accusatory tone. "Hold on," she began, but Reece interrupted her.

"I *was* watching the whole time. Except for when I was tending to Dawn. Because she was making *un*happy sounds, and I needed to make sure she was okay."

Joanie sighed and stretched her arms over her head. "God, I feel weird. That was a very—*colorful* experience." She cleared her throat. Reece handed her a bottle of water.

Joanie and Graham had described the palette of their trips, as if bright colors had been the main effect of the drug. Odd, Dawn thought, that she hadn't noticed the colors in hers; her experience had been far deeper than mere visuals. Then again, maybe it wasn't odd. Her experiences tended to be more anxiety-laden than those of her friends. How often did Mia, Craig, or Summer, even Quinn, command her to *chill*? To *relax*?

Joanie drained her water. "You know how Summer is. She probably sobered up, got annoyed, and headed back to the cabin. Or the yurt."

"Did she take a lantern?" asked Dawn.

"One, two, three." Mia poked her index finger with the broken nail at each lantern in the room. "Nope. All the lanterns are here."

"Thanks again for confiscating our phones, Meadows," said Graham.

"You're welcome."

"Aren't you worried about Summer?" said Dawn. "It's so unlike her to ditch a party."

Mia shrugged. "She's not stupid. Maybe the drug didn't work and she got bored. Anyway, no stressing on your b-day, Dawnie. Let's just go find everyone and have a debrief at the yurt. Jax should have some après-trip refreshments ready."

"It's cool, Dawnie," said Joanie. Dawn thought she sounded unusually calm.

"Summer's a grown woman," said Reece. "And a highly capable one at that."

"Give or take," said Joanie. "Wait—I'm sorry. I shouldn't have said that. I'm just kind of—discombobulated. I'm only

used to weed. Of course you're right, Reece. Summer's a bad-ass. I just didn't expect to come back from that and find her missing."

"Well, let's go search for her then, shall we?" said Mia, picking up a lantern and stepping toward the opening of the shed.

"Thank God," said Dawn. "Let's go." Just then, a wave of nausea rippled through her, and she fought the urge to gag. "Ugh. I think I'm going to throw up."

"Deep breaths," said Reece.

"Don't worry, honey," said Mia. "Just relax, and let that stuff wear off. Nausea is a super-common side effect of DMT. It'll pass."

"Do—do you guys feel nauseous?" Dawn's heart began to pound, on top of her queasy stomach. Could she be having some belated reaction to the drug? What had she been *thinking*, swilling some laced tea Mia had allegedly scored from another actress?

Joanie shrugged. "Nah. A little spacey, but no nausea."

"Me neither," said Graham.

Dawn suddenly longed for Summer's throaty laugh and reliable wisecracks to fill the space, lift the mood. Why had she left?

"Come on, birthday girl, let's walk it off," Mia said, stepping outside. "A little night air will set you straight. I bet Summer and Jaxxy are down in the yurt, getting hammered and singing Cat Stevens. Let's go join them and talk about what just went down. I'm dying to hear your experience, Dawnie." She beckoned toward the open hillside. "Down we go, beautiful people. Follow me."

Reece took Dawn's hand, and they walked down the hill.

2011

Santa Monica

DAWN AND REECE HUDDLED TOGETHER OVER REECE'S NEW iMac, purchased by Mia for the Project and installed on Reece's desk in the Nurtury. Also on the desk was a thick stack of papers, each page cluttered with checkboxes and handwritten signatures.

Vaccination records. Collected from all over the country.

Reece filled out a spreadsheet to log their progress. Dawn scanned each document into the computer, then imported it into Photoshop. She tweaked dates, checked boxes, added pediatricians' signatures, not finishing until every curl and loop and slash of the signed names was perfect.

She wouldn't stop her work, the first *important* work she'd done (*take that, ever-important Dr. Craig*), until every parent, anywhere in the United States, who wanted to send their child to school without subjecting them to a possibly toxic injection could, through the Project, obtain a foolproof facsimile of a vaccine record, confirming their child had received all vaccines required for school admission.

The interest in the Project was overwhelming. Thousands of parents from across the country, clambering for their records. Reece had devised a beautiful system of parent activists who assembled copies of real vaccination records and repurposed them in the name of the Project. The Nurtury group worked in shifts: Mia was on parent outreach, using carefully worded emails and phone calls scripted by Graham. Summer and Joanie handled all the FedEx mailings. Dawn Photoshopped the documents. Reece handled the payments. The service was free, but donations were encouraged, to cover the costs.

"Consider the ostrich," Reece told the group. "The bird is virtually unkillable by disease. Naturally resistant to SARS, MERS, Ebola, even HIV. So, if the ostrich, why not us? If intelligent design has created an immune system like the ostrich's, then why should individuals be denied the choice to say no to the artificial manipulation of our own immune systems? Who might your child be, at this moment, had she not received a mandatory injection?"

Hearing the question aloud, with all it implied, stunned Dawn. She couldn't help but see Quinn as damaged—by Big Pharma, the lobbyists, the government, the school system. She put herself on that list—wasn't she to blame, most of all? She had taken Quinn for all her shots, held her still each time the nurse plunged the needle in Quinn's beautiful rolls of baby fat, comforted her after with a bottle, and later, a lollipop. As much as it sickened her to think of her daughter as hurt, impaired, broken, it strengthened her commitment to the Project.

They made signs, posted them all over the Nurtury, to remember their purpose:

EDUCATION WITHOUT INJECTION!

MY IMMUNITY = MY HUMANITY!

I TRUST MY BODY MORE THAN THE FDA.

MY BODY, MY BLOODSTREAM.

WAKEMAN WAS SILENCED!

NOTHING IN NATURE IS NOT NORMAL.

As they worked, they blasted Billy Joel's "Goodnight Saigon" and belted out the chorus together:

> *And we would all go down together*
> *We said we'd all go down together*
> *Yes we would all go . . .*

The song became the mantra of their Project.

Dawn had meant the words every time she screamed them along. *Together.* All for one, one for all. Then again, she'd never considered getting caught. She'd never considered that Craig, who was working a relentless shift schedule at Cedars-Sinai at the time, would ever find out. She never doubted the Project, not for a second. Working on it had been the most meaningful experience of her life. Harmonious and beautiful, teeming with purpose.

Until Reece had gotten sloppy with the donation payments—she'd never cared about money, her purpose always on a higher plane.

Until the feds showed up at the Nurtury and flashed their search warrants.

Then, one morning, Craig read a headline from the Huffington Post aloud to Dawn at breakfast, in a flat, hard voice Dawn had never heard him use.

"LOCAL CHILD PSYCH GURU BUSTED IN ANTI-VAX FORGERY RING."

He turned to Dawn, eyes blazing. "So help me god," he said, through clenched teeth. "If you're publicly affiliated with this fringy bullshit, my career's over, and so's your life as you know it. And I can assure you, I'll get custody, so you can get ready to see Quinn for a maximum of three supervised hours per week, if you're lucky."

Later, the feds visited Dawn's house. Two chiseled guys in navy suits. When they sat down in the living room, she saw the handguns strapped to their ankles.

Blessedly, Quinn had been at school, and Craig at work in the hospital.

Dawn denied everything. She looked the big, blue-suited guys right in the eyes and said she knew nothing about any sort of illicit activities at the Nurtury. As she lied, she knew she wouldn't get away with it, that she was simply postponing the inevitable, but then Craig's threat blared in her mind: *"three supervised hours per week, if you're lucky,"* and the absurd denials rolled off her tongue.

"I was only there to learn how to help my child, who's special needs."

The men nodded. On Dawn's coffee table, their black recording device pulsed with a little bead of red light.

"Reece Mayall is a wonderful, empathetic therapist. So passionate about her work."

"How passionate, would you say?"

Dawn paused.

"Let me rephrase. Would you say Ms. Mayall's passion ever clouded her judgment?"

Very quietly, Dawn said yes.

The others were doomed by outside witnesses. A few of the parents Mia had contacted caved in panic and supplied her name. The staff at FedEx on Wilshire identified Summer and Joanie. Graham fell apart and confessed mere seconds after the navy suits rang his apartment buzzer.

Reece, of course, was ruined, thousands of dollars in donations traced straight to the Nurtury's bank account.

Dawn's work on the Project, the countless hours she'd logged on the iMac in the Nurtury, bore only *inside* witnesses: Graham and Mia. Summer and Joanie. Reece.

They'd kept their mouths shut. Not one of Dawn's friends breathed a word about her involvement. They corroborated her clumsy denial to the feds, standing behind her every false word.

In the meantime, they *went down together.*

All except Dawn.

Thanks to her friends—her loyal, selfless, incredible friends—she'd never had to spend a single night away from Quinn.

33

Twyla (the Hostess)

TWYLA PULLED THE CURTAINS OF HER BEDROOM CLOSED WITH A HARD tug, releasing a cloud of dust from the ancient velvet folds. The house was quiet, although she thought she'd heard noises from the basement.

She'd been staring out the window for too long, scanning the dark landscape, looking for Arnold's lumbering shape, or the ghostly smear of Klondike's white-gray coat. Nothing but starlight and earth, hills and trees. No human shape. She longed to throw open the front door, to blaze outside into the night and scream Arnold's name, slashing the ray of her flashlight into the darkness, asking the goddess to please, *please,* let the beam land on her husband.

Where had he gone?

She wished Sibyl were here in the house. Sibyl always knew what to do. But she was down in the barn for the night, on call to do her readings whenever the urge struck Ms. Meadows and her guests. Sibyl had seemed unfazed by the brazen request that she stay up all night, just *in case* some self-important, champagne-drunk urbanite felt like having their energy read at two a.m. She hated the idea of Sibyl at Ms. Meadows's beck and call, bleary-eyed and struggling to stay awake. At least, Twyla thought, as she watched shadows from the leaves of the massive oak quiver on the bedroom wall, Sibyl would have the goats for company. Twyla suddenly missed Nocturne and Diurn; she'd been so busy tending to her high-maintenance guests, she'd had no time to visit her little friends.

Speaking of animal friends, it was reassuring to think that Arnold had taken Klondike with him. Twyla had no doubt Klonnie would protect him. She just hoped they stayed far from Ms. Meadows and her friends.

But why couldn't he have just stayed home tonight? When did his anger at her grow so large? Why must he make her feel like a villain for wanting to stay at Celestial Ranch? Twyla had read the average American life span was around seventy-eight years, just around the corner, and most of their friends were already dead. It wasn't as if her goal was to make their property into a five-star resort. She simply wanted to restore it to a bare standard of decency, so she and Arnold might enjoy whatever time they had left, surrounded by the majesty of nature, in the place she loved more than anywhere else. *This* was why Twyla didn't think twice about spending the little money they had on the ranch: she did it for love. The way, she told herself, parents didn't hesitate to spend money on improving their children's lives.

Twyla and Arnold had tried for years to conceive, back when "trying" simply meant sex a few times a week, sometimes aligned with an awareness of her menstrual cycle, sometimes followed by the "legs up" method she'd read about in *Our Bodies, Ourselves*, which supposedly encouraged Arnold's sperm to do its work more effectively. This was in the seventies, long before "trying" meant tens of thousands of dollars in fertility treatments. When they weren't pregnant by the time Twyla was forty-one, they agreed it wasn't in the cards, and talked at length about overpopulation's decimating effect on the planet. They were artists, anyway, Twyla a sculptress and Arnold a woodworker. Arnold had reminded her, again and again, how children were anathema to a life in art.

She'd had her "tubes tied" in the nineties. It wasn't a premeditated decision, but one casually suggested by her GP, along with a few menacing statistics on the hazards of "geriatric motherhood." She'd made an appointment for the next week, mentioning it to Arnold. Arnold had agreed immediately. The possibility of children was over for them anyway, so why not guarantee that their bodies wouldn't veer from the decision?

What her doctor had implied would be akin to a tooth extraction had turned out to be major surgery from which Twyla took ten days to recover. A dull but insistent ache in the center of her belly, like a deep, radiant bruise. It throbbed day and night, often in sync with her heartbeat. She had a prescription for Percocet but didn't fill it; blunting the feeling seemed like a cheat somehow. She'd made the conscious decision to alter her body from nature's course and believed she should endure the fullness of the pain.

The duration of the pain was unexpected, but what shocked Twyla was her grief. A scraped-out feeling she couldn't shake, no matter how many sculptures she made or vases she threw on the pottery wheel. What art once did for her—giving her a sense of possibility, of expanse, that there was always more joy to discover in the world—no longer worked.

It occurred to her that the ways in which Americans lived their lives—before so many began practicing yoga and claiming

Buddhism—were anchored in attaining the same goal: the avail-
ability of the future. Even the most hedonistic pleasure-seekers
were sustained by anticipation of the *next* round of pleasure. A
brightness ahead. The most obvious source, she'd realized, after
officially closing the door on motherhood, was having children.

Twyla's barrenness marked the end of possibility. Then
the money from her mother came, allowing her to buy the land
that she and Arnold made into Celestial Ranch, and her sense
of possibility returned. She would never call the property "her
baby"—it repelled her when people compared some acquisition
to a child—but Celestial Ranch *was* the thing that gave her a
permanent sense of the future.

Now Arnold wanted to take that away.

Perhaps, she thought, slipping her fingers through the
curtains and peering into the darkness, he did not understand
because he was a man. Like all men, he'd arrived at some internal destination in which all his needs were met. His art had
been made—Arnold had sold his cabinetry company in the
nineties—his dick had permanently softened, he had a library
full of books, and of course, he had Klondike and Twyla. What
else was there to *want*?

Celestial Ranch simply got in the way of his needs, Twyla
decided. Fractured how she gave of herself to Arnold. The way
having a baby would have fractured it. The way her Airbnb
venture diverted her attention away from him, gave her a long
to-do list that didn't revolve around Arnold.

This was why he wanted to move to a retirement community. To have her all to himself.

It was why, at this very moment, he was sabotaging her
weekend. Ensuring her guests would leave a spate of one-star
reviews and stinging comments.

Well, she thought, a new swell of anger rising, she would not give him that.

She sat on her bed and stretched her legs out, leaning against the headboard, a faded cherrywood slab that Arnold had made for her fiftieth birthday. Fifty (how young it seemed now!), the very milestone being reached by one of the guests this weekend.

What happened to old-fashioned celebrations? Twyla rolled her ankles in slow circles. Even in the wildest days of her youth, it would never have occurred to her to *plan* fun with such strategy and effort. When one of her Airbnb guests, a pale woman in her thirties who wore her hair in cornrows, told Twyla about the Burning Man festival she attended every year, Twyla had asked if it was modeled after Woodstock. The woman had laughed and explained that artists spent the entire year making "installations" they would display at the festival, and that the desert area was transformed into an entire *city*, complete with street names. The tickets, Twyla had been shocked to hear, cost hundreds of dollars! By the time the young woman had finished describing the planning and building and money that went into the festival, it sounded more like a corporate retreat than a free-spirited art festival. ,

This birthday weekend organized by Ms. Meadows seemed like the Burning Man festival on a much smaller scale. There was a schedule and activities and rules. There were catered meals and games. None of it required participation on Twyla's part, Mia had assured her over the phone, back in the spring. Ms. Meadows had also mentioned that while Celestial Ranch looked "absolutely perfect" for the party, she'd need to come up for a "preview" first.

Twyla conceded and set up a time to show Mia around,

frantically cleaning the bungalows, weeding the footpaths and clearing branches, spraying the buildings with a power hose. Then Mia had arrived and barely paid attention as Twyla drove her around the property, trying her best to be a courteous and informative guide, pointing out the oak grove behind Betelgeuse where the Tongva people had ground acorn flour, the trail on which John Muir had once hiked, and emphasizing the brand-new yurt and all its amenities.

Mia had nodded and inserted bland comments—*cool, wow, amazing*—while seeming to search the surroundings the entire time, as if she were on safari hoping to spot wildlife. As if she were *looking* for something to which Twyla was oblivious.

Twyla had looped around the barn, making mention of Nocturne and Diurn, but Mia only said she'd eaten goat a few times, from a Mexican food truck that always had a line around the block, which left Twyla at a loss as she maneuvered over the uneven ground at the base of Hydra Hill, knotted with tree roots. Suddenly, Mia jabbed her finger in the direction of the top of the hill and said, *"Oh, what's that?"*

The shed. The sagging, ancient shed atop Hydra Hill that Arnold had once used to store tools. It was off-limits to guests; what use would they have for a half shelter with a rusted roof and dirt floor?

Confused, Twyla had explained that it was scheduled to be torn down.

Mia had perked up in a similar fashion when Twyla led her around the back of the main house, with the intention of showing off her chicken coop. Mia had veered over to where weeds and dandelions grew along the foundation, stopping beside the wooden doors abutting the house's weathered siding. She pointed a red-nailed finger at the hatch, which Twyla hadn't opened in ages, and asked, *"What's this ramp-thing?"*

"Oh, just an access door to the basement," Twyla said, embarrassed about the back of her house, which was years overdue for a paint job.

Later, when Mia bid her farewell, Twyla stood in the dust kicked up by Mia's large SUV and wondered if she'd ever hear from the actress again.

A few hours later, Twyla received a message from Mia through the Airbnb app: Thanks for the delightful tour of your stunning property! It was just what I needed. I'd like to confirm my reservation for the weekend of June 25th, with one small additional stipulation, per the legally enforceable verbiage below, for which I'll insist on paying an extra fee. . . .

Twyla's eyes ached as she squinted at the screen:

The Airbnb Host will grant the Guest full access to the Main House basement, via the "ramp hatch door," which shall remain unlocked from sunset (8:43pm) on Saturday, June 25, until sunrise (6:23am) on Sunday, June 26. During this time, the Host forfeits all access to the basement of the Main House. Failure to abide by this agreement results in forfeiture of the additional fee of $2500 paid by the Guest to guarantee fulfillment of this request.

Now Mia's interest in the hatch made sense. It was merely some part of the elaborate Burning Man–style party she was planning. Giving up access to Hydra Hill and her disaster of a basement for one night seemed a low price for the reward of paying the minimum amount required to stave off a lien on her years-overdue property taxes.

She lay back on the mattress and curled onto her side. Without Arnold, the bed felt empty.

Could *he* have wandered into the basement? She'd left the

hatch unlocked, per Ms. Meadows's contract, but she hadn't mentioned anything to Arnold.

Arnold loathed the basement. *A room full of shit,* he called it. *"We should sell as-is. Or find someone to burn it all. It's nothing but wreckage down there."*

Specifically: the wreckage of *her life.* Twyla had stopped using the basement years ago, after filling it with broken chairs, bicycles, and plastic tubs filled with the paperback spy novels Arnold had once devoured. The wire and metal and wood she'd used to create shapes and forms that, somehow, helped her make sense of the world. Notebooks and old clothes and tchotchkes. Giant pots used to make big batches of elaborate veggie stews for a dozen or more guests, back when she and Arnold still entertained; handblown goblets from a thrift store in Berkeley forty years ago—so big her guests' faces were obscured with every sip. Mannequins from her clothes-making period; stretched canvas from the years she dabbled in acrylics, paintbrushes with petrified bristles. Her old wooden rifle in its metal case, a Mossberg Arnold gave her in the early eighties, when Twyla went through a target-shooting phase. She once thought the long, chestnut-brown .22 truly beautiful, and had been a decent markswoman, but as she'd grown older and shootings became rampant all over the country, she was ashamed to own the gun and kept it in the basement, out of sight.

Perhaps the basement wasn't so much a storage space for junk as an archive of her memories. As if the ancient, dust-coated objects held her sadness, so she didn't have to. It was, for example, too painful to think of Mira, the half Percheron, half Thoroughbred mare she'd ridden on the ranch for fifteen years before the horse had died. Twyla had found her lying in the middle of Andromeadow, belly swollen and flies buzzing around her eyes. Twyla had lain down beside the mare and wept, resting her head on the animal's quivering flank. Mira was long gone, but the two saddles Twyla had used to ride her were in the basement.

Surely Arnold wasn't down there now.

Twyla took some deep prana breaths. She reminded herself that Arnold vanished daily, going off with Klondike to check on his bees or clear the trails or just wander the rain-starved hills.

Most likely, Twyla told herself as she counted to five on her exhale, he was at the broken hive in the far woods by Ursa Ridge.

What if he ran into the birthday guests galivanting in the moonlight during yet another preplanned activity?

She groaned in the darkness, surrendering to the anger and hurt.

Let him stay out all night. Let him experience the solitude of Twyla ceasing to fret over his safety, anticipate his every need.

Though of course, she would never stop.

The minutes crept past. No familiar two-note creak of the front door opening, no thud of Arnold's booted feet on the warped hardwood. The hands of her bedside clock were pushing midnight. Her anger morphed into worry.

She sat up and sighed, lowering her feet to the floor. She reached for her fleece vest from its hook on the wall, then groped for a light wool beanie in her sock drawer. The room was bathed in moonlight, the window misted with light dew. Twyla loved Topanga most of all late at night. She stepped down the stairs into the darkness, wishing Arnold still loved it too.

34

Sibyl (the Visionnaire)

JAX'S HAND WAS WARM. IN SOME OTHER CONTEXT—SAY, ONE IN WHICH he was not gripping Sibyl's upper arm quite so securely, or one in which her wrists were not bound with twine from a bale of hay, so tightly she could feel it cutting into her flesh—she might have found his touch reassuring.

The moment he'd come up behind her and tied the blindfold over her eyes had happened so quickly and fluidly that Sibyl, for a flash, thought the lights might have gone out in the barn. When he spoke, his voice was so changed from the inflected, theatrical swing he'd been using that Sibyl thought she was being abducted by someone else altogether. She had cried out to him for help: *Jax!*

The new voice, his real voice, was deep and measured, a voice of authority. A voice for issuing orders.

"You will do everything I say. Follow every instruction. You will not speak except to answer my questions in the briefest, most direct fashion. If not—" Sibyl felt the tip of something at the back of her neck. Its sharpness was so pure she hardly felt the pressure, only a faint pinch, followed by an itch.

She recognized the sensation. As a child, she'd been to the doctor exactly once, when a fever had gripped her for almost a week, her nights trippy with weird, fragmented dreams, the days long and melted. Her throat hurt. Her head itched. Finally, her mother drove her to the walk-in clinic an hour away in Shastaville, complaining under her breath, as if she were being supremely inconvenienced. Sibyl was eight at the time, or so her mother told her, rehearsing the facts in the crowded waiting room. *"May fifth, nineteen seventy-four. You got that? YOU GOT THAT?"* The doctor was kind but harried, a man who was probably in his fifties but who seemed ancient to Sibyl. He took her temperature, listened to her heartbeat. Parted her hair with his fingers and peered at her scalp. Murmured *"Jesus."* From the way he shifted his gaze from Sibyl to Amity Crabb, wife of the Supreme Reverend Crabb of Harmony Church, his grimace shifting to accusation, Sibyl understood the doctor was displeased with her mother. She had felt a flare of defensiveness, an urge to protect her mother, when the doctor asked to have a word, alone, with her mother in the hall.

When they returned, her mother's eyes were cast to the floor and stayed there as the doctor explained gently to Sibyl that she had strep throat and lice, and that it was *very, very important* that she take the medicine he was prescribing her. Also, she must allow her mother to comb lye through her hair for five days straight to get rid of the bugs. *"Are we clear, Deborah?"* the doctor said to Sibyl, but he kept his eyes trained on Amity. *"Are we clear, Mrs. Crabb?"*

Her mother said yes in the tight, clipped way she answered Sibyl's father when he told her to bring him a drink.

"And I want to take a blood sample before you leave."

The doctor pricked her finger, and she felt the stab, followed by the itch of freed blood.

Now she felt that same sensation at the back of her neck as the man who was not Jax said, in his new voice, "Feel that?"

A whimper flew from her lips. "Yes."

"That's a knife. A very sharp one. As long as you follow my instructions exactly, we won't need to use it."

Her eyes burned, and she felt tears leak into the fabric of her blindfold.

"Are we clear, Deborah?"

Time collapsed. She was back in the doctor's office, the doctor blanching with concern and disapproval, saying, *"Are we clear, Deborah?"*

Sibyl said yes. She was clear.

"Very good," said the man who was not Jax. "Come with me then." He tugged Sibyl forward, and she took a step. Then another. Her wrists were jammed together. Her eyes useless.

They were near the barn doors. She smelled the night air—jasmine and sage and the brine of the sea far below the canyon.

She wanted to run, fling herself forward, reach that fresh air.

"Step lively now," said the man.

Sibyl stepped. They had walked past the doors. They were still in the barn. A door creaked. The ground crisped under her feet. She was walking on straw. The door creaked again, and she knew where she was. Her chest clenched.

He was putting her in the goat stall; the gamy, intestinal scent of the animals was unmistakable. She gagged, then fought to control herself, forcing long breaths of the fetid air into her lungs, willing herself to adjust.

When she was sure she would not vomit, she said softly, "Who are you?"

The man chuckled. "Such a subjective question, isn't it? Who is *anyone*, really?"

Sibyl's toe caught something on the ground, and she lost her footing. The man caught her by the elbow. "Easy now."

He placed a palm on the top of her head and pushed gently. "Sit and stay."

She dropped to her knees, the straw damp and sharp. Beneath her right shin, she felt a soft mound of mud flatten and cling to her skin. She winced at the mushy feel of it, realizing with dismay that it was probably not mud, but goat shit.

She felt the man's elbow press into the center of her back, holding her in position on the stall floor. His breath became louder, and she heard a grunt, then a ripping sound.

Tape. He was tearing tape with his teeth.

He exhaled, and she heard the soft thud of something dropped into the straw. Then his hands were on her hands, maneuvering her wrists so they pressed together, and she felt the tape winding around them.

"No," she said, pointlessly, knowing it was already too late. "Please, don't."

He finished taping her wrists, then he slid his hand beneath her right arm and threaded something strap-like under it. When she felt the sensation of leather closing around the soft flesh of her triceps, she knew exactly what he was doing: tying her up with the shank Twyla used to lead the goats when they were too stubborn to move on their own. Sibyl felt a stab of guilt over not bothering to use the shank earlier today, for merely yelling and kicking at the blameless animals instead of guiding them.

Where were *the goats?* she wondered suddenly.

The strap was very tight now; Sibyl's arm was flush against the metal grate of the stall door, nearly immovable.

"Stay quiet," the man told her. "Don't try to go anywhere, or you'll just hurt yourself. I'll be back soon."

"Please, wait," Sibyl pleaded, terrified of being left alone this way, her vision blocked, her bound arm throbbing from lack of blood flow. "Don't leave me like this. Tell me who you are."

The man gave a short, bitter laugh. "You know, that's a great question. I'm not entirely sure who I am. Funny, it's a feeling I've had ever since I can remember."

"Then tell me who you *think* you are," Sibyl begged, desperate to stall him.

The man went quiet. She heard him breathing.

"I have an idea," he said finally. "Why don't *you* tell me who I am? Isn't that your thing? Telling people what they don't know? Using your *visions* and whatnot?"

"I—I." Her voice quavered. "I can't just do that, on command. It's a process. You would have to—"

"Cut the shit," the man snapped. "I don't have time for this. I'm already late. But let me leave you with one little clue. Something for you to chew on 'til I get back. Fodder for your *process*, if you will."

Her panic swelled. Was she going to die here, wrists bound, kneeling in goat shit? "When are you coming back?" She choked back a sob.

"Quit being such a crybaby, *sis*."

"What?"

"You heard me. I'm asking you to get it together, sister. Just sit here like a bump on a log 'til I get back. Is that too much to ask? And when I'm back, well, then we can finally get to know each other."

Before she could form an answer, he taped her mouth shut.

"Make any noise, sis, or Debbie, or as you prefer, *Sibyl the Seer,* and I promise, you'll feel that knife again. Except next time I won't go so light. Okay? Don't answer."

Sibyl did not answer.

She sensed him standing up and heard his steps as he moved across the stall, the straw crunching under his feet. The latch to the outer stall door slid open with a soft metal clang, and he was gone.

35

Dawn (the Birthday Girl)

THE YURT—ORION—WAS LIT AGAINST THE NIGHT, A GLOWING SAFFRON orb. Dawn had never been so happy to see it. Her nausea was finally abating, and now that she'd gotten off godforsaken Hydra Hill, and out of the decaying shed, she was starting to feel better. The night was almost over, no matter what Mia decreed. Dawn needed sleep to blot out the strange intensity of the DMT. A *respite*, for God's sake, the very thing Mia had promised on her original invitation to the party.

A respite from reality.

It had been a far cry from reality, the thing Dawn experienced when she'd drunk the tea, but still, she needed distance from it. Sleep was the only answer.

"I bet Summer's inside," said Mia, skipping up the front steps of the yurt. "Let's go give her shit."

"Gladly," said Joanie.

"Guys, hang on," said Dawn, trying to sound casual, yet assertive. Mia turned around, chin tilted with a hint of challenge. Dawn's breath shortened. Reece squeezed her hand hard, then let go, as if to say, *You can do this, all by yourself.* "Just to be, um, set expectations, I'm staying for ten minutes, max. One drink. It's been such an amazing night, unforgettable really, but I've got to get to bed. You know, I'm officially *old.*"

The pull back to Betelgeuse felt gravitational. She *knew* Quinn was there—her daughter was the last person who'd venture out into the night for no reason—yet Dawn wouldn't be able to relax until she saw her daughter with her own eyes.

"We'll see," said Mia, flinging open the door and stepping inside. Joanie hurried after her. Then Graham.

Dawn didn't move. Neither did Reece. They held each other's eyes. And then Reece whispered, *"I forgive you."*

At least, that's what Dawn thought she said. Her mind was still hazy, gauzed over from the drug. She must have heard wrong—*forgive her for what?*

"What?" said Dawn.

"You heard me." Reece smiled and nodded at the yurt. "Now let's go."

"Actually, I didn't hear you," said Dawn, but Reece had already disappeared inside.

Dawn followed her up the steps to the threshold, heart hammering. Could she still be under the influence of the drug? Everything seemed slightly off, like reality, but askance.

Inside the circular room, soft music spilled over Dawn, some sort of African jazz, full of sensual woodwinds. The now-familiar string lights glimmered along the ceiling. The cavernous room was larger and darker than Dawn remembered from dinner, just hours ago.

It seemed like years.

"Well well well!" Jax's theatrical voice sailed across the room. He sounded a bit out of breath. "Look who's come down from the hill, *quite literally.* The birthday girl! I hear Hunter S. Johnson has truly met his match."

Dawn blinked at him. His good looks seemed almost mawkish to her now: his lips too pouty, cheeks too sculpted, the splay of curls over his forehead too deliberate. "Who?"

"Hunter S. *Thompson,* you doofus!" Mia beelined from the bar in the kitchen and circled Jax's waist from behind, running her hands up and down his abdomen.

"Literature's not his strong suit," Mia cooed, "but Jaxxy's a genius at *other* things." Her fingers kneaded Jax's sides, as if stroking a pet, and his eyes fell shut with pleasure. Still massaging, Mia peered around Jax's buff arm and met Dawn's eyes. Her pink mouth lifted into a smile, and she winked at Dawn.

Dawn turned away. But not before she'd stared long enough at Jax to notice that, despite his conspicuous handsomeness, he looked rather, well, *grimy.* Sweat rings darkened his underarms. There were a few brownish stains across his designer T-shirt and a faint ashy smudge on his high cheekbone. Strange. All weekend he'd kept his appearance impeccable.

"Sorry if the PDA's a bother, Dawnie," Mia said. "Has Jaxxy even offered you a drink?"

"My bad!" said Jax, regaining his usual flamboyance. "Let me pour you a nightcap, Dawnie. I call it the Midnight Toker. It's basically a Manhattan, but hemp-infused."

"Thanks, but I'll pass," said Dawn. "I've ingested enough substances tonight." She peered around Jax and Mia to the seating area, craning her neck for a glimpse of Summer. But she saw only Graham stretched out on one of the couches, elbow tented over his eyes, and Reece seated in one of the chairs, legs tucked beneath her, flipping through an issue of *Sunset* magazine. She seemed suddenly distant, as if she'd detached from the party.

The whole room felt oddly empty to Dawn. Bereft.

"Hey, we figure out where Summer went?" Dawn asked. "And where's Joanie?"

No one answered.

What the hell was wrong with everyone? Wasn't *she* the one who'd had the bad trip on some obscure drug?

Graham sat up. "Sorry, Dawnie. I just got super tired. No, Summer wasn't here. Right, Jax?"

Jax saluted him. "Scout's honor. Haven't seen the lovely lady since dinner."

"No worries though, babe," said Mia to Dawn. "The mystery's solved. While you and Reecie were telling your secrets outside, Joanie realized Summer must've gone back to the cabin. Apparently, it's something she *does* once in a while. Just bails, so Joanie has to go find her."

"What?" said Dawn. "I don't get it. Summer just takes off—for what?"

"Oh, come *on*," Mia cried. "Don't get all prudish on me. Jax, can you translate?"

Jax cleared his throat. "Dawn, what Mia's trying to say is, Summer took off to the cabin so that Joanie would follow and—"

"Get nasty!" Mia finished gleefully. "Now come." She half skipped over to the couch opposite Graham and flopped down, the tips of her cowgirl boots jutting into the air. She pulled the boots off, dropped them on the floor, and patted the spot beside her. "Sit with me, Dawnie-babe, and Jax will make us a drink."

"Coming right up!" said Jax, striding with new purpose back to the bar.

"Could I get a Macallan's neat, my good man?" asked Graham.

"Amen, brother," said Jax.

Dawn felt glued to her spot near the door. Hell if she was going to cozy up between Mia and Graham with a cocktail—it was after midnight.

"I'm done for the night," she said, hearing the tremor in her voice, hating it. "It's been, um, magical, but it's time to call it quits. I'm going to swing by and give Summer and Jo a hug, then hit the hay."

Mia laughed. "Nonsense. Get over here, silly girl. When's the next time we'll have a chance to be together like this? You can sleep all day tomorrow."

Dawn felt herself soften, the too-familiar urge to comply pulling her toward Mia.

"Let her go, Meadows," Graham said.

"No one asked you."

"No pressure, Dawn," said Reece, looking up from her magazine. "You need to do whatever's best for *you*, but if you do change your mind, I can probably be convinced to hang a bit longer. I do have to get on the road pretty early tomorrow, so I'm not sure we'll have another chance."

"Hear *that*, Dawnie?" said Mia, grinning.

Now Dawn was even more confused: *Reece,* sober, exhausted Reece, was encouraging Dawn to stay up?

Quinn.

Dawn forced a deep breath. "Sorry, guys, I'm touched that—"

"Hey, we're not *dictators* here," Mia said. "It's just your besties, wanting more of your delightful presence. So why don't we compromise? You go tell Summer and Jo nighty-night, and give Quinn a little kiss, then come back for a little nightcap. Does that sound better?"

"I'm happy to walk you there and back," said Graham. "I've got Twyla's treasure map nailed at this point." He tapped a finger to his temple. "It'll be like twenty minutes, round trip, if we cut across the meadow."

"Right on!" called Jax, from the bar. Dawn had the urge to strangle him. Who *was* this idiot Mia was supposedly infatuated with?

"So, what's the verdict, Dawnie?" said Mia.

It occurred to Dawn that Mia was giving her the opportunity to exit. The answer was obvious: she could simply *leave* and not return. Graham would understand. And if Summer could do it, why couldn't she?

It was *her* birthday party, after all.

"Yes," said Dawn, smiling. "That's a perfect solution. I'll go give good-night kisses and be right back for"—she paused, trying to remember Jax's stupid cocktail—"my Midnight Toker."

"Fan-fucking-tastic," said Mia.

"Yay," said Reece. "Graham, you'll take her, right?"

"Chivalry's my middle name," said Graham, standing up.

Dawn hated lying to Reece, but they'd see each other in the morning, and very soon, she'd drive up to Oakland and visit her. She and Quinn would make a road trip of it.

"After you, milady," said Graham, meeting Dawn by the door.

"Oh, hey, Mia," said Dawn, trying to sound casual. "Can I have my phone back? It's been a whole day."

"A whole day was not the pledge. Twenty-four hours was the pledge. Tomorrow morning, ten a.m. sharp, you'll all get your precious little machines back. Cross my heart."

"Are you serious?" said Dawn. How many components of this day—this *night*, everything—did Mia have to control?

"Serious as suicide," said Mia, batting her eyes.

Dawn felt like she'd been punched in the gut. She looked to Reece, but she'd returned to reading the magazine.

"Cancer, babe," Jax called out. "I think the expression is serious as *cancer*."

Mia shrugged. "Poetic license. No phones yet, lovelies, but I can offer this." She worked her hand into the pocket of her jeans. "Hey, Graham, think fast."

Dawn saw something red fly across the room. Graham reached to catch it, but missed, and it bounced off his fingers and onto the floor. He bent over and retrieved a small flashlight.

"You throw like a girl, Meadows," he muttered.

Mia threw back her head and laughed. "You're welcome, Grahammy. Didn't want you getting lost in the dark. Now scoot, you two. I want you back here in under thirty."

Mia blew Dawn a kiss. Dawn blew one back, then followed Graham out of the yurt and into the night.

Raj (the Drifter)

RAJ HAD FOLLOWED THE OLD MAN'S ORDERS TO PUNISH THE TRES-
passers for their destructive ways: he'd snuck bear scat into
the shower. He'd filled a bed with pine cones. Finally, this
afternoon, he'd set the bees free to sting the trespassers' nude
flesh.

Sheshnaag had been pleased when Raj saw him to-
day, over by the ridge in the late afternoon, just after Raj had
bid farewell to Quinn. The old man had smiled behind his
hooded eyes, laid a cracked hand on Raj's own. Called him a
good, brave boy.

There would be just one more favor, the man had told him.
The biggest and noblest one yet. If Raj could complete this
final assignment, he and Candace would be welcome to stay
at Celestial Ranch forever. Their safety, this time, would be
guaranteed.

"How?" Raj had asked. Sheshnaag had promised him safety
many times before.

"Wait here," the old man said, and disappeared behind the massive trunk of a nearby oak.

When he'd returned, he was carrying a gun.

Raj felt every muscle stand at attention. He knew nothing about guns except that he hated them. Or rather, that Candace passionately hated them. At a beachfront bar on the island in Florida, she'd gotten into an argument with some locals about background checks and bans on automatics, and Raj had steered her away from the conversation by the shoulder, heart hammering. Too often, Candace let her feelings put her safety at risk.

It was, he thought, with a sickening feeling, as Sheshnaag stood before him, rifle extended (*Mossberg '79*, he identified the curved brown gun to Raj, with pride), exactly what she'd done for Raj.

Put her feelings for Raj in front of everything else.

Raj took the rifle from Sheshnaag. He didn't know what else to do. It was about the weight of his binoculars, the wood grain of the handle worn and smooth.

Then Sheshnaag told him his final assignment.

"No, no," he had repeated. *"I can't."*

It was the first time Raj had told Sheshnaag the Great Protector, no.

The old man had given a shrug of his mighty shoulders, squinted his cloudy blue eyes at Raj with disappointment.

"Okay then. You wanna be a pussy, that's fine. But you and your so-called girlfriend are on your own now."

The words had cut Raj like a blade: *pussy, so-called girlfriend.* Sheshnaag had never spoken this way to him.

"I'm not—I'm not," Raj had begun.

"Do it, then," Sheshnaag had said. *"Do it, and you're safe for life. I'll let you keep the gun. And the dog can even sleep with you every damn night."*

Raj imagined the big wolf dog curled in the cave between him and Candace, keeping watch as the two of them slept against his deep gray fur, the pistol lodged deep in Raj's sleeping bag, never to be used, but there to keep Candace safe.

He imagined the peace he would feel if he and Candace had the wolf dog and the gun.

Perhaps, they could finally relax. Finally return to the joy of being together.

Perhaps, he thought, as a beechie darted through the narrow space between the old man and him, that joy was worth being a murderer once again. Right here, on Celestial Ranch.

In his mind, the hashtag flashed:

#MurdererRajPatel.

He'd already done it once. He supposed he could do it again.

This time, though, it would be for Candace.

He thought of Quinn, how he'd promised to see her tonight, to show her more animals in the woods. How full of trust her green eyes had been when he'd found her on the tire swing, how shocked she'd been when he'd hurled the pine cone into her back.

The thought of hurting her made him want to die. To crumple into the parched forest floor, disappear into the earth.

But he could not die now. Not when Candace was still hidden in the cave.

Raj lifted his eyes to Sheshnaag's, the gun warm in his hand, sunshine hot on the back of his neck. Overhead, the birds crooned louder, as if cheering him on.

At the corner of the old man's lips, the faintest hint of a smile.

"I'll do it," Raj had said. *"I promise."*

37

Dawn (the Birthday Girl)

DAWN AND GRAHAM WALKED THROUGH THE DARK MEADOW, THE BEAM of Mia's flashlight cutting a few feet ahead, the battery low. The temperature had dropped, leaving a faint chill in the air, and Dawn clutched her arms over her chest to keep from shivering. Overhead, the stars had dimmed, and the moon had risen high above the trees.

"Oh hey, take this," Graham said. He began to unzip his hoodie, but Dawn waved him off.

"I'm fine," she said, accelerating her stride. To think she'd been frolicking across this very meadow just a dozen or so hours ago, without a stitch of clothing. Even now, fully dressed, Dawn hardly recognized herself. Had she really just ingested a powerful psychedelic on the edge of a steep canyon and gone to some wild, terrifying place in her mind?

All because Mia had told her to do it.

What had come over her lately? What sort of mother was she? What sort of *person*?

Well, she would redeem herself. Starting now. In just a few minutes, Dawn would reunite with her daughter and start behaving like the *fifty*-year-old adult she had just become.

"I can see you're cold." Graham tried again, panting to keep pace. Dawn was exhausted, but her desire to get back to Quinn was stronger.

He thrust the sweatshirt toward her. Dawn almost took it, but something stopped her. Graham had been behaving strangely all night. Perfectly nice, but *distant,* issuing almost none of the inappropriate jokes or caustic, hilarious observations he usually shared with Dawn. He'd been cordial, and given a complimentary, though careful and generic, mini toast at the end of her birthday dinner, but he just hadn't been himself. As if he were keeping her at arm's length.

Perhaps he was ashamed of what they'd done last night and thought that if he ignored her, it would go away. Graham was probably behaving like every man who'd cheated on his significant other and regretted it.

Well, she had regrets too. She wouldn't accept the charity of his stupid Nirvana hoodie.

"Keep it," she said, and broke into a light jog, her sore legs protesting.

"Okay, Flo-Jo," Graham said, a few full paces behind her, straining for breath. "You have to hang a right up there, over that slope." He pointed the dim beam of the flashlight.

"I *know,*" Dawn lied.

She veered right, crested the slope, and on the other side she spotted Betelgeuse, a single window lit, a yellow stamp against the night.

No more than a hundred yards away, she broke into a full-blown run.

"Dawn," Graham gasped behind her. "Can you *please* wait the fuck up?"

She ignored him, closing the gap to the cabin, feeling a renewed power. Perhaps she would take up running again. She sprinted the last dozen yards, then leaped over the three steps to the splintered porch. Outside the front door, she placed her hands on her knees to slow her breath and calm down—she didn't want to alarm Quinn by bursting in red-faced.

Once she'd collected herself, she turned back toward the meadow to check for Graham.

He was gone.

"Graham?" she called out.

No answer.

She'd run so fast she'd left him behind completely. He must still be trudging up the slope, paying the price for all those secret cigarettes.

She considered waiting for him but decided against it. Her breath steadied, Dawn blotted her sweaty cheeks against her T-shirt, then opened the door of the cabin and stepped inside.

The lights in the living room were off, but the moonlight suffused it with a ghostly glow, and—*dear god!*—there was a votive candle burning on the small table in the kitchen area. Dawn blew them out, the rising smoke stinging her eyes. She had read Twyla's emphatic host notes aloud to Quinn and had repeated, several times, the *"No fires in any way or form! NO BONFIRES, NO SMOKING, NO CANDLES. Celestial Canyon, like most of our beautiful Earth, is in a drought and the wildfire risk is HIGH. Protect our land, cherish the gift that it is, and DO NOT LIGHT FIRES!"*

What was Quinn thinking? Thank goodness Dawn had returned to check on her or Quinn might've burned down the cabin—the entirety of Topanga, for that matter.

Quinn wasn't on the couch, though the rumpled blanket

and scattering of paperback books suggested she'd just been there. Dawn eased the front door closed, leaving a small crack to signal Graham to come in, and crossed the living room to the beaded curtain leading to the bedroom. She pushed through, the beads clacking softly behind her.

The bedroom door was open.

Dawn peered inside. The room was dark, but she could see that both beds were empty, each ancient wool blanket pulled drum-tight across the thin mattress. The way Quinn liked her bed made. Dawn remembered how disheveled her bed had been when she'd left the cabin for the meadow that morning, head and knees throbbing. The thought of her daughter tidying up, so that her hungover mother could slink off and run nude with her friends, then do drugs—Dawn released a low wail of shame.

"Quinn?" She reached for the light switch on the wall.

The room leaped into an anemic glow.

Quinn was not there.

38

Sibyl (the Visionnaire)

"DEAR LORD JESUS, I KNOW THAT I AM A SINNER, AND I ASK FOR YOUR forgiveness. I believe You died for my sins and rose from the dead. I turn from my sins and invite You to come into my heart and life. I want to trust and follow You as my Lord and Savior."

Sibyl was on her sixth recitation of the Sinner's Prayer, her father the Reverend's favorite prayer, one he'd make the congregation recite with him, line by line, every Sunday service.

Her arms had gone numb, and her blindfold was sopped with tears.

"Dear Lord Jesus, I know that I am a sinner—"

The man had returned. She heard his footsteps on the barn floor, the lever lifting on the outer stall door. She'd been praying, conjuring Twyla and her constant appeals to *the goddess*, for someone—anyone—to find her, but now that the man was back, a fresh terror gripped her. Maybe he'd come back to kill her. She remembered the bite of his knife against the back of her neck and bile rose in the back of her throat.

"Hey, Debbie, old gal, I'm back. As promised."

She felt him kneel beside her, his hands busy near her shoulder. The strap around her arm went taut, then slack. He'd cut her loose from the stall door. She nearly thanked him.

"Hold still," he said, gripping her taped wrists. "Got to use my knife now, I don't wanna cut you. Not yet anyway." Sibyl whimpered, and he barked a laugh. "Kidding, kidding."

She held as still as she could, but she was shaking. From fear, from the cool night air. She felt the sharp metal blade slide between her wrists, and then a brief sawing sensation as the man worked the knife against the layers of tape.

He pulled off the tape roughly, the glue tugging at her skin. She sucked in a breath. And then her hands were free.

"Stand up," he ordered, yanking her wrist upward. Slowly, Sibyl stood. Her knees ached and she couldn't feel her feet. He tightened his grip on her wrist. "Don't get excited. Just because the tape's off doesn't mean you're home free. We're going to go outside, and it's going to *look* as though we're just taking a nice late-night stroll together. You know, looking at the stars and shit. But the truth is, my wish is your command. You're going to do exactly what I say, and if you don't—"

The tip of the knife pricked her neck. Closer to her throat this time.

"Are we clear? No funny business, whatsoever?"

She tried to answer, but the tape still sealed her mouth.

"Oh, right," he said. "I better take that off. And your blind-fold. You can't be walking around looking like a kidnapping victim, now, can you? Though that would really be a beautiful sight. Debbie the kidnapper getting kidnapped herself! Poetic justice if I've ever heard it."

What? Sibyl longed to say but couldn't. *What are you talking about?*

"It's a damn shame I can't just keep you like this," he went on. "Taped and blindfolded. But it might cause me some trouble if one of those old hippies who own this shithole property happens to be looking out the window. Old people don't sleep, I hear. But hey, at least you got a little taste of what it *feels* like to get kidnapped."

Sibyl moaned. She wanted to tell him she knew what it felt like to be a prisoner. To take him back to the boxy white church in desperate need of fresh paint and a termite treatment, little Debbie watching her parents work themselves into frenzied states of—what? They claimed it was ecstasy, that they were inhabited directly by the Lord on those blazing-hot summer Sundays in Harmony Township, Pennsylvania, population 562, filling them with so much joy their bodies were overtaken with the sensation, causing them to jerk and leap and collapse on the mealy, half-rotted floor of the church.

For as long as she could remember, she'd dreamed of getting out, far from the farmlands of Pennsylvania, far from her father's altar, to a place where she could finally begin to *live*.

All at once, the man who used to be Jax yanked the tape from her mouth, and the blindfold from her eyes.

She yelped and clamped her hands to her lips, struggling to focus in the faint light. Blurrily, she could see Jax's face—though he was no longer Jax to her at all—peering scornfully down at her.

"Spare me the waterworks, Debbie," he said. "Take my hand. Come on."

Sibyl swallowed the urge to scream it this time: *Don't call me Debbie!* Then she thought of her sessions with the guests earlier, how angry and defensive Graham and Summer and Joanie had become each time Sibyl had confronted them with even a vague suggestion that they were withholding the truth.

She would not become defensive now, she decided; it would only make her appear desperate and weak.

She took his hand and let him lead her through the door to the pen where Sibyl had shooed the goats that very afternoon. Poor Diurn and Nocturne. She hoped they were somewhere safe, maybe with Twyla at the house.

"Hurry up," he said, tugging her hand and lengthening his stride. She obeyed.

The night was deep and still. The moon had moved high in the sky and the stars seemed to have dimmed. The man who had called himself Jax walked fast over the coarse earth, around the base of Hydra Hill, onto the faint trail leading through the trees. Even the leaves overhead did not move as Sibyl panted and struggled to keep pace. Was this the same world she had left behind when she entered the barn for her session with Jax, what she had hoped would be her last session of the night? It felt changed. Or maybe it was just she who had changed.

The trail ended at a clearing, and they continued up a long slope. It grew steeper, but he did not slow his stride or relax his iron grip on her hand. Pressed against his, Sibyl's palm had turned cold and sweaty. Her lungs squeezed, and then she felt a familiar bloom of pain open behind her eyes.

She knew the feeling as well as her own face. When the pain started this way, there was no stopping it. The migraine was irreversible now, a sickening inevitability: a runaway train on a downslope, a foot stepped off the roof of a tall building.

In the same instant the pain announced itself, Sibyl recognized the man leading her through the night. The migraines worked this way: with the sentence of pain came the gift of knowledge.

Every time.

"Abel," she said, her voice shaky but finally certain in her knowledge. "It's you. My little brother."

He stopped in his tracks, jerking Sibyl's arm.

"Obviously," he said. "For a psychic, you sure aren't very perceptive. Now keep walking."

She walked, her heart and head throbbing in sync, the pain possessing her completely. She closed her eyes and let him guide her, knowing she could trip on a root and break her ankle, or step on a rattlesnake. Knowing he could be escorting her to her death. Not caring. All that mattered was the pain, filling her, taking shape around her like a membrane.

Minutes passed. The baked ground crunched underfoot. Sibyl's feet kept moving. Somewhere, an owl hooted; seconds later, another returned the call.

Sibyl understood they were bidding each other farewell. Through the burnt-orange glow of her pain, she felt a well of infinite sadness.

"We're here," he said. "Final destination."

She forced her eyes open. Her vision swam, then cleared. She blinked and looked around her. The familiarity of what she saw was both a shock and a comfort.

She was standing in Twyla's backyard, right next to the house, beside the triangular hatch that led to the basement. The slanted door was propped open with a brick, revealing a strip of light below.

"Sisters first," Abel said, heaving open the door and placing his hand on the back of her neck, forcing her down.

39

SUNDAY, JUNE 26, 2022

Raj (the Drifter)

RAJ SLIPPED THROUGH THE SHADOWS OF THE TREES RINGING THE meadow, on his way to Betelgeuse, the sky no longer an inky black but a grainy slate gray, offering the faintest hint of morning.

He was taking a great risk, he knew, going to find Quinn like this, but then, he'd already broken his promise to Sheshnaag. Defied the old man's wishes, abandoned the gun. Left the gate to the goats' pen wide open, rather than shooting them between the eyes, the way Sheshnaag had instructed.

Instead, Raj had freed them, like he'd done with the bees.

In doing so, he'd lost his Great Protector. Lost Sheshnaag. Left in his place, Raj understood now, was an angry, frightened old man with big, stooped shoulders and a great crack in his heart.

And Raj was on his own.

The old man would never forgive him. He was no longer

the Protector. No longer Sheshnaag the Great. Now, he would return to Candace and protect her himself. He no longer needed the old man. He didn't need the gun, or the massive wolf dog.

He needed only to see the green-eyed girl from the tire swing, Quinn, *MacQuinn, Ó Cuinn,* one more time.

He ran faster, his feet flying over the rocks and scrub grass without the slightest stumble or pause.

His body knew the way.

If he could be in Quinn's presence, if only for a moment.

If only he could touch her pale, smooth skin. Feel the life-giving warmth of her flesh against his.

Then he would be strong enough to survive.

SHE OPENED THE cabin door wearing—a dress. Blue and flowy, with a white sash tied at her hip. As if she'd been expecting him.

"Good evening," she said, not sounding like the same Quinn who had soothed a wild beast in the woods. More formal, as if she'd rehearsed.

"You look pretty," he said.

She shifted in place, dropped her eyes. He had embarrassed her.

"I'm sorry," he said. "I just—need to speak the truth."

"Come inside," she said, beckoning, and he followed her into the cabin's dingy living room. Instantly, Raj spotted a candle on the table, its flame dancing inside a mason jar beside two wineglasses filled to the brim. His mouth went dry. He eyed the exposed wood walls of the room, and remembered how the old man had warned Raj to never *ever* light a fire on Celestial Ranch. Not even on the rare winter night when frost glittered on the heart-shaped leaves of the bougainvillea that wrapped the barn in a deep pink cloak.

"Are you pyrophobic?" Quinn asked, sitting down on the ratty brown couch in the living room.

He continued to stand.

"Uh—what's that?" Raj tried to steady himself.

"A rare phobia—fear of fire. Wikipedia says some people can't even stand next to a burning candle. No birthday cakes. You look like maybe you have that?"

He forced a deep breath, reminding himself it was only a single candle, contained in glass. Nothing bad would happen.

She handed him a wineglass and took one for herself.

"Thank you," he said, taking a sip. It was cheap and sweet but the taste of it thrilled him because, he realized, beautiful Quinn had been planning for his visit. Had gone to the trouble of making the shabby little cabin romantic, with a candle and wine.

His chest tightened. He knew he should leave, very soon, and go to Candace in the cave.

But he found himself sitting down beside Quinn on the couch. The springs groaned under his weight, and Quinn giggled.

"Do you like the wine?" she asked.

"Yes," Raj lied. "I haven't had alcohol in a very long time." This was true; two sips and his head was already buzzing.

"The bottle came with the cabin. My mom says it tastes like crap, but she drank some anyway. She was nervous."

"Why?"

"Seeing old friends. Especially Aunt Mia, who was, like, mad at Mom for years. And Aunt Reece. But that is more of a sad thing, because she almost died."

"How?"

Quinn paused. "She tried to kill herself. A long time ago. Because of something bad my mom did, I think."

"What was it?"

"Oh." Quinn shrugged. "My mom let Reece take the blame for a big mistake. Like, a really big one. I don't know what it was exactly, but Reece lost her job and got really sad. And then . . . she had to go into the hospital for a long time."

"I'm—I'm sorry," Raj faltered. He sat in silence, his mind racing, searching for the right words to comfort Quinn. He'd never been good at giving comfort. That was Candace's magic power. She gave and gave, and Raj took and took.

His eyes filled with tears of shame. He blinked them back and took a long drink of the bad wine. Then he turned to face Quinn.

"I've done bad things too."

Quinn's green eyes held his. He braced himself for her question, *Like what?*, but it didn't come. Instead, she inched closer to him on the couch, folding one long leg beneath her body, until her knee pressed against his thigh.

"They'll forgive you," she said, putting her wineglass back on the table, untouched. "Reece forgave my mom. At least, I think so."

Raj could not move. His heart felt like wild horses in his chest.

"Put your glass down too," Quinn whispered, and Raj did.

Then she pulled him toward her and kissed him.

Her lips were soft, with a faint trace of salt. He'd never tasted anything so wonderful. He moaned and leaned into her, feeling the delicate slickness of her tongue in his mouth.

Then, on the steps outside the cabin, footsteps.

Quinn sprang away from him, onto her feet with the grace of a cat.

"It's my mom. She's here! Get into the bathroom. Follow me."

She pulled him up from the sofa with a strength he had not imagined, and led him through a beaded curtain and down a hallway, into the ugly pink bathroom where he'd planted the bear scat just yesterday, never letting go of his hand.

40

Dawn (the Birthday Girl)

DAWN STARED AT THE EMPTY ROOM, THE IMPECCABLY MADE BEDS AND an open suitcase at the foot of each, her brain refusing to register that *Quinn was gone.*

She slapped off the light switch, as if to erase the scene before her. A sob gathered in her throat.

She stepped back into the hall and nearly collided with Quinn.

"Baby!" Dawn yelped. She flung her arms around her daughter.

Quinn kept her arms at her sides like a toy soldier.

"Why are you yelling?" said Quinn.

"If you heard me yelling, why didn't you answer me?"

"I was busy."

"Busy? Doing what? It's after mid—" Dawn stopped herself; Mia's voice in her mind admonishing her to *let it go.*

Quinn took a step back, pulling out of Dawn's embrace. Dawn noticed that her daughter looked disheveled, her cheeks flushed and dark hair flat against one side of her face, mussed on the other. Dawn reached out to smooth the puffy side, but Quinn dodged her hand.

"I'm sorry for interrupting," said Dawn, trying not to feel hurt by Quinn's avoidance of her touch, the same feeling of rebuff she'd been dealing with for twenty years. "And yes, I was at my birthday party. And it was, um, lovely. But it's over now."

"Okay," said Quinn. She adjusted her stance so she was standing in the center of the hallway, squarely facing Dawn, as if blocking her.

"Were you—getting ready for bed?" Dawn asked. "Or," she revised, noticing that Quinn was still wearing her "day clothes"—a baggy black T-shirt and sweats.

Quinn paused. "Yes. I was getting ready for bed. I have my—you know—" Quinn trailed off and angled her gaze to the floor. Dawn watched her pale cheeks color with discomfort.

And then Dawn got it. Relief coursed through her. Not only was Quinn *not* missing, but her hiding in the bathroom now made perfect sense: she had her period. It had been happening for nearly a decade, and yet she was nearly as uncomfortable with it now as she'd been at thirteen. Her embarrassment usually irritated Dawn, how if Dawn dared to ask her if she needed tampons, or if she wanted Motrin for cramps, Quinn would turn her head to the side and mumble an inaudible answer, if she even answered at all. Now Dawn felt almost grateful for her daughter's quasi-phobia.

She offered Quinn an understanding smile. "Got it, honey. I'll let you finish up in the bathroom, okay? Then I'll have my turn. And then we can go to bed. I don't know about you, but I'm exhausted."

"I'm not," said Quinn. "I'm going to stay up and read."

"Helloooo?" Graham's voice came from the living room. "Anybody home?"

"One sec!" called Dawn. "Be right out!"

"Why is *he* here?"

Before Dawn could answer, the beaded curtains parted and Graham stepped into the hallway, red-faced and winded. "*There* you are." He placed his hands on his upper thighs, panting. "Quinn, hi! Sorry to barge in so late. Gosh, it's been a long time. You're so, ah, grown up. It's amazing."

Quinn didn't answer but latched her eyes to Dawn's. *Get him out of here.*

Dawn tried to explain. "Graham was just walking across the meadow with me, so I wouldn't get lost."

"You could just use the map," said Quinn. "It's a good map."

"I'm bad with maps, honey, you know that. And my sense of direction's not great."

"Yeah, I know," said Quinn, with a certainty that stung. How many *more* of Dawn's deficiencies did Quinn "know" beyond a shadow of a doubt? That Dawn was anxious practically all the time? That twenty-two years into motherhood, she still felt she didn't know how to do it? That last night she'd gotten so drunk and needy, she'd accidentally had sex with the tall, stooped, bespectacled man Quinn was regarding with palpable disdain?

She felt herself wither. She wanted nothing more than to crawl deep under the scratchy wool blanket on the cabin's flimsy bed and sleep until the morning sun blazed over Celestial Ranch and she and Quinn could drive out of Topanga Canyon and back into their lives. Then, she vowed, *then* she would begin her second act—or was it her third?—as an entirely new Dawn. A Dawn who behaved like the self-assured, clear-eyed, forward-thinking woman she was supposed to have become long ago. A person who could hold her own in the presence of

Mia Meadows. A person worthy of respect in the heart of someone as pure as Reece Mayall.

As soon as she got out of Topanga Canyon, so help her, she
would become *that person*.

Graham cleared his throat. "Uh, guys? Did Summer and
Joanie stop by here?"

Dawn snapped back to attention. "Quinny, did Aunt Joanie
or Aunt Summer stop by?"

"They're not my *aunts*," said Quinn.

"Oh—r-right." Dawn blinked in confusion. Why had she
said *Aunt*? Quinn hadn't called Summer and Joanie *Aunt* in
years. Since just before the Project fell apart.

Why did time seem to be collapsing tonight? Was it the
spiked tea she'd drunk? No, Dawn reminded herself, she'd
felt it from the moment she'd set foot on Celestial Ranch, this
sense of the present and past shuffling together like bridged
cards.

"Summer and Joanie then?" Dawn corrected herself.

"No." Quinn sounded defensive. "I haven't seen anyone
since you left for your party. I've been here alone."

"Oh, honey." Dawn's guilt spiked. "I'm so sorry, I—"

"Well then, I'll get your mom back to you ASAP," Graham
said. "We're just going to pop back out and say good night to
Summer and Joanie, then head over to the yurt to close out the
party. Your mom will be back like—" He snapped his fingers.

"Oh, I'm way too tired for that." Dawn had also forgotten
her false promise to Mia to return to the yurt for a final nightcap. The thought was absurd now. It was far too late, her eyes
heavy and aching from the dry canyon air. Surely Graham would
understand. "In fact, Graham, could you possibly go check
on Summer and Jo without me? I don't think they're waiting
around for me to kiss them good night."

She didn't want to leave Quinn again. Yes, Summer's sudden absence had worried her, but Joanie had already gone after her. If Graham went too, was it necessary for Dawn to abandon her poor daughter yet again?

"Of course, you don't need to go all the way back to Orion," said Graham. "Mia will deal. But I think we should at least check on Jo and Summer. It'll take fifteen minutes, tops. I mean, we haven't seen Summer since we drank the . . ."

"I know, I know," Dawn said. "You should check on them. I mean, I'm sure they're fine—you know how those two are when they're fighting—"

"They weren't fighting."

"They're *always* fighting."

"Come with me." Graham's voice was flat but insistent.

"Please," Dawn said, exasperated. "I just want to go to bed. I'll see them in the morning. My daughter is—"

"*Mom*." Quinn spoke with such uncharacteristic sharpness, Dawn almost jumped. "Go with him."

"What?"

"Just go with him." She crossed her long arms over her chest, as if the decision were final. Dawn couldn't remember the last time her daughter had spoken so assertively. Or suggested that Dawn *leave*. She told herself to be glad—this was what she'd been wanting, wasn't it? This was the goal: for Quinn to behave like a typical independent adult who didn't want to be doted on by her mother.

It was the goal. And yet, it hurt.

"Mom," Quinn repeated. She took a few steps back, widening the gap between her and Dawn, as if saying: *go.*

"Quinn, what's going on with you?" Dawn asked, moving down the hallway toward her. "Why are you acting like this?"

"Like what?"

"Uh, I think I'll wait outside," said Graham. "I'll be on the porch." He pushed back through the beaded curtain. Dawn waited until she heard the front door shut.

"Look, Quinn, I know you're upset with me for leaving you alone so much this weekend. I just want you to understand that I love you *so* much, sweetheart. I never intended to drag you here like this. Your father was supposed to—"

"Stop it! Stop saying you're sorry!" Quinn whirled around and charged back down the hall. "Stop saying you love me!" She pressed her hands over her ears as she bounded away from Dawn, her elbows poking out from her head like sharp wings.

As if she wished to fly away.

Quinn stomped into the bathroom and slammed the door shut.

Dawn felt the cabin walls shudder.

Empty of Quinn, the hallway became an unbearable space. The single bulb on the ceiling threw its harsh LED glow across the nubbed brown carpet, its too-high wattage an affront to Dawn's eyes. She thought suddenly of a doctor shining a wand into the eyes of a patient, searching for signs of life, lifting one eyelid, then the other, and then in her mind, she saw Reece, the long slender shape of her on the gurney, somehow retaining her grace even beneath the white sheet as the EMTs hoisted her into the—

Dawn screamed.

"Graham, wait!" she cried, and bolted through the beaded curtain, through the living room, and onto the porch, where he said he'd be waiting. She shut the cabin door behind her, hot tears flooding her vision.

She blotted her eyes with her knuckles and stood blinking. Graham hadn't waited. He'd given up on her, apparently, and had already started walking. Dawn could see the weak glow of the flashlight knifing over the ground up ahead, in time with his long stride.

"Graham!" she called. "Wait! I'm coming."

She saw Graham's light change direction, back toward her, then go still.

He was waiting for her.

From some far-off place in the canyon, Dawn heard the coyotes' crooning wails. *How-woo. How-wooooo.*

Had the howling just begun, or had it been carrying on all this time and she'd simply failed to notice until now?

Dawn took a deep breath and jumped from the porch to the dry, dark ground.

41

SUNDAY, JUNE 26, 2022

Twyla (the Hostess)

TWYLA HURRIED DOWN THE FRONT STEPS, MAKING SURE TO LEAVE THE porch light on, in case Arnold came home. She cut across the lawn, dodging her sculptures in the dark of the wee morning hours. She was proud of how intimately she knew Celestial Ranch, like the body of a longtime lover.

She reached her golf cart parked under the big live oak and turned the key. She stepped hard on the gas and steered the cart onto the path that led down the long slope into a thicket of woods. She gained speed on the descent, enjoying the feel of her long hair loose from its usual tight braid, and caught the trail leading through the trees. She wove around one bend and another, the headlights catching glints of animal eyes through the trees, and felt a flush of pride that even in the dead of night, the sight of creatures in the woods didn't scare her.

This was her home. Forever. She had grown into her truest self here, the real Twyla, and she would die here too.

As she drove, she plotted the route in her mind: At the end

of the woods, where the path cleaved toward the barn in one direction and Andromeadow in the other, she'd swing east into another forested swath, where the beehive lay cracked open.

The thought of Arnold crouching in the dark woods beside the wrecked hive, as if mourning a ransacked grave, Klondike waiting at his feet—it was too sad. She reached the clearing where the path forked and angled toward the meadow, driving faster as her desire to find Arnold reached an urgent pitch.

What if he'd hurt himself? What if he'd tried to climb a tree and fallen, broken his neck, or—

"No," she said into the night. She couldn't leave Celestial Ranch, but she couldn't live here alone either.

The golf cart shuddered. Twyla pressed harder on the gas, but the cart began to slow, and in seconds, came to a stop.

Only then did she notice the little orange light in the center of the dashboard.

She'd run out of gas.

She slapped her hand on her forehead, disgusted that she could be so careless.

Well, at least she hadn't gotten far. She was still a three-minute drive (or a twenty-minute walk) from the hive, but the barn, where she kept her gas canisters, was no more than a hundred yards away. She would walk to the barn, say a quick hello to poor Sibyl, give the sleeping goats a little pat, then grab her spare fuel and be on her way. She pulled her headlamp from the pocket of her fleece and hopped out of the golf cart, leaving the key in the ignition. She flicked on the headlamp and walked as fast as she could toward the barn.

The heavy, rotted doors were shut. She heaved them open and stepped into the dim, cavernous space, waking the barn swallows in the rafters above.

"Sibyl? It's me! Surprise."

She hurried down the shed row, wishing she had a slice of peach bread or leftover lentils to offer. Poor Sibyl must be peckish after all those hours in the barn, and tired of sitting on a bale of hay behind Twyla's old card table.

When Twyla reached the far end of the barn, Sibyl was nowhere to be found. The purple tapestry Sibyl used as a tablecloth was lopsided, baring the faux-wood surface of the card table on one side and hanging nearly to the ground on the other. Twyla straightened it, smoothing the thin fabric. Sibyl had taken a break, apparently. In the morning, Twyla would make Sibyl a breakfast fit for a queen.

She couldn't resist taking a minute to peek at the goats. She loved watching them sleep, curled in the hay side by side in their stall, noses tucked against each other's shoulders. Nocturne and Diurn brought her such reliable joy, the sort she used to find in Arnold's presence.

First, she stopped in the tack room, making sure to rustle enough to warn the mice and beechies of her presence before flipping on the light and lifting a red fuel canister from a shelf.

Then she made her way to the goats' stall, quieting her footsteps as she approached; her little friends were light sleepers.

Except Nocturne and Diurn were not there. The outer door to the pen stood wide open, and when Twyla peered out into the pen, she knew the goats weren't outside the barn either.

They were missing.

Twyla charged across the pen, fuel canister banging her hip, the light of her headlamp stuttering across the ground. She reached the gate at the other side, where the safety of the enclosed pen ended, the wilds of the unfenced property began, and where the coyotes and mountain lions and bobcats roamed hungry and free.

The gate stood wide open.

On its top slat, in the center, was Twyla's old gun.

The Mossberg rifle Arnold had given her for target practice decades ago, before Twyla had understood the evils of gun ownership.

The gun had been locked in its case down in the basement for years. Nearly impossible to find, unless you knew where to look.

Someone knew.

Fear seeped through her, melding with disbelief at her own stupidity.

How could she have trusted these people, her so-called *guests*, to run wild and booze-soaked across her property all weekend and *not* disturb the natural order of Celestial Ranch? The signs had been everywhere, for goodness' sake: in the way Klondike had responded to puffy-lipped Ms. Meadows, in the bear that'd found them so distasteful he'd shat right in their shower, and in the angry swarm of bees descending upon their naked frolic in the meadow.

They'd even found her gun. Left it on top of the gate as some joke, a sick prank.

Or perhaps they'd just been drunk, too immersed in their own pleasure to bother doing whatever they'd intended to do with the rifle.

She should have known. She'd been warned of their menace, yet she'd chosen not to see it. Chosen the tawdry promise of their money instead. In doing so, she'd put her sweet goats at risk. Sibyl, Twyla knew, would never be so careless as to leave any gates open.

This was all the work of her guests. Twyla was sure of it. Only Mia Meadows and her self-important, self-indulgent friends would be so rude and unthinking as to let her goats out.

To play with guns.

Twyla grabbed the rifle from the fence, the gas canister swinging from her other hand, and headed back to the trail where she'd left the golf cart. Her breath came short and fast as she jogged; moonlight slatted through the trees. She reached the cart and poured the fuel into the empty tank.

First, she would find Arnold, then she would go down into the basement—*her* basement, beneath *her* house—and tell the guests exactly what she thought of them. That they would never, ever be welcome at Celestial Ranch again.

Twyla closed the cap over the gas tank and hopped into the driver's seat.

The key was gone from the ignition.

Her rage turned to cold, hard fear.

Letting the goats out by accident was one thing. But if one of the guests had taken her key too—well, what did that mean?

Could the guests have harmed Arnold? Sibyl too?

Twyla couldn't imagine why they would, but she did know, as she ran back to her house, that something was very, very wrong.

She would get to the bottom of it, right now. She would stop kowtowing to the pushy, greedy city folk who'd taken over her land, those trespassers, and she would make sure her husband and dear friend and beloved goats were safe.

Twyla would take charge. She'd infuse herself with the power of the goddess and make things *right* at Celestial Ranch.

Dawn (the Birthday Girl)

DAWN STUMBLED OVER A BUCKLED ROOT, KEEPING HER EYES ON THE faint glow of Graham's flashlight up ahead. He was waiting for her on the edge of Andromeadow. Dawn seemed to remember from Twyla's map that Vega, Summer, and Joanie's cabin, was in the other direction, around the *back* of Betelgeuse.

"Hurry up!" Graham called. His voice sounded small and distant. His light looked fainter and farther away than it had just seconds ago, as if he'd taken a flying leap down the edge of the meadow, but Dawn figured it was merely a trick of the darkness, or the late hour, or her weary, addled mind. All of the above.

She pushed faster—just how many miles had she run on her own damn birthday?—feeling ridiculous for chasing after Graham, but Quinn's disdain had hurt too much. She hadn't known what to *do* with it. Her daughter had never behaved so scornfully and had never pushed Dawn away. She missed the long-past days of the Nurtury, when she could share Quinn's most confounding behaviors with the group every week and count on their understanding. On Reece's wise, compassionate advice. The topic of parenting felt off-limits to Dawn in the company of her friends now. With the exception of Mia and her unsolicited advice, they'd all avoided speaking of their children this weekend. No one had offered anything beyond basic information: Summer had mentioned Maisie attending college in Washington State, a special program for students on the spectrum. Mia's Nate, Dawn knew, worked as a software developer and competed in open-water swim races. Graham planned to visit Ethan in Park City, where he worked as a chairlift operator. And as for Quinn, well, Dawn hadn't really said much of anything.

Reece, of course, never had children of her own.

It was if they'd tacitly agreed the topic was too risky. As if talk of their now-grown children might slide them into the dark places they never wished to return to, into the *toxic topics*.

Dawn was jogging through a patch of tall, scraggly weeds when she felt a hot prick stab her ankle. She yelped and crouched down, groping her leg for whatever had lodged itself in her flesh. She found a burr the size of a coffee bean and yanked it out. When she stood again, her ankle smarting, she could no longer see Graham's light.

"Graham?" she called.

There was a long beat of silence.

Then, from somewhere in the trees ahead, his voice came: "Over here!"

There it was—the light. Even fainter than before, but Dawn saw its dim ray in the trees. He'd gone ahead and started on the path through the woods. The asshole couldn't be bothered to wait two minutes. Patience had never been his strong suit, she thought, wincing at the memory of last night, when they were rolling on the ground together.

"Dawn!" he called to her again. "Follow me! Come on."

She looked to the pale slash of light in the trees, then back to the cabin, but she'd followed Graham so far across the meadow that Betelgeuse was way behind her now. She didn't want to make her way back to the cabin by herself. She suddenly felt acutely alone.

Where had everyone gone? She was supposedly running in the direction of Summer and Joanie, yes, and she remembered leaving Mia and Reece back in the yurt, and Quinn in Betelgeuse, and yet . . . they all seemed impossibly far away. As if they'd never really come to Topanga Canyon at all.

But Graham *was* just ahead in the woods, she reminded herself, fighting for breath as she charged ahead. She could still make out the thin column from his dying flashlight, cutting toward the sky, as if he were holding his arm in the air. When she was parallel to the beam, she veered from the edge of the meadow and into the trees. She'd assumed she would find the path here. The one Graham had taken, leading them to Vega. As if saying good night to Joanie and Summer even mattered now. Dawn had lost all sense of purpose. A pure animal fear overtook her, an instinct as base as hunger. She needed to *not* be alone. Even if it meant being with Graham in the woods again.

She ran through the trees, abandoning all hope of a path, branches and leaves snagging at her face, tearing at her clothes. The beam grew closer.

"Graham!" she yelled.

Then she was beside the vertical ray of light. Except Graham wasn't holding it. The red flashlight was stuck into the ground.

Graham was nowhere.

Dawn grabbed the flashlight and shone it ahead, searching for a way out. But she saw nothing but trees. She whirled the dying light in a full circle around her, checking to make sure someone, or something, wasn't waiting to—what? Attack her? The thought felt silly, but the feeling was undeniably real. She wasn't safe out here.

Everywhere looked the same: woods and more woods. Except—wait. Off to her left was a clearing. A bare spot of tree-less ground. An opening, a respite.

"Respite from reality." Dawn saw the line in her head, printed on Mia's fancy invitation.

She moved toward the clearing. Perhaps Reece would be there. Waiting with open arms to hold Dawn close and murmur into her ear, *"Everything will be okay, baby girl."*

Dawn stepped into the clearing. A bald patch of hard, dry earth ringed by endless trees. In the center, a strange hulking structure, like a giant, wide corncob. Pocked across its surface and lopped off jaggedly at the top, as if something had bitten it.

It was, Dawn realized, as she stepped closer, flicking what was left of the light across the surface of the thing, a beehive. Or *part* of a beehive. The bottom half. The rest of it torn off by, Dawn somehow knew, some angry, ravenous thing.

She felt a sudden strong presence. The clear knowledge that she was no longer alone. She flicked her dying flashlight beam through the darkness.

It caught two lumpy, furred shapes standing in the tall ferns nearby.

A pair of goats, staring at her, their eyes like lit marbles.

Dawn stared back, frozen.

Then the goats moved in sudden unison, leaping straight toward Dawn, bearing down on her.

"Reece!" Dawn screamed, the name flying from her lips before she'd even tried to form it. She whirled and ran out of the clearing, back into the labyrinth of woods.

43

Dawn (the Birthday Girl)

DAWN RAN THROUGH THE WOODS, EYES BLURRED AND STINGING WITH tears, legs and lungs on fire. She had no idea where she was going. Only that she needed to get away from the charging goats. Out of the woods.

Finally, the trees parted, and she burst into a clearing. Two lights beckoned: the moon high above, a bleached thumbprint, and a round yellow glow up ahead. The light of a house. Betelgeuse? No—Betelgeuse was smaller. It was, she realized, Twyla's house. She summoned her muscles and charged, ascending a hill. She reached the top and kept running, through the arch of a grand oak tree and up to the porch, where the light burned beside the front door. She knocked and waited, knocked and waited. Nothing. She turned the knob, and the door opened into a foyer. The house beyond it was pitch-dark. She groped for a light switch along the wall but couldn't locate one.

"Twyla!" she called. "Knock knock, hello! It's Dawn Sanders, your Airbnb guest. You know, the birthday girl. I'm so sorry, but I seem to have gotten lost . . ."

No answer. She stepped into the living room.

"Hello?"

No one was home; the sense of absence in the house was palpable. But where would Twyla have gone? How many times had the woman reminded Dawn she'd be *right here*, ready to help with anything at a moment's notice?

Dawn stepped to the bottom of the staircase and rapped her knuckles against the wall. The banister quivered.

She cupped her hands to her mouth and called up the stairs, "Twyla? I hate to wake you, but it's a . . . semi-emergency." Was it though? Maybe she'd simply lost track of her friends. Imagined the goats who had appeared like ghosts. She *had* taken one of the world's strongest hallucinogenic drugs only a few hours ago.

No. She remembered the impossibly white eyes of the goats; the extinguished look of something that had once been alive.

Dawn moved into the kitchen, a big room with copper pots hanging from a rack over the center island. A door to her left, an unlit hallway to her right. Glasses and plates with forks still resting across the remains of a meal, as if Twyla and her husband had just finished dinner. Then vanished.

The silence of the kitchen engulfed her. She felt like the last person on earth.

She leaned on the tiled island and breathed.

Where had everyone gone?

Then she heard it.

A soft whimpering. Like a puppy begging to be let out.

Where was it coming from? She held her breath.

It came again, louder this time. A sustained moan.

It was coming from somewhere in the floor.

As if the house itself were afraid.

She leaped to the front door and stumbled back outside, stepping carefully across the open ground behind Twyla's house; a dried-up yard without grass, only weeds and a large patch of withered plants in neat rows: a dead garden.

Her fear softened with the relief of being outside the big house and its suffocating silence. She turned in a circle, trying to orient herself. How long had she been gone? Was Quinn awaiting her return in a panic, pacing the slanted floors and chewing on her shirt? Or was she the *new* Quinn now, glad her mother was gone?

And what of Summer and Joanie? Had they made it back to Vega? Why had Graham rushed ahead? Had Mia and Reece been worried when Dawn never returned?

What if something terrible had also hurt her friends? Could her own daughter be in great danger too? Or worse, could Quinn already be—

Dawn screamed.

Her voice echoed off the ancient walls of the canyon and returned.

She closed her eyes, willing the night to end.

When she opened them, she saw the light.

Not the soft orange-pink light of dawn, but a strip of electric light along the side of Twyla's house. The glow came from beside the stairs; she hadn't noticed it before. A wood-slatted triangle tipped on its side.

It was, she realized, a door. A hatch leading underground, propped open a few inches.

She stepped closer, heart thudding. She saw a brick wedged

beneath the hatch. A metal handle protruding from the center of the thick wood. She reached down and pulled the door.

It was heavy. She struggled to lift it, had to use both hands. Once open, she peered into the luminous square in the ground. A staircase slanted down. Was this fucking real? Maybe she was still tripping, stuck inside her own mind, on a never-ending journey into madness. And this was the gate to hell.

She lowered herself into the hatch, bracing against the cold metal opening, then felt for the top stair with her feet.

Please, God, please don't let something, someone, reach up and grab me.

Slowly, she began to descend the metal stairs. She heard a faint echo of her steps far below.

She began to cry softly, terrified, but unable to make herself turn around.

She'd taken three steps down when the light from below flicked off and on. Then it flickered manically for a few seconds before dying completely.

"Help me!" Dawn sobbed into the darkness. "Oh, God, please. Please!" She squeezed her eyes shut and stood still, too frightened to take another step. Her body shook, making the metal steps creak and groan.

Someone, something, was nearby. She felt movement below. She smelled sweat. Perfume. Candle wax.

"Oh, oh—Jesus, no! Stay away from me!"

The light leaped on.

"*Surprise!*" screamed a chorus of voices below, and she felt hands on her legs, helping her down.

She stepped off the last stair and onto solid ground, blinking away tears, struggling to see. To understand.

Finally, the space around her came into focus. She'd entered a large, cluttered space lit by soft lamplight and flickering candles. Piles of wicker furniture, odd sculptures of twisted metal, stacks of canvases leaning against the wall, boxes and crates and bins full of stuff.

Her friends. They were all here, standing in a circle around her—Mia in a wispy black dress and Jax at her side, Graham in a fresh linen blazer. Summer and Joanie, perfectly intact, holding hands. And Reece, beautiful Reece, in the same pretty dress she'd worn earlier. They all wore jaunty party hats and held full champagne glasses.

Dawn stood gaping, unable to speak.

"You made it!" said Mia, placing a party hat on Dawn's head. "You did it, Dawnie-girl! We knew you could. Hey Jax, how 'bout some champagne for the birthday girl!"

Jax pushed a cold glass into Dawn's hand. She was still shaking. The champagne spilled onto the concrete floor.

Reece took Dawn's other hand and gripped it tightly. She leaned close and whispered: "I never lost faith in you, baby girl. Here you are. Everything's going to be okay."

The group burst into song, their voices clear and bright:

"HAPPY BIRTHDAY TO YOU, HAPPY BIRTHDAY TO YOU . . . HAPPY BIRTHDAY, DEAR DAW-AWWWN . . ."

Dawn watched them singing, their faces burnished and beautiful in the soft light. Especially Reece, in her yellow silk dress, her skin aglow, eyes shining. Looking as vibrant and youthful as she had the first day Dawn had met her at the Nurtury.

As Dawn's old, dear friends—her lifeblood—sang to her, she was mesmerized, transported to a place of pure gratitude. Nothing terrible was happening, after all. Perhaps the goats were a figment of her imagination, an aftereffect of the tea she'd swilled.

"How old are you now? How old are you now?"

It was hard sometimes, Dawn thought, as her friends belted the original verse once more, to know what was real and what was merely a trick of the mind.

The two confused her all the time: the real and the unreal. Now, for example, as Dawn stood in the center of her singing friends, she could have sworn she saw Sibyl the Seer, the Visionnaire, crouched in a far corner of the basement, but then, Dawn couldn't be sure. Of anything.

44

Arnold (the Husband)

HIS WORK DONE, ARNOLD MADE HIS WAY AROUND THE EDGE OF THE property, toward the cave where Raj lived. They would wait there together, along with the young woman, until Twyla and the guests made their discoveries and finally, Arnold's life would begin. He'd never spoken to Raj's friend, the woman with the beanpole frame and nervous green eyes and dark cascade of hair, but Raj cared for her, and said Candance did too.

When Arnold had met them in the woods outside Betelgeuse, Raj and the young woman, Quinn, hand in hand, she had looked more like a girl in her too big dress. Skittish like a nervous filly. But Raj had promised she was one of them. Both a prisoner and a noble warrior, fighting for her life. Just like Arnold and Raj and Candace.

Arnold made his way through the trees to the clearing near the barn and hooked left toward the far ridge. Overhead, the moon was faint in the sky, soon to be banished by the bloody hues of sunrise, to another endless day in the canyon.

When had the prospect of a new day begun to bring him such dread? There had been a time when the sunrise—as sunrises were supposed to do, and as the poets and songwriters promised—brought him a feeling of hope, of expansive possibility. *Another day, another chance.* At some point, soon after Twyla's third, or maybe even fourth, venture—the avocado farm—had failed, the inverse had begun to creep in. Lightly at first: *another day, one less chance*; it finally landed with a thud when the godforsaken virus had hit, when it became clear that Twyla would never go anywhere, would never let *him* go anywhere: *another day, another step closer to death.*

He needed a change. From the monotony of isolation. From the relentless chores of the ranch—he yearned to never again lift a shovelful of goat shit. It began to feel like a war. The canyon versus Arnold and Twyla. Why repair holes that termites would only reopen in a week's time? Why water vegetables when the sky refused to open, and the land was as dry as the Sahara? There was no point in anything but surrender to the beechies, who were as plentiful and indestructible as cockroaches.

He'd tried all the reasonable methods to convince Twyla to leave. Presented, gently and without pressure, all the sensible reasons to leave Celestial Ranch for an easier life.

They were drowning in debt. Twyla thought he was oblivious, but Arnold had no trouble logging into accounts on his wife's phone during the long stretches she went "screen free." Bills stamped with OVERDUE in red ink arrived in the mail weekly.

They were all alone. The hard-to-access location of the canyon, combined with quarantine, had brought Arnold to a level of isolation so extreme he often felt he was living in a cage some cruel god had dropped from the sky.

Not only had Twyla refused to even consider selling the

ranch, but she also wouldn't venture down into the Valley for something as noncommittal as an open house at one of the airy, modern complexes they could live in for a fraction of what it cost to maintain Celestial Ranch. A place where their water simply flowed from a faucet without a well having to be primed first, where air-conditioning was a basic option of life instead of an impossible luxury. Twyla would rather die of heat stroke than cool their house during the broiling, rainless Topanga summers.

And then, of course, there were the goats.

The ornery, ever-shitting animals were yet another reason Twyla refused to leave the ranch. Never mind that *he* had offered to give up Klondike—an animal infinitely superior to the goats—if they moved to a senior community. But Twyla said the goats were her *children*. That she could not make them orphans.

Arnold was trapped. Trapped by the goats, and the guests, and this drought-racked mountainside his wife would not leave. All he wanted was a little comfort. Was that so much to ask, in the twilight of one's life? A little comfort in the way of appliances that worked and stairs he wasn't terrified of falling down, and a bit of company here and there. Twyla had stopped needing (wanting?) his company long ago. He'd come to feel like nothing more than a nuisance in her presence, yet another task to check off her to-do list.

He'd almost given up. He was ready to kiss Klondike's velvety nose and step right off the steep edge of the canyon. Twyla, on the other hand, did not seem lonely. She had Sibyl, the quack psychic who practically lived with them, and her hoity-toity city-slicker guests from the website.

The rotating weekend guests had been the nail in the coffin. They'd transformed Twyla, once the most authentic person

Arnold had ever known, one who saw right through the loud, phony chaos of the world, into a phony herself. Into someone who ran herself ragged all over the ranch in order to please her "guests"—utter strangers! Trespassers! She drove all the way to Topanga Village—sometimes as far as the Palisades—to buy garbage for the guests with money she and Arnold did not have, insisting the "guests" have soap that smelled like a specific flower, all because she'd read an article on the internet on how to be a great Airbnb host!

When Arnold thought of the money she'd spent to please rich people from the city—building the ridiculous yurt, fixing the plumbing and the flooring in the cabins—he felt ill. Ill, then angry, his rage building until the force of it scared him.

It was when he began complaining about the Airbnb funny business, which Twyla considered a *legit* business, that she began using words like *dementia* and *Alzheimer's*, and made appointments for Arnold with Dr. Belk, the goddamn geriatric specialist.

He knew about the pills, had known all along. He heard her drag the stool over to the fridge each night so she could pluck out a pill, mash it into powder, and slip it into his tea. His Twyla, the love of his life, had tried to drug him. Most nights he found a way to dump the tea and make her think he drank it. Other nights, he had to drink it and woke the next morning in a fog, forced to trudge through the day even more depressed than he already was.

It had been Twyla's insistence that there was something wrong with him that had revealed to Arnold his *plan*. If she wanted so badly for him to be a dumb, drooling senior citizen, well, he'd give her what she wanted.

He made her believe he was going soft in the head, fast becoming a confused old geezer who wanted nothing more than the love of his dog and the bland meals Twyla set out before him three times a day and praised him for eating, as if he were a stubborn toddler.

It was easier, he found, to have Twyla think he was succumbing to dementia. Easier than going head-to-head with her in battles he was destined to lose.

Then, by some miracle, Raj had come into his life, the strange young man with haunted eyes and dirt-caked skin beneath his matted beard Arnold had found half dead in the cave behind Hydra Hill. Raj who talked to the cave walls and insisted a woman named Candace slept in the darkest corner.

It was Raj who helped Arnold realize there were ways to get off Celestial Ranch that did not require the direct persuasion of Twyla. The young man's total independence from the stranglehold of the regular world, while born from great tragedy, made Arnold believe that he, too, could be free.

Raj was all too happy to help. Together, they became a team, working to liberate each other: Raj from the corporeal struggles of living in a high, waterless canyon, and Arnold from the lonely vortex of his life. The deal they struck was simple: Arnold would keep Raj nourished and protected from the dangers of the canyon. And in turn, Raj would help Arnold break free of each shackle that bound him to Celestial Ranch: The guests. The goats. Twyla.

Raj had not let him down. This weekend, he'd shone more than ever, rattling the guests with bear shit in the shower, bee swarms at their picnic, sharp pine cones in the bedsheets, and beechies at their silly psychic readings.

Just hours ago, Raj had performed the ultimate feat. Arnold had wrestled with the idea for weeks before finally proposing it to Raj.

"You can keep the meat," Arnold had said, after explaining what needed to be done. *"Klonnie can have some too."*

But Raj had refused. At first. Arnold had been forced to make a threat—it was the goats or Raj. One of them was leaving the ranch.

Raj's eyes had grown wide with horror.

Then, acceptance.

They understood each other, Arnold and Raj.

Arnold knew Twyla would grieve for the goats. He also knew that grief passed, leaving new strength and clarity in its place.

Grief woke you up.

Raj had taught him this.

Twyla needed waking. A good strong dose of reality.

It was for this reason that Arnold had stopped when he'd seen her golf cart, parked in a seemingly random spot on the trail between their house and the now-destroyed hive. He had checked the ignition for the key. There it was. The round metal head gleaming in the soft moonlight.

Twyla assumed that the world waited for *her*, bent to her will.

Well, Arnold thought, as he fingered the key now deep in his pocket, he had news for her.

45

Dawn (the Birthday Girl)

AFTER THREE LONG ROUNDS OF "HAPPY BIRTHDAY," DAWN'S FRIENDS stopped singing, and Mia spoke.

"Okay, everybody, have a seat. Except for Jax." Mia batted her eyes at him. "You may be excused."

Jax slunk away into the dark fringes of the basement.

"As for the rest of you, butts to the ground. It's not the most comfortable, or hygienic, but we work with what we've got, right?" She turned to Dawn. "I know you're overwhelmed, babe, but the hard stuff is done. All you need to do now is go with the flow. And then you get to sleep. Right next to your precious Quinny-bee."

At the mention of her daughter, Dawn's heart clenched. "Is—is Quinn okay?"

Reece squeezed her hand. "Of course she is, baby girl. She's back in the cabin, waiting for you." Then she let go of Dawn's hand and sat on the floor. The others followed: Joanie and Summer sat cross-legged, knee to knee, Graham leaned back on his hands, and Mia tilted to one side, legs tucked under her. Shadows danced and played over the walls.

Dawn was the only one still standing. Paralyzed by the strangeness of her surroundings. By the thought of Quinn, far across the meadow, alone.

She swallowed hard and found her voice.

"Uh, guys. Before I sit down, can someone please tell me what's going on?"

"Whatever could you possibly mean?" said Summer, mock-incredulous.

The group laughed.

Had she really reveled in that laughter, felt drunk with gratitude for her friends, just hours ago at dinner? Now, it sounded ugly and mean.

"Now, now," said Mia. "Let's be extra nice to our birthday girl. It's been a long night, and she's done an incredible job."

"An incredible job—at what?" asked Dawn. Mia defending her—Mia!—made her feel like she was going to vomit again.

"At playing your birthday game!" said Mia, with glee. "We hid, and you found us."

"What?" said Dawn. "You hid?"

"That's right."

"Why?"

"So that we could give you your present!" Mia waved her palms through the air.

"What present? This entire *weekend* was my present."

"Oh, no, my love," said Mia, shaking her head. "The weekend was just the *setting* we needed to give you your present. To give you the right context."

"What she means is," Reece spoke, "we needed to prepare you to receive your gift. So that when the time came you wouldn't be startled."

"Not startled?" Dawn felt as if her heart might stop.

"Exactly," said Summer.

"Bear with us, Dawnie," said Graham.

Dawn looked at him. "You left me in the middle of no-where, in the dark."

Graham shrugged. "Worse things can happen."

"Oh god," she muttered. This was the man she'd fucked in the woods last night. The man who had made her feel wanted and safe. It had all been a lie.

She scanned the room for something to catch her vomit. Instead, she threw up in a dark corner on top of a box holding old saddles.

"This is too much," Reece said behind her. "I told you—"

"That's enough chatter, people," said Mia. "You good now, Dawn? If you'll have a seat, we'll get to the main event."

Dawn used her T-shirt to wipe her mouth and her tearing eyes, then lowered to her knees on the basement's grimy floor.

"I want to go home," she said.

"Perfect," said Mia. "Now, Dawnie, does this remind you of anything?"

"Does *what* remind me of anything?" Her head was pounding. She needed to lie down.

Mia lifted a finger, her broken nail jagged at the tip, and moved it in a circle through the air. "*This*," she said. "The six of us, sitting in a circle together."

"Oh. Well." She looked to Reece, but Reece was staring at Mia.

"You can say it, babe," Mia pressed. "We're back together again. The six of us. The original Nurtury crew. The creators of the Project. Now, I know I made everyone promise *no toxic topics* during the party, but the party's over. We can be totally *real* with each other now."

"Okay, I think," said Dawn.

"But you know, sometimes it's hard to speak the truth. We have the best intentions, but then, when the moment presents itself, we clam up. Our feet get cold. We mean one thing but say another. Which is why we've written everything down."

"Written what down?"

"The F-List, of course!" said Mia. "The *new* F-List. The Oh-Fuck-We're-Old List!"

"Come on, Mia," said Joanie. "Tell her what it really stands for."

"Geez, do you people not understand *buildup*?" said Mia. "Dawnie, my love, my bestie, the full title of the new and improved F-List, updated for the year 2022, designed especially for *you* on your fiftieth birthday, is . . ." She inhaled dramatically. "The long-awaited sequel to the Freedom List. It's the . . . FORGIVENESS LIST!" She clapped, and the others whooped and cheered. Summer gave a loud wolf whistle.

Dawn knew then: this was about the Project. This was about revenge. But Reece? Again, she tried to catch Reece's attention, but her friend, her mentor, had her eyes glued on Mia.

Mia cleared her throat. "And here with us tonight, to present the F-List, we've got an extra-special guest. A neutral third party, if you will. So, without further ado, I invite Miz Deborah Crabb to come on up!"

"Who?" said Graham, sitting up.

"You're not going rogue on us, are you, Meadows?" asked Summer.

"Of course not, lovelies," said Mia. "We're right on script. This is just a cameo."

The psychic, whose face Dawn had seen on so many magazines and websites and TV clips, shuffled to the center of the circle with downcast eyes, a sheet of paper in her hand. She lifted her head slightly and addressed the group. "Hi, everyone," she said, her voice a whisper. "My name is Deborah Crabb, and—"

"I can't hear you!" Jax broke in from his unseen place in the darkness. "Start over."

Graham cut in. "Hey Mia? What's this about? It's not what we planned."

We planned?

"Roll with it, Grahammy," said Mia. "I decided it couldn't hurt to add a little more *truth* to the evening. You can never have too much of it, can you? Go on, Debbie. Louder this time!"

"Sorry," Sibyl mumbled. Then, louder: "My name is Deborah Crabb. You know me by my professional name, Sibyl, but Deborah is my true name. I was born in Harmony Township, Pennsylvania, in Beaver County. When I was eighteen, I ran away to Los Angeles, on a Greyhound bus. I took my infant brother, Abel, with me."

"Kidnapped," corrected Jax. "The correct term is *kidnapped*."

"I don't like this," Dawn said. She searched the faces of the people she thought were her friends. The mood had shifted. Graham looked annoyed, Joanie scared, Summer confused. Reece sat with her hands clasped in her lap and her eyes closed.

"Kidnapped," said Sibyl. "And on the way to California, I gave Abel up for adopt—"

"Sold him!" corrected Jax, from the shadows.

"Sold him," repeated Sibyl. "And I went on to have a good and successful life in Los Angeles, while my younger brother struggled for much—"

Jax again: "*Suffered*, Deborah. Stop glossing over the truth."

"Dude," Summer said. "This is, like, totally illegal. She looks hurt."

"Mia," Joanie said, "so help me, if you get our asses arrested . . ."

The paper in the psychic's bruised hands trembled. Dawn wanted to take her into her arms and run to Betelgeuse.

The psychic went on. "I'm here to apologize tonight to my brother, Abel, with the six of you as my witnesses, so that I might ask forgive—"

A loud bang overhead interrupted her.

Someone had closed the hatch to the basement.

Another thud came, and another: feet descending.

"Who," Mia said, eyes wide, "the *fuck* is that?"

"I'm scared!" Summer cried, pulling Joanie into a tight hug.

Graham stood, searching the dark corners of the basement. Dawn was pleased to see his double chin quivering. He was terrified.

Dawn began to laugh—uncontrollable bursts that rose like bubbles and burst into the room.

Even Mia was startled. "Jax, baby . . ."

One hiking boot dropped into view, then another, and Twyla appeared.

Dawn laughed harder. Her bladder released, and instead of being ashamed, she found it hilarious.

"Sibyl!" Twyla cried. "Thank the goddess. Is Arnold here too?"

"What the *fuck* are *you* doing here?" snapped Mia, jumping to her feet. "Didn't we sign a contract?"

"We certainly did," said Twyla. "But I'm breaking it."

"You can't," said Mia. "Not now. It's too late."

"Oh, but I can," said Twyla. "I believe this is *my* house?"

Dawn wanted to cheer for Twyla, who seemed transformed, nothing like the flaky, apologetic woman who'd driven Dawn and Quinn to their cabin. *Quinn.* She had to get back to Quinn. She would wait until the chaos grew worse—at this rate, Mia and Twyla would be in a fistfight at any minute—and escape through the hatch door.

"Hey, Jax?" called Mia. "Can you help me out here with Twy-la?"

"For sure," said Jax, gliding out of the shadows.

Dawn watched in disbelief as he grabbed the gray-haired woman's arms and pinned them behind her back.

"Whoa!" Summer stood, shoving her sleeves up to her elbows like she was going to jump in.

Twyla gasped. "How dare you!"

"Come on, guys," Graham said, in a ridiculously reasonable voice. "This lady is the same age as our moms."

Reece was on her feet. *Thank God!* Dawn thought. Reece would make this better. She'd make all this bad go away. Just as she always had.

"Unhand her, young man," Reece said, and Dawn saw the fire in her eyes.

"Don't mind her," said Mia. "It's only for a minute, Twyla. Then we'll let you go. Now, Debbie, what were you saying?"

Sibyl (the Visionnaire)

SIBYL NEARLY BURST INTO TEARS WHEN TWYLA APPEARED IN THE basement. Like an angel descending to the earth instead of rising to the heavens.

She longed to bolt from the circle and into Twyla's strong, ropy arms, to bury her face in the soft fleece of Twyla's vest and weep. Then she remembered Abel's words as they had stood in the backyard together, just before he'd pulled open the hatch to the basement and forced her down.

"You will not cry." He had whispered the command forcefully in her ear, his breath hot and sour, his hand clamped to the back of her neck. If someone had seen them, Sibyl thought blearily, through the pulsing pain in her head, they might be mistaken for a couple, sharing a secret. *"You will not scream. You will stand up in front of the group, and you will confess your sins. If you don't, well, Celestial Ranch is a beautiful place to be buried, don't you think?"*

"What—please—" Above her, the stars had begun to wheel.

"Just kidding, sis." He'd laughed, harsh and bitter. *"I can't murder you. It'd be terrible for my career. You think it's been easy, following in your footsteps here in LA? I'm just glad I went with a more conventional type of acting. Playing a psychic seems like a real bitch."*

"I'm not—"

He cut her off. *"Let me give you some advice, sis. Next time you decide to sell a baby, do a little more research on your buyers. This might come as a shock, but usually the folks on the black market looking for a kid aren't the most upstanding citizens. Make sense?"*

Sibyl's heart and head had throbbed in cruel sync, every cell in her body aching, her gut roiling. *"I—I only wanted to give you a better life. I didn't mean for any harm to come to you. The opposite, Abel. I wanted to save you. Our parents, they weren't fit to—"*

"Shut up!" She felt his nails cut into the underside of her wrist. *"Just shut your mouth, Debbie! The decision wasn't yours to make. They were struggling. They suffered. Dad's dead, you know. A long, painful death. And Mom has a heart of gold. You wouldn't know, because you never bothered to look back. But I looked back, and I found her. She told me you were always too good for our family. That you thought you were destined for bigger things. Like a big shiny life out in Hollywood, right? How'd that work out for you, huh, sis? Pretty glamorous, right? How's it feel to be a D-list has-been famous person whose claim to fame is killing a talk show host?"*

"I"—Sibyl struggled to speak—*"didn't kill Merry Williams. It was an accident. She wanted to jump. The parachute didn't—"*

"Tomato, tomahto," Abel had cut in, jauntily. *"Anyway, here's the deal. I'm taking you downstairs to meet my girlfriend and her nice little group of Hollywood pals. She's a kindred spirit, Mia. You know that? So, you're going to get up, and tell her and the gang your story. You'll keep it short and sweet. But I need to hear you say it, or you're going to be very, very sorry. I think you've had enough legal*

troubles for one lifetime, wouldn't you agree? So, you're going down-
stairs, and you're going to repent. Just like our daddy the Reverend
taught us. Are we clear, sis?"

Then he'd opened the hatch and shoved her down.

"Forgot your line?" said Mia to Sibyl now, in the basement. "Happens to the best of us."

Sibyl's headache had finally begun to subside. She'd found the two pain pills she had put in her pocket, backup, and had shoved them into her mouth when Abel hadn't been looking. She took a deep breath and the words tumbled from her lips: "That's all. I'm confessing that I made a terrible mistake when I was young, and that my brother Abel suffered because of it. Tonight—I want to—want to confess my sin and ask for forgiveness."

"Who the fuck is Abel?" said Summer.

"Right here, bitches," said Abel, from behind Twyla, returning to the theatrical inflection of Jax's voice. "In da house."

"Oh my God," groaned Joanie.

Mia clapped her hands. "Well done, Deborah! You've set a great example for the rest of us. You may take a seat in the circle now. How about right there?" She pointed to a spot just in front of where Twyla stood helplessly, her arms pinned behind her by Abel's iron grip. "Close to your little bro, so both he and I can keep an eye on you."

Sibyl looked to Twyla and for a beat, the two women's eyes locked. Twyla blinked, and Sibyl saw the tiniest hint of a smile at the corner of her old friend's mouth.

She understood Twyla was telling her to be brave. To have faith in the goddess.

Sibyl did not believe in the goddess, but she believed in Twyla.

A flicker of understanding passed between them. Sibyl

realized she was no longer in pain; the migraine had passed. The air in the basement suffused with the gauzy light that followed the pain.

She walked to the edge of the circle and sat down.

Mia spoke again. "Brava to our opening act! And now, on to the main event. Dawn Leigh Sanders, come on up!"

47

Twyla (the Hostess)

TWYLA WATCHED DAWN, THE SO-CALLED BIRTHDAY GIRL, PUSH TO HER feet and step to the center of the circle. She tried to ignore the pain in her shoulders as the man squeezed her arms behind her back.

She'd known he was no good from the moment she'd laid eyes on him, this too-handsome young actor with lips as delicate as a seashell's edge and catlike eyes that slid past you when you spoke to him. You couldn't trust someone who looked that way.

Klondike had been the first to know, of course, that Mia Meadows and her boyfriend were no good. The big wolf dog had tried to warn Twyla. She should have listened better: Animals always saw the truth. They were incapable of seeing anything else.

If only humans could be so pure.

She thought of Nocturne and Diurn, the image of their empty stall and pen. The two gates wide open. Tears burned in her eyes, and she resisted the urge to scream.

And Arnold. Where was he?

She glanced at Sibyl, seated at Twyla's feet, facing away. She tried to communicate a message to her. If Sibyl had taught Twyla anything, it was to believe in the power of the mind.

Twyla stared at the back of Sibyl's head and told her friend, using only her mind, what she needed her to do.

Then Twyla took the deepest prana breath and asked the goddess to please, please help her.

48

Dawn (the Birthday Girl)

DAWN STOOD IN THE CENTER OF HER RING OF—FRIENDS. HER MIND churned. This was real, after all. Not a trip or a dream she would wake from.

Mia reached into the back pocket of her jeans and withdrew a folded square of paper.

"Don't worry, birthday girl. You've got it easier than Ms. Crabb. We've written everything down for you." She stepped forward and handed the paper to Dawn. "Here it is. The new F-List, twenty twenty-two edition. All you need to do is read it aloud. And make sure you look straight at the person in question, shall we say, while you're reading. You'll know where to look. Trust me."

Dawn took the paper from Mia and unfolded it, her fingers trembling. It was crowded with printed type, the font too small for her eyes in the dim basement light.

"Go on!" said Mia.

Dawn squinted at the page.

"You can do it, baby girl," said Reece.

"It's too dark," said Dawn.

"Here, let me help," said Reece. She reached for a candle burning atop a metal storage shelf and carried it over to Dawn. Dawn heard Twyla suck in a breath of disapproval, and she felt a pang of pity for the sweet older woman, remembering how desperate she'd been yesterday for Mia's approval, how hard she'd tried to make Celestial Ranch a special place of peace.

Dawn understood now, more than ever, that it was impossible to please Mia.

She'd spent most of her life trying.

Reece angled the light from the candle's flame toward the paper, casting just enough light for Dawn to discern the words.

"I, Dawn Leigh Sanders, am reading these words at the conclusion of the night celebrating my fiftieth journey around the sun. Over the course of the preceding night, my friends created a unique and intense experience for me"—Dawn's sweat-slicked hands began to shake—"designed to help me learn and grow, so that I may live the third act of my life with greater integrity and awareness. Now that I've successfully completed the special challenges of my birthday party, I would like to apologize to each of my guests, to my former fellow members"—her mouth had gone dry, and she paused to swallow—"of the Nurtury Center for Child Development and crr-cree—"

"Speak up, Dawnie!" shouted Mia. "We can't hear you!"

"—creators of the Project for Vaccine Choice, or simply the Project."

She stopped, unable to read any more. "Mia, why? What is this? I just want to see my daughter and go home."

"No one cares what you *want*, Dawn. That's not the point of this exercise."

Reece spoke. "Just keep going, baby girl. You're almost there. Can someone give her water?"

Joanie leaned forward and handed Dawn a plastic bottle. Dawn uncapped it and took a long drink, almost choking. She'd had no idea how thirsty she was.

"Proceed," commanded Mia.

"And that they grant me forgiveness for the following transgressions. One. To Summer Hemsworth and Joanie Ahn—"

"Look at them," Mia commanded.

Dawn looked at Summer and Joanie, nestled together on the floor. They stared back at her, Summer's eyes blazing, Joanie's rimmed with tears.

Dawn read on. "I apologize for the financial hardship I caused you, directly and indirectly, and for my failure to mention it over the course of the past eleven years." She looked up. "What?"

"Unbelievable," said Summer. "It's like she *still* has no idea."

"So, explain it to her," said Reece.

Joanie spoke. "Ninety-five thousand dollars."

"Ninety-*seven* thousand dollars," Summer corrected. "That's what it cost us after you turned us in to the feds. Fines, legal fees, and penalties after our house went into foreclosure."

"We had to move in with my *parents*," said Joanie. "It was humiliating. Summer and me *and* the girls in one room for eight months. My mom yelled at them constantly, especially Maisie. You know how my mom doesn't believe in special needs; well, Maisie was traumatized."

"But, I thought—"

"You *didn't* think," said Summer. "All you wanted was to cover your own ass. Yours, and your precious Quinny-bee. You didn't even call to—"

"That's enough, Summer," Mia snapped. "This isn't therapy."

"It's therapeutic, though," grumbled Summer.

"Keep going, Dawn," said Mia.

"To Graham Caldwell, I apologize for the emotional, phys- ical, and"—her cheeks flamed—"s-sexual manipulations I've initiated over the years, including during the time of the Proj- ect, when such behaviors were devastating to you and your family. I acknowledge that I have hurt you immeasurably over the years, and disregarded your feelings to satisfy my own"— she could hardly finish the sentence—"wh-whims and needs."

Dawn looked at Graham. He was crying.

"Whoa, bro," Jax said.

Reece shushed him.

"Sorry, Mama Reece," Jax said snarkily.

"It's true," Graham whispered, his voice breaking. "You hurt me, Dawn. So many times."

"I'm sorry," she whispered back. Why couldn't he have told her all of this last night? Why tell her now in this twisted the- atrical production?

"Onward!" said Mia.

Dawn found her place on the page. "To Mia Meadows, I apologize for making choices that resulted not only in your in- carceration, but in a lengthy separation from your young son and severe damage to your career and finances."

With great effort, Dawn lifted her face from the page to meet Mia's wolf-blue eyes. She wondered if her old friend would weep, like the others, but Mia only laughed. "Well, that sure was good to hear! Too bad you're about a dozen years late, Dawnie. Was that *really* so hard to say? Keep up the good work, you're almost there."

Dawn forced air into her lungs and started the final para- graph. It was the longest on the page.

"And finally, to Reece Mayall—"

The sobs broke through as soon as she said her dear friend's name.

"Okay, I'm sorry. I'll keep going. I apologize for betraying your trust and destroying your career and reputation. I apologize for unjustly blaming you for executing the mission of the Project, when in fact, I was as critically involved as anyone. I acknowledge that, in doing so, I bear responsibility for damaging your mental health to such a degree that—"

Dawn's eyes swam with tears. She turned to Reece, blinking. "I can't . . . go on."

"You have to," whispered Reece.

"But it's not true. What's written here—it's a lie."

"But honey, it's not." Reece looked at her with the bottomless compassion Dawn had relied on in the toughest moments of her life since Quinn was born. "It's all true. You just don't want to see it. You never have. That's how you operate, love. I thought you'd gotten better, I really did. I was ready to forgive you, without all this hassle. But then, you wrote me the letter."

"Letter? Which letter? I love our letters! They're the only things that've kept me connected to you all this time."

"I loved them too. But then, you sent me the one about your salon. Your Covid speakeasy, or whatever you called it. How you gave women access to Botox during the pandemic."

"I was doing what I had to! I was desperate, going broke. And Craig was divorc—"

"I know. It was a hard time. But did you truly believe your illegal vanity business getting busted was the same as what happened to me with the Project? That getting a fine and your license to wax people's eyebrows suspended was comparable to my entire life getting torn down? Because you said that, in your letter. *I understand what you went through.* That's what you wrote. Word for word. Remember?"

"I—I guess. But I was just trying to—"

"To what?" said Reece. Slowly, she lifted her hand and closed it into a fist. Then she raised the candle in her other hand so the light shone on her bare wrist. "To let me know that you were suffering just like *this*?"

In the candlelight, Dawn saw the ropy crisscrossing of scars that ran vertically from the heel of Reece's palm to the inside of her elbow.

"Did you try to kill yourself, Dawnie? When you couldn't fix the rich ladies' wrinkles anymore? Did it make you do *this*, like I did after I couldn't help people's children anymore, because my therapy license was *permanently* revoked, and I became a national laughingstock? Was it apples to apples, Dawn, what you did to my life and what that pesky pandemic did to your work as an *esthetician*?"

"But I thought—I thought you were already depressed," said Dawn. "That you were struggling before the Project. That you'd founded the Nurtury not only to help parents with the mental health of their children, but to help yourself too."

"Maybe so," said Reece, her face lit by a nimbus of candlelight. "But, baby girl, I only tried to kill myself because of—"

"Ouch! Goddammit!"

Jax released Twyla, then doubled over. "She bit me!" he screamed. "That fucking crazy psychic bitch!" He gripped his calf with both hands. "I mean, Debbie! Debbie fucking bit me!"

Sibyl leaped to her feet and darted across the room to Twyla, who had crouched behind a metal shelving unit, groping for something beneath it.

When Twyla rose to her feet, she was holding a long gun, its butt resting on her shoulder, muzzle pointing straight at Jax.

Dawn heard two clicks and a thump.

"Jesus Christ," said Graham.

"Seriously?" said Mia.

"Hands in the air, everybody," said Twyla. "No one moves until I know what you've done with my husband and my goats. And even if you dodge my bullet, well, I closed the door to this basement, and it's rather heavy to open in a rush. Somebody better tell me, right this gosh-darn minute, or I'll pull the trigger. I'm old, but shooting a rifle's like riding a bike. Also, I'm old, so I don't have much to lose."

No one spoke.

She may be holding a loaded gun, Dawn thought, *I am one hundred percent Team Twyla.*

"Excuse me, Twyla," Dawn said. "My daughter is all alone in—"

"I don't want to hear anything about anything *but* the location of my husband. And my goats."

"Those goats stink," Mia said.

"You think I'm joking?" Twyla pointed the gun at Mia. "Do you think this is all one big game, Ms. Meadows? Is this just more play-acting to you, you selfish bi—"

"I'm bleeding!" Jax screamed. "I'm really bleeding."

"Glad to hear it," said Twyla.

Sibyl shrugged. "Guess my teeth are sharp."

"It hurts!" Jax howled, and began hopping around on one foot, lurching forward.

He lost his balance and tumbled, colliding with Reece. The candle she'd been holding flew out of her hand and landed in a crate of papers beside the tower of wicker furniture.

The paper caught fire, then the wicker pile burst into flames.

Quinn (the Daughter)

THE HOUSE WAS BURNING. HER MOTHER WAS INSIDE IT. HOW QUINN knew this, she could not explain. Normally, she had to look for signs that her thoughts were valid in the real world, the one outside Quinn's inside world. She studied the changes—in the light, the weather, the taste of the air. On people's faces, which seemed to Quinn to change as frequently as a traffic stoplight.

Quinn had been sitting in the cave with Raj and the old man and his dog. Klondike was letting her scratch his bunny-soft ears.

It felt like a scene straight out of Unbridled number three, *The Wild Wild West,* in which Harmony Fairbanks, the heroine, went full cowgirl and traveled to old-school Gold Rush California on her trusty horse, Foxglove. Once there, of course, Harmony ran into a super-hot guy who also happened to be a train robber wanted by the law. Her mom had read part of that book—Quinn knew she was being nice, trying to bond and stuff. But then her mom had asked who *on earth* would want to have sex on the hard ground of a desert cave.

Well, here Quinn was. Except Raj's cave smelled like the school gym lockers at her old high school and unwashed hair and that cream made from clay her mom used to paint women's faces and make their wrinkles vanish.

Quinn had been thinking how she should go back to the cabin, that her mother would be worried *to death*. Her mother, her aunts, all the adults she knew said things like that when they got excited. They weren't actually going to die from worrying. Quinn had to remind herself of this every time her mom said that. It was like adults couldn't prove their point without making whatever it was—an argument with their boss, a bad haircut, a difficult kid (Quinn knew *she* was a difficult kid)— sound super bad, the absolute worst. *Death* being the absolute worst, Quinn guessed.

Quinn was an adult now too. Just not the kind her mother and aunts were.

Last night, the things she and Raj had done on the sofa in the cabin—those were adult things. Quinn touching Raj, him touching her, had felt good. Had given her this buzzy feeling in her stomach like when she jumped from the high board at the YMCA pool near her house back home.

Her mother treated her like a baby. Raj treated her like a woman.

Still, her mother would be worrying *to death* all over the cabin, maybe all over the ranch. But Quinn did not want to leave Raj. She did not know when she would see him again, or when she would get to feel the way he made her feel. Important. Necessary. Special in a way that had zero to do with Special Ed, or what the jerks at her old high school called SpedEd. Like when she walked past the lockers outside the senior common area and they shouted, *"Alert, alert. Spedhead! Spedhead!"*

She noticed Raj pacing in circles in the darkest corner of the cave. His lips moving. Fast, like he was arguing with someone. She didn't like it—him walking in little circles in a corner like that. It reminded her of some of the kids who had been in her SpedEd class at school before she'd graduated—Ricky and Lorenzo and Marianne, kids who needed help to eat and go to the bathroom and hold a pencil. When Ricky got upset, he paced. There was nothing their teacher, Ms. DePaul, could do to make Ricky stop, and so she let him walk back and forth all afternoon in the back of the classroom where the iguana, Phyllis, lived in a heated tank. It had made Quinn sad that Ricky couldn't stop to take a break.

Then she smelled it, in the cool, still air of the cave: smoke.

She felt her heartbeat was different—faster—and her left eye started its twitching thing. Maybe she was wrong.

She looked to Raj, still whispering into the corner. The old man was half asleep against the stone wall.

No. She was not wrong. She didn't need evidence to know she smelled smoke. She didn't need proof to know that her mother was in danger.

"I need to go." She stood so quickly she stepped on the big dog's paw. He let out a whimper. "Something bad is happening."

Arnold looked at her, then to Raj's corner and back to Quinn; she could *feel* the old man thinking. He was thinking she was strange. Odd. Maybe even crazy. She knew what people thought of her; worse, how they felt around her.

"Well," the old man said, slowly rising to his feet, his shoulders bent so he didn't hit his head. "I suppose Klonnie and I ought to come too. Raj? Your friend here has to go, she says."

Raj left his corner. "I—I can't go just yet." He looked different to Quinn. His eyes too big, his forehead slick with sweat.

He smelled scared. Angry.

"We'll come back for her, Raj," the old man said. "I promise."

Quinn didn't know who this *her* was. She knew it was not the her that was Quinn.

She knew she needed to find her mother now.

Quinn, the old man, and Raj stepped out of the cave and into the smoke-filled night. Quinn saw the faint orange glow behind the meadow.

"There," she whispered, pointing.

She ran, Raj and the old man behind her, the wolf dog at their heels.

50

Dawn (the Birthday Girl)

A SMOKY, ACRID DARKNESS ENVELOPED DAWN. SHE COULDN'T SEE. SHE couldn't breathe or even think. Her mind was a black cavern, burning hot.

Her throat narrowed, then closed. Nothing could enter.

The brightness swallowed her.

She gave herself over.

Something gripped her by the arms and pulled her up. It hurt.

Everything hurt.

Her throat opened, and air moved in.

At the edges of her vision, a brightness.

In the center of it, a blotch of light. Undecipherable, yet somehow familiar.

Slowly, the shape came into focus, and Dawn saw Quinn's face hovering over her.

Overhead, framing her daughter's face, was the violet-tinged morning sky.

"Mom!" said Quinn. "You woke up."

Dawn tried to speak, but only a croaking sound emerged.

Another face appeared above Dawn. A young man, dark-skinned and bearded, his face smudged with ash. Eyes wide and urgent.

"They're all out," he said to Quinn. As if he knew her daughter, Dawn thought. "Sheshnaag and I got them all out."

"Who?" said Dawn, blinking against the pearled light.

"It's going to burn. The whole house," the young man said. "You need to run, Quinn. You and your mother. Go."

"But what about you?" said Quinn, and Dawn heard the note of alarm in her daughter's voice. Quinn sounded as if she needed this man.

"Go," said the man. "Please."

"Mom," said Quinn. "We have to go."

She held out her hand. Dawn grabbed it and let her daughter pull her up.

Raj (the Drifter)

THEY WERE MERE MEN AND WOMEN.

Not demons.

Demons, Raj understood as he watched the house burn, would not fear fire like these mortal men and women. Demons fed on destruction.

And what a feast, Raj thought bitterly, Yama the god of death had enjoyed those last few years, dancing on bones in the hellscape of Naraka deep inside the earth. Surely the death of millions from the virus must have tasted sweet.

Surely his beloved Candace had tasted like pure crystalline honey.

Raj sucked in the cool night air, willing his lungs to accept it.

He scanned the soot-streaked faces of the trespassers. They coughed and coughed until they doubled over and got sick on the ashy grass. One woman, the guide with the braids, she was confused, shuffling over the lawn shoeless as the house burned behind her, crying, "The babies! Where are the babies?! Make sure the babies are safe!"

Mr. Secret Cigarette had passed out. And the blond demon, the one the old man had called the ringleader, she had collapsed to the ground, wailing as if, Raj thought, she had just buried her child.

The Witch was no witch but only a pretender—she and the old woman were locked in an embrace watching the house burn. With every beam that fell, sending a cloud of burning embers shooting into the gray sky above the house, the old woman let out a cry.

Even Sheshnaag the Protector had returned to human form. The old man crouched at the edge of the yard, the wolf dog's collar held tight in his strong hand. He had gotten his wish, Raj thought. He would not be holding the land steady tonight.

Quinn and her mother were huddled on the ground, arms wrapped tight around each other so Raj could not see where one woman ended and the other began.

The trespassers, the Witch, even the old man and his wife, they may be wicked but only as much as Raj had been wicked in the life before.

Raj had been just like them, wanting what he wanted, when he wanted it. As if he were a god and the world his toy.

Candace had tried to warn him, begging him to cancel the party on Sanibel Island, sending him article after article about the surge and the CDC prediction of exactly when every state's ICUs would be full. She sent him articles with stories about families in New York, South Dakota, Texas, even Los Angeles, unable to hold their loved ones' hands in the moment of death, forced to say goodbye on FaceTime.

The stories had shaken him.

But they were young and healthy, and the world was their

oyster, he told Candace. And, he added, *"I have a surprise for you."* It was the ring with a pink-orange gem the color of lotus flowers, and he was to ask her to be his bride, his queen.

But this had only angered her—*"You are not listening to me, Raj"*—and sparked an argument that went on and on, him saying things like *"We can't let fear rule our life!"*

In his mind, his heart, he and Candace were *one life*. He had known as soon as she showed up for her interview in his steel-and-glass office at Plasteeq that he would not be able to breathe without her. It embarrassed him even now, the comp package he'd offered her, *double* what she'd been making at her biotech start-up in Cupertino, so much that her cheeks had flushed pink, and she'd stammered as she read the offer aloud, right there in his office, at his insistence. He had done everything in his power to impress her. Bought an entirely new wardrobe at a boutique on Abbot Kinney in Venice. Started taking surf and skateboarding lessons. With time, it became clear to him that what she liked best were the things he, too, liked best about himself: his corny jokes and knowledge of niche topics like the precise amount of plastic at the bottom of the Mariana Trench.

If only he'd understood that those things had been enough. That he hadn't needed to rent out an island and throw a party mid-pandemic to prove to her how much he loved her.

In the end, he won. Candace climbed the steps into the chartered plane to Sanibel Island.

She had been the picture of health. Thirty-two years old, a dozen half-marathons under her belt, a plant-based diet, slim as a reed. No underlying conditions. She rarely even got a cold.

The terrible prophecy printed in the newspapers came true.

He said goodbye to her on the screen of his phone, hers held up by a masked ICU nurse in a hazmat suit and face shield wearing an ID that said HI! MY NAME IS LYDIA. Candace was unconscious and tubed. Her eyelids taped shut to prevent drying out.

Had she heard him wail, *"I am sorry, I am sorry!"* Had she seen him slap his own face until his cheeks burned, yelling, *"Stupid, stupid Raj!"*

Had she heard his final words to her? *"I love you, my lotus flower."*

Had she known he was there and that he would be with her always?

Candace had not been alone. Four Plasteeq employees who had attended the party died from the virus. All young, all healthy. A *superspreader event*, the media vultures called it, with hashtags that had trended on Twitter for days.

#MurdererRajPatel

#PlasteeqDeathParty

#CovidiotPatel

#RIPCandaceLu

Then, she returned. He'd been on the deck overlooking the white-tipped ocean waves, watching through his binoculars, searching the sky for the media scum's drones. He had felt movement at his back, on the other side of the wall-to-wall windows—someone crossing the living room.

It was Candace. Different—quieter, prone to letting her dark hair hang over her face—but still, it was her.

Then came the night the shutter roaches attacked— *click-clack, clickity-clack*—crawling across the roof, down the windows, their camera strobes blinding him through the skylights.

They fled. Candace had wanted to stay, begged Raj to let them stay. He'd had to carry her out of the house and on the long walk down the Pacific Coast Highway, cars blaring their horns as he tried to stay in the narrow shoulder. But Candace was so heavy and so sad. Her tears had soaked his T-shirt.

The cave had calmed her. She had her corner, and once the old man found them, she had her blanket.

But she had never returned to the cave, not after the night Raj woke to the trespassers' howling and saw Candace's corner was empty. He had been sure she would be there when he brought Quinn and the old man back. They were to get a night's rest and then set out for the Valley, where the old man promised Raj he would help him and Candace, and now Quinn too, find a place as safe and quiet as the ranch. Where Raj and Candace could remain invisible.

The corner had been empty but for Candace's blanket, and then Raj had seen it for what it was: a torn and dirty rag. He had paced the back of the cave, calling her name quietly, not wanting Quinn and the old man to know Candace had abandoned them. Him. He told her, in whispers, all about the escape plan to the Valley, hoping it would make her appear, convince her to leave her hiding spot. He had begged her to return to him.

Now he understood. Candace was gone. She had ascended to the Good Kingdom without him, the reward for her righteous actions on earth. Raj knew he was not worthy of oneness with Brahman, the supreme spirit. He did not deserve to dance in the clouds with the celestial deities. He did not deserve to spend eternity in paradise.

His heaven had been on earth. With Candace.

And he had wasted his chance for happiness. Like his friend Orpheus, whom Twyla had reincarnated in sculpted steel, Raj would be forever looking back, waiting for his dead queen.

The roof of the burning house collapsed with a roar. The

wolf dog wailed along with Twyla. Ash rained down like giant black snowflakes.

He heard his name and looked to Quinn, but she was still locked in her mother's arms. Or, Raj wondered, was it her mother who was in Quinn's arms?

Raj stepped closer to the fire. The heat seared his forehead and cheeks. He struggled to keep his eyes open.

Voices behind him, yelling. Someone pulled at the back of his shirt.

"No, listen!" he shouted. "I hear—"

Candace danced in the flames. She wore a dress of orange silk, and her shiny hair was loose.

She smiled at him and waved. The gem on her finger caught the firelight, and as she twirled, a floor of bright gold spread from the ring like a velvet carpet unfurling.

"*Ever after,*" Candace called in her singsong voice.

Raj stepped to the edge of the gold floor.

His path.

He ignored the screams at his back, eager to leave them behind.

She had returned for him.

Hot rivulets of sweat streamed down his cheeks like sudden tears.

He closed his eyes and stepped into the fire.

ABOUT THE AUTHOR

Cassidy Lucas is the pen name of best friend–writing duo Julia Fierro and Caeli Wolfson Widger. *The Last Party* is their second book together, and they've published two novels each under their individual names. Julia and Caeli met in Brooklyn in 2004 and now live in Los Angeles with their families.

READ MORE BY
CASSIDY LUCAS

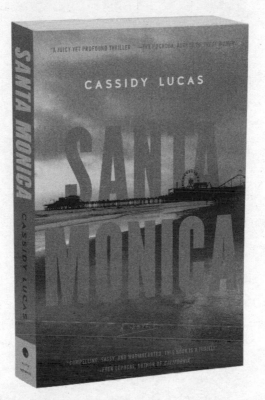

"Part riveting mystery, part incisive domestic drama, *Santa Monica* is a sharp look at the superficial lives of the pretending-to-be-perfect in gorgeous seaside California, expertly walking the line between satire, suspense and biting social commentary."

—KIMBERLY McCREIGHT
New York Times bestselling author of *Reconstructing Amelia* and *A Good Marriage*